PENGUIN BOOKS
DAUGHTERS OF ALBION

A. N. Wilson was born in 1950 and educated at Rugby and New College, Oxford. He is the Literary Editor of the *Evening Standard*. His other novels include *The Sweets of Pimlico* (awarded the 1978 John Llewellyn Rhys Memorial Prize), *Unguarded Hours*, *Kindly Light*, *The Healing Art* (1980 Somerset Maugham Award), *Who Was Oswald Fish?*, *Wise Virgin* (1983 W.H. Smith Literary Award), *Scandal*, *Gentlemen in England*, *Love Unknown*, *Stray*, *Incline Our Hearts* and *A Bottle in the Smoke*. He has written biographies of Walter Scott, Milton, Hilaire Belloc, Tolstoy and C. S. Lewis. Other books by A. N. Wilson include *Penfriends from Porlock* and *Eminent Victorians*. Many of his books are published by Penguin.

D0608773

A. N. WILSON

DAUGHTERS OF ALBION

It was one of those journeys on which a man
perpetually feels that now at last
he must have come to the end of the universe,
and then finds he has only come to the
beginning of Tufnell Park.
G. K. CHESTERTON

PENGUIN BOOKS

PENGUIN BOOKS

Published by the Penguin Group
Penguin Books Ltd, 27 Wrights Lane, London W8 5TZ, England
Penguin Books USA Inc., 375 Hudson Street, New York, New York 10014, USA
Penguin Books Australia Ltd, Ringwood, Victoria, Australia
Penguin Books Canada Ltd, 10 Alcorn Avenue, Toronto, Ontario, Canada M4V 3B2
Penguin Books (NZ) Ltd, 182–190 Wairau Road, Auckland 10, New Zealand

Penguin Books Ltd, Registered Offices: Harmondsworth, Middlesex, England

First published by Sinclair-Stevenson Ltd 1991
Published in Penguin Books 1993
1 3 5 7 9 10 8 6 4 2

Printed in England by Clays Ltd, St Ives plc

TO
R.

A List of Characters Mentioned in the Story

If a character has made a first appearance in some other volume of *The Lampitt Papers*, this is indicated in brackets. IH is an abbreviation for *Incline Our Hearts*, BS for *A Bottle in the Smoke*.

DEBORAH ARNOTT	A popular novelist. As Mrs Maddock (IH) she had lived in Timplingham during Julian's childhood. She and Julian had a brief affair in the late 1950s. (BS)
BARBARA	The maid at Les Mouettes, a house in Brittany where Julian spent some time during his adolescence. (IH)
DR BARCLAY	Fellow of Rawlinson College, Oxford. Specialist in German Romantic literature.
BERYL BEACH	The art mistress at Seaforth Grange school in 1947 (IH) subsequently better known as the sculptor Beryl Lewis. (BS)
MISS BEAN	A close friend of the late Angelica Lampitt.
BEATTIE	A girl in the typing pool at the Ministry of Works to whom Rice Robey was briefly devoted.
ALICE BLOOM	William Bloom's American wife.
WILLIAM BLOOM	Army friend of Julian (IH) subsequently a publisher (BS) who undertakes the publication of the present work.
GLORIA BOYD-FLEET	A sister of the late Mrs Lampitt of Timplingham.
BRENDA	Civil servant, colleague of Felicity and Rice

vii

	Robey. Lives in Putney with Henri, a gym mistress, and breeds cocker spaniels.
GEORGE BROWN	Later Lord George-Brown. Deputy Prime Minister at the time of Miles Darnley's wedding.
CELIA	A temporary secretary at the Ministry of Works.
PROFESSOR GEOFFREY CORMAC	A right-wing Oxford Professor of History. An Ulsterman.
PETER CORNFORTH	A wounded jockey who earns a living as an occasional journalist. Habitué of the Black Bottle. (BS)
MADGE CRUDEN	Publisher at Rosen and Starmer, whose authors include Raphael Hunter and Vernon Lampitt. She published Julian's novella, *The Vicar's Nephew*. (BS)
CYRIL	Landlord of the Black Bottle. Famed for his extreme rudeness and his uncanny resemblance to T. S. Eliot. (BS)
MISS DRAKE	English tutor at Rawlinson College, Oxford. Expert on Spenser's numerology.
MISS DARE	Devotee of the Sarum Rite and of the Rev. Roy Ramsay.
ELIZABETH DARNLEY	Miles Darnley's sister. (BS)
MILES DARNLEY	Schoolfriend of Julian. (IH) Editor of *The Spark*.
CAMPBELL DILKES	Minor composer. Married to Lavinia Lampitt. His 'Surrey Rhapsody' is used as the theme music for 'The Mulberrys'.
SIR ALEC DOUGLAS-HOME	Prime Minister after Harold Macmillan.
MIA EGGSCLIFFE	'One of the last great hostesses.'
VIRGIL D. EVERETT	The American collector who purchased the Lampitt Papers. (BS)
FRANCES FITZGERALD	Miles Darnley's mother.
RAPHAEL HUNTER	The biographer of James Petworth Lampitt. Columnist in the literary pages of Sunday

newspapers, TV broadcaster and man about literary London. Nicknames Hinter (Pat Lampitt's nickname for him) and Lover Boy (Sargent Lampitt's nickname for him). (IH, BS)

GEORGE ISLEWORTH | Owner of Mallington Hall in the late eighteenth century.

DR JACK | A civil servant in the Ministry of Works.

FENELLA KEMPE | An unsuccessful actress. She was once Julian's landlady. (BS)

RIKKO KEMPE | Fenella Kempe's husband. He plays Stan Mulberry in the radio drama series 'The Mulberrys'. (BS)

LORD LAMPITT | The first Baron Lampitt, who lived at Mallington Hall. The father of Vernon Lampitt. He was a Liberal MP who joined the Labour Party.

MRS LAMPITT | She lived at Timplingham Place in Norfolk. The mother of Martin, James Petworth, Michael, who was killed at Mons, Vivian, Sargent and Sybil. (IH)

ANGELICA LAMPITT | A feminist, who committed suicide upon the marriage of her close friend Miss Bean.

BOBBY LAMPITT | A cousin of the Timplingham Lampitts, who emigrated to Rhodesia. (IH)

CECILY LAMPITT | Married to Sargent Lampitt (IH) and the close companion of James Petworth Lampitt.

THE HON. CHRISTOPHER LAMPITT | Son of Vernon Lampitt.

JAMES PETWORTH LAMPITT | Son of Mrs Lampitt of Timplingham; famed as a belle-lettrist historian in the early to mid-twentieth century. The subject of a scandalous biographical study by Raphael Hunter. (IH)

THE HON. JOANNA LAMPITT | Daughter of Vernon Lampitt.

JOSEPH LAMPITT I | A late eighteenth-century brewer of radical political leanings; friend of Benjamin Franklin, Josiah Wedgwood, *et al.* Purchased Mallington Hall with his fortune. Known as 'Radical Jo'.

JOSEPH LAMPITT II — The son of 'Radical Jo', he married Selina Isleworth, who was the heiress to Mallington Hall.

THE HON. KIRSTY LAMPITT — Daughter of Vernon Lampitt.

LAVINIA LAMPITT — The sister of old Michael Lampitt of Timplingham, she married the composer Campbell Dilkes.

NAOMI LAMPITT — The Quaker wife of 'Radical Jo'.

PAT LAMPITT — Married to Vernon Lampitt (second Baron Lampitt) of Mallington Hall. A former Wren officer.

PENELOPE LAMPITT — Vernon Lampitt's sister, always referred to by Roy Ramsay as the Honourable Penny-lope.

SARGENT LAMPITT — The fifth child of Mrs Lampitt of Timplingham, he was a Fellow of New College, Oxford, and regarded by many as the best political theorist of the age. Nervous disabilities compelled him to lead a retired life in the country where he relied heavily on the friendship of the Rev. Roy Ramsay. They fell out, an irreconcilable quarrel at the time of the demolition of Timplingham Place. Julian becomes his companion and factotum. (IH, BS)

URSULA LAMPITT — Dame Ursula Lampitt, Principal of Rawlinson College, Oxford. An expert in Anglo-Norman literature. (BS)

VERNON LAMPITT — The second Baron Lampitt. As the Hon. Vernon Lampitt, he served in Attlee's cabinet. Now an extreme left-winger known popularly as Ernie Lampitt. Occasional contributor to Darnley's magazine *The Spark*. (IH, BS)

THE HON. WILLIAM LAMPITT	Son of Vernon.
MARGOT LARMER	Wife of the former headmaster of Seaforth Grange, Great Malvern, Worcestershire. Known to the boys as 'Mrs Binker'. (IH)
ROBBIE LARMER	Headmaster of Seaforth Grange, known to the boys as 'The Binker'. The brother of Audrey Paxton. (IH)
LESLEY	A friend of Anne Starling's from her student days at the Courtauld Institute.
MR LEWIS	A teacher at Seaforth Grange, known to the boys as 'Lollipop Lew', who married Miss Beach, the art mistress. (IH)
HAROLD MACMILLAN	Prime Minister and leader of the Conservative Party until 1963.
ISABELLA MARNO	A distinguished actress, once the lover of Raphael Hunter. (BS)
'THE MULBERRYS'	A radio drama series of great popularity. Julian plays a character called Jason Grainger in this series. (IH, BS)
MISS NOLAN	Lead singer in 'The Newnham Norns'. A Cambridge undergraduate.
MME DE NORMANDIN	Julian's French hostess during summer holidays from school. (IH)
AUDREY PAXTON	The widow of Graham Paxton, she lives at 77, Twisden Road with Rice Robey. She was painted by P. J. Pilbright.
GRAHAM PAXTON	Alcoholic former headmaster who gave employment to Rice Robey.
P. J. PILBRIGHT	He worked in the Accounts department of Tempest and Holmes, a shirt factory, for forty years, where he was a colleague of Julian Ramsay and of Julian's father. He subsequently became famous as a painter. (BS)
MISS PLUMB	A Fellow of Rawlinson College Oxford, she specialised in Pure Maths.

DAVID RAMSAY	Julian Ramsay's father. Killed during the Second World War. (IH)
DEIRDRE RAMSAY	Wife of the Rev. Roy Ramsay. (IH; BS)
FELICITY RAMSAY	Fellow of Rawlinson College, Oxford, a philosopher. Julian Ramsay's cousin, they were brought up together as children in Timplingham Rectory. Felicity has given up teaching, at the beginning of the present volume, in order to be a civil servant at the Ministry of Works. (IH)
JILL RAMSAY	Julian Ramsay's mother, killed during the Second World War. (IH)
JULIAN RAMSAY	The narrator. He works in radio as a free-lance actor and is beginning his research for a book about the Lampitts. (IH, BS)
ROY RAMSAY	The rector of Timplingham, in whose house Julian was brought up when Jill and David were killed in an air raid. It is Roy Ramsay's obsession with the Lampitts which shapes Julian's childhood imagination. (IH; BS)
THORA RAMSAY	The mother of David and Roy, the grandmother of Felicity and Julian. Lately, she lived at Timplingham Rectory. (IH; BS)
RICE ROBEY	A civil servant, who is also an expert on the sites and legends of ancient Britain and the Middle Ages. During his twenties, when employed as a teacher by Graham Paxton, Rice Robey wrote four novels under the pseudonym 'Albion Pugh'.
RODNEY SMITH	The producer of 'The Mulberrys'. (BS)
AARON SAMUELSON	Former pupil of Treadmill's, now a banker, married to William Bloom's sister Hedda.
HEDDA SAMUELSON	The sister of William Bloom; probably having an affair with Patrick Garforth-Thoms.
ANNE STARLING	The daughter of Rupert and Sybil Starling. Art historian, formerly married to Julian. (BS)

xii

SYBIL STARLING	Married to a Treasury official, Sir Rupert Starling. The mother of Anne. (BS)
THÉRÈSE	The cook at Mme de Normandin's house, Les Mouettes, mother of Barbara. (IH)
PATRICK GARFORTH-THOMS	School friend of Julian's, now seeking political office. Probably having an affair with Hedda Samuelson. (IH)
TIMPSON	Head boy of Seaforth Grange during Julian's time in the school, now a clergyman. (IH)
MR TONGUE	A clerk, articled to the firm of Widdell and Blair.
VAL TREADMILL	The inspiring English teacher at Julian's public school, who also does some work in radio and writes occasional scripts for 'The Mulberrys'. (IH)
GODFREY TUCKER	Opinionated journalist, much doted upon by Mrs Eggscliffe.
FREDDIE VANCE	Producer of a books programme for the BBC World Service.
MRS WEBB	The best friend of Julian's grandmother. (IH)
JAMES HAROLD WILSON	Prime Minister from 1964 until 1970, and again 1974–1976.
MARY WILSON	The wife of James Harold Wilson.
LADY AUGUSTA WIMBISH	The wife of Professor Tommy Wimbish.
PROFESSOR TOMMY WIMBISH	Oxford historian. Author of various popular histories of the Tudor age, and a three-volume history of the Labour Party.

ONE

Love was in the air.

At one end of the formica-topped table they spoke of the prostitute, and at the other of the bishop. I was caught between the two colloquies; I sat opposite Darnley who was always exactly halfway down the table, a position from which he could hear as much as possible of what was being said.

'I can't see what difference it makes if a Cabinet minister, like most other healthy individuals in the fucking world. . . .'

The speaker, Peter Cornforth, was interrupted by Vernon Lampitt.

'With great respect, Pete, that's not the point.'

'How do you think the world got populated?' asked Peter. 'You got children.'

'That isn't the point. The world is not populated by public figures exploiting the services of young girls. . . .'

'Exploitation!' Peter laughed and ignited a Park Drive. Understandably, he seemed weary of the food placed before him. A school dinner chosen by Darnley. We had eaten our way through steak and kidney, suet, boiled potatoes, cabbage, gravy. Now the rhubarb crumble lay in front of us, poking above the custard, rocky islands in small yellow seas.

Peter Cornforth, a wounded jockey who had made a sporadic living as a freelance hack, contributed a page of racing notes to Darnley's little magazine *The Spark*, which had been running a bit less than a year. It was a strangely miscellaneous publication, reflecting the disjointed nature of Darnley's own personality. The general verdict, when, as inevitably happened, it folded, was that Darnley had not made up his mind what sort of magazine it should be. I don't think this view is altogether correct. Darnley did make up

1

his mind what the paper should be like, but his mind was not the easiest of things to fathom, and the general public evidently did not think, at 6d, that it was worth the effort. Those who might have enjoyed Pete Cornforth's gossip about trainers, bookies, or race-horse owners, or the even more scurrilous passages of social and political comment in the 'Diary' at the front of the paper, would not necessarily have wished to wade through the longish articles about literature, politics or religion in the second half of *The Spark*. Darnley had the idea that if he produced a paper which contained nothing but items of interest to himself, then the public was bound to follow him. He was wrong, even though one now sees that *The Spark* was of its time; little papers were springing up all over London in those days. Some were to turn into national institutions, like *Private Eye*; others, more identifiably political than *The Spark*, would enjoy specific moments of notoriety before running out of cash or being closed down by the law. *The Spark* had something in common with these semi-underground rags, though in other ways it was more a throwback to earlier traditions of journalism, *Night and Day*, *Horizon*, even *GK's Weekly*.

Almost more important to Darnley than the paper itself was the regular lunch which he held for contributors and friends. His zest for the dingy made it inevitable that he should have decided the Black Bottle to be a suitable venue for these symposia. It was a pub where I had worked as a barman and spent more time than was useful in my early twenties. Now that my thirtieth birthday approached, I felt sheepish about going to the place. Cyril, the proprietor, laid aside a small back room, which it would appear was now being used as a store for domestic rubbish, since the dozen or so guests for lunch that day had squeezed past a broken standard lamp and a mangle which were half blocking the door.

Talk of the politician's downfall, and his association with the young woman, was for a moment drowned by the group on my right talking of the bishop. A fat journalist was speaking in gravely northern tones.

'Either you believe in God or you don't, and if you don't believe in God, you shouldn't be a bishop.'

'Oh, but it's less simple than that!' screamed some woman, whom I have never seen since. Beehive hairstyle and big teeth.

To my left, Vernon Lampitt and Peter Cornforth were now setting to.

'You may be completely virtuous,' said Pete. 'He is.' He stabbed the air with an ignited Park Drive in the direction of Darnley who sniffed imperiously, and then roared with laughter. If sexual coyness is to be associated with virtue, then I think Darnley was extremely virtuous, though this was one of the many ways in which the adult Darnley was unlike the ten-year-old whom I had first befriended at our private school, Seaforth Grange. In grown-up life, we did not see much of one another for long periods. Then there would be spells when we picked up the threads. I had only the haziest idea of his emotional make-up, beyond having decided that he was one of those people to whom sex, or rather his own sexual nature, was not very important. Other people's tastes in these areas were a different matter, so long as their proclivities led them to behave in a way which Darnley considered risible.

'Look,' said Pete, 'Members of Parliament are away from their wives all week, lucky bastards. Most of them are too horrible to make friends with nice girls.'

Darnley put on his High Court judge voice.

'Are we going to allow that to pass?' he enquired. 'Ernie?'

'No,' said Vernon. 'And yer missing the point, Pete. This is a matter uv national security. We're talking about a minister uv the Crown. . . .'

As often happened when Vernon was enunciating an argument, he began to speak more slowly, as to a classroom of backward schoolchildren. He removed his pipe from his lips and counted out each phrase, holding the pipe in one hand and touching a separate finger of the other with its dottle-wet stem for each separate point he wanted his hearers to understand.

'We're talking about a Cabinet minister responsible for the defence uv the realm, friend uv the Prime Minister and the ruling establishment. . . .'

'What do you think you are if you aren't the ruling establishment?' asked Peter.

'I'm not the establishment. The Lampitts, that's me family, have always bin anti-establishment and I could give yer chapter and verse for that. But let's stick to the issues. . . .'

'So you think he's been muttering military secrets to this girl as he flops back on the pillow. "Was that nice for you, darling, and by the way, I've been meaning to tell you, nearly forgot, we're thinking of sending a tank regiment over to Aden."'

'She's bin seein' a man from the Russian Embassy,' said Vernon.

'Friend of yours?' shouted the fat northern journalist.

'Ernie,' said Pete with sudden intensity. 'When did you last do it?'

Pete had moved into a new phase of drunkenness. His brilliant blue eyes were flecked with red, and his cheeks had become scarlet. Vernon hummed and hawed. I wondered if he was seriously trying to retrieve the information Pete demanded from the cobwebs of memory.

'Would you speak about military secrets to a woman?' asked Pete.

'In principle, I don't see why not,' I volunteered.

'Because they're too fucking stupid to understand military secrets, that's why not,' Pete explained.

'It's all a symptom,' said Vernon who with his dottle-drip was preparing to count out another list on his fingers. 'A symptom of moral bankruptcy in the established class, a symptom of the real emptiness of the capitalist system, yes you can laugh.'

Most of them did.

'Pugh will never tell us,' said Darnley, 'how he managed to know about this distressing affair months before the journalists. Will you, Pughie?'

As he gazed down to the end of the table where they were discussing the bishop, a look of something like adoration passed over Darnley's face.

'It was bound to materialise at the last,' said the man to whom we all turned. 'And Lord Lampitt is surely right. . . .'

'Ernie, Ernie!' protested Vernon. 'None of this "lord" rubbish.'

'There is a place for a hierarchy of nobilities, Lord Lampitt, you are wrong to deny it,' said the man whom Darnley called Pugh. 'But you are right to discern that these events have symptomatic reverberations. Here is a portentous conjunction. You meditate upon the Harlot, while we discuss the Episkopos.'

He intoned, more than spoke, in a nasal cockney voice and stared at the ceiling as the strange words passed his grinning lips. Very thick lenses, bottle glass, magnified his dark eyes into bulbous marbles. For the fashion of those days, his hair was unusually long, brownish grey, receding from a Shakespearian brow. He was unbearded but 'clean' would be an inappropriate adjective for the manner in which he was shaven. He wore a crumpled dark blue double-breasted suit. Between the greasy tie and a quarter inch of greyish neck a stud jutted between collar and shirt. Mr Pilbright, my superior in the Accounts department of the shirt factory where I was once employed, would have approved that here was 'no nonsense about collar-attached'. I had no idea who the man was, though I formed the instantaneous impression that it was 'typical' of Darnley to have collected him.

'I've heard of the Bishop and the Actress,' said Pete. 'But this is a new one. The Harlot and the Piss what?'

The portly northern hack, whose name was Godfrey Tucker, and who for years had an 'opinion' column in one of the middlebrow Sunday newspapers, laid an odoriferous miniature cigar in the remains of his rhubarb crumble and repeated, 'Either you believe in God or you don't. As it happens, I am not a believer myself, but for a bishop, a bishop of the *Church*. . . .'

'What other sorts of bishop are there?' asked Darnley.

'I could tell you,' said Pugh darkly.

'To say in a public article, in a high-falutin Sunday newspaper, read by all the Hampstead intellectuals, that he doesn't even believe in the Resurrection. . . .'

Darnley beamed at Tucker, satisfied, as always when people parodied themselves. From early days together, I had noticed in Darnley what I came to think of as the ringmaster's expression. The poodles were about to stand on their hind legs and teeter through the hoops. 'I think a piece is coming on,' he muttered, pointing to Godfrey Tucker with his thumb.

'The bishops are appointed to give a lead in matters of faith,' grumbled Tucker. 'Not to sow doubts.'

'New para!' shouted Darnley.

I have never been much interested in 'the news', and I shared none of Darnley's fascination with journalistic ephemera. I had missed the article in which some bishop, famous at the time, had expressed the usual Anglican incredulity about the Christian story. The other matter – the scandal in the Cabinet – I could not avoid knowing about. It was one of those nauseating moments in English life when a sexual débâcle gripped the public mind and, wherever you went, intruded itself into every conversation. There was talk of the Government being brought down by it. Any connection between this semi-comic, if sordid chain of events and the desire of some cleric to make a splash in the newspapers by a declaration of unbelief was not one which I should have made myself but, as I came to feel, it was highly characteristic of 'Pugh', who was never more in

5

his element than when sacred and erotic love were enmeshed or confused.

'The Episkopos, like many Englishmen, is imprisoned in the empiricist fallacy,' he enunciated. 'Either/or – the two falsest words in the English language.'

'You're not saying the bishop's involved in all this other business?' asked Tucker. He had cottoned on to 'Pugh''s ability to form bizarre connections, and also to his genius for esoteric gossip. Tucker was suddenly very interested. If a bishop, albeit a suffragan, could be found to have shared the favours of the young woman with a Soviet Embassy attaché and a Cabinet minister, this was the sort of thing his editor would like to hear.

'Randy Bishop in Sex Romp,' said Pete.

'The Frolics I Mitre Had,' said Darnley.

'The Episkopos is chaste,' said 'Pugh'.

Disappointment was visible on every face round the table, including Vernon's.

'His thought is vapid, impotent,' added our sage.

'Do you mean, he can't get it up?' asked Tucker. 'Now, how would you know a thing like that?'

For the moment, it was evident that everyone in the room had come to believe that 'Pugh' might conceivably know such things; might even be omniscient.

'The Episkopos has lost his vision of the Mystery. The Harlot has her grip on the Cabinet minister for similar reasons. We can't live without believing in Mythos. Belief is not just something which you accept with a part of your mind, it is what you live by. England has lived by a Mythos ever since Dunkirk, the Island Race against the powers of Darkness. Now it has all evaporated. No one believes in the Mother of Parliaments or the new Commonwealth or the Flag. Until another Mythos replaces these old ones, the sludge at the bottom of the collective mind rises up as in dreams, and we have filthy little stories. The Harlot and the Statesman become interchangeable. Secrets are sold like human flesh and the Church has lost its Christ.'

'Why not call a bishop a bishop?' asked Pete. 'Why all this Episkopos crap?'

Vernon spoke. 'Yer right. We have lost touch with something. But yer see, Mr – er – Mr Pugh, there's always bin another England apart from the privileged little class who are at last being dethroned.

Yer right ter think it is appropriate they should be brought down by a prostitute because prostitution is at the core of the capitalist system. It's buying people, and that's what yer factory owners have done, yer mill-owners, yer mine-owners. . . .'

'It isn't buying people,' said Pete, 'it's buying a fuck. Most of the girls do quite well out of it, better than if they were waitresses, or barmaids in this fucking horrible pub. I'd sell my body if anyone would buy it.'

> 'The Whore & Gambler, by the State
> Licenc'd, build that Nation's Fate,'

chanted 'Pugh'.

It wasn't a surprise to hear the words of William Blake on his lips. 'A fuck, as you call it, my friend, unites us to the Sacred Fire,' he said. 'It's not that it shouldn't be paid for, so much as that it can't be paid for.'

'They've been quoting you too high a price,' said Pete.

'It can't be paid for any more than you could pay for Holy Communion or buy a ray of the sun.'

'Pugh' was unable to develop this line because Vernon was in full flight.

'Ever since 1689, a little moneyed class have had it all their own way, they've run the whole show – they've put in their own tame monarchs from Holland and Germany, oh yes, and they've made governments out of their own class to protect their own interests, but it's all over for them now. The people uv England 'll see 'em off. That's the true England, the true tradition.' Another finger-counting exercise began. 'Yuv got Wat Tyler, yuv got the Pilgrimage of Grace, yuv got the Diggers and they saw what Landowner Cromwell was up to by Golly, yuv got Wilkes and Liberty, yuv got the Chartists. . . .'

Vernon was running out of fingers in his catalogue of radical high watermarks in English legend.

'People often say ter me, "Ernie yer some kind a Marxist" – yer made the same easy joke just now, assumin' I was friends with the Russian Embassy bloke, and I like ter reply, "Long before Karl Marx, and good luck ter 'im, came and took refuge in the British Museum, and 'e'd uv bin lucky ter do that with this new Immigration Bill comin' up, there was this strong healthy native tradition which saw through the lies uv the ruling class."'

'There has to be a ruling class,' said Tucker. 'All you want to do is to boot out the educated classes, all right and the rich like yourself, and make the proles the ruling class. Instead of having a country run by reasonably civilised individuals with two or three hundred years' practice at it, you'll have it incompetently run by a lot of bullying trade unionists. It's champagne bottles or sauce bottles.'

We all groaned.

'The time of refreshment is past, and toil must resume,' said 'Pugh' consulting a watch which hung from his broad lapel on a leather strap. He rose to his feet. 'No, please, Mr Darnley, I do not wish to disrupt the continuum of the tabula.' He said goodbye to all those around him – 'Lord Lampitt, Mr Cornforth, Mr Tucker,' and when he came to me, 'Mr Grainger.'

Jason Grainger was the character whom I played in the radio drama series 'The Mulberrys'. Darnley habitually called me by the name and must have thus introduced me to his other friends. It did not, however, occur to me to wonder whether 'Pugh' was a real name or another of Darnley's joke sobriquets. I hesitated and wondered whether to correct him. It seemed pompous to do so, and he was in any case wrestling with the detritus of domestic rubbish by the door. It was surprising to see him pick up the broken standard lamp in one hand as if it were a bishop's crosier, and somehow get a grip with the other hand on the mangle.

'Cyril'll give you a hand with those, Pughie,' said Darnley, for the publican was at that moment coming into the room, staring at us all with a contemptuous smile as if he never saw such a collection of cretins in his life.

'Cyril fucking won't,' said Cyril. 'What d'you want to cart all that rubbish round London for anyway?'

'There is an electrical shop near here which will mend the lamp,' said Pugh, in a much more matter-of-fact tone than had informed his conversation at the table, 'and an ironmonger in Berwick Street said he would look at the mangle. I think it's just rusty.'

'It *is* just fucking rusty,' said Cyril. 'You should throw it out.'

'That isn't a possibility,' said Pugh's voice.

He was invisible now, having negotiated his way out of the room, dragging the mangle behind him.

When he was gone, Darnley smiled satirically and whispered, 'Domestic troubles.'

'He was a rum cove,' said Godfrey Tucker. 'Gave me the shivers, actually. Continuum of the tabula? What's that meant to mean when it's at home?'

Professor Cormac, who until this point had been asleep at Tucker's elbow, awoke with a snort. He was deceptively young in appearance in a cherubically Dylan Thomas style. He spoke in a broad Ulster brogue.

'Didn't catch that man's name,' said the professor. Though still far gone in drink, he had not lost his desire, transparent at the beginning of the meal, to tick off in his mind, like a schoolboy spotting trains, the names of potentially famous people he had met on his day-trip to London from Oxford.

'Great man, Pugh,' said Darnley and burst out laughing. You momentarily wondered whether he was joking, and whether he could not see that Pugh was ridiculous. Then he screwed up his eyes and I saw that he meant what he said. Whether or not he was 'great', the man called Pugh was a disturbing figure from the first. His mind seemed full of subjects normally considered serious about which he pronounced with alarming vigour and confidence. He spoke about solemn things not as if they were a joke but with this mildly satanic grin on his face. Such matters as political and social gossip, by contrast, made his face become stern. As I came to learn, he was proud of having his ear to the ground. It was he who contributed much of the gossip to the 'Diary' in *The Spark*. Where did he get his information? Did he overhear it in bars, or invent it? His belief in the importance of Myth is apparent in the pages of his unfinished book about Christ. Perhaps those fragmentary pages were trying to illuminate the interesting question raised at that lunch by 'Pugh' – the myths we live by. My life as a radio actor involved me in a very minor way in a part of national mythology. The popularity of 'The Mulberrys', unabated to this day, must owe something to the way the English view themselves. The bucolically unreal Barleybrook, the village where the Mulberrys farm, where old Harold Grainger was the blacksmith and I, Jason, was his wastrel son, was perhaps a place where all Mulberry fans longed to be. The Mulberrys are not art, but their saga touches a place in the soul similar to those images of England which had been memorably drawn by true artists. We find it in the realism of Constable's skies and landscapes, in the native airs of Elgar and Vaughan Williams, in the novels of Thomas Hardy, all of which appeal to the rural fantasies of a race who for the most part live in towns and suburbs but like to think of themselves as countrydwellers.

The professor, Cormac, was drunk enough not to mind being a bore, but sober enough to be able to brag about his powers of recall: he knew 'who Pugh was'.

'Albion Pugh,' he said, 'those extraordinary novels.'

'Never heard of them,' I said, remembering as I did so that this was not quite true.

'There are four. He wrote them ages ago,' said Darnley. 'He has never done anything in that line since. There's nothing quite like them.'

'There's one about King Arthur,' said the professor. '*Towered Camelot*. A couple are staying somewhere in Wales, and there's this classic country-house murder. Only it isn't. It's more than that. Excuse me.' Cormac protruded his very moist lower lip and belched. Looking less dazed, he continued. 'One of the characters turns out to be a witch, and the lost body of King Arthur, sleeping in Avalon until his people need him again, is found in the caves near the house. Anyway, the detective character. . . .'

'Pugh's got this way of making the supernatural seem totally real,' said Darnley.

'Like our friend Blake?'

'Very much like Blake, Pugh,' said Darnley. 'Same weird thing of having a vision of England. Similar, too, in the way the sublime stuff goes hand in hand with absolute balls.'

'How did you meet Pugh?'

'Sent a letter, care of his publishers, to say how much I liked the books. I didn't even know if he was still alive. He wrote back, pretty chuffed, said he hadn't had a fan letter since the war. We took it from there. The best of the novels is set in Egypt.'

'*Memphian Mystery*, oh, now that's a *delicious* one,' said Professor Cormac, with the perky air of a child doing well in a quiz. 'A party of travellers, mainly English, some Americans, cruising in the Med. Typical Agatha Christie stuff, you might have thought. One of them is carrying this sacred scarab – he doesn't know what it is, of course. Anyhow. . . .'

But Darnley and I turned away. Albion Pugh. *Memphian Mystery*, *Towered Camelot*. I could place them now, though I could not say that I had ever read them. I remembered the green and white covers of the pre-war Penguins lying about in my uncle's rectory at Timplingham during my childhood. I had a visual memory of my uncle's daughter Felicity, truculently absorbed in *Memphian Mystery* whose plot Professor Cormac was even now rehearsing as he sat at the table in the Black Bottle. He was speaking to himself. All the other guests had risen to their feet and were dispersing.

A few stragglers leaving the pub hovered on the pavement. Vernon Lampitt was there – Ernie, as it now seemed more polite to call him. He was in his early sixties, and his hair had turned quite snowy since our last encounter. My uncle liked to quote a Lampitt family saying that Vernon was very much more a Charles than a Lampitt, Charles being the maiden name of Vernon's mother. It is true that physically Vernon did not have the classic Lampitt features, as my ex-wife Anne had, or her mother Sibs, or her uncle Sargie – that long face with a protuberant chin. Vernon's sister, always referred to by Uncle Roy as the Honourable Penny-lope (as a boy I never realised that this was a joke pronunciation) had these features. So did Dame Ursula Lampitt, the Principal of Rawlinson College, Oxford. Vernon's face was rounder, and softer, with large, popping blue eyes. (Old Mrs Lampitt, Sargie's mother, wondered if Vernon suffered from thyroid trouble, though she would never say so to the boy's father. 'A *wonderful* woman,' Uncle Roy would add.)

Standing outside the pub with Vernon, it occurred to be that his pop-out eyes, often described by journalists as penetrating, were the very opposite of Albion Pugh's. You had the sense in 'Pugh's' presence, in spite or because of his evidently defective vision and thick spectacles, that he could see through you. Vernon's eyes gleamed and stared, but when they fixed on a person, there was no indication that he took in what he saw.

We did not know one another well, and beyond a general recognition of my presence at the lunch table, Vernon did not give me any clue that he remembered who I was. Since Darnley insisted on introducing me to everyone as Jason Grainger, there would have been every reason for a certain vagueness in the matter. I wasn't even sure, having some years earlier split up with his cousin Anne, whether Vernon would regard me in a friendly light. But as we stood there in Poland Street he seized my upper arm in a comradely fashion and squeezed it in a manner suggestive of a boxing trainer anxious about a featherweight's biceps.

'We don't see enough of yer, Julian. We *hear* yer all right. Pat's a great Bilberry fan.'

11

'Mulberry.'

'I don't have time for it meself unfortunately.'

'Of course not.'

The very idea that Vernon could spare quarter of an hour in the midst of his political concerns to listen to the Mulberrys was a preposterous one.

'Yer still with us, I hope?'

'Us?'

'Yer've not gone all right wing or anything? I know yer uncle Roy's still *dong le mouvemong*. Saw him not so long ago.'

I was disgracefully lazy about keeping in touch with my uncle, particularly since I now shared a house with Felicity and felt that I kept in touch with her parents vicariously, through her.

'Where did you run across him?'

'That's right.' Vernon seldom gave answers which suggested he had attended to one's questions. Had he not been a professional politician you might have supposed him to be deaf, which, for all I know, he might have been. 'Yah. Yer never met me poor old cousin Bobby.'

'The one who farmed in Rhodesia? Didn't he once make a rather amusing remark about a duckling?'

From earliest times I could remember my uncle hardly able to contain himself at the repetition of this 'famous' *mot*, made to a waiter at the Adelphi Hotel in Brighton. Vernon either had never heard the duckling story or chose to forget it. He showed no surprise at my absolute grasp of his extended and complicated family tree.

'Poor old Bobby was a bit of a fascist really. Came back to London to die – his boys took over the farm. He finally passed on three weeks ur so ago. Yer uncle came up and took the funeral.'

'He didn't tell me.'

I felt unjustifiably aggrieved.

'It was Sibs's idea to have Roy.'

There was that phrase of Jimbo's (i.e. of James Petworth Lampitt) which had so annoyed my uncle: 'Sargie's tame parson'.

'Very appropriate,' I said.

Like all people lacking in social confidence, I respond to unexpected information as if it were somehow designed to trick me, or show me up. Vernon could not possibly have cared whether I knew about my uncle's visit to London, but I felt the need to lie about it.

'Now you mention it,' I said. 'Felicity did say something about her father coming to London to conduct a funeral.'

She had not done so. She spoke about very little except her work, and I formed the impression that Roy's visit to London had been kept a secret even from his daughter; not for any sinister reasons, but simply because he saw the Lampitts all too rarely these days and would want to concentrate on solid joys and lasting treasure without dissipating the experience by exposure to his own flesh and blood.

'You remember Felicity?' I needled Vernon.

'Good *Lord* yes.'

His overemphasis suggested that the reverse was true.

'Foreign Office?' he fished.

'As it happens, Ministry of Works,' I said, 'but she's only been a civil servant a short time. It's an experiment. She got fed up with being a don and they're giving her a few years off from Rawlinson to see how she likes something different.'

'Rawlinson. *Course*. With Ursula. Don't know why I thought Felicity was in the Foreign Office. Anyway, come down to Mallington, both of yer. Do.'

'That would be nice.'

'Ridiculous place, uv course. I long ter be rid uv it. Pat 'n I debate its future all the time. Should be nationalised like all these dirty great houses. A conference centre, or mebbe a place for youngsters, a place fer thum ter come at weekends, mebbe learn a trade.'

Any less likely setting for an apprentice to perfect his skills in, say, electrical maintenance or welding, would have been difficult to devise.

Cyril, mine host of the Bottle, came to the pub door to address Darnley.

'That fat bugger's still in there.'

'The prof?' smiled Darnley.

'Still sitting at the fucking table talking about the fucking pharaohs. I've told him to sod off but he's too heavy to lift. Irish, inne?'

'I'll come and have a word with him,' said Darnley.

'These lunches 'll have to stop if you can't clear out the piss artists after closing time,' explained Cyril.

'It's Professor Cormac,' said Vernon. ''E's practically fascist, yer know. Wrote a really foul review uv me friend Tommy Wimbish's history of the party. Did yer see it?'

13

'No,' I said, though I rather enjoyed Professor Wimbish's books, which were written for people like myself, intelligent 'general' readers, who can't be bothered with footnotes. 'Don't all dons hate one another, as moles are supposed to do?' I asked.

This was certainly the impression I received from conversation with Felicity.

While Darnley tried to shift the recalcitrant professor from his chair, Vernon and I took our leave.

'I'll walk with yer ter the Tube. Got ter get back to the Chamber. We're inter the second reading of this Immigration Bill. Between ourselves, I hope we send it back to the Commons for reconsideration. Our party's got it wrong I'm afraid ter say.'

It slightly surprised me, in view of his principles, that Vernon was prepared to take his seat in the Lords. There was much talk in the family of his renouncing his peerage, but this did not seem to have happened yet. He appeared to me to have a very muddled attitude to the Immigration Bill, on the one hand reacting to the issue like any Little Englander, and on the other seeing it as an opportunity to trounce the Conservatives.

'You can't be for the Bill?' I asked.

'Lord, no. But I think it's scandalous, if we're honest, ter hold out the hope of British citizenship ter folk in Africa und the West Indies when we haven't bothered ter provide indoor toilets for our own people.'

'So, you might vote with the Tories?'

He waved any such absurdity aside.

'No, we'll get rid uv the Bill, we'll get rid uv the Government, we'll get rid uv the Tories and start to rebuild. . . .'

'Jerusalem, in England's green and pleasant land?'

'If yer like, if yer like. If I may, Julian, I'll write ter yer and suggest a date when yer can come down ter Mallington. Perhaps yer could bring Darnley? I see quite a future for this little paper uv his.'

I refrained from mentioning Vernon's own prolix article in the present issue on the nationalism of the clearing banks.

'I don't know who feeds Darnley half his stories for the "Diary",' he said.

'Albion Pugh, it would seem.'

'The funny bloke with glasses?' Vernon laughed. 'I thought he had a bit of a screw loose.'

It takes one to know one. At Tottenham Court Road station we parted, he for an Embankment train, and I for one in the opposition direction, Camden Town.

The encounter with Vernon set off a reverie in my mind which drove away Darnley, Albion Pugh, the harlot and the bishop. Too much execrable wine with the meal, followed by a ride in a stuffy train took me back to the day which I had almost forgotten when I first saw Mallington Hall, and my mind was so full of it that I forgot to get out at Camden Town and sat in a daze until Tufnell Park, where I alighted and walked home southwards thinking of the day God pulled the plug out.

Mrs Webb, my grandmother's close friend, was saying, 'It's not proper sea, not what I would call proper sea. We've walked for miles, and just look at it – it's *still* miles away.'

My tiny legs were certainly tired. I was barely five years old. We had walked and walked, past shining mudflats where oyster-catchers, terns and black-headed gulls patterned the wet surface of the empty creeks with their thousands of intricate footprints, and made our way over sandy paths alongside still ditches and dunes where the grass was coarse and thick and springy, and yet the sea was still far off. The small village where we were staying seemed equally distant now. Further off were the clumps of flat-topped pines. Before and behind, the distance stretched with apparent infinitude and in that very clear September light no detail of it was faded; it was all bright as some Dutch landscape painting of the seventeenth century.

'That's Mallington Hall,' said Daddy. 'We might go there tomorrow.'

I was sitting on my father's shoulders. He pointed.

'Look, Julian. Do you see the lovely house?'

The brick and stucco shape was too far away for my eyes to take in, in any detail, but I could see it, far away, safe in its own inaccessible beauty. We did not go there the next day. Our holiday was to be cut short.

'Come on now, son, try and walk for yourself a bit more. Daddy's shoulders are getting tired.'

He lifted me down, and I ran to hold Mummy's hand.

My grandmother stood still and tried to focus her eyes on Mallington.

'I can't see it,' she said.

'There!' Daddy often laughed at his mother, but in an affectionate, rather than satirical way. 'There!'

Before any comment could be made upon the view, Mrs Webb leapt to Granny's defence.

'It's a shame to bring Thora here with her feet,' she announced.

Daddy did not answer. He strode ahead, indicating that the walk, or route march (which was what it felt like) had resumed, regardless of discontent in the ranks. He wore very capacious shorts so that only a little of his pale legs was revealed. His white shirt was rolled up to his elbows, and his forearms were brown.

We traipsed in single file, all of us. I held a small spade, which, while I had been astride his shoulders, Daddy had been afraid would poke his eyes. I also carried a bucket. It was decorated with a transfer of Mickey Mouse. Granny had bought it for me earlier in the summer when she and Mrs Webb had taken me to Westgate, where the sea was unimpeachably proper, fully equipped with bathing huts, toilets (though these had been denounced by the two ladies as 'a disgrace'), a pier, ice-cream stalls, and cafés serving 'nice' cups of tea and the full variety of light meals on toast – beans, roes, eggs, sardines, what not. I myself much preferred Westgate to this new sort of sea.

'Mummy,' I said.

'Not *another* stitch?' she asked.

The reason that my father had consented to carry me on his shoulders was that, a few minutes before, we had all had to stop while I relieved a stitch, touching my toes and gulping with the pain of it. The stitch was indeed returning, but I did not want to admit this, in case Mrs Webb crowed and triumphed too much over my parents. There had been no question of a stitch at Westgate. The whole visit there had been a riotous success, with donkey rides, and an attendance at the Punch and Judy show, followed by a positively delicious plate of egg and chips for tea. It was all too imaginable how Mrs Webb would make use of the present situation. Silly, wearing the boy out before we even reached the sands. Thus she would rail, putting Daddy in the wrong.

'It's gone,' I said, referring to the stitch. 'Only, Mummy. . . .'

'What is it now, Julian?'

She wore a straw hat over her thick brown hair and her loose, short-sleeved dress was splashed with a floral print of yellow and green. The skirt was perfectly ironed and stiff and stuck out as a triangle around her pink smooth legs. I wished we weren't walking in single file, because I desperately wanted to hold Mummy's hand. Do I deceive myself? Was this the very same dress which she wore on that terrible day, several years later, when I set eyes on her for the last time on the platform at Paddington station?

'Was it like this when Moses dried up the sea, Mummy?'

'Probably,' she said.

'Not far now,' said Daddy.

We had passed the mudflats and could see the glistening sand, stretching in every direction, a huge expanse. The sea, infinitely beyond, was lower than the shore. It was a vast, brooding, dark blue bath, heaving beneath the sky, but too distant for us to reach.

Behind me, Mrs Webb observed, 'It isn't nice to think of *them* just over the water. Probably *in* the water, with submarines and swastikas stuck all over them. It's disgusting.'

This frightened me. I did not know who 'they' were. If any more of the sea were to disappear, however, there would be a limitless stretch of sand and they, swastikas and all, could merely climb out of their beached submarines and walk up to us, as the children of Israel had walked across the bed of the Sea of Reeds.

'Has God pulled the plug out?' I enquired.

Granny and Mrs Webb were always on the look-out for jokes, and this remark was often repeated in later years. That fateful day in European history became, in our family, 'the day God pulled the plug out'.

'He'll let the water back in again,' said Mummy. 'You'll see.'

I was not so sure that He would. My earliest impression was that He was not necessarily to be trusted, and I had imbibed some of Mrs Webb's distrust of religion. At Westgate, we had given a very wide berth to a beach 'mission', and Granny had given full assent to Mrs Webb's view that there was a time and a place for everything, but that it somehow was not quite nice to be singing songs about Jesus where the kiddies were making sandcastles and trying to enjoy themselves.

We struggled on in silence until we had passed the grass-grown dunes and came to the shore itself and settled ourselves with rugs and two picnic baskets and the old ladies' books, and my bucket and spade. Daddy said that he and I should go in search of sea-shells.

'It's nearly one,' he said with a glance at his wrist-watch. 'They should be here very soon.'

'It'll take them ages in that contraption of theirs,' said Mummy.

This exchange filled me with alarm. First Mrs Webb had let the cat out of the bag with the information that 'they' were hiding in the sea. Now, my parents calmly announced that 'they' would be arriving in a contraption. I did not realise that Mrs Webb was talking about the Germans, and that my parents were discussing the arrival of Aunt Deirdre, Felicity and Uncle Roy, Daddy's brother. Leaving Granny and Mrs Webb with their Warwick Deepings and their Craven As, my parents took me further on to the sand, following a shallow inlet which ran down towards the sea and which Daddy said was good for shells. Mummy collected the most, lifting the hem of her skirt to form a sort of marsupial pouch which I helped her to fill with whelks, scallops, razor-shells, giant mussels, oysters, limpets, cockles and clams.

'Mrs Webb's right, really,' said Daddy, referring to an earlier altercation. 'We should have seen if we couldn't get to a wireless to listen in. There's probably one at the hotel we could have heard.'

Our holiday cottage was primitive. I seem to remember that there was no electricity and that water was drawn from a pump in the back yard. There was certainly no wireless.

Mummy stroked my father's shoulders.

'Maybe it will all blow over,' she said. 'It did last time.'

Daddy sighed. 'Oh, Jill,' he said.

'They can't' – she faltered, and then with the hand which was not holding up her skirt she stretched and gestured towards the wide sand, like Moses stretching forth his rod over the waters. 'They can never bring all this to an end.'

All this: the huge sea-shore and the wide flat land which stretched as far as the eye could strain over staithes and dykes, fields and woods to the squat tower of Mallington church and beyond that, in its well-planted park, to the Hall itself. I do not know why, Londoners, my parents had chosen this particular village as a suitable holiday place. Presumably they liked that strange bit of the north Norfolk coast, unlike anywhere else in the world, and felt it was sufficiently close to Daddy's brother to allow for family visits while being far enough away to maintain a safe distance – an hour in the 'contraption', an extraordinary old car called a Trojan which had solid tyres. I am sure that the proximity of our cottage to Mallington Hall played no part

18

in my parents' fondness for the place. I have no reason to suppose that they were interested in architecture and I know that they did not share my uncle Roy's consuming passion, the genealogy and doings of the Lampitt family, a branch of whom lived in the noble pile which could be glimpsed beyond the flats and pines.

My uncle Roy's parish, Timplingham, was about twenty-five miles inland, to the south, and contained another branch of this, to him, inexhaustibly fascinating family: 'our Lampitts', as I came to think of them: old Mrs Lampitt, her 'hopeless' son Sargie, who was Uncle Roy's best friend, his brother, the writer James Petworth Lampitt (Jimbo) and their sister Sibs (destined for a time to be my mother-in-law). These others, the Lampitts of Mallington, were cousins, leftish politicians by calling.

Quarter of a century after 'God pulled the plug out', I met 'Albion Pugh' and heard expressed the commonplace view that we cannot live without myths. (It sounded impressive on 'Pugh''s lips, not least because he used the word 'mythos' rather than 'myth' and said it in his strange cockney sing-song.) Uncle Roy's saving mythology was the Lampitt family, more interesting, it would seem, then his own, more capable of engaging the imgination and providing life with a shape.

I was too young when Daddy died to be able to form a realistic impression of how well he got on with my uncle Roy. The fact that a man speaks satirically of his brother by no means implies lack of fondness but, with the literalness of a child, I imagined that Daddy did not much like Uncle Roy and that it would be wrong, even disloyal, of me to do so. As I write this down, I see how this fact must have complicated the sometimes painful relationship I had with my uncle when he had taken me to live in his house after my parents were killed in the air raid.

'When they *do* come,' said Mrs Webb, 'I hope we don't have to hear too much about the Lampitts. We'll have Lampitts coming out of our ears, the way Roy talks about them.'

There was a general, laughing assent to this surreal possibility.

'Lord Lampitt' – Daddy put on his cruelly accurate 'Uncle Roy' voice, which was rather posher than his own – 'a charming man, but I'm sorry to say. . . .'

Mummy was already laughing and even I, at barely five years old, knew the chorus by heart.

'Just a tiny little bit of a humbug.'

We said it in unison, and it partially resolved my fears. From everything the grown-ups had been saying during the past few days it was obvious that something was about to happen, something big and disastrous which the Prime Minister would tell us on the wireless. 'They' were coming.

I now realised that they were not going to kill me or take my Mummy away. When they had completed the tedious journey across the North Sea in their contraption, 'they' would emerge in their swastikas; but, as I now learnt, all we had to dread was the possibility of Lampitts coming out of our ears. I had never realised before that the Germans shared with my uncle Roy this Lampitt obsession. For all I knew, everyone in the world was interested in them except us. I had not yet been imprisoned in what Albion Pugh would have termed the empiricist fallacy. I had never knowingly set eyes on a Lampitt, unless perhaps to be given the occasional gin-flavoured kiss on the top of my head by Sargie, and I was not of an age to ask whether stories were true or false. All that mattered was whether stories were interesting, funny, or frightening. If two children came across a house made of gingerbread and candy in the middle of a wood, this was no more improbable than Lord Lampitt being a humbug. I imagined him as part human, part boiled sugar, the sort of figure Tenniel would have drawn well, his cheeks striped and shiny with hard minty surfaces, the pointed corners of the asymmetrical cube serving him for nose and ears.

'They should be here by now,' said Daddy – we had walked back to rejoin Granny and Mrs Webb – 'though I know that Roy has to finish his service thing.'

Granny and Mrs Webb, unwilling to 'wait about all day' had already consumed a quantity of cress sandwiches, hard-boiled eggs and cold chipolatas. Eager eyes were already being cast on the fruit cake. I was desperately hungry and accepted the sandwich which Mrs Webb held out to me.

'Sit up again on Daddy's shoulder,' said my father – has anyone ever explained why so many grown-ups, when addressing children, refer to themselves in the third person? – 'and tell him if you can see Uncle Roy.'

Daddy pretended to be a camel and lolloped up the sand dunes until we had found a good vantage point.

'Someone is coming,' I said uncertainly.

'Is it your uncle Roy?'

Anxious to give an answer which would please, I said 'I think so,' even though I could not in fact see my uncle. I saw Aunt Deirdre, though. Over her fleshy shoulders, the thick canvas straps of a haversack were tightly drawn. She wore a white floppy sunhat, Christopher Robin style. Her white blouse and blue skirt could have been – though in fact were not – uniform. Behind her, in almost identical rig, certainly wearing the same sort of floppy sunhat, came her daughter Felicity. Their ages at this time were, perhaps, twelve and thirty-eight, but in appearance they could have been sisters. Felicity in childhood always seemed old before her time, while Aunt Deirdre, roundfaced and crop-haired, retained an ageless innocence.

Aunt Deirdre waved. As was her wont, she looked slightly cross. I seldom saw this expression vanish from her face, in the course of her entire life, except for those rare occasions when she actually lost her temper and 'let rip'. Very occasionally, when gardening, one would see the disgruntlement vanish from her features, but for the most part, she seemed to be holding back sharp words. Slightly before she reached us, she began her explanation of Uncle Roy's absence from the scene.

'Of course, as soon as he heard the news, Roy felt he had to stay behind and comfort Sargie. He was in a terrible tizz, Sargie I mean.'

It was of Sargent Lampitt she spoke, the humbug's cousin.

'Mrs Lampitt and he heard it on the wireless of course, up at the Place. Sargie came straight down to church, if you please, and that made history in itself. I knew something was up, because I happened to turn round and see him hovering while Roy was chanting the last of the versicles. When Roy got to the third collect, first Sunday in the month, so it's Mattins which I *much* prefer, Sargie boomed out, "You'd better all know we are finally at war". . . .'

'At war with Germany,' Felicity corrected her mother. 'Uncle Sargie said we were at war with Germany.'

'How many were in church?' asked Mrs Webb, with merciless directness.

'Roy kept his nerve, of course,' continued the messenger. 'No point in doing anything else. He said "Before you all rush off, I think we should. . . ."'

'"Hasten away",' said Felicity. 'Pa said "hasten away", not "rush off".'

'Same thing,' said Granny.

'They're not the same words,' said Felicity. 'They're not what Pa actually said.'

'He asked us all to stand,' persisted Aunt Deirdre, 'and sing "Jerusalem". So we did.'

'How many of you, though?' Mrs Webb wanted to know. Family pride or perhaps the dark suspicion that my grandmother's friend might be chapel or, worse, RC (and therefore with no business to know what went on in proper churches) made my aunt instinctively cagey about revealing the numbers at Mattins at Timplingham that morning.

'Naturally there were fewer than usual,' said Aunt Deirdre. 'People were staying at home to listen in.'

'I can't believe it,' said Mummy. 'I just can't take it in. I thought it would all blow over.'

'There were six of us,' said Felicity, 'if you count Mrs Collins who was playing the organ. Seven for "Jerusalem", because Uncle Sargie joined in.'

'I should have called that more a Women's Institute hymn,' said Mrs Webb. '"Fight the Good Fight"'s more like it now. Or the National Anthem.'

'Well,' said Aunt Deirdre, choosing to ignore this impertinence, 'this time he's gone far enough.' She spoke in the same impatient, cross tone with which she might describe a child whose behaviour had become raucous at a parish tea party, and who had been sent to 'cool off' in the corner while the rest of us passed the parcel. 'We gave him Czechoslovakia on a plate and he should have been jolly grateful for that, though Roy and Sargie both said it was wrong at the time. But he just wants more and more and more. No satisfying some people. Now he's gone and invaded Poland when we *told* him he couldn't, and – well, enough's enough.'

'Always nice weather when a war breaks out,' said Granny. 'Do you remember the last one? Lovely weather then.'

Larks rose vertically from the springy dunes and the gorse was brilliant with flowers. Nothing looked different from five minutes before, in spite of the news my aunt had brought. The wind blew, but by the standards of that coast, it blew gently. The sun continued to shine.

'Only, Roy said at once, we couldn't leave you stranded; you might have been waiting here all day.'

'There's no wireless in the cottage,' said Mummy. 'This was the first we heard of it.'

'I said I'd drive Fliss over, the air would do us good. No good moping, just because there's a war, and I'd already made the potted meat sandwiches. Got to eat, Hitler or no Hitler.'

'Uncle Sargie's upset,' said Felicity. 'He was crying during "Jerusalem". He said it was all bloody nonsense, but it made him blub.'

'It is quite unnecessary to repeat that word,' said my aunt hotly. Felicity went so red that I thought she herself would cry.

'Fliss is right, actually,' said my aunt, perhaps fearing her daughter's tears. 'Sargie was bitterly upset. Roy had to stay with him.'

'Naturally,' said my father. 'A war breaks out, and where is Roy? With his own family? Comforting the troops? Oh, no. He has to stay with Sargent blooming Lampitt.'

An awkward silence followed that observation. When I lived in the rectory and became acquainted with its routines, I learnt that my aunt also resented the amount of time spent by Uncle Roy in Sargie's company, but marital loyalty would not allow her to admit this to my parents. She merely seemed 'browned off' – that would have been her phrase – with Hitler. The mad dictator should have been more thoughtful. Invading Poland was bound to upset Sargie and, as she often said, 'When Sargie suffers, we all suffer.'

'Roy was really looking forward to coming today,' she said in his defence. 'He had hoped some of us would want to call at Mallington, bless him.'

'That's where the Honourable Vernon Lampitt lives,' said Felicity with intense seriousness. 'Pa says that he is a brilliant economist.'

'Oh bother the Lampitts!' Mummy exclaimed. 'The world is about to be destroyed, and all we can do is to stand here and talk about the Lampitts.'

'They do say,' added Mrs Webb, 'that London will be flattened. Levelled to the ground.'

Her lips were set firm at the prospect. It was not, exactly, a defiant expression: it was not saying, 'Come on, Hitler, do your worst!' It seemed to accept the tragic destiny of London, of its inhabitants, including herself, perhaps the tragic destiny of the entire human race, but to refuse, quite, to bow to its inevitability.

'Well, I do think it's *hard*,' said Granny. 'Hard.'

·

23

Aeons pass. With the indifference of a clumsy child, throwing broken toys into a corner, Fate removes characters from the scene. Mummy and Daddy and Mrs Webb had been long since dead when I met Vernon Lampitt round Darnley's lunch table with Albion Pugh, Pete Cornforth and the rest. (The Honourable Vernon was himself Lord Lampitt now, and it remained to be seen whether his party inclined to Uncle Roy's high views of his skills as an economist, or whether they would endorse Sibs's malevolent judgement that Vernon was 'a dimwit – the dimwit of the family, really'.) Hitler himself, and his threats to destroy England, had vanished. Twenty-four years had passed since God pulled the plug out and since Aunt Deirdre, Uncle Roy, Felicity, Sargie and the others had sung Blake's words, speculating about the legend of Christ visiting Britain as a child, and declaring their refusal to cease from mental fight until they had seen Jerusalem built in England's green and pleasant land: all matters of vital interest to Darnley's new friend Albion Pugh. England had passed out of austerity into a phase when we were supposed never to have had it so good.

Certainly, this political cliché implied more than economic prosperity. Perhaps the Harlot and the Episkopos were indeed tokens. The vapid agnosticism of the bishop, surely shared by the majority of churchmen, reminded us of how much had been eroded of the old certainties. The Ten Commandments had been left behind with our ration books. The public threw up its hands at the Cabinet minister's unsuitable choice of companion, but the simple fact was, that people envied him. They too, had they been able to afford it, would have liked to romp naked by the swimming pool at Cliveden, and attend wild parties, and disregard their marriage vows, and put sex before their tedious jobs. The scandal became a signal for a general whoopee which would engulf England for at least a decade.

In this new arrangement of the scenery we all stood poised to play our parts. The brilliant economist (or family dimwit), in his new incarnation as Ernie Lampitt, the people's friend, was quite possibly destined for high office in the new Britain which was waiting to be born. He had managed to laugh aside his inherited barony as 'me dad's little bit o' nonsense'. His large house in Norfolk, to which I had just been invited, was spoken of as a burden. Neither title nor property seemed to deter Vernon's advancement as a working-class hero. Presumably, if the chance of really high political office came his way, he would discard the peerage, and become plain Mr Lampitt. A Lampitt Prime Minister! My uncle had been speaking of the possibility for as long as I could recall. I had never taken him seriously, since in his vision of the universe, only Lampitts fully existed, the other inhabitants of the planet being shadowy, ethereal beings in whom it was eccentric, by the standards of Timplingham rectory, to take very much interest. It was natural that Uncle Roy should have seen Vernon as the next Prime Minister. Now, by an extraordinary chance, the world seemed to be of Uncle Roy's mind.

The Lampitts, who had seemed to be a purely private obsession of my uncle's, did, as I now realised, have some place in the public consciousness. Since Raphael Hunter had published that notorious volume of biography, the world knew more than it needed to know of James Petworth Lampitt, the man of letters. There had been a great revival of interest in his works and even talk of Jimbo's biography of Prince Albert being made into a film. Hunter showed no signs of writing a continuation of the biography, taking it from Jimbo's young manhood to his death, but he had kept the Lampitt flame aglow with several 'spin-offs'. There had been a reissue of some of Jimbo's books with introductions by Hunter, and there was a projected television series, scripted and 'fronted' by Hunter, based on some of Jimbo's sketches from Victorian life. Jimbo himself, in Hunter's version of the story, had become an emblematic figure, though one less tuppence-coloured than the Bishop and the Harlot. If, as Hunter implied, Jimbo had been a promiscuous homosexual, this was all to the good, as far as his current sales and popularity were concerned. At the period when Hunter was researching the book in Sargie's house, the period when he formed his disastrous attachment to my cousin Felicity, homosexuality was, generally speaking, frowned upon except by the enlightened few. Even those of homosexual disposition themselves might well share the general view that having a particular preference somehow constituted a handicap, even a form of spiritual disease from which a cure could or should be sought. Different mythologies were about to burst upon the world and Jimbo's supposedly limitless sexual appetite, his ability to seduce members of his own sex however heterosexual they might have been (the Lloyd George incident is the one most often referred to), made him a potential hero in the age of the Harlot and the Bishop. Whether the real Jimbo bore any resemblance to the

Petworth Lampitt in Hunter's biography was a matter of hot dispute. His brother Sargie still denied it vigorously, and doubts had been sown in my own mind by Felicity, the only person I knew, apart from Hunter, who had even cast an eye over the 'Lampitt papers' now safely housed with a private collector in New York.

These matters occupied my thoughts as I walked southwards to Camden Town. As sometimes happens to me when I am mildly drunk, whole scenes and conversations replayed themselves inside my head, sometimes from long ago (the day on the beach when we heard that war had broken out), sometimes from the most recent past (the lunch, Darnley, his new friend Albion Pugh – sage, prophet, gossip, religious charlatan, failed writer, mystery man).

It was of Pugh that I thought as my feet passed the litter-strewn pavements by Camden Town station: his high brow, not dissimilar, it now seemed, from William Blake's, his long hair awry, his marble eyes distorted by the lenses of those ancient specs.

'Either/or' – his cockney voice sang inside my brain – 'the two falsest words in the English language.' What had he meant by that?

I turned into Parkway. The road where I lived was first on the left past a pub called the Camden Stores. The street was lined by a middling-sized terrace of brick houses built in the 1840s when London was expanding northwards beyond Regent's Park and when those regions were inhabited by just such poor waifs as William Blake had pitied – industrial child-slaves whose Irish parents had been enlisted as navvies on the railway as it extended through Chalk Farm and Primrose Hill, or who worked in the factories dotted around Camden itself. Now, the terrace had a handsome, peeling gentility which I found congenial. Twenty years were to pass before this part of London became in any sense fashionable, though it had, I suppose, a certain Bohemian chic. (Dylan Thomas had occupied a house round the corner from my own.)

I say 'my own' but, again, these were the days before anyone of my limited means would contemplate taking out a mortgage. Like the huge majority of Londoners, I paid rent.

After my marriage to Anne broke up, I did not really care where I lived so long as it was not in the area on the edges of Chelsea where we had become so miserable together. Anything with SW in the address was to be avoided. NW seemed as different as possible, and my present address was very convenient for Euston station. I now earned my living, such as it was, as a radio voice. Two or three times a month, I had to make the journey from London to Birmingham, where the Mulberry programmes were recorded. Euston was where I caught my train. My other radio stint was a weekly broadcast from London, at Bush House in the Aldwych, a book programme on the World Service of the BBC. I liked the producer of this programme and he would usually give me work reading aloud extracts from writers under discussion.

The money was not good, and I was poor. I am fortunate enough never to have greatly minded about these things. I did not aspire to live grandly, I dressed like a scruff, and initially, in the first couple of years on my own, I had all that I needed. Little by little, however, an early harbinger of middle age, I found that my domestic needs were becoming marginally more – how shall I phrase it? It was not comfort or luxury which I needed, it was privacy. I had moved from various lodgings and then I found myself sharing a house with two other actors and someone who worked on the technical side of things at Broadcasting House, a sound recordist. We all four kept ourselves to ourselves, had separate bed-sitting rooms, sharing only the bathroom and kitchen. There was a communal sitting room but we seldom all sat in it together. When one of the four left the household to get married, I took his room, not because I needed any extra space, but because I did not want the risk of an uncongenial neighbour on the same landing. I could not really afford the extra rent – if I named the sum here, it would seem ludicrously modest – but it was worth it. The two actors eventually moved on, and I took over the whole house and sublet the top floor to lodgers. It was not a success. The desire to be alone, to be my own master, had taken possession of me, and I was an intolerable landlord, complaining about the noise of their gramophone, seething with rage if 'they' put food in 'my' refrigerator (even though it was part of the agreement that they were allowed to do so) and generally making myself unpleasant. I retained the fourth bedroom as a 'spare', though I had few enough friends to occupy it, a fact which eventually dawned on my cousin Felicity, at that time a lecturer in philosophy at Oxford. She took to coming to stay fairly frequently during the university vacations. Camden Town was conveniently placed for the British Museum where she liked to work in the reading room, and she had various friends, of vaguely intellectual flavouring, who lived within a short bus ride of me. At the height of my trouble with the lodgers, Felicity put to me a scheme which seemed at the time irresistible.

She would pay half the rent for the whole house in exchange for being able to come and stay whenever she liked. We would lead separate lives. She would occupy the top half of the house, and I the bottom, and we would continue the arrangement of a shared kitchen and bathroom. The lodgers were dispatched and their rooms were refurnished with objects familiar to me since childhood, since Uncle Roy and Aunt Deirdre had more than enough furniture at the rectory and were probably despairing of Felicity ever setting up house in a 'conventional' way with a husband.

For some time this arrangement worked very well. For half the year Felicity was in Oxford, and for half the year she occupied the top half of the house in Arlington Road. Then, a year or more before I met Albion Pugh at the Black Bottle, all this changed quite dramatically. I do not think that Felicity was deliberately manipulative or dishonest; I do not think she undertook to share the house with me knowing that she would soon be living there all the time, but I do believe that having a house in London helped her towards the rather precipitate step of changing her career. It was after Christmas dinner at Timplingham that she broached the subject with me. Uncle Roy was reading aloud a Margery Allingham to Granny while Aunt Deirdre pored over gardening catalogues, and Felicity and I were washing up in the kitchen.

'Julian, there's something I should have told you.'

She blushed. For some reason, I spontaneously recalled the time, so far away emotionally that it might have been in a previous life, when she was recovering from her abortion, the necessary consequence of her entanglement with Hunter. She looked sheepish and vulnerable. Her resemblance to her mother, so strong in childhood, had grown much less marked with the years. Aunt Deirdre still looked like a disgruntled sea scout with a round, unchanging jawline. Felicity had her hair cut short too these days, but her cheeks were hollowed and she had become much paler than her mother. As I knew from sharing a house with her, she was an insomniac and her large eyes were shadowed beneath with sleeplessness. Her oval features were very lightly freckled. Her eyes were green, and something about the shape of the brow had come to resemble Uncle Roy, a point of likeness which had never showed itself in earlier times. One of the strangest features of Felicity's face was that her lips had become almost indistinguishable in colour from the flesh of her cheeks. They were full, rather sensual lips, particularly when opened to reveal those big teeth, but no girl ever had less rosy lips. She was several inches taller than Aunt Deirdre, who had once taken grave offence when someone, I think a gym mistress at school, had described Felicity as 'gawky'. In shoes, another fact I had not known until she moved into Arlington Road, she took size eights. As I stood in her mother's kitchen and looked at Felicity, blushing, and looking down with such seriousness, I guessed that she was about to say she was engaged to be married and I at once began to wonder whether her husband was coming to live in London too.

This was not what she had to say.

'I'm giving up philosophy,' she blurted out. There was a long silence, and then she added, 'Perhaps for ever.'

'Do you mean that you want to give up teaching?'

'That as well. I am giving up teaching because I am giving up philosophy.'

'You make it sound like giving up smoking.'

'I know. It would perhaps be as true to say that philosophy has given up me. It's not exactly that I can no longer do it.'

Family loyalty made me rush to her defence. I was sure that old Fliss could 'do it' with the best of them, whatever 'it' was. Like the rest of the family, I had never been too sure what philosophy was, though I more inclined to Aunt Deirdre's opinion that Fliss was jolly clever and should be given all encouragement than to Granny's view, enunciated with heartless vehemence on those occasions (these days rare) when she was awake, that philosophy was 'a lot of nonsense' – an absurdist definition which would, I suspect, have found an echo in the the bosom of the ever-lamented Mrs Webb. Felicity, when rattled once too often by this line of her grand-mother's, had snootily pointed out that some Frenchman, himself a philosopher, had come to this very conclusion in one of the most interesting books of the century.

'It's not that I can't do it,' she repeated, ignoring my expressions of certainty that she could, 'even though it is the most devilishly difficult thing in the world to do, and it may be that there is a madness in trying.' She paused and was silent for about a minute. 'Not in considering it important, that's not mad, but trying might be mad. The devil of it is, that except in a very limited number of mathematical and scientific statements, we are obliged to use language as the means to discuss the important matters before us.'

'You mean, like whether there's a God or not?'

'That's not often discussed these days.'

She laughed lightly.

I had introduced this question because I did genuinely suppose that it was the sort of thing with which philosophers were occupied. I also, however, felt a gossipy curiosity. That Christmas was the first since childhood at which Felicity had attended her father's Midnight Mass. I always went. As a conscious unbeliever I positively enjoyed the shape of the liturgical year. The Mass, with its gospel story of angelic salutations to the shepherds, its carols, its lights, was for me an essential part of Christmas and I was untroubled by an inability to regard it as anything but folktale. Felicity, for reasons which had never been spoken, but which I took to be ones of intellectual scruple, had stayed away from church altogether.

'Shouldn't philosophers be interested in the existence of God?' I asked her again.

'It depends by what criterion you are using the word *shouldn't*.'

'Surely it is important whether there is a God or not.'

'Yes, but equally important is where you derive your standards of importance, how they may be usefully discussed. . . . But you don't need me to say this. It's common sense. It is the difficulty of what happens when we go beyond common sense which is reducing me to silence.'

'Do we ever need to go beyond common sense?'

'I don't know. We choose to do so often enough, if by "we", you mean the human race. Oh, Julian, I need *time*.' She ran a large white hand through her short hair and raked it back from her waxy brow. 'Time, not to think, but to stop thinking. The brain tires itself out by thinking, it becomes sore with it, and can't go any further. I very much want to go further, but I don't like the directions in which my thoughts – which have stopped being thoughts and have become something else – are appearing to push me. I like common sense as much as you do, dear.'

'So, you're giving up teaching.'

'Most philosophers and mathematicians give up thinking before they reach my age. That doesn't matter. You have to be a genius actually to *do* philosophy, rather than merely being able to see what it is. For the purposes of my job, giving tutorials to young women, that's enough, that's all I need.'

'You mean, you can tell them the gist of what Hegel said, Kant,

Plato, the kind of thing you get in Russell's *History of Western Philosophy*.'

'My approach would not be the same as Russell's, but I see what you mean.'

'It is the only philosophical work I have found even remotely readable.'

'It is a silly and unfair book.'

'Oh.'

We continued to bang about in the kitchen but I did not speak. These lofty, snubbing remarks of Felicity's had been putting me in my place since childhood. I still hated it when she went all superior. I wrenched open cupboard doors and piled saucepans and baking trays with a clatter. She showed no conciousness that she had made an offensive remark.

'Who was that one who gave up philosophy because there was no more to be said – it was something like that, wasn't it?' I said. 'You saw him once in Cambridge. He became a village schoolmaster? No?'

'I'm not going to be a great philosopher like him,' she smiled sadly. I saw how much she would have wished to be in the same league as Wittgenstein. Through most of the years when we had shared our childhood home, I, similarly, had nursed all manner of ambitions: I wanted to be a great actor, a great writer. Perhaps those who achieve greatness in life are not those with the most talent, but those who never lose the childish self-confidence that they can walk on water. Once they question their ability to do so, they sink. Such a moment had evidently occurred in Felicity's life.

'Ursula Lampitt is being terribly good about it,' she said. 'When I told her why I wanted to give up my job, she insisted upon keeping my options open. They've appointed a temporary lecturer for three years. I can go back after that if I want to.'

'And what will you do?'

'I want to do ordinary work which doesn't leave the mind churning in the small hours.'

'A market garden?'

'Anyway, I'm fed up with Oxford.'

'I shall miss hearing all about the Fellows at Rawlinson.'

'I've been there nearly ten years. You have visited me perhaps twice.'

'I didn't want to *meet* your colleagues. I liked hearing about them.

Better than the Mulberrys, or your father's stories about the Lampitts.'

'Poor old Pa.'

Felicity had a quiet capacity to bring her colleagues to life. I knew each of the Fellows at Rawlinson so exactly from her verbal portraits that when I did eventually pay one of those rare visits to the college, I had no difficulty in recognising any of them. I knew before being introduced, that I was about to shake hands with Dr Barclay, an expert in the literature of the German Romantic period, who was said never to have crossed the Channel, spoke German with a Roedean accent and had the habit of lifting a cardiganed sleeve to cover the protuberant yellow teeth as she gave utterance. And there was the generously filled sailor's suit of Miss Plumb; pure maths, but vaguely impure, if unrequited, feelings for her pupils. Miss Darke, the pinched, snobbish English don, liked to make the girls cry and had a bee in her bonnet about the numerology of Spenser's *Faerie Queene*. How well, without anything so overt as an imitation, Felicity had conveyed to me Miss Darke's lips; the way, when she had delivered herself of some particularly barbed comment, Miss Darke's lips would implode, so that her mean little mouth would momentarily disappear, leaving nothing but a pencil line between the sharp nose and the triangular chin. With the imminent removal from my life of this gallery of entertaining figures, I felt as the listening public might feel if the Broadcasting Corporation chose to take 'The Mulberrys' off the air.

'What, then,' I asked, 'if not a market garden?'

'I've joined the Civil Service.' She blushed very deeply now. 'I suppose we should have talked about this sooner, because it will mean I'll be living in London all the time.'

Thus it began. Felicity started work at her ministry that January, and since then, she had been a permanent feature of life in Arlington Road. We still nominally led separate lives, ate most of our meals apart, and occupied separate floors of the house, but from that moment, everything was different . . . I was no longer able to tell myself with complete accuracy that I lived alone. Initially, I resented this; I knew that Felicity had every right to spend as much time in the house as she liked; after all, she paid half the rent. But my solitude was threatened. It was an alteration to the original agreement. I was no longer, quite, an independent being in the sense that I had been before. I found myself involuntarily developing irritation with

Felicity which was just like my fury with the lodgers; only, it was deeper because it revived ancient childhood hostility between us. The clumsy way she filled a teapot, her large talcum-powdery footprints on the landing linoleum – these annoyed me. Much worse was her intrusive interest in my 'work'. For as long as I was alone, I could hide from myself the fact that I was a professional failure, that I was not doing with my life what I had initially wanted to do, that my 'writing' had come to nothing, that radio work for the most part bored me, and that my private life was pathetically empty. I did not spell these things out to myself, still less to Felicity, but they became starkly obvious as soon as our shared life began. There was too much curiosity in her, too much intrusive sympathy, real but crushing. But the worst feature of her presence at Arlington Road was that, while finding it maddening, I also came to depend upon it. The evenings when Felicity was 'good' and did not intrude upon my time started to feel empty. We had the unwritten, unspoken agreement that we should continue to lead quite separate lives, but that, should we happen to coincide in the sitting room at about 6.30 p.m., we would have a drink together before our separate suppers. In time, these separate suppers turned into joint suppers. I found myself deliberately hovering in the sitting room wanting her to return, eager for the glass of sherry, and the latest instalment of office gossip, while 'our' supper was cooking. By this stage, I was not quite sure who had taken over whom, or whether it was merely an arrangement which suited us both; perhaps it was a reversion to childhood, simply.

The rehearsals of Felicity's office day were among the features of the new dispensation which I valued most highly. Even more than when she had been a university teacher, Felicity now needed to talk about her colleagues. At the end of each working day, she had to relive it for at least a quarter of an hour before drifting into silence, or talk of something else. Sometimes, if the desire for work-talk was strong, or the details too esoteric for the layman's ear, she needed to share it with some colleague in the same department, and she would come home later than usual having been to a pub to discuss the minutiae of office politics with a colleague, usually with Rice Robey. At other times, my company would satisfy, particularly if she wished to speak of Rice Robey himself. These talks were the mental equivalent of stretching tired limbs in a hot bath after a strenuous walk; and because of them, I came to know, as well as I knew the Lampitts, or the Mulberrys, or the Fellows of Rawlinson, a whole new cast-list of the people who worked on Felicity's corridor, or those whom she encountered in the course of her work. She was in a department of the Ministry of Public Works which had charge of Ancient Monuments. Her work was purely administrative, and she never left the office, but there were colleagues, such as the much-quoted Rice Robey, who was occasionally in the office, and who spent much of his time 'in the field'. Rice Robey was not Felicity's superior – I never did quite work out the Civil Service hierarchy – but I gathered that he worked several doors down from herself on the same corridor; he had charge of ancient sites in the southern region of England – stone circles, earthworks, Iron Age camps, White Horses, cairns, burial mounds, Romano-British floors. Sometimes, if no one else could be found to take them on, Rice Robey took an interest in later stuff, ruined castles and abbeys of Norman times, but his chief interest died out in the Dark Ages.

Rice Robey was by far the most colourful figure in Felicity's new box of puppets and I found him interesting from the first, not least because of Felicity's rapidly changing attitude towards him. So fast did the attitude change that I was slow in the early months to recognise that 'a really very tiresome man on the same corridor as myself', mentioned in her first week, was the same person to whom she contemptuously referred as the 'bull's-eyed poet' or that either of these individuals were to be associated with 'Mr Robey – he is a most fascinating conversationalist – he knows about everything – the Welsh Triads, theology, Egyptian hieroglyphics, William James's *Varieties of Religious Experience*'.

'That's everything?'

'Yes.'

She had laughed, a quite new laugh, liberated from the old despotism of fact which had enchained her academic existence.

'Whatever came of your theory that Mr Robey was a spy?'

'He certainly has the most extraordinary store of knowledge about people.'

She repeated the scandalous information which Rice Robey had told her about the newly elected Leader of the Labour Party.

'He should know. Mr Robey did work under the man during the last Labour Government.'

'You mean, Harold Wilson was Minister of Works, and Mr Robey happened to have a minor job in the ministry at the time. This made Mr Robey privy to the secrets of the minister's bedchamber?'

'I consider it rummer than this other business,' said Felicity, 'this stuff with the Cabinet minister.'

'If true, it would be *as* rum.' Now it was my turn to be pedantic. Since meeting Rice Robey, Felicity appeared to have an altogether looser attitude to language, and to truth. So much so, that it was difficult to build up a picture of the man which hung together or 'made sense', in the way that one always wants a two-dimensional figure to make sense. When Felicity had first described Rice Robey to me as 'tiresome', she had not expanded, and I assumed that some minor verbal badinage had irritated her. As her picture of him grew rosier, she started to deny her early descriptions of the man if ever they were repeated back to her. Thus:

'How's the man with the squint?'

'What man with a squint?'

'You know, the poet. The man who's rewriting Dante's *Divine Comedy* on the back of memo-slips.'

'Rice Robey does not have a squint. But I do wish he did not always have a cigarette hanging from his lips when he pokes his head around my office door.'

When, a week or two later, I referred to his habit, which she had vividly described, of 'flicking ash all over the place', Felicity had crossly asked me what was wrong with 'having the odd cigarette' and reminded me that I myself smoked heavily.

A similar rewriting of recent office history took place with regard to Rice Robey and the women.

'He's auditioning us for the role of Beatrice in his *Divine Comedy*,' she had said, in the days when she could still describe him with detachment. 'I've no hope. He likes trecento maidens with long hair. Beattie – the girl I told you about in the typing pool – is the likeliest candidate at the moment.'

'You said she despised him; handed round the note he had written to her.'

'Only because she couldn't understand the quotation he had written on her blotter – she needed someone to translate it for her. *Incipit vita nuova*. How could he expect a girl like Beattie to understand such words? Perhaps he wants women to despise him. Some men need that. Anyway, he certainly likes hair. You know when we had a temporary typist with a high bun of hair on her head, he took her down to the basement of our building, supposedly to sort through some additional filing cabinets which

35

we keep down there. Well, Brenda went down there quite by chance. . . .'

'Wait a minute. Brenda? She's the one two doors along from you. . . .'

'Yes. She's been transferred from Crown Buildings. Lives in Putney with a gym mistress, breeds cockers, it was her. She went down to the basement and found the two of them standing there. Rice Robey had a hairbrush in his hands, and the girl's bun of hair had been unwound. It was hanging loosely down her back. Brenda did not say anything.'

'Merely told you, and everyone else in the building.'

Since this incident had been related to me, I had more than once alluded to it. For some reasons, the image of the temporary secretarial assistant with her long hair falling about her shoulders haunted my imagination. I wondered why she had consented to play Rice Robey's probably harmless, if mildly unusual game. Felicity, it was clear, regretted having told me about it. The first time I mentioned it again, she dismissed my allusion with a crossness which reminded me of her mother. The next time I spoke about it, she more or less denied that the hairbrushing incident had taken place. She was in the middle of a fairly complicated narrative about some contretemps between the Head of her Department and the Head of Personnel. Not enough typists provided, something of the sort. I forget the details. I remember only that I made some facetious comment to the effect that I hoped any typists enlisted would have long tresses suitable for Rice Robey's requirements.

'I really don't know what you're talking about,' said Felicity.

'You know. Rice Robey in the basement with a hairbrush and the temporary secretary; Celia, you said she was called.'

'I don't remember a secretary called Celia. This sounds like one of Brenda's tall stories.'

'It was Brenda who discovered them together.'

'Brenda doesn't like Rice Robey. I don't remember the story. It sounds very unlikely to me.'

She fell to a meticulous analysis of a budget report and its ramifications. For most of our working lives, mind and emotions are caught up in details which, with the passage of the years, vanish totally from consciousness. I had taken to boring Felicity with analogous twingle-twangle in relation to my work for the BBC. I minded desperately, from week to week (not least because I was a freelance and my income depended on it) about the whim of the producer of 'The Mulberrys' and I was obsessed by the internal affairs of Bush House. It took Felicity no time at all after leaving Oxford to be neck deep in the trivia of office life at A.1., as her branch of 'Accommodation and Buildings' was called in the Ministry of Works. Where the money was coming from for this or that project; the fate of particular papers, précis and memos; the abuse or exercise of power by those who pushed these documents from in-tray to out-tray: these things filled Felicity's mind, kept her awake at nights, throbbed through her waking thoughts as she caught her bus, or kept at bay those more disturbing thoughts of love and age and whither we were all hurtling as the weeks sped by. But they are gone now, these preoccupations, like the food we eat, and I find that I only recall those things which, at the time, seemed extraneous to work, supposedly unimportant matters of gossip such as who was in love with whom; and even those details became distorted and forgotten.

A myth to live by – that, Albion Pugh had suggested, was the one thing needful. An exercise such as the present narrative in which one selectively reclaims the past is such a piece of myth-making, no doubt, or a discovery of what myths I have been involuntarily weaving in my brain out of the day-to-day ordinariness of things. The lunch with Darnley had made me mildly drunk, but it had also awoken a disturbing chain of reflections. Memories of childhood, of the part played in life by the Lampitts, had all arisen, murky ghosts in the mind, drawing back further curtains of memory to reveal the north Norfolk coast, and my lost parents in the bright sunshine of September 3, 1939, a day which, for everyone who can remember it, however dimly, links the personal myth to the national. Albion Pugh was right. Everything since the war had broken up and old myths had not been replaced by anything with analogously cohesive power. And now the Cabinet minister was in disgrace and the bishop did not believe in Christ. Whether or not these two facts were, as Albion Pugh averred, mystically linked, they both threw into focus within my own head an atrophy which had overtaken me since my divorce. I had been living without love. What I had known with Anne had been for a short and delightful period something so real to me that I could no longer imagine consoling myself for its absence with casual affairs or the ersatz escapades apparently enjoyed by senior government ministers. With the sealing off of this area of experience, however, something within me had died and I had begun to fear that what I had lost was whatever gave one a motive for wanting to wake up in the mornings – the imaginative faculty or the capacity in any active role to love. I felt myself beginning to be doomed to be a spectator rather than a participant in life. That was why I derived such interest and satisfaction from Felicity's narratives of office politics and scandal. I could enjoy them at a voyeuristic distance with no danger of involvement. The very act of enjoyment filled me with the dread that I was turning into a figure like the Lady of Shalott who could not face life head on, but could only view it through her looking glass. When she turned to look on Camelot, rather than its mirror image, she was cursed. Plato's figures in the cave, satisfying themselves with shadows cast by the fire and un-aware of the existence, behind them, of the brightness of the sun, would have provided another image of my plight. And Albion Pugh's censure of the unimaginative bishop who could no longer believe in Christianity emphasised what was growing stronger in me with the years, a sadness at my own incurable agnosticism. As Uncle Roy's nephew, I had spent so many hours in church that I knew the Psalter and the Prayer Book and many passages from the Bible by heart. It did not worry me that I could not, in a conventional sense, believe: indeed, I did not see how an intelligent person could adhere to the orthodoxies. But it had begun to sadden me that I could put all this religious inheritance to no good or imaginative use. It lay around like lumber in my mind, but it did not quicken the heart. Stories from the Bible had inspired some of the noblest lives in history, some of the greatest music and paintings and architecture. As nothing else had done, it had provided a 'myth' for people to live by, and just as I regretted my present incapacity to love (or even to feel sexual desire), so I also regretted my unbelief, my failure to respond imaginatively to the Old Story. The great majority of Europeans for the last 1,900 years had lived with this story as a background to their lives and somehow made use of it. Imaginatively, I was cut off from them, and from it, unable to find the mental or emotional equip-ment with which to respond to it. I did not even share the vacuous bishop's worries about whether it was true. This, I think, was what Felicity had in mind when she spoke of a desire or need to go beyond common sense. At least she was now involved in the supposedly real world of work. Even this was denied me. I earned my living by pretending to be Jason Grainger, pretending to live in Barleybrook and purveying, each time the Mulberry theme music crackled through the loudspeakers into British homes, a fake England, disembodied and unreal.

With some such reflections adding melancholy to the late afternoon hangover, I fumbled for my doorkeys and entered my house. When I woke up in an armchair, having only slept for an hour or two, Felicity was entering our shared sitting room and putting down her briefcase on the upright chair beside the gas fire. I instantaneously wondered if she was about to launch into another Rice Robey saga, but in fact she was to do better than that. Her lips were pouting excitedly, moving noiselessly before she spoke in wheedling, uncharacteristically cooing tones.

'I hope you don't mind – I've brought Rice Robey home for a bit. Something' – her voice sank to a whisper – 'something has cropped up.'

'Use this room if you don't want to' – my mind flew instantly to hairbrushes – 'if you don't want to take him upstairs.'

'Could I. . . .'

She hesitated. It was clear that she wanted me to leave the sitting room while she entertained her friend; on the other hand, she felt embarrassed to say that this was what she wanted.

'I've got to wash socks,' I said.

'Just say hallo to him anyway.'

'OK.'

I was not sure that I really wanted to meet the legendary Rice Robey of whom so many strong and conflicting reports had been delivered over the last year. He was a figure, evidently, whom Felicity could not get out of her mind, and nor could I. But was he not, from my point of view, better kept, like a character in 'The Mulberrys', unseen but vividly imagined? I had no choice in the matter, however, since Felicity was calling to him.

'Come in, do, and meet my cousin.'

A strong cockney voice in the hall said, 'Not if it necessitates the disturbance of the domestic tranquillities.'

The man who entered the room was the figure at Darnley's lunch table, the man called Albion Pugh.

'Mr Grainger,' he said, shaking my hand.

'Mr Pugh! What a coincidence!'

Felicity looked puzzled, and rather cross, as if we were excluding her from some private joke.

'A conjunction of personal destinies – it's not necessarily to be regarded as a matter of chance.' As he spoke, he tossed his head backwards and his eyes became temporarily invisible as the lenses of his specs caught the reflection of the 100-watt bulb suspended from the middle of the ceiling.

Felicity, with a literalness which recalled her childhood self, explained to each of us that we were really named Julian Ramsay and Rice Robey.

'You two will want to discuss. . . .' I hesitated, 'whatever it was you had to discuss.' I made to leave the room.

Rice Robey grinned.

'Connections, connections. What do you think of Lord Lampitt's chances of rising high in his party?'

'Negligible, surely? For a start, he's a peer.'

'He has the backing of the Marxians,' said Rice Robey. 'They are an important voice. If they dislike his title, they could find little in his private life which could bring down scandal on the party. Some day, someone is going to pin a great deal to the name of James Harold Wilson.'

'Really?'

'Oh, yes.'

His face became cruel and slightly mad as he spoke of these political matters. He turned down the corners of his mouth and fumbled in his pocket for Fragrant Cloud. There is something particularly irritating about two friends, whom one had thought to belong to entirely different worlds, turning out to have topics in common which exclude oneself. I felt that Felicity was owed an explanation, if not an apology.

'Mr Robey met me at *The Spark* lunch,' I said. 'Vernon was there.'

'They are an interesting consanguinity, the Lampitts.'

'We've known some of them,' said Felicity. 'Someone called Sargent Lampitt is my godfather.'

'You never said' – Rice Robey's tone was sharp. 'The brother of James Petworth? Well, well!' His face broadened once more into a grin, and I supposed that he was going to repeat some Hunter-style scurrilous legend about Jimbo's private life. Felicity scowled and, standing beside the mantelpiece, moved from foot to foot.

'R.R.,' she said, 'Julian doesn't want to hear about our problem at the office.'

She normally had reasonable manners, but on this occasion she was desperate to have Rice Robey to herself, and there was a danger, if the Lampitt conversation continued, that I should hover about for the duration of his visit.

'You must forgive us, Mr Ramsay, if a little later we talk shop,' he said. 'A little trouble at the office.'

'Things are getting quite out of control,' she said wildly. Presumably she spoke of the behaviour of the Head of Department, but from her tone she could have been describing her own emotional condition.

'I knew Mr James Petworth Lampitt very well,' said Rice Robey.

He was, I should guess, a little more than fifty, which would mean that he was in his mid-thirties when Jimbo died. The belle-lettrist and biographer had occupied a flat in Hinde Street just off Manchester Square and had met his end falling from a fire escape just outside his kitchen door on the fourth floor. His young friend Raphael Hunter, subsequently the author of that indiscreet volume about him, had been in the flat at the time, but had been unable to prevent the old man cascading into the area. (It was said that he was found upside down in a dustbin by a policeman who was nearby at the time.) I remembered Hunter describing the incident (omitting the dustbin detail) when he came down to address the Literary Society when I was at school.

'In my youth I too wrote books,' said Rice Robey.

'I had no idea,' said Felicity.

'They're largely forgotten now.'

'Darnley is a great fan,' I said. 'So too is the professor who fell asleep at the lunch table.'

'Cormac? He wrote a very amusing article the other week about old Professor Wimbish.'

'Vernon mentioned it.'

'They are deadly enemies, of course, Cormac and Wimbish. There was said to have been more than academic rivalry.'

'Do you mean over a woman?'

'A neaniskos,' he said, without removing his cigarette from his lips. Smoke poured from his mouth and nostrils as he laughed. 'No, I am out of print, and out of mind. I could never write in that manner again.'

'Mr Robey wrote as Albion Pugh,' I said.

'*Memphian Mystery!*' exclaimed Felicity. 'I loved that book. Reading it was one of the great imaginative experiences of my adolescence. That scene between Pharaoh's daughter and Moses.'

She flushed with excitement.

'Incest is one method of not dissipating the sexual energy which unites the race of man to the cosmos,' he declaimed, 'and binds the humanities to the angelicals.'

'I was not talking about incest,' said Felicity. 'I was thinking of that discussion about the religious destiny of Moses, doomed to lead his people into the wilderness, but destined never himself to enter the Promised Land.'

'Because he was an Egyptian, not a Hebrew,' said Robey.

'It's a wonderful idea.'

'It's *true!*'

Felicity would never have allowed such an assertion of fancy in her early days as a philosopher. Now, evidently, the rules had changed. 'You see,' he continued, 'while I was writing those *fabulae*, I lived like young Samuel.'

'Consecrated to the Lord in the Temple at Shiloh?' she said hopefully.

'Samuel Johnson, not Samuel the prophet. The *fabulae* came to me in the evenings when I had finished teaching. It was not merely that I had time to write. My teaching did not consume me, as this job does, and we speak, of course, about the days before the commencement of the Great Attachment. All creation small "c" is part of the same process as Creation big "c" and the energies of Eros for the race of men are the channels through which creativity flows. When the distractions of Eros commence, the stream is diverted from Parnassus.'

I took him to mean that too much sex puts writers off their work.

'Surely if that were true,' I said, 'all true writers would be celibate which has not, historically, been the case.'

'It is probably truer than we know,' he said, 'but these mysteries are contained within the still heart of the Primum Mobile, and whether we make love or make art, we make ourselves not merely the partakers of that divine energy but also its rivals. Therefore a revenge is exacted. As we read in the Upanishads, there is Malice as well as Love in that still heart, though the malice was never shewn in a more paradoxical chiaroscuro than on Golgotha-hill.'

If Godfrey Tucker had been given the shivers by Rice Robey's comparatively mild talk at lunch, there is no knowing what he would have felt at these words. As I heard them, I had the sensation of cold slugs making their progress up my spine. If Felicity was seeking conversations in which it was possible to stray beyond the confines of common sense she had clearly found an ideal companion.

'James Petworth Lampitt was the vessel of grace for me,' Robey continued. 'Without Mr Lampitt. . . . It was not just that he helped me to get my *fabulae* into print, found me my first job. . . . He was an enabler. He lent me books, gave me books. Books have been a sacred life-blood to me, Mr Ramsay. Mr Lampitt gave me a ticket to the London Library, no less. As far as I was concerned, it was a ticket to Paradise. You know how they tell you that if you wish to get on in the world you need an on-tray, you need to be introduced to all the right people? Well, Mr Lampitt introduced me to all the right people. He introduced me to Paracelsus and to John Milton and to the Pseudo-Dionysus and to Wilkie Collins. They were all there waiting to meet me on the shelves in St James's Square.'

It was almost independently of my uncle Roy's Lampitt mania that I developed my own preoccupation with James Petworth Lampitt. At a certain point of my career at school, I had fallen under his spell as a stylist and had too often re-read his mannered biographical studies of nineteenth-century life. Strangely enough there weren't, as I recall, many Jimbo stories in Uncle Roy's inexhaustible repertoire. Uncle Roy had the indiscriminate interest in the genus which marks the true collector. *N'importe quel Lampitt.* Stories of far-flung Lampitt cousins catching wrong trains or diseases or saying unremarkable things in shops and hotels ('Typical Lampitt saying, that,' he would murmur, satisfied, as he repeated their words) were just as fascinating to my uncle as those members of the Lampitt family who might by any dispassionate standards have been considered interesting. Jimbo was interesting to me not as a Lampitt, primarily, but as a writer. The fact that I had known his brother since childhood and later married his niece added to the interest, but it did not diminish his status in my eyes. As I changed my mind about 'style', so I changed my mind about Jimbo as a writer, but I could never entirely discard a feeling of gratitude to him, for the aesthetic pleasure which his writing had awoken in me, but more, because it was in reading his pages that I first consciously became aware of my own desire to be a writer, to encapsulate truth in words. The whirlygig of time brings in its revenges, and Jimbo, who had pinioned so many lives to his collecting case like the specimens of butterflies or moths, was

43

destined himself to be the subject of a biography, that of Hunter, who never seemed even remotely appreciative of the distinctive features of Jimbo's prose and who regarded him merely as an appropriate coat-hanger from which to suspend social and literary history of a not unclodhopping kind. Most offensive to the family, as I have already mentioned, was Hunter's contention that Jimbo had been a rampantly promiscuous homosexual, at least in his youth. Where my new-found acquaintance Rice Robey fitted into all this, I was not sure, but his sudden appearances, twice in one day, and his three independent connections with Darnley, with Felicity, and now, with the Lampitts, gave plausibility to his theory of 'conjunction of personal destinies'.

In trying to convey the quality of Rice Robey's utterances, it is not enough to record his peculiar autodidactic idiolects, or his cockney accent. He had the power of drawing you in to his own peculiar imaginative world so that whether he was generalising about the supernatural or gossiping about the sex lives of politicians or giving the gist of an admired book, you had the same sense of being a child, led into a magic grotto by a grown-up whom the other grown-ups would not consider suitable company. Gooseflesh sometimes came and went as he spoke.

I now forget at what speed, and at what stages, I came to learn the outlines of Rice Robey's life, but I might as well set down a brief résumé here. His parents ran a small sweets and newspapers business in Gospel Oak. He was an only child of exceptional talents, but his education was interrupted by domestic tragedy, the death of his father when Rice Robey was twelve. The boy was compelled to leave school a year later, working as an office boy, first in a legal firm, and then at a publishers – James Petworth Lampitt's publishers. Duties included acting as a messenger to addresses in central London, and he came Lampitt's way when delivering parcels to the apartment which the writer occupied in Hinde Street. An invitation to tea turned into a conversation about literature. Jimbo lent Rice Robey a book – Jessie L. Weston's *From Ritual to Romance*. The next week, when he came to tea, the boy borrowed a volume of Fraser's *Golden Bough*, and, another week, some Yeats. This was the period of Rice Robey's real education. Jimbo obviously liked the boy's company, and perhaps he was flattered that someone so young, and so different from himself, should wish to return, week after week, for tea and anchovy toast and literary talk. Self-taught, Rice Robey had an intellectual range which was idiosyncratic, but he was obviously clever. When he was about eighteen, and had known Jimbo for a number of years, the old man conceived a scheme for the furtherance of the boy's education. He was to be attached to a small private school on the borders of Metroland, somewhere near Chorleywood, an establishment with whose headmaster Jimbo was somehow acquainted. Rice Robey was given free board and lodging and a small allowance in exchange for teaching the younger boys. The headmaster for his part agreed to coach Rice Robey for the public examinations necessary to qualify for matriculation at the university. All this took place in the late 1920s and early 1930s. Jimbo's plans for his protégé, however, went badly askew. The headmaster of the school was an alcoholic and the academy was far from flourishing. When Rice Robey first went to work there, some thirty boys were in attendance, but after only a few years their number dwindled to twenty, fifteen . . . and the future of the school looked uncertain. Mention of Rice Robey's tuition for matric. was somehow forgotten, and as all the other teachers drifted away, the young man was left responsible for shoring up a collapsed system. Jimbo could, perhaps, have rescued him, or Rice Robey could simply have left, but this did not happen. Had he been serious about wanting to go to university, perhaps he would have left, but the circumstances were ideal for an aspirant writer.

It was at this period that he wrote his Albion Pugh novels. (Pugh was the maiden name of his mother, and a Blakean preoccupation must have made him choose Albion as a first name for his pseudonym.) The four novels so admired by a tiny coterie were all composed very rapidly when he was in his early twenties, and still nominally looking after the school. By now the headmaster was himself graduating from three-quarters of a bottle to two bottles of Scotch per day, and there were almost no pupils. Rice Robey had time, and stationery, to indulge his imaginative bent.

It was the period when he first read Malory's *Morte d'Arthur*. Since he saw everything in analogical terms, he was easily able to envisage the collapse of the tenth-rate little school through the lens of high Arthurian fantasy; the departure of (doubtless ill-qualified) colleagues seemed like the dismantlement of Camelot when the friendship of the knights was broken partly because of the unattainable lure of a religious vision, the quest for the Sangreal, partly because of the adultery of Queen Guinevere and Arthur's most trusted knight, Sir

Lancelot. From what he subsequently told me – the crack-brained idea that the exercise of the sexual faculty somehow or another diminishes the creative urge – I would guess that Rice Robey did not actually become Mrs Paxton's lover until he had finished *Towered Camelot*, though some of the steamier passages in that might suggest, to a relentlessly biographical critic of the Albion Pugh *oeuvre*, the direction in which his heart was leading him. An affair of some sort began with the headmaster's wife. I don't think anyone ever satisfactorily explained to me all the details of the final débâcle, but the upshot of it was that Rice Robey and Mrs Paxton eloped, leaving the school and the husband to sink into alcoholic collapse. We are speaking of a time close to the outbreak of the Second World War. Rice Robey was in his late twenties, Mrs Paxton getting on for twice this age. Her 'little bit of money' soon evaporated. They lived in hired lodgings, sometimes unable to afford more than one shared room. He tried to make a living as a writer, but the prose no longer flowed, and he was too eccentric a stylist to make much of a living from hack work. (A short spell of reviewing for the *New Statesman* – he covered crime writing – came to an end because he was unable to perform the task which the literary editor set him, that is, to give short notices of the latest detective stories; he was unable to write about anything without his metaphysical preoccupations rising to the surface, just as he was incapable of using 'ordinary' language – bishops became 'episkopoi', young men, 'neaniskoi'; Marxists, 'Marxians'; families, 'consanguinities'; and so on. Once removed from the squalid little school – 'the Dotheboys of the suburbs', he had once described it to me – he could not get on with work. A projected novel about druids never progressed beyond the stage of notes. He had the curious habit, which I had never come across before in a prose writer, of doing the first draft of everything he composed, including the published thrillers, in verse. The habit of doodling poetry continued, and he was still at work on an English version of his English *Commedia* (in execrable *terza rima*) when I first met him.

Money came his way from this source and that. Jimbo helped him on an irregular basis. Some of his cheques, as I learnt from Cecily Lampitt, were very generous. I myself disbelieve the suggestion (Darnley had heard it too and repeated it to me long after my first meeting with the man) that Rice Robey was formally employed in Military Intelligence. True, that branch of government service has employed some strange types in its time, but how would they have enlisted Rice Robey? How would he have come their way? I think he probably was in touch with those who did work for Intelligence. He had an astonishingly large acquaintanceship, and would seem to have known a little bit about everyone – politicians, churchmen, lawyers, senior civil servants and journalists. How this came about, that an unemployed young schoolmaster should have built up such a store of information, I shall never guess; but perhaps Rice Robey was merely an extreme example of the commonplace fact that one thing leads to another, and if you are prepared to follow up connections, to remember names, to work at gossip with the appropriate reference books and newspapers in your hand, it does not take long to build up a mental filing cabinet chock-a-block with damaging dossiers. It could well be the case that his friendship with Jimbo was the start of all this. The Lampitts may not be as important in the scheme of things as Uncle Roy supposed, but they are a large family with cousins and friends in the worlds of politics, business, universities and in what might once have been termed 'society'. Anyone wishing to build up a thoroughgoing knowledge of English life could do worse than to start with the cultivation of a Lampitt. Rice Robey was also a man who liked bars. He was not alcoholic, but he could hold a certain amount of liquor and was known to enjoy visits to pubs on his way home to Mrs Paxton. At the beginning of the Blitz, he and Mrs Paxton moved in with his mother, in the borderlands between Kentish Town and Gospel Oak. I do not know whether Mrs Robey and Mrs Paxton enjoyed one another's society, but Rice Robey's mother died some time during the war. His poor eyesight disqualified him for military service. He entered the Civil Service at the executive level, and was attached to an area of no immediate interest to his friends in MI5 – the Ministry of Works. It was a propitious moment to be starting a career as a civil servant. There were few rivals in the office of his own age or sex and his wide range of knowledge about ancient or prehistoric sites was soon recognised. Before long, he had been promoted and transferred to a job which carried the status and salary of the 'officer' class of civil servant, the so-called grade.

Since boyhood, all spare time had been spent exploring London on foot, and any available holidays had been devoted to walking or cycling in the British Isles. He had an encyclopaedic knowledge of the very sites which it was his task in the Ministry of Works to conserve. There was no henge, barrow, stone circle, or earthworks in the south of England about which he could not display knowledge (and, it is perhaps needless to add, cranky theories).

In peacetime, his job would doubtless have been given to someone with better paper qualifications, such as a degree in archaeology or medieval architecture. Needs must, however, and he was soon exercising a considerable responsibility for those sites which were under his control. After the war, the new government reorganised the Civil Service and greatly increased its numbers. Rice Robey felt himself diminished in importance. If there was truth in half Felicity's stories about him in her early months as his colleague, it was possible to see that he was not everyone's idea of the perfect civil servant. There was the gossip, and the compulsive trouble-making, perhaps exacerbated by the drying-up of his pen. He needed to weave romances, and when it was no longer possible to do so in print, the compulsion to do so in life became unstoppable. He came to believe, after one markedly unsuccessful year when he came up for his Board, failed to get promotion for which he had applied and found himself being 'shoved sideways' in some departmental reorganisation, into a job with less status or influence than he had been doing before, that 'they' were out to get him; that he was passed over for promotion not because of professional incompetence but because he 'knew too much', most notably about the Minister of Works in Attlee's administration, James Harold Wilson, the future leader of the Labour Party and three times Prime Minister. Others felt that Rice Robey ditched his chances by gross inefficiency at all matters of office administration, failure to do necessary paper work, while among academics and archaeologists he was not taken seriously because of his unashamed willingness to link all the ancient sites with their supposed legendary or mythical background. There was also the talk of Robey and the women, and his eccentric, romantic ways of passing time with female colleagues.

Now he stood before me, this legend, and Felicity was conspicuously anxious to have him to herself. An expression of true anguish passed over her features when he looked at his watch and said that he should have been home half an hour earlier.

'The Great Attachment?' asked Felicity impishly.

'Masters' commands come with a power resistless,' he quoted, with a malicious grin.

There was scarcely going to be time to discuss whatever 'import-

48

ant' piece of business they had used as a pretext for this extension of their day together.

'I must leave you to it,' I said, 'but how fascinating – isn't it, Felicity? – that Mr Robey knew Jimbo Lampitt. We must talk of this some other time.'

I put down my sherry glass and overacted the part of a man bustling about his business, anxious to get on with chores.

'I not only knew him,' said Rice Robey. 'I also know something about him which I think escaped the *speculum* of the authorities, unless they chose to ignore it, unless there were a conspiracy of the magistrature.'

'You're not talking about that filth of Raphael Hunter's?' asked Felicity. 'Sargie and all the Lampitts are agreed that Hunter's book is a pack of lies.'

'Ah!' said Rice Robey. 'Raphael Hunter, a name which could not for long remain unmentioned in this connection.'

Felicity looked decidedly uncomfortable. It was inconceivable to me that she had ever spoken to Rice Robey of her own miserable time with Raphael Hunter; nevertheless, I believed it was possible that Rice Robey knew about it.

'I wasn't referring to Raphael Hunter's book, as a matter of fact,' he said. 'I was referring to Mr Lampitt's death, and the manner of his dying.'

'He fell to his death from the top of a fire escape,' I said.

In the brief silence which followed I thought of Jimbo, whom I had never seen; I thought of dead legs in tweed trousers sticking out of a dustbin.

'So we have been informed,' said Rice Robey.

'By Hunter. Who witnessed, or almost witnessed, the accident.'

'Ah, yes. Mr Hunter.'

Rice Robey's manner, smile, general demeanour, had already begun to give me the shivers, as they had done to Godfrey Tucker at lunch. I was now turning to such gooseflesh that it would not have surprised me to know that my hair was actually standing on end. He was a master of the pause. We waited breathlessly for him to spell out what he meant.

'One thing about Mr Lampitt is certain. He was not a self-slayer. Another certain thing in my mind' – again, a melodramatic pause – 'is that in recording a verdict of accidental death, the coroner was stretching the meaning of the word "accidental". I often stood at the top of that fire escape outside Mr Lampitt's kitchen door. He liked to stand there because on a summer evening, he could see the sunset behind the Wallace Collection, a view redolent for him of Italy and old Roman days. He was the lover, Mr Lampitt – but you know this. . . .'

What morsel was to follow this appetising pause?

'. . . of the *Italianate*.'

Perhaps pruriently, I found this revelation a little tame.

'There are no accidents in my creed, Mr Ramsay; certainly, there are no accidental deaths.'

'But, let's get this clear,' I said, ' and then I really will leave you in peace with Felicity. Are you just saying that Mr Lampitt's death was in some way foreordained, fated?'

He turned to Felicity with a smile.

'I like your cousin's use of the word "just",' he observed. 'If the concept of Fate is a useful one, then the hour of our death is fore-resolved. But that is not all that I am saying. Outside the kitchen door at the top of the fire escape there are some railings. They came up to Mr Lampitt's chest, effectually. He was, I am sure you know, a small man. Now, the coroner said nothing about Mr Lampitt falling down the fire-escape stairs. He did not fall down the stairs. He fell over the railing which he would have considerable difficulty in climbing. If Despair had possessed his *anima* he would not have chosen to end his life in that way; not while he was in the middle of entertaining a neaniskos. He was the soul of courtesy.'

'You can't be saying that he was pushed? You're suggesting that Mr Lampitt was murdered?'

Rice Robey, however, would say no more at this meeting. His marbly eyes became mysteriously dead, almost invisible behind the thick lenses and he smiled his inscrutable smile.

TWO

Lunch at the Rectory was over, and we were almost ready to depart for Mallington, Darnley and I. Throughout the meal, Uncle Roy had beamed at us with loving indulgence, as if, after the lamentable false start of my divorce from Anne, I was at last on the point of doing something sensible, that is, hobnobbing with Lampitts, extending and deepening my Lampitt acquaintance, brushing up on my Lampitt lore. Anecdotes and sayings of the great family had poured from his lips throughout the meal. The others round the table were Felicity, Aunt Deirdre and Granny.

Darnley did not go in for politeness. If someone bored him, he made no pretence to be interested in what they were saying. At the first possible pause in the Lampitt narratives he turned to my grandmother on his right and spoke to her, not uncondescendingly, but almost desperately, suggesting that any subject was better than my uncle's favourite topic of conversation.

'So Mary said – that's Sargie's second cousin – brilliant woman – "Oui, mon capitaine" – you do know French, don't you?'

'Enough to understand that,' said Darnley. Hoping we had reached the end of this particular story, he added, 'Is that it?'

'I've heard this one so often before,' said my grandmother without opening her eyes.

'"Oui, mon capitaine, mais ça, c'est tout à fait une jolie bouilloire". . . .'

He blushed, shook with the hilarity of it. Would he manage to finish his sentence before Aunt Deirdre snapped out the punchline for him?

'Bouilloire de poissons, we know,' she said.

While my uncle, convulsed, dabbed his lips with a napkin and murmured, 'Typical Lampitt story, that,' Darnley plunged in.

'Whatever happened to your nice friend who drove us about in a Riley? Do you remember, Mrs Ramsay? We all went out to lunch together in Worcester.'

'Oh, Miles, that was ages ago, and you were a little lad,' said Granny. 'I'm afraid poor Mrs Webb has been gone a long time now.'

'Mrs Webb, that was it. Charming person. Laughed at all my jokes.'

'Mrs Webb and I always said as how Miles should go on the stage,' said Granny, making Uncle Roy wince at the phrase 'as how'.

Because it was Granny who said this, Aunt Deirdre reacted as if the remark had been mildly insulting.

'Different people want to do different things,' she said.

'Did I say otherwise?' asked Granny. 'I haven't seen this magazine of yours, Miles. Julian was telling me about it. Would it be this new satire?'

'Partly, some of it's serious.'

'I stayed up watching, you know, on the television.'

She laughed, just at the memory of it.

'It's far too late and it's absolute rubbish,' put in Aunt Deirdre.

'That was a Week, that was,' said Granny, at last able to remember the programme.

'*The* week, *the* week,' said Felicity. '"That was the Week that was".'

'Very rude about the Prime Minister,' said Granny with a chuckle, 'and the other Harold. Both the Harolds.'

As she spoke, the very word *Harold* seemed richly comic. Granny had not opened her eyes for some minutes, and even now, as she indicated the need for cigarettes, she merely made her bodily gestures, from side to side, rather than opening her eyes to look for the packet of Craven A. '*Very* funny imitations,' she said, 'though I didn't like it when they made a joke about the Queen.'

'Honestly!' exclaimed Aunt Deirdre, 'I think that the standard of the wireless is vulgar enough, but the things they show on the television, not that I watch it. . . .'

'It was different in Lord Reith's time,' said Uncle Roy.

'They hardly had television in Lord Reith's time,' said Darnley, failing to see the importance of the BBC in the scheme of things – not that it was a great broadcasting corporation, in which many interesting people had worked, but that it had once figured in a Lampitt anecdote.

'Do you remember when they enlisted Jimbo Lampitt on to a committee advising the BBC on how to pronounce words? There was George Bernard Shaw, who was a bit of a chum of Vernon's papa, by the way – people sometimes make the mistake of thinking he only knew Angelica – and who else was there? Rose Macaulay, and dear old Jimbo.'

'We know,' snapped Aunt Deirdre, '*sausage* pronounced *sors-ij*.'

It was a little unkind of her to cut this particular story so relentlessly short, render it indeed into telegraphese. I began to think of reducing the other famous stories to palatable mouthfuls of less than ten words. 'Bobby Lampitt. Waiter. Duckling young duck not old horse.' Or, 'Tony – should have said you meant by *aeroplane*' or 'Sargie – poop-poop – car tyres – brilliant mind'.

'I heard a strange thing the other week about Jimbo's death,' I said.

'Do you need to worry about clothes, old thing?' my aunt asked, 'For Mallington, I mean? I dare say Roy's old dinner jacket's still wearable, if you need it for tonight.'

My aunt was manifestly unable to endure another Lampitt story, even if it were a murder story. Perhaps it was tactless of me to have embarked on the story of Jimbo's death. It could only upset Uncle Roy to think of a Lampitt being murdered, and I did not wish to revive the distressing memories of Raphael Hunter's book, nor of Uncle Roy's painful estrangement from Sargie. Probably, the idea that Jimbo had not met an accidental death was one of Rice Robey's fantasies.

'You won't need a dinner jacket at Mallington, of course,' said Uncle Roy, quietly amused at this little mistake of his wife's. '*Old* Lord Lampitt dressed for dinner, and of course down here at the Place, old Mrs Lampitt always liked men to put on a black tie. Sargie, bless him, always. . . .'

'Penguin outfits,' said my aunt quickly.

'Yes, he always called them penguin outfits. But the Honourable Vernon – which is how I shall always think of him – is almost self-consciously informal.'

'It's all so put *on*, this Ernie nonsense,' said my aunt. 'I can't bear it on the wireless when they refer to him as Ernie Lampitt.'

'His father had that side to his nature,' said Uncle Roy. 'I'm sorry to say that Old Lord Lampitt was just a *tiny* little bit of a humbug.'

Felicity had resolved to stay with her parents, while Darnley and I went over to Mallington for the night. I did not blame Felicity for wriggling out of the engagement. I did not much want to go myself, as the time for departure approached, though I liked the idea of a jaunt with Darnley. I knew that I would be interested to see the house again, though, and a small part of myself was excited by the knowledge that Vernon was now a man of potential influence in the Labour Party. Mallington was known to be a place where senior trade unionists and members of the Shadow Cabinet sometimes congregated. I led such a very sheltered life that I was able to be snobbishly attracted to the notion of proximity to famous people, famous moreover in fields which were different from my own. Darnley, I think, was similarly fascinated by those who wished to exercise political power. He spoke a bit about this when, an hour after lunch, he was leaning forward in the passenger seat of his red Morris Minor, an ancient car which I liked to drive when I had the chance.

'I wonder who Ernie's got lined up for us,' said Darnley. 'Hope there aren't any other hacks. I could do with a rest from hacksville.'

'Really? You never seem to tire of it.'

'I shouldn't mind if Harold were there.'

'Harold Wilson? Is that likely?'

'Ernie was one of the people chiefly instrumental in getting Harold the leadership. Harold was the left's candidate, but the left knew they couldn't have a *real* lefty like Footy. They needed a man who would look after their interests and con the general public into voting for them.'

'What about Vernon? Is he a real lefty, as you call it?'

'Och, he's practically a communist.'

This last sentence of Darnley's was, for some reason, delivered in the voice of the Binker, our hateful old headmaster at Seaforth Grange. Darnley broke into different voices quite arbitrarily, and there seldom seemed much connection between the voice and the content – he could be Humphrey Bogart while talking about the Archbishop of Canterbury, Vernon Lampitt while telling me about his sister's latest (and unsuitable) bloke, which he did, as the car left Timplingham behind us, roared through the beech avenue beyond the church, passed the new bungalows and the petrol station until it found blank, mildly undulating country. The matter of Elizabeth's man disposed of, we fell to other areas of gossip, snatches of memory of Seaforth Grange and the army, and then – Rice Robey.

'Pughie's done a brilliant collection of diary snippets for *The Spark*,' said Darnley. 'Brilliant. It's miraculous how he gets hold of half his information.'

'Perhaps he makes it up.'

'Oh, no,' said Darnley airily. 'Pughie'd never do a thing like that. Besides' – he sniffed loud and long as if trying to inhale snuff through pints of mucus – 'all these little stories of his have the ring of truth. He's also given me some bits and pieces of this book he's writing about Jesus. I'll give them to you to read if I may. See what you think.'

'What sort of gossip has he fed you?'

'Well, there's some pretty good dirt on poor old Harold.'

'Which Harold?'

'Harold the younger. Pughie did work under the man when he was at the Ministry of Works. I must remember to ask Ernie about that – he and Harold were both in Attlee's Cabinet together, you know. He'd know the gossip. Then, on a completely different subject, Pughie's got a bee in his bonnet about Aldingbury Ring, this stone circle near Windsor which Pughie thinks they are going to demolish or plough up to build a road. He's trying to have it stopped.'

'He was in such a flat spin about it all,' I said, 'that he actually came round to my house, supposedly to discuss it with Felicity. You realise they work in the same office, she and Pugh?'

'Yes.' Darnley showed no interest in this at all. I was not actually sure that he did realise that Felicity and 'Pughie' were colleagues.

'From what Felicity said,' I continued, 'I thought they were both getting things out of proportion. They seemed to believe that people were out to get Robey, that they would somehow use this stone circle as a means to engineer his downfall.'

'I should think plenty of people would love to see Pughie sacked,' said Darnley. 'He's a dangerous man, he knows too much; and you see, you can't say that Pughie is motivated by malice.'

'Why not?'

'Pughie has nothing to gain by spreading these stories about.'

It was possibly true that Robey had nothing to gain in material terms by scandalmongering, but if this activity provided him with its own distasteful form of satisfaction, then this surely was malice? Did not malice provide its own satisfactions?

Darnley, it disturbed me to believe, did not quite understand what malice was, or did not choose to recognise it in his own nature. Yet,

55

trying to be fair to Robey, I was conscious that my own reaction to him was instinctual rather than rational. He sent shivers up and down my spine, but this was not a reason for supposing he was a liar. The reason that I did not like him probably had to do with the fact that Darnley and Felicity did so. I was jealous of the man.

'Felicity is exactly of your opinion,' I said. 'She thinks they are doing their utmost at work to get rid of him. She wishes he did not make trouble, and she has tried to dissuade him from writing stuff for *The Spark*.'

I did not have enough imagination to suppose that Darnley might feel extremely jealous of Felicity for whatever degree of intimacy she had achieved with Rice Robey. One of Rice Robey's emotional talents was in the ability to make his devotees compete with one another. They all wanted to show that they knew him better than the others – hence, presumably, their willingness to believe the worst about the Great Attachment, the woman with whom he shared his domestic life and who, presumably, in fact knew him best.

'Apparently,' I continued tactlessly, 'he has threatened to make a real stink in the office if they go ahead with plans to demolish this little henge. Rice Robey and Felicity and several others in their department have been sending in reports recommending that the Minister be informed, and that if necessary, there should be a show-down with the Ministry of Transport. Oh, they've been going on about it for weeks. Fliss'll speak of little else.'

'It's not very interesting,' said Darnley. 'But the stuff about Harold *is*.'

It was odd that Rice Robey now dominated so many of my waking thoughts. Before Felicity changed her job, I had not even known that he existed. Then, in that mysterious way that sometimes happens, his name cropped up in several miscellaneous and hitherto unconnected areas, rather as circuses, before their arrival in a provincial town, advertise themselves by posters stuck arbitrarily on trees and fences where you might least expect them. I can remember my excitement as a child when the beech avenue going into Timplingham suddenly sprouted a crop of these brightly coloured posters. A clown smiled out – over his head was the name of the circus, and in the background, the hastily daubed rendition of the big top, a ringmaster, performing beasts, awoke in me a longing to attend the performance. Felicity (I could easily have killed her for this) announced that circuses were boring and, worse, demeaning to animals. Uncle Roy had kept repeating that, had old Mrs Lampitt been alive, there would have been a rumpus about the circus sticking posters to the beautiful beeches in the avenue. He had also made some dismissive and contemptuous remark about circuses in general, and I could see that by his standards they were bound to be dull since, as far as history can shed light on the matter, no Lampitt is known to have passed their life balancing from a high wire on a monocycle, or jumping through a hoop of fire, or coaxing elephants to stand one-legged on tubs. Only Aunt Deirdre saw how much I wanted to attend the circus, and she took me. The act which thrilled me the most was when a firmly built young woman, her body taut inside a glittering silver lamé bathing dress, spun round and round from the summit of the Big Top, suspended only by her teeth. Afterwards, Aunt Deirdre had said that Uncle Roy had spoilt the suspense by talking; the sight of the girl spinning there had awakened, by an inevitable train of association, the latest quarrel which Sargie had contrived with his dentist.

Anyhow, if the analogy holds, the circus posters had by now been going up for some time inside my head. A new show was coming to town. Its name was Albion Pugh or Rice Robey. As a grotesque, Rice Robey made me laugh, and I still could not quite believe that Darnley meant it when he insisted that 'Pughie's a great man'. Nevertheless, in that annoyingly proprietorial spirit with which we regard our blood relatives, I was worried by the growing attachment between Rice Robey and Felicity. Disregarding the fact that she was a grown-up person who was allowed to make whatever mess she chose of life, I was anxious that she would get hurt, as she had done during her fling with Raphael Hunter. There was something decidedly odd about Rice Robey, sexually odd, I felt. Felicity spoke of the relationship in terms of Robey's need of her. He needed her as an ally, as an office friend, as a confidante. I was less sure than she was about all this, and not in the least sure that he had told her, or anyone else, the truth about 'the Great Attachment'.

There seemed such an absence of good taste, putting it at its mildest, in sharing his domestic secrets so openly with the world. I was astonished that Felicity felt sorry for Robey being 'shackled' to Mrs Paxton. Though specific instances of his antics were no longer referred to (we heard nothing now of hairbrushes nor of stenographers) there was a general, sniggering acceptance on Felicity's side that a man in Rice Robey's position deserved the occasional indulgence, added to the conceited (and I thought manifestly untrue) implication that, now that he had Felicity as a friend, he would be unlikely to look elsewhere. Felicity never spelt any of these things out; they were what I read from her manner, all of which suggested that he had found everything he needed in her company – intelligence and understanding hitherto lacking in colleagues; sympathy long absent from his relationship with Mrs Paxton. . . . God knows what fantasies she allowed herself on the erotic plane.

'Rice Robey – is he quite . . . ?' I had begun the question but I did not know how to put it into words without sounding priggish or snobbish. My ex-mother-in-law Sibs would have been anxious to know if Rice Robey was 'quite the thing', and this was the question which I actually wanted answered. How could it be translated into inoffensive terms?

'Pughie has a completely original vision,' said Darnley, 'a poet's vision.'

'What of?' I asked, realising as I asked the question that I am almost devoid, in this sense, of 'poetry'.

'You could call it a vision of England, but that would make it sound patriotic and boring; if you called it a vision of Jesus Christ, you would sound conventionally pious – and I'm never actually sure what Pughie *does* in that department.'

'You mean, whether or where he goes to church?'

Another big sniff answered this. Then Darnley continued, 'The thing about Pughie is that he makes categories redundant. He's *sui generis*. I used to think he was a bit bogus.'

'What made you change your mind?'

'The fact that he is so obviously genuine, the real thing.'

'The real what, though?'

When describing the foibles or weaknesses of those whom he liked, Darnley had a peculiar way of laughing. It involved shaking his head from side to side and slightly closing his eyes, as though any explanation for his laughter would have been impossible to put into words.

'This Jesus book' – more laughter – 'it will never get published.'

'He's published books before.'

'Ages ago. And they are thrillers, really. I forget if you ever read one.'

'No.'

'Well, the Pugh ideas are all buried in quite good yarns. Whereas this new thing he's writing. . . .'

'It's fiction?'

'He's inclined to get a bit poetic, Pughie, if you don't watch him. And to have an idea which you can't tell – it might be batty, it might be rather brilliant. This new one's got two such ideas. The first is, that Jesus came to England.'

'That's hardly new. *And did those feet in ancient time?*'

'Well, old Pughie has Jesus going to Stonehenge, seeing the druids, popping up to London, all that sort of thing.'

'What's he up to?'

'Jesus or Pugh?'

'The former.'

'Some kind of travelling salesman, or at any rate his uncle is, Joseph of Arimathea. I see signs that Pugh wants to extend the story into a vast epic history, so you will get the old legend of Sir Lancelot being a cousin in the ninth degree of Jesus, and the symbolic links continuing into modern times. I'm not sure that William Blake isn't scheduled to put in an appearance if the book ever gets finished.'

'You said the book has two ideas. What's the other, apart from the Holy Lamb of God on England's pleasant pasture?'

'It's about St Paul. Pughie thinks St Paul was one of the original scribes or Pharisees who followed Jesus about and agitated for his death. Batty idea in some ways.'

'Why?'

Darnley just laughed and did not say.

'Pughie's a mixture of things,' he remarked at length, 'an old-fashioned mystic, a newfangled psychological man. I'm not so sure about the newfangled bits. He sort of hints that St Paul was queer, almost in love with Jesus, couldn't get him out of his head. After the Crucifixion, Paul developed a bee in his bonnet about the Cross, couldn't shake off his guilt feelings. Then he has his moment on the Damascus Road – 'I am Jesus whom Thou persecutest' and the whole thing gets turned round for Paul. Sublimated. The Cross which has been the greatest shame, becomes a thing of Glory. He feels it's all right after all. The wickedest thing he'd ever done, killing Jesus, has actually been a means of salvation, for him, and for the world.'

'Sounds terrible.'

Darnley sniffed.

We drove on for about five minutes without speaking. We passed a ruined windmill, beyond which stretched miles of flat fields.

'He's on to something, though,' said Darnley. 'You see, this bishop. . . .'

'The one who doesn't believe in God?'

'It's hopeless, really, that. What old Pughie is so good at is seeing that if this thing is true, then it's true, and there's no getting round the fact that the material world just isn't what half the clever people say it is. There's *more*.'

'Of course there's more. But you surely don't believe all *that* rubbish do you?'

I blurted out these words too fast. It was obvious, from what Darnley had just said, that he was, in some sense, a believer. He must have known that by 'all that rubbish' I meant the whole Christian way of viewing the world, but he tactfully chose to assume that I referred merely to Rice Robey's particular idea about St Paul.

'Dunno. Pugh has a sort of intuition, you know. On the other hand, I don't believe everything he says or writes. This queer thing that St Paul is supposed to have about. . . .' He ended his reflection with laughter.

'Is Rice Robey really queer underneath it all?'

This might have explained much, the early devotion to Jimbo, the need for a mother-figure in Mrs Paxton.

'Lord, no. Dirty old man with the girls, or so they always say.'

I was aware, as on other occasions, of Darnley's contrasting scale of values. He was loud in his condemnation of public figures who stepped aside from the strictest codes of chastity. The matter of the Cabinet minister, who had by now retreated in disgrace, with positively Dostoyevskian resolves to purge his guilt among the poor, had largely been dropped by the newspapers, but *The Spark* continued to mention it in every issue. Darnley must have half believed, as Rice Robey had been suggesting at that lunch in the Black Bottle, that such scandal spelt the end of something in Old England. In relation to his own personal heroes, however, Darnley took an entirely different line. Rice Robey could be described with a loving smile as 'a dirty old man'. Behaviour or proclivities which would have been abominated in Darnley's enemies here became rather endearing qualities which if anything enhanced our affection for the 'great man'.

'His home life is said to be absolutely wretched, so I suppose that's partly why he chases the girls,' said Darnley.

'I don't know why philandering should be regarding as a symptom of domestic unhappiness. It must often be the opposite. Having enjoyed something is a greater incentive for wanting more of it than not having enjoyed it. . . .'

'That's all too clever for me,' said Darnley. 'I've never met the Great Attachment.'

'Felicity talks about the Great Attachment. Does this mean that Rice Robey's married?'

I knew a bit about Mrs Paxton from Felicity's accounts, but I wanted to hear Darnley's version of events, and to see whether Rice Robey span the same story to all his friends, or whether he varied it.

'Pughie lives with this woman, they're not married. He met her when he was a schoolmaster, I believe. . . .'

He gave me an account of Rice Robey's early life which corresponded to what I already knew, or to what I have already set down in this narrative.

'So she ran away from her husband because of Rice Robey?' I asked.

'I forget all the details. He's very attractive to women. I don't know if you've seen enough of him to notice.'

'I have. Felicity, you know. . . .'

'Anyhow, Pugh and the Great Attachment have been shacked up together for years, in Kentish Town or somewhere. He works in some government department – he's a civil servant now. Pathetic, really.'

'He works with Felicity.'

'So you were saying. Good old Pughie.'

He smiled, as if the mere contemplation of Rice Robey's character brought peace and benediction. A similar expression would take hold of Uncle Roy's eyes and mouth when speaking of the Lampitts.

'I am actually very worried about Felicity and Rice Robey,' I said. 'She is obviously becoming very fond of him, and he doesn't strike me as the sort of person it is quite safe to love.'

This silenced Darnley. He was incapable of discussing the emotional life. When my marriage was tottering to an end, I had tried several times to treat Darnley as a confidant, and been greeted only by silence. I do not think it was failure of sympathy so much as a lack of rhetoric. All topics of conversation need a set of conventions to

61

carry them along. An inability to handle these conventions leads either to brilliant originality of talk, or to no talk at all. Darnley simply did not know how to begin conversations about matters of the heart. It made me wish, sometimes, that he would 'grow up', and with a colossal failure of sympathy on my own part, I wished he would enter into my worries about Felicity and Rice Robey. It did not quite dawn on me that his own perspective on the matter was so different from my own that he could not have been sympathetic, even had he been able to speak of it. I was tacitly taking it for granted that Rice Robey was a grotesque joke, a figure whom it would be potentially calamitous to take seriously; and this fact seemed to me so fixed, so obvious, that I blinded myself, even then, to the extent to which Darnley did take him seriously.

After a longish silence, Darnley said, 'Pugh's given me some truly extraordinary tit-bits for the "Diary". Can't decide whether to use them.'

'What sort of thing?'

'Well, do you remember that shit Raphael Hunter?'

I could hardly fail to remember Hunter, even if he had not been, at that date, a figure who was constantly on television and radio, as well as writing regularly for the Sunday newspapers. After all, he had dogged my steps ever since my boyhood, seducing the art mistress with whom I was so much in love at Seaforth Grange, ruining Felicity's life, destroying, by the rows set in motion after his life of Jimbo, the friendship between Sargie Lampitt and my uncle Roy, alienating the affections of my wife. . . . Yes, I remembered Hunter.

'He wrote that big biog which so annoyed your family.'

'Not my family, my wife's family.'

'The one about the old homo.'

'James Petworth Lampitt. He claimed to be an intimate friend of Lampitt's, but it would seem that in fact he hardly knew the man.'

'Well, guess what Pughie thinks.'

'He told me himself. Unfortunately, Felicity was so anxious to have a tête-à-tête with Rice Robey that I could not get him to expand, but he thinks Jimbo Lampitt was murdered.'

'Who's Jimbo?'

'It's what they called Petworth Lampitt in the family.'

'So Jimbo was the old shirt-lifter.'

Darnley laughed again, a snigger turning into a continuous burst of laughter.

'The homosexuality was only alleged,' I said.

For some reason, this produced near hysterics in Darnley. At one point I thought he was going to put his head through the windscreen, he was laughing so much.

'It's only a hunch of Rice Robey's,' I said. 'He could have committed suicide; he could have died by accident, whatever Rice Robey says. I'd take anything he said with a pinch of salt.'

'I'd trust old Pughie's hunches,' said Darnley lovingly, still chuckling a little.

'Evidently, you would.'

'It has a kind of plausibility, don't you think?'

It would have seemed churlish to point out to Darnley that he did not know anything about Jimbo, nor about Hunter, so that the criteria by which he judged the plausibility of any information concerning them must be completely valueless. Without having any of Felicity's academic interests or ratiocinative skills, I was beginning to notice how few people in my acquaintance ever employed rational processes of thought to arrive at conclusions. Darnley was not unique in this regard; in fact, I do not remember meeting a journalist who was capable of 'thinking', in Felicity's sense, that is, of sifting evidence, or of seeing that one thing either does or does not necessarily follow from another.

'It all has the ring of truth to me,' said Darnley. 'I'll probably run the story.'

'What – say Hunter murdered Jimbo Lampitt?'

'I don't see why not.'

'Won't you be sued for libel?'

It was like asking someone at a firework party on November the fifth whether there might not be a danger, should lighted tapers be put to the fuses, of catherine wheels revolving, or Roman candles shooting their brilliant fountains of sparklight into the dark sky, or of rockets making their satisfyingly noisy ascent beyond the treetops. Darnley's laugh reminded me of school. Teasing people, 'rotting them up' had been the phrase then, was fun, but it was not enough to give him his real kicks. For pure satisfaction to result, he needed to go too far, to make the other person, master or prefect, lose control, lash out with (in those days) lines, runs or the cane, or (nowadays) writs. There had already been several threatened libel cases in *The Spark*'s short history, a sure sign to Darnley that he was holding the strings and making the grown-ups dance to his tune.

'In a way, it is stronger stuff than his Harold Wilson stories. I mean, the Wilson stuff is all predictable, though I'm not sure I quite believe Pughie's suspicions about Harold's contacts behind the Iron Curtain. The smutty stuff has the ring of truth, though. Perhaps it will all come out, and Harold will resign. Then we might have Ernie as the next Prime Minister.'

'I wouldn't mind a chimpanzee as Prime Minister so long as he wasn't Conservative.'

'Ernie's a bit like Pugh in this way. He's got a vision of England. His whole political philosophy is really summed up in that Chesterton poem. You know the thing.'

'"The Donkey"?'

'No – "We are the people of England, and we haven't spoken yet".'

'He sees a sort of invisible thread connecting Magna Carta, the Peasants' Revolt, oh, all the predictable things, leading up to Tom Paine and all those enthusiasts for the French Revolution, of whom his ancestor, Jo Lampitt, was one.'

Darnley said, 'I don't know much about Ernie's family,' and I said, 'I don't know much about anything else,' realising with a thud that these words, intended as a joke, were probably true.

'Well, Jo Lampitt – radical Jo – was really the founding father of the dynasty,' I said. 'Rolling in money from his successful brewery, and wildly revolutionary in politics.'

'Sounds much like Ernie himself.'

'He was one of the first provincial brewers to open alehouses in London, and he made a fortune out of property. He bought a lot of burnt-out houses at the time of the Gordon riots and refurbished them as inns. At the same time, he was a genuine radical, an intellectual. He was friends with men like Benjamin Franklin, Josiah Wedgwood, Joseph Priestley, Godwin. It was he and his Quaker wife Naomi who bought Mallington. The house was the ancestral home of the Isleworths. Funnily enough, radical Jo's son Joseph, Jo the Second as Uncle Roy calls him, married an Isleworth heiress, Selina. They were already advancing themselves in the world, the Lampitts, and when Selina Isleworth's Uncle George sat up all night in Brooks's playing whist with Charles James Fox, he was said to have lost £40,000 in a single session – though the session lasted through two nights and a day, as Isleworth tried to win back his fortune, only losing more and more heavily. Mallington had to be sold, and the Lampitts had the money to buy it.'

'So all that passed into the hands of the lefties,' said Darnley waving at the view which suddenly came before us, as we turned the corner of the coast road and found ourselves at the south gates of the park. A long drive stretched before us, and beyond the clumps of ilex were pines, and beyond the pines the light of the sea. But in the distance was the house. Twisted brick Jacobean chimneys rose from the gabled roof. The stucco had been allowed to crumble, revealing here brick, here flint, the whole a pleasing variety of gentle colours surrounding the high oriel windows. Emblazoned at the top of the bays was the stone legend in simple capitals, the heraldic motto of the Isleworths: HONOR INSULAE AMOR PATRIAE. The house nestled in the trees which, to the east, crept up to the stable wings and garden rooms. The west front was in complete contrast to the remainder of the building, a stately wing added in the mid-eighteenth century, of pale pink brick symmetrically spaced with tall, well-proportioned windows. Further west still, beyond the smooth velvety lawns, stood the orangery, now housing a riot of azaleas.

I stopped the car.

'Yes,' said Darnley. 'Let's enjoy the view and prepare ourselves inwardly for a dose of old Ern.'

He chuckled, but I had not stopped in order to savour an aesthetic moment, irresistible and strong as that was, seeing Mallington in the haze of a warm summer afternoon. I had been jolted back with unexpected violence to the day the war broke out, quarter of a century earlier, and reminded with horrifying clarity of the happiness of my early childhood. I had known, with my mind, that those days were happy, but it felt at that moment in the car as if I was remembering it all for the first time. I remembered with an intense vividness, the cottage a mile or two away which my parents had rented that summer. The holiday had never been so clear in my mind as it was then, sitting with Darnley. It had been summoned up for me more luminously than if a film of it had been made at the time and was now being replayed to me for the first time. I remembered quite uninteresting facts like the texture of the wooden draining board beside the sink, and the sliminess of the soap suds which had splashed there from the washing-up bowl. I was too small to see the draining board, I could just reach it and touch the edge, this mixture of rough, slightly splintery wood and soapy slime. And I remembered Mummy saying, 'Don't get a splinter, darling,' and reaching down – all this had been forgotten until this second – and moving my hands, and kissing them, and then stooping down to kiss me. I remembered the exact texture of her lips and cheeks and arms as she embraced me then, and the smell of her was brought cruelly back, a wonderful smell in which the sweetness of soap was mingled with a very faint suggestion of sweat. Even as I sat there, I could feel my nose pressing into the softness of my mother's bosom. This particular snapshot of memory, overpoweringly strong and beautiful, retreated before recollections which were perhaps not memories in the same sense of the word. I think they were part memories, and part recollections of things I had been saying to myself about my childhood ever since. I remembered Daddy laughing at the idea that Uncle Roy aspired to know people such as the Lampitts. Now, what separated me from my parents was not the trivial barrier of class but the unbridgeable gulf of time. God had pulled the plug out and my parents were gone. They had been dead for more than twenty years and yet I was not sure as I sat beside Darnley in the Morris whether I had ever come to terms with their deaths, still less accepted them. With unquenchable longing, I still wanted them, and only them. I think that ever since they died, I had been waiting for the moment when this alarming state of things would be undone; surely, my subsconscious hoped, they would come back, and life could resume its 'normal' course, when Mummy and Daddy and I lived together in harmony, with only the occasional interruption from the likes of Granny, Mrs Webb or Uncle Roy. Until Mummy comes back, I had felt throughout life, I am just marking time. There seemed no need to pursue a 'proper career' with a university degree or a professional training, no need either to put my emotional or personal life on a more grown-up footing. Why did I put up with the unsatisfactory arrangement of sharing a small rented house with a cousin I only half liked? Was it not because at the back of my mind there was this crazy idea that one day things would right themselves, return to normal, and until that day, there was no need to make an effort, no need to get life right? I sat there at the wheel of the car looking over the thick grasses and cow parsley and buttercups which occupied the foreground of the view and knowing with chilling clarity and certainty that there would be no getting back to normal, no reunion, no healing of old wounds, no sham wiping away of tears from every eye.

All that was an illusion. I wanted Mummy then with a desire which was so strong that I felt myself shaking, heaving with grief. If Darnley noticed, he would have been deeply embarrassed.

I started the engine of the car. Darnley, once more, was speculating about the composition of the house party.

'Ernie and Pat are pretty thick with the Foots. I shouldn't be surprised to see Dick Crossman.'

These were not names which were above every name; they were no Lampitts; but I had heard them in childhood on the lips of Sargie and Uncle Roy. The Labour Party had a shadowy pre-existence until the moment (after his quarrel with Lloyd George) that Lord Lampitt (humbug and father of Vernon) had decided to join it. Thereafter, the Labour movement becomes a subject of interest to the historian, it becomes real, and the names of its luminaries, in so far as they were known and loved by the humbug and the Honourable Vernon, came to be learnt as part of the Lampitt catechism. Thus, from early years, I could lisp the names of Nye, and Ellen Wilkinson, and Stafford Cripps. They did not figure largely in any great, central stories, but flitted in and out of the narrative rather like the lesser-known angels in Milton, attendant upon the great characters upon whom our fullest attention was fixed. Clem Attlee, for example, was not an important figure in himself; it did not matter in the least that he was the Prime Minister. The important thing, from the Timplingham perspective, was that the Honourable Vernon was a member of his Cabinet.

In those days, Vernon had not been very far to the left of the party, though he had shown early signs of subsequent developments by resigning, with the others, over the issue of National Health charges. ('They say it cost him the Chancellorship – a great misfortune because the Honourable Vernon, as you may know, is a brilliant economist' – Uncle Roy.)

Now that the party was poised to resume power, after more than a dozen years of Conservative governments, it was a very different thing from the Labour Party of Clem Attlee. Nevertheless, Vernon had somehow overcome the disadvantages of his upbringing and won the favour of the left wing. The surprising thing about this when I came to analyse it, had nothing to do with class. The title could be dismissed as his 'dad's little bit o' nonsense'. There was no reason, once prejudice had been discarded, why the more revolutionary wing of the party should not have been happy to welcome as their champion a man who was extremely rich and sat in the House of Lords. What was surprising about their enthusiasm for Vernon was the lack of Marxist, doctrinaire bite in any of his reported speeches, published articles, or, in my experience, private utterance.

He stood for an old-fashioned, sentimental radicalism – the abolition of the monarchy, the House of Lords, the honours system. These were things which, as far as I could see, could be removed from the scene without changing the fabric of English society in the slightest degree. There was nothing in Vernon's programme of reforms, set of private fantasies, call them what you will, which even remotely resembled Stalinism, Trotskyism or Leninism – still less a fashionable new variety of the creed now gaining popularity, Maoism. The newspapers, however, had chosen to depict Vernon as a communist. He was always adorned with hammers and sickles in the cartoons, and the role of 'mad Red' was evidently one which he was happy enough to act out if interviewers or reporters came his way.

Now, after its spell of political impotence, the left was in a position where it could once more exercise power in Britain. Having seemed electorally immovable for years, the Conservatives had become unstuck. Economic and political reasons for this were advanced by the pundits, but perhaps it was just as plausible to believe that portents had appeared in the sky, and that the Harlot and the Episkopos were ushering in a new era, uncertain in its creeds, morals or social order.

The Morris made its slow way down the rutty drive towards the house. I was recovering from my sad reverie, but was not sufficiently concentrating on the driving, and was taken completely by surprise when a large black limousine swooped towards us at great speed in the opposite direction. For a second, a head-on collision seemed an inevitability, but lucky instinct made me swerve, and we juddered to a halt on the grass beside the drive, and the engine stalled.

'Bloody fool! Driving at us as if they wanted to kill us!'

'You saw who it was,' Darnley asked, 'in the back of the car?'

'No.'

He adopted the voice of the pompous High Court judge.

'The Leader of Her Majesty's Opposition.'

'That's no excuse for driving like a maniac.'

'He wasn't driving.'

I tried to be as blasé as Darnley seemed, and assented to the derogatory remarks which he was offering about our leader. I did not hold his views or career in any particular veneration; but I did revere the fact that he was powerful and famous, and the thought that we had nearly been involved in a motor accident with him produced an excitement which dispelled all my previous anger and fear, an excitement which was absolutely snobbish, based purely on a sense of proximity to the mighty in their seats.

The tall woman in slacks, waiting by the front door as the Morris scrunched to a halt in the gravel was Vernon's wife Pat, whom I had only met a couple of times before. The trousers were made of green artificial fibre and she had on a pink blouse. She was substantially built with rather mottled brown skin and thick silver hair.

'We nearly didn't make it here alive,' said Darnley. 'Your Leader almost collided with us in the drive.'

She shook us both warmly by the hand. My childhood catechism had told me that Pat Lampitt (née Dawnay) had been in the Wrens during the war. At seven years old, I could have told you, 'If Pat hadn't been a woman, she'd be fighting this war as an admiral'. Not Uncle Roy's own words, of course, but a 'famous' quip of old Mr Michael Lampitt, bless him.

Pat spoke with rather a surprising voice, in its way as idiosyncratic as Vernon's. It was fundamentally posh, but it had a nasal, cock-neyfied twang to it, and one wondered whether she had always spoken in that way or whether she had adopted the vowels in early adulthood. Her voice could have been based on the Edwardian cockney known to have been spoken in some aristocratic families in her parents' time, but it is conceivable that she had decided that this highly eccentric way of speaking the English language would put Vernon's proletarian supporters and constituents at their ease.

'Let's go round the back way' (pronounced *why*), 'and then we can have a nice cupper in the kitchen.'

She led us through the conservatory at the side of the house and into a stone-flagged corridor littered with decades' attrition of junk. The bells on the walls, each with a coil of metal attached to them and, beneath, the name of a room, were rusty and cobwebby, eloquently indicative of the present generation of Lampitts' un-willingness to summon, or employ, servants. The shabby gloss paint, peeling from the walls, was a remainder of Mallington's incarnation as a field hospital during the war. Old prams, one of Edwardian vintage, groaned under the weight not of baby clothes but of political leaflets and pamphlets. The urgency of the headlines and the excitement of the exclamation marks on these documents were mocked by the yellowing and curling of the paper on which these messages, once so arresting, now so obsolete, were printed. In one ancient pram which might well have conveyed Vernon for walks, pushed by his nurse, there was a pile of papers headed, in scarlet capitals, A LIST OF TORY MISDEEDS. I paused to read them. They included the usual Conservative faults and flaws, but they concluded PRIVATEERING FROM THE SOUTH AFRICAN WAR. The advice VOTE LAMPITT FOR A FAIRER WORLD had been addressed not to our generation, but to the electorate of 1906 – one of the last elections he fought, before purchasing his barony from Lloyd George. Political bumf from Vernon's career outnumbered his father's relics. There must have been a thousand copies each of his pamphlets STOP THIS SUEZ MADNESS!, THE TRUTH ABOUT HANGING, and HAVE YOU REALLY HAD IT SO GOOD?, an essay composed in 1960 but which, on brief perusal, seemed almost identical in its general thrust to A LIST OF TORY MISDEEDS of the 1906 era. There were also many posters lying around, begging us to VOTE LAMPITT.

'Do you know Harold?' Pat asked. 'He likes journalists. He mixes with them all the time; image-building, I call it.'

'I've met him a couple of times,' said Darnley.

This was news to me.

'He brought that secretary woman with him.' Pat sighed. She heaved a huge black steaming kettle from the range and made tea. As she did so she pulled a 'funny face' as though it was perhaps wiser to say nothing of the secretary. It was almost the expression of a woman who thought her kitchen was 'bugged' and that anything she said might one day be taken down and used in evidence.

'We last met when you were married to Anne,' she said with a violent change of theme. 'And that was quite a little time ago now.'

She was a Joe Blunt, Pat. I felt reassured that we did not have to tiptoe round the subject of my divorce or feel that it was un-mentionable.

'It was at Sibs's house, right?' (roit).

'Wasn't it when Jimbo's papers were being sold to that American?'

'That's right. There was a great family pow-wow' (piaow-wiaow).

'We thought we'd all been so clever taking the papers out of the hands of that man who wrote the book. In fact, he was ahead of us in the game. He had the Americans eating out of his hands, long before we came on the scene. We were conned!'

This series of events, which Pat was describing fairly accurately, had made most of the Lampitts extremely angry at the time. Now, it made her roar with laughter.

'Like ginger biscuits?' she resumed abruptly. 'I made 'em moiself.'

Momentarily, we were schoolboys being given a treat by matron.

'Still, he's a right little bastard, our Mr Hinter.'

She saw the puzzlement on my face. Was 'Hinter' her funny way of pronouncing, or had she forgotten Hunter's actual name? I felt very stupid when she had to explain.

''Cause he hints! You're thick. Hints about Jimbo being a pansy; never says so much, but hints. Mr Hinter.'

Now we had got the general idea, it seemed unnecessary to spell it out so repetitively.

'And did you see the paperback of *Prince Albert*, Jimbo's book?'

'No.'

'Didn't you? I'll show it to you.'

She went over to the dresser where she fumbled for a spectacle case amid electricity bills, seed packets, cookery books. On the shelves of the dresser stood ranks of Staffordshire figures, an enthusiasm of the late Humbug's. They were mainly political characters of the last century: Gladstone, Disraeli, Peel, Parnell, the Prince Consort, Bradlaugh (a great hero of the Lampitts) and Palmerston all stared down in their unreal garishness of whites, blues, oranges and reds. Other characters from the radical past – Wat Tyler and Milton caught the eye – were joined by a few religious figures. Wesley held up a glossy black sleeve from his pottery pulpit. Ridley and Latimer were eternally confined to streaks of red and orange earthenware flame. Some of these figurines recalled the subjects of Jimbo's popular biographies, most noticeably that of the Prince Consort. Others, if Jimbo's own biographer could be believed, had actually crossed the penman's path in his boyhood. The austere little statue of Cardinal Manning, the glaze faded from its biretta and its emaciated features, stared across Pat's kitchen icily unaware of the scabrous suggestions made in Hunter's book about that tea party, some time in the 1880s, when the prince of the church supposedly took the infant James Petworth Lampitt on the knees of his watered-silk cassock.

Hunter's life of Jimbo seemed to have ground to a halt after

71

Volume One. Other things had happened in my life and I had not given any thought to it all until Rice Robey had revived my interest in the matter.

'Here we are,' said Pat, who had donned some surprising American-looking spectacles of butterfly design and retrieved the paperback of *Prince Albert* from the pile of rubbish on the dresser. She was reading from the blurb on the back of the book.

'Listen to this. "The engagingly written introduction is by Raphael Hunter, Lampitt's biographer, and for many years his close friend and private secretary." Well, that's a whopper. Jimbo had no need of a secretary. He always had Cecily.'

'Do you mean Sargie's wife?'

Sometimes one makes a remark to another person which reveals that one knows nothing, absolutely nothing, about the matter under discussion. Such blunders elicit looks which are akin to pity. As such an expression passed over Pat's face, I remembered, from my Lampitt catechism, that Cecily and Jimbo had been 'as thick as thieves'. But, Jimbo's relationship with Cecily, still less my ignorance of it, were not what Pat wished us to consider.

'You know,' she said, 'there is no one close to Jimbo' – she listed some members of the family and one or two writers – 'who ever met Mr Hinter until Jimbo died. Elizabeth Cameron said, I remember, when these books started to come out, "Pat, who *is* Hunter, we never heard Jimbo mention him?" That's the truth. Isn't it the *limit*? Sibs has written to the publishers to complain.'

We drank our tea and ate our biscuits.

'Was the Leader staying with you?' Darnley, perhaps understandably, was more interested in the recent departure of a man who, in a matter of months, was bound to become the next Prime Minister, than in the length or extent of Hunter's acquaintanceship with one of Vernon's cousins.

'Harold? Just came to lunch. Now, I haven't told you who *is* staying,' said Pat.

Even as she spoke, I could hear two familiar voices in the stone-flagged corridor outside the kitchen door.

'I said to the man, "Syringe the bloody things again. They're my ears. I'm paying."'

'Payin'? Shame on yer, Sargie, fer not usin' the Health Service.'

'Anyway, bang goes another bloody doctor. Had to sack him. I'm not deaf. Just needed my bloody ears syringing. I couldn't get

72

another doctor that night. Though I rang three, it was past midnight by the time the other bugger was finished. . . .'

Sargie's narrative continued as he entered the room. Whether he was deaf was in the nature of an academic question since in my recollection of him, going back to my early childhood, he had never been interested in anything that anyone beside himself was saying. He was always affectionate towards me, however, and when he saw me in the kitchen, he abandoned his ear saga and exclaimed, 'Julie, my dear!' with apparent pleasure.

I introduced Darnley and while Vernon pumped my hand and said how glad he was we could spare the time to come to this 'dirty great place – absurd intit?', Sargie said, 'So you edit *The Spark*.'

Darnley grinned. It wasn't often he met a reader of his paper.

'Bloody amusing cartoon in the last issue. The one about old Harold Mac's water-works.'

'That was several issues ago.'

There was a paradox about Darnley's journalistic efforts to be outrageous. He truly wanted to be offensive, indeed considered it almost a duty to make those in authority squeal; but he also coveted praise and Sargie's expressed enjoyment of *The Spark*, whether or not genuine, caused a sheepish grin of uncomplicated pride to appear on Darnley's face.

'Wouldn't have laughed some years ago when I was having wee-wee trouble myself. I asked my bloody doctor then, "Why do we *need* a prostate gland?" He couldn't answer. Have you noticed how many doctors are stupid? I mean, really stupid, much stupider than average? Anyway, I couldn't help chuckling over your thing about Harold Mac. But how did you know about it? That little tit-bit of yours appeared about a fortnight before Harold actually went into hospital, and no one knew – except his friends.'

'A bloke told me. Friend of Julian's.'

Darnley smiled at me and it was somehow immediately apparent that he spoke of 'Pughie'. I could not begin to guess then, nor can I now, how Rice Robey was *au fait*, before the great majority of the British people, with the Prime Minister's urinary difficulties.

'The Tories will have to have a new leader, Mac's on the way out,' Sargie decreed. 'Who'll put up the best fight against our Harold? Rab's the man they oughta have. Vebba clebba febba, Rab. But my guess is that they will choose Quintin – bloody fools that they are.'

Darnley laughed. I laughed. We all laughed.

73

'You could be right there, Sargie,' said Vernon, applying his light to his pipe and speaking jerkily between puffs. 'It'll be hard for Quintin ter lead iz party frum the Lords but it could be done, it could be done.'

The slightly insane gleam as he said this made me aware that Vernon would not be averse, if the chance came his way, to exercising power without abandoning his peerage.

'Verra much betwin a-selves,' added Vernon, 'Harold was here ter-day. Jus' came ter this terribly informal lunch, but it was nice uv 'im to come.'

'He's a devious bugger,' said Sargie. 'You always wonder what he's up to. He's not really left-wing, not *innocently* left-wing, like you, Vernon.'

'Oh, I think yer wrong, there, Sargie. I'm sure Harold's got a real socialist commitment. We wouldn't 'uv backed 'im if 'e hadn't. No. We're going to see real economic planning for the first time since 'fifty-one. We're going ter see an extension uv the nationalised industries, a total reform uv the educational system. My old school will go!'

'Julie's old school,' said Sargie.

'So it is.' Vernon could not possibly have remembered where I had been to school but he nodded as if this were the best-known fact in the world.

My school had been chosen for its Lampitt connections. Old Mr Lampitt, who married a sister of Archbishop Benson's, had been headmaster there during the last century; James Petworth Lampitt himself was one of the school's more illustrious literary sons.

'I'd be happy to see it nationalised,' I said.

'We'll see the House of Lords go,' said Vernon, ' – in the very first session I shouldn't wonder. We'll see the American air-bases wound up, we'll see the banks nationalised, and the money put where it belongs.'

'Down the drain,' said Sargie, and laughed. 'You were right to back Harold, my dear, but don't get carried away. He only hinted about that Cabinet post anyway. You thought he was promising you something, but I listened to his words very carefully.'

'Sargie, we did agree not to talk about that,' said Vernon. 'For Harold's sake. It really was confidential.'

'Have some tea and stop talking about boring politics,' said Pat.

As he sat down at the kitchen table, the cigarette-holder clenched

74

between his yellowing dentures, I noticed for the first time that Sargie was carrying my novel. It was the only book I had ever published and by now, five or six years on, I was so heartily ashamed of it that I was almost literally unable to bear the sight of it. I wondered what conceivable reason there could be for Sargie to carry it in his hand. He was no devotee of contemporary literature and, with the visitation of each bad bout of depression over the years, the habit of reading had slowly left him. If the Leader of the Labour Party could have been described as devious, it was an art in which he could have taken lessons from Sargent Lampitt who was the most successfully manipulative person I had ever known.

'Our house revolves around Sargie's moods,' my aunt once crossly and accurately averred; and certainly, during the days of their friendship, Sargie was able to command in my uncle Roy the most unwavering and spaniel-like devotion. If high spirits seized Sargie and he felt like a few days in London, accompanied by a friend, then Uncle Roy would go with him, at a moment's notice, cancelling church services and leaving his own household to manage without him. Similarly, when Sargie was in the thrall of one of his very terrible black moods, wanting only to sit in Timplingham Place and watch the rain trickle down the window-panes, Uncle Roy would be there, to sit in silence with his friend, sometimes, when the gloom was at its worst, holding Sargie's hand. Whether as chauffeur, dinner companion, reader aloud, chess partner, or in other dogsbody roles, my uncle never failed Sargie. Now that they had quarrelled and neither met nor spoke, there was a great emptiness in Uncle Roy's life. He jabbered more obsessively than ever about the Lampitts, but was this a substitute for Sargie's daily, hourly companionship? Sargie must have missed my uncle, too, though he would have been too arrogantly proud to admit it. He found a succession of Roy-substitutes. My ex – Anne – had for a time run errands for him; for all I knew, she still did so. Any paid employee, whether medical or domestic, was lucky to last six months before some impossible quarrel necessitated an end to their association with Sargie, who was never happy with helpers or servants; slaves and serfs were what his nature craved.

He looked at me though his horn-rimmed spectacles and exhaled cigarette smoke through both nostrils over the well-trimmed moustaches. My eyes fell to the dust-wrapper of the book and passed up to his again. We eyed one another like two strange cats unable to decide whether the other wanted to rub noses or scratch eyes. I braved it out and said nothing about the book. It was too soon after my arrival at Mallington to be drawn into one of Sargie's plots. I was already experiencing the sinking sensation which had visited me more than once before in life, of having believed myself to be moving into uncharted territory only to find that I was still in the same, circumscribed world of childhood.

'Yer've told 'em we've got the kids comin'?' asked Vernon, gesturing towards Darnley and me with his pipe. 'Jus' the girls. Yer've not met me lads have yer?'

'Christopher I've met once or twice at Rupert Starling's,' I said. 'William was in America at that period.'

This parrot-knowledge of the names, doings and whereabouts of the Lampitts flew out of my lips easily. Sargie smiled. Vernon showed no surprise that I should remember, some five years after, his younger son's period in Massachusetts, the exact course he was pursuing at the MIT.

'No, Bill's in advertisin' now,' said Vernon. For a good socialist like Vernon to have spawned a boy who wanted to go into advertising seemed a bit sad. Hearing the information on his lips was like hearing a director of the Bank of England inform his company that a child of his loins was a dab hand at forging bank notes, or a Moderator of the Methodist Church inform his brethren that a daughter of his had a prominent position in the chorus line of the Folies Bergères. I have noticed, however, that parents who are ashamed of their children's activities often speak about them with an added heartiness, and this was what Vernon did now.

'And then there's Tommy Wimbish upstairs. Have you met Professor Wimbish?'

'No, but I like his books.'

'Verra disciplined man, Wimbish. He's writing the history uv the party. He's done one volume. Not everyone was kind about it.'

Cormac, the portly young academic I had met at *The Spark*, was one of those who had been less than generous.

'You had to laugh at the review of Wimbish's book by young Cormac,' said Sargie.

'No yer didn't. It was malicious.'

'That's why you had to laugh at it. They're too similar, Cormac and Wimbish. That's why they hate each other. They are both good historians, they both became professors young, and wrote their books, but that wasn't enough for them. They wanted to make a splash. Always a mistake for academics to want that. So, Cormac hasn't written a word about the Crusades since he got his chair; he's written pop biographies of Nazis and articles for the Beaverbrook press.'

'Cormac's revoltingly right-wing,' said Vernon. 'Wimbish is loyal to 'is working-class roots.'

'In his fashion, doubtless. But there again, they are similar. They're both clever grammar-school boys. It just happens that Cormac is so-called right-wing and Wimbish is so-called left-wing. I more and more think it doesn't matter *what* opinions people have. Both Cormac and Wimbish just use their opinions as instruments of self-publicity.'

Not knowing either of the professors, I could not contribute to this discussion. I had not read Professor Cormac's books. Wimbish's briskly written popular histories of the Tudor Age had entertained me, though. The history of the Labour Party, in which he was now engaged, was evidently a work which would bring him less cash or kudos, and he was loyally pressing on with his task, in spite of the vilification of his colleagues.

'There's masses uv stuff me Dad left behind. Wimbish could tell the whole story from Dad's diaries alone,' said Vernon.

'If he wanted to get the story wrong,' said Sargie.

'He writes 3,000 words every day,' said Vernon admiringly. 'Rain or shine. So 'e wuz tellin' Harold.'

'It's not often you see Harold stumped for words,' said Sargie, 'but since Wimbish wouldn't stop talking about himself, our dear leader hardly had time to spell out his policies or offer Vernon the job, or whatever it was he had come for. We had to hear all about Wimbish's low social origins, Wimbish's brilliant mind that rescued him from the gutter, Wimbish's original historical research. And you'd think Wimbish had invented the bloody Labour Party from the way he talks about this book he's writing.'

'Anyway,' said Pat. 'That's who we've got for you, Julian. Not exactly a glittering house party, I'm afraid.'

She stood behind the seated figure of Vernon and ran an affectionate hand through his hair as she spoke.

'The girls are coming by train,' she continued. 'If you were feeling like an angel, Julian, you'd drive over to Lynn and meet them at the station. Such a bore since they Beechinged all the railway lines in these parts. Some of the trains always stopped at Mallington Halt in the past, and if they didn't, you could always get out at Burnham, Wells, Walsingham.'

'All the LMS trains, of which me dad was a director.'

'And my brother Martin was LNER,' said Sargie wistfully. 'They were rivals in trade. We had decent railways in this country until this Great Movement of Ours nationalised the bloody things.'

'Closin' the branch lines had nothing ter do with nationalisation. If I'd a' bin Minister of Transport, I'd 've kept 'em open.'

I thought of this claim as I waited on King's Lynn station for the arrival of the Lampitt girls. It was strange to think that there were some people in the world sufficiently interested, or adult, to make decisions about our system of transport. I had never conceived, for a single instant, of being involved with the practical running of affairs. Felicity, with her files and in-trays, was now involved with such matters in a minor way. Her obsessive conversations with Rice Robey, animated as they were with an emotional interest which extended far beyond the prosaic sphere of civil service departments, were nevertheless concerned with such practical matters as whether the Ministry of Transport should be allowed to build roads through ancient archaeological sites.

I was glad of the chance to be alone. I had left Mallington with some eagerness. Darnley sank into a chair with *The Fifth Form at St Dominic's*. Sargie, still clutching *The Vicar's Nephew*, with no comment made upon it, had 'things to do' in his room, a compulsion which grew more conspicuous as the minutes in the kitchen had ticked past and Pat had poured him nothing stronger than tea. Vernon had gone to confer with Professor Wimbish, who had not yet descended from the library. Pat, who had beguilingly hinted at the existence of another member of the party by hoping that Gussy was all right on her own (who was she?) sliced peppers and counted plates in preparation for supper.

The drive along the coast road through Wells and Brancaster and Sandringham had brought many jumbled thoughts of past and present into my mind. I thought of Uncle Roy and Sargie driving me to London on the day of Jimbo's funeral and putting me on the train to Malvern, where I had been at school with Darnley. I thought of the moment, later that summer term, when I first glimpsed Raphael Hunter through a window in the school, embracing the art mistress with whom I was in love. The Lampitts' continued concern with

Hunter's book and Jimbo's reputation came as something of a surprise. I did not know what to make of it. I was not having consecutive thoughts. Impressions, like a cascade of unsorted snapshots, filled the consciousness. I thought of Rice Robey and his youthful connection with Jimbo. All these images, apparently disparate, seemed linked by a golden string. It was ages since I had set eyes on Hunter's book *Petworth Lampitt: The Hidden Years 1881– 1910*, but the whole strangely connected matter did not seem to go away. The string of incidents which had begun on the day of Jimbo's funeral, begun, that is to say, in my own imagination and consciousness, had become one of those focuses provided by life as a way of observing the truth itself. Was it, simply, possible to be objectively truthful about the past? Hunter had based his book, or so he claimed, on Jimbo's diaries which no one but himself (and, fleetingly, Felicity) had ever seen. The family disputed the interpretation he had placed on these documents, now lodged in the Everett Foundation in New York. The Lampitts even went so far as to suppose that Hunter, for his own impenetrable motives, had fabricated the evidence. Certainly, the issue was complicated by the feelings we all had about Hunter himself. Were he, however, a purely blameless and scrupulous recorder, his selection and arrangement of evidence from Jimbo's diaries would still have been an interpretative act. Wishing to tell an objective story about another human life was perhaps an illusory desire. As I stood on King's Lynn station, mulling these ideas over, I think I began to have the glimmering of a wish which would one day turn into the present narrative. The half-thought, the almost-perception, was that all truth comes to us filtered through a mythological process. Was this what Rice Robey meant by saying that we could not live without myths? Wisdom would come, if it ever came, when we ceased to worry about the truthfulness or authenticity of the mythological instrument, language, memory, by which we discerned or shaped experience. It would be a mistake to try to make the focus of the image too sharp, for the most truthful impression of life's experience would have to convey its ambiguities, its smudginess, its half-enlightenments. Myths themselves help us use the inchoate collection of impressions we receive because they lack such fogginess, but even myths, or the best ones, are riven with ambiguities, we can take them both ways. The myths concerning Christ, for example, are riven with contradictions which give them a troublingly realistic quality of chiaroscuro, a quality garishly lacking (as it seemed to me when I read it) in Rice Robey's reworkings of the story.

And now I stood on the station platform, my mind full of confused remembrance, and tingling with the excitement, however slight, which must always come before meeting strangers of the opposite sex for the first time. I remembered that Kirsty was an undergraduate at Cambridge. Jo, her elder sister, was by all accounts save those of Uncle Roy a bit thick. I was to await them at the ticket barrier carrying a piece of card which had started life as a stiffener for one of Vernon's new shirts. On the back of it, Pat had written in bold characters the single word LAMPITT.

Like so much which had happened to me lately, this seemed portentous, emblematic. Was this a little image of what my life had been, and was to be, standing at a barrier where others came and went, with the legend LAMPITT on my cardboard shield? As I stood there, I tried to remember the various Homeric formulae or heroic kennings by which Uncle Roy labelled these two girls. He could scarcely have met them very often if at all; this would not have prevented him from thinking about them so long as Lampitt blood flowed in their veins. One of the more formidable female members of the family, perhaps Sibs, or possibly Ida (daughter of Bobby of duckling-in-Brighton fame) had pronounced Kirsty to be a 'handful' when a child. Jo's teeth, protuberant when she was twelve, had been put in a brace by an expensive dentist, said by Sargie to be 'an absolute something something' – Uncle Roy's way of conveying his friend's strong habits of speech. My wife Anne, several years older than these cousins of hers, used to speak of Jo as if she were mentally retarded, and it was true that there had been difficulty 'getting her settled' after she failed her resits at the secretarial college. It was then that Uncle Roy had pulled strings with someone he knew in the Diocesan offices in Ely. The job entailed 'light office duties'. The world of archdeacons and minor canons' wives was not thought to be one where Jo would fit in cheerfully, but it was considered safer than letting her loose on London; Cambridge and Kirsty were near in one direction, Mallington and the parents in another. These were hazy snatches of Lampitt lore on which to construct any premonitory impressions; but there was not long to wait before coming face to face with the sisters themselves. Passengers were coming off the Cambridge train with that variety of unguarded facial expressions so often on display at points of arrival and departure. Some peered about, expecting a friend or relative to greet them, their anxiety melting suddenly into relief and glee and love at the sight of another human being standing there; it prompted the thought of how strangely arbitrary human affection is. Why should they be so delighted to see this person rather than that? Why did they gaze so fervently through the crowds of individuals, all similarly composed, all (or most) with their full complement of faces, arms, legs, desperate for the sight of one face, the clasp of one pair of arms? And I thought, too, of how vulnerable this made them, this rushing forward to be met, and how easily such expressions of happiness could be shattered, for example by the announcement over the loud-hailer that some named individual was not waiting at the station, but lying unconscious in the Intensive Care Unit of the local hospital.

Two girls came up to me. Both had short, blonded hair and duffel bags suspended from a shoulder; both had mouths wide with an-archic toothy grins, and both had an arm round Rice Robey. The trio were so intertwined as they approached, that they could almost have been some mannerist sculpture brought to life. At first glance, it was hard to see whose limb was whose, or where greasy navy blue sleeve ended and fluffy black jumper began.

'Fab!' said Jo as soon as she had made out the word on my piece of cardboard. 'I was expecting Mum. Nice to have a bloke. You're not married or anything, or queer?'

'Your mother's cooking supper. She asked if I'd drive over and fetch you.'

Rudimentary introductions began.

'Mr Robey's been giving this really brilliant talk at Cambridge to the archaeological society,' said Kirsty. 'Sorry – what's your name?'

'Mr Grainger and I are already acquainted,' said Rice Robey. 'This is indeed a propitious conjunction of the consanguinities.'

'He's nice, isn't he?' Jo asked me, with a sideways jerk of her head towards Rice Robey and a slightly crazy squint.

'It was all about stone circles, and ley-lines and temples and druids,' said Kirsty, 'and it was quite simply the most brilliant talk I ever heard in my life. It beats all the lectures I ever heard in Cambridge.'

'Far too flattering a testimonial.'

'No, it was, it was.'

All these remarks passed as we walked to the Morris in the station

81

car park. There was no need for Jo to spell out a reason for their bubbling merriment.

'G. and t. on the train!'

'I told Mr Robey that he must come home for the night and nobble Papa, and whoever else is staying. There's bound to be some Labour Party high-ups hanging around the place. . . .'

'I think not,' I warned her. 'It seems to be more of a domestic occasion.'

Rice Robey was basking in the glow of the two girls' affection. To be squeezed by two nymphs who took seriously his view of legendary Britain must have come close to his personal definition of Paradise, the equivalent of *foie gras* to the sound of trumpets. Kirsty never confided in me what her thoughts had been, but Jo, who was not noticeably reticent, announced when the effect of the gin and tonic had worn off that she was glad to get home.

'He's *sinister*! His fingers went too far in the back of the car.'

'How far's that?'

'That's a real wanker's question.'

We were standing about waiting for dinner by the time Jo and I had exchanged these words. Pat Lampitt was evidently so accustomed to unannounced arrivals that she completely accepted Rice Robey's eruption on to that scene. The only surprising thing, I found, was its unsurprisingness. One now expected him to turn up everywhere until what he called 'the symphony of destinies' had played its final chord, or at least reached the end of a movement. I knew, Felicity had so often reiterated it, that Rice Robey was much in demand as a freelance lecturer, and as a guide around the ancient sites of Britain. Given the fact that he managed to fit this in on top of a busy schedule of journalistic malice and office chores, it was perhaps not so very surprising that he had come Kirsty Lampitt's way. As soon as one began thinking of it as a coincidence, one began to remember that in his peculiar vision of things, such concepts as chance, coincidence and luck were to be discarded.

'Your friend – what's he called?' Jo persisted. She had sobered up a bit and become prosaically anxious to get things straight, sort out identities.

'Miles Darnley.'

'Miles, right. Why does he call you Percy Grainger?'

'Because . . . difficult to explain, really.' Difficult, that is, to someone who seemed virtually incapable of thought. I felt coy to admit that I was 'Jason Grainger' on 'The Mulberrys'; it would be too embarrassing if she never listened to the programme, and worse if she did. Darnley's tortuous need to relabel the human race with nicknames of his own devising was too wearisome to disentangle, particularly since the general family consensus that Jo was 'thick as a plank' seemed at that moment far more plausible than something Uncle Roy claimed to have heard from the Diocesan Secretary in Ely – 'that Lampitt girl's a live wire'. Darnley's doodling sort of brain had not been content to leave me as Jason Grainger. He had had to change it to Percy Grainger, a musical composer of whom Jo had almost certainly never heard. It was too boring to unravel nonsense of this kind.

'Anyway, he seems to be getting on well with Kirsty,' said Jo. 'Kirsty's just bust up with her boyfriend. It's really, really sad, I think.'

Kirsty, who certainly seemed to have hit it off well with Darnley, was unmistakably Jo's sister: they had the same sort of hair, straight and thick, which they had deliberately made more alike by cutting and dyeing it identically; both had the same rather beaky noses sticking out of fleshy faces; both had blue eyes. Both faces, however, were completely different; where Kirsty's was animated, Jo's was not. Jo stared uncomprehendingly, her eyes seemed half dead and the way in which she jutted out her lower lip somehow recalled the more truculent inhabitants of the ape house at London Zoo. Kirsty's face, by contrast, was lit up with intelligence; it seemed brightly and comprehendingly amused by the world it confronted.

'Bitch,' said Jo. 'She's always bagging blokes I fancy.'

'If you want to pitch in and break it all up,' I said, 'don't feel you have to waste time talking to me.'

'Oh, what's the use?'

She crossly exhaled a noseful of Number Six.

We were standing in the Cabinet, an octagonal room, whose high walls were hung with faded torn crimson damask. Ormolu candle brackets and mirror-frames sprouted from the wall above the chaste white chimneypiece. Most of the furniture was gilt except for two or three large Boule *bureaux plats* which echoed the crimson of the wall hangings and added to the claustrophobic and vaguely infernal feeling of the place.

'Red curtains always make me think of *naughty* Lord Byron, you know,' Professor Wimbish's excited contralto rang out over the company. It was more like song than speech, the singing of some conceited bird or the uncontrolled warblings of some crazed old dowager. His pencil-thin wife, said to be rather grand, stood by, twitching her little lips with disapproval as he thrilled out – 'You see! Byron woke up in the middle of the night and saw the red curtains hanging round the bed. He said he thought he was already in hell!'

Pat politely rocked with laughter.

'Horrible man, Lord Byron,' said Lady Augusta Wimbish. She looked so very old, and so wirily indestructible, that it was on the verge of credible that she spoke from actual memory of the poet.

'But, I say!' exclaimed Wimbish, ignoring his wife completely. 'What a mind Harold has!'

'He's brilliant,' Vernon agreed.

'You know, I've been thinking,' said Wimbish, 'all afternoon while I worked in your beautiful library, Harold is really the same as Henry VIII.'

Professor Wimbish was a small man, several inches shorter than his wife, with thick crinkly dark hair and nut-brown eyes which smiled madly behind specs. Joe and I had run out of things to say to one another, so we gathered round Wimbish in a circle while he expounded his theory of likeness between the Leader of the Labour Party and the sixteenth-century despot.

'Henry, you see! He was master of setting one faction against another. On the one hand you have your Boleyns, who might correspond, let us say, to some section of the party. Let's say the TGWU. Or Northumberland and the Fabian Society that Sargie's so fond of. Michael Foot and the Abbot of Glastonbury, you see!'

The comparisons were rather detailed and since the personalities of Henry VIII's courtiers and subjects were as real to the professor as the personalities of the modern Labour Party, it was difficult at times to follow his drift. Vernon protested at the likening of his new hero to the man who had put down the Pilgrimage of Grace which, in his view had been primarily an uprising of the poeple rather than a specifically religious movement. It was all rather lost on me, and probably on Jo, and it was something of a relief when Rice Robey turned towards our group and intervened.

'You speak of Henry VIII. What do you know, Professor, of Herne the Hunter?' he asked.

Wimbish cast a look of utter disdain in Rice Robey's direction, perhaps amazed that anyone with such proletarian diction should dare to open his lips at all.

'And what do *you* know about anything?' He wiggled his finger as he indulged in this ludicrous parody of point-scoring.

'I merely wondered, Professor Wimbish, whether you had come across references to Herne the Hunter in your extensive researches into the history of the Great Despoiler.'

'The Despoiler of *what*, pray?'

'Oh, come *on*.' Vernon leapt to Rice Robey's defence. 'Henry VIII was the Despoiler uv the Monasteries. Yer can't deny Henry did that, and brought into bein', at one stroke, the privileged classes. Gave the lands and the houses ter the people who could pay – all good Tory stuff. What uv we here – Fountains Abbey? Who's the highest bidder? Goin', goin', gone!'

'Well, Herne, you see, might well have existed,' said Wimbish. 'You probably remember that he is mentioned in Shakespeare. Mistress Page, in *The Merry Wives of Windsor* says,

> There is an old tale goes that Herne the Hunter
> Sometime a keeper here in Windsor Forest,
> Doth all the winter-time at still midnight,
> Walk round about an oak, with great ragg'd horns,
> And there he blasts the tree and takes the cattle,
> And makes milch-kine yield blood, and shakes a chain
> In a most hideous and dreadful manner.'

'The legend is that he was a keeper, either of Henry VIII's time or earlier,' said Rice Robey. 'He was a follower of the Old Faith, one of the *wicca*. He hanged himself, or so it is said.'

'All that is pure conjecture,' said Wimbish. 'There is not one shred of historical evidence for it. Why *do* second- or third-rate individuals insist on leaping to conclusions for themselves rather than coming to those of us who *know*, the professional historians? Here are you. I don't know who you are, but you are offering us opinions about a legendary character from Tudor times, without having consulted the most authoritative and important book ever written about the Court of Henry VIII.'

'I have read your books, Wimbish, with great admiration,' said Rice Robey firmly.

At this confession, Wimbish became quite kittenish. His stern-ness melted into a coquettish smirk. He patted Rice Robey's wrist and said, 'Well in that case, dear, you're forgiven.'

'You ask all the old, empirical English questions,' said Rice Robey. 'It is your job to do so, or so you may consider it; but this is not the way that the collective unconscious operates.'

'What I think you are saying,' said Wimbish, 'is that people in the main are too bloody stupid to know the difference between truth and falsehood, which is why there will always be political oppression in the world. Tyrants like Hitler and Lenin knew this – they saw that people were far too stupid to see through their lies.'

'Lenin wasn't the same as Hitler,' said Vernon. 'Lenin was a good man, Hitler was a bad man – there's no gainsaying that.'

This assertion, which sounded uncomfortably like something out of Orwell's *Animal Farm*, was interrupted by Rice Robey.

'It isn't a matter of stupidity, Wimbish, it's a matter of the *way* we perceive truth.'

'Those of us with minds perceive truth by thinking. Those who can't bloody think – which means the majority of the human race – should just shut up, and leave the thinking to those of us who can.'

'We don't know our parents by thinking, we don't know ourselves by thinking, not by the narrowly empirical processes which you would call thought,' said Rice Robey. 'We recover the past by mythologising it, by forming connections which have no empirical reality but which possess what I call the verities of correspondence.'

'That's just waffle-talk,' said Wimbish.

'There's no such thing as "what actually happened",' said Rice Robey. 'It is a fantasy of the Age of Voltaire. Until that point, the race of man lived by myth and inference, not by what could be proved by the narrow rules of Leibniz or Hume.'

'No such thing as "what actually happened"? Are you trying to tell a professional historian, the foremost historian of the Tudor Age, that the Field of the Cloth of Gold did not happen, or the Dissolution of the Monasteries or the execution of Thomas More, or the Defeat of the Spanish Armada? And are you saying that we cannot distinguish between these events, which *did* take place, and those which did not – fairy tales about Herne the Hunter, for instance? Because, if you are saying that, then you can't bloody *think*! It is as simple as that.'

'I can think, but I can also breathe and feel. Those events which you describe were mythologies before they were even recorded in history. Their significance is not that they happened, but what they became in the collective mind. And this, incidentally, is why the current vogue for small-scale and local history is so dubious. In 1588, Jess Bundle of this parish shifted a bale of corn in Lammas-tide and, come Michaelmas, died of an ague. That may be true, but it isn't history, not in the sense the Armada is history. That was a mythology in the collective mind long ere your Froudes wrote about it in their books. Herne, likewise: just a man, perhaps, "sometime a keeper here in Windsor Forest". But in death he was translated, his verity corresponded to the deeper verities, to the memories in the collective mind which have their own necessity, or they would not be there. Perhaps, in life, he was no more than one Richard Horne, arraigned for poaching in the royal forests. In death – who knows how or why – he became identified with the great Antlered Huntsman whom we meet in the old Northern and Celtic mythologies. Cerunnos, the Antlered God and lord of the animals, brought fecundity. The Germanic tradition of the wild hunt saw the Antlered One as a sky-god, leading his pack of lost souls across the heavens. Garanhir, as the Stalker or Hunter is known in the English tongue, leading the Herlathing, the Einheriar as it is called in Norse. Herne the Hunter is a greater figure to me than Jess Bundle, and you have said nothing, O Empirical Dryasdust, nothing about him whatsoever, if you merely say that he does not exist; for to say that he does not exist is to say that human consciousness, human imagination itself does not exist! He appears, Herne, at times of national emergency. Herne flew in Windsor sky at the time of the Abdication crisis in 1936, and again at the commencement of the Germanic hostilities, and again when sixth Monarch George perished in 1952. Now, at the time of the Harlot and the Episkopos, might he not fly again?'

'These old folktales are interesting to an historian, of course they are.' Wimbish was visibly taken aback by this exhibition of knowledge and opinion, expressed by someone other than himself. 'But, to say that there is no empirical reality, or no distinction to be made between myths and pure historical fact, is just silly.'

'It depends what you call fact,' said Rice Robey.

'Fact is what happened, fiction is what didn't happen. I shouldn't have supposed *that* was difficult to grasp!'

'The piperade will be turning into rubber if we don't eat it soon,' said Pat, coming back into the room. 'Do we go into dinner without Sargie, or will you go and rouse him, darling?'

Although she addressed Vernon, I heard myself interrupting with the suggestion that I should go in search of Sargie, and that they should start the meal without me.

Knowing Sargie of old, it was no surprise that he was unable to put in an appearance on time for dinner. Not least, he would have hated the notion of competing with Wimbish, Rice Robey or Vernon to be the centre of attention. Pat the Wren officer gave such clear directions, that I had no difficulty in finding Sargie's room, while the others trooped in to the dining room.

Upstairs, the house continued, just, to contain its chaos. As in the kitchen corridors, so on the landings, heaps of paper littered the furniture. A bicycle – what was it doing upstairs? – was propped against turn-of-eighteenth-century Chinese wallpaper. A bust by Westmacott of old George Isleworth was adorned with a dusty opera hat. At the feet of the plinth on which it stood, piles of the *New Statesman*. Stuffed into the corner of the sub-Claude Lorraine harbour scene was a Vicky caricature of Vernon dressed as a matador, baiting a Tory bull – Selwyn Lloyd, I think. Some carved tables by James Whittle were scarcely visible beneath the mountains of newspapers.

Sargie was in a large, rather cold room at the front of the house, a room dominated by a huge four-poster bed festooned with shreds of moth-eaten green curtain. He sat on a little nursing chair as close as possible to the gas fire, staring at his trouserless legs and stockinged feet.

'Began to get dressed and couldn't finish,' he said, when he was aware of another presence in the room. He was still clutching my novel, *The Vicar's Nephew*.

'Bloody good book, this.'

'It's not really, Sargie.'

'Gets old Roy to the life.'

I pompously wanted to say that this wasn't the purpose of fiction, to caricature real people. (Now, I'm not so sure.) It was perhaps the first time Sargie had spoken to me about my uncle since their estrangement. Here would have been a chance to make a grand, intrusive, potentially embarrassing speech to Sargie; to say that I knew my uncle had missed him every day of the seven years or so which had elapsed since their quarrel, and that it would take nothing to effect a reconciliation, nothing at all. Roy hated scenes, and he would have picked up with Sargie as if nothing had happened, basking in his company, delighting in all his most infuriating characteristics, running his errands, listening to his talk.

There was a very long silence in which I could not speak, could not find the right words, felt sure that Sargie wanted me to speak about himself and Uncle Roy and for that reason felt unable to say anything.

At length, I said, 'I think Pat's starting dinner.'

'Don't give you much to drink, these people. Sittee down, Julie dear, have a little snifter with your Uncle Sargie.'

By the side of the nursing chair, on the floor, there was a bottle of gin and a tooth mug.

'Is there another glass?' I enquired.

He waved his cigarette-holder in the direction of the washstand. I found a chipped cut-glass tumbler there and wiped off the traces of denture-fixative with a grubby face-towel. I found that the faintly minty taste was not disagreeable when doused with two inches of gin.

'You should write another book.'

'I think about it a lot. Easier said than done.'

'Doesn't have to be a novel.'

The gas fire hissed. The chance to urge him to patch up the quarrel with Uncle Roy had floated away like a wisp of cigarette smoke.

'Know what I think?'

'Hardly ever.'

'I think you should beat Lover Boy at his own game, and write about old Jimbo.'

'Lover Boy' was Sargie's sobriquet for Raphael Hunter. Not realising that this was a considered suggestion – indeed the whole reason, I now believe, for my having been invited to stay at Mallington for the weekend – I responded at once with a little laugh.

'Don't know enough, Sargie.'

'Nonsense. You know all about my family. Roy's told you so much over the years. Sibs says you know more about the Lampitts than we do ourselves. You'd write a magnificent book about Jimbo. You could make it into a bit of family history, too. It needn't be just about him. You could even start the story with Old Jo and this place, if you liked. Radical Jo.'

Since Sargie's proposal was completely unexpected, I had no

language to reply. I assumed that what he was saying belonged wholly to the realm of fantasy. Even supposing that I wished to write the book, and could rediscover within myself the energy to start writing once more, who would want to publish it? Certainly not Madge Cruden, who had published Hunter's first volume and anxiously awaited the arrival of the second.

'Think it over,' said Sargie. 'We'll have lunch one day, eh? Clabbages? Vebby clebber febbers, Clabbages.'

I drained my gin and rose to my feet.

'Well, Sargie, I think I had better go downstairs.'

'What's going on?'

'Dinner.'

'I know, but what are they talking about? Harold, I suppose. He's a bit of a shit, Harold. Between you and me and the bedpost, I think he'll keep Vernon out of the Cabinet when the time comes.'

'I thought he'd come over to lunch to suggest the opposite.'

'To suggest, yes; not to promise. Vernon's really the last of the radicals. Our comrades on the left like him because he is always prepared to argue their case, but by modern political standards, he is a dodo. The IP don't want to hear about the Chartists. They want tellies, fitted carpets, nursery schools and polytechnics for the nippers. Harold'll dish it all out to them and persuade Conference that this is socialism, even if it ruins the exchequer, which it will. He's just the same as Harold Mac, only he wears a Gannex raincoat instead of a norfolk jacket. They've both got the same cynical ideas. There won't be any social revolution of the kind which Vernon and the Comrades want. Our Harold's conning them, just as old Harold conned his party into thinking that Disraeli's One-Nation Toryism meant unlimited public spending, roaring inflation and indoor toilets for the masses.'

'In short, "Not Amurath an Amurath succeeds,
        But Harold Harold".'

'Worse luck, my dear. So we'll have to wait a few years before Vernon is able to Build Jerusalem.'

We sang the last few lines of the poem in slightly tuneless unison.

In England's green and pleasant land!

'Better go downstairs, anyway,' I said.

'Wimbish is a bore. Thinks he's the only living historian who knows anything.'

'He was just saying something to that effect.'

'Hope someone will shut him up. Your friend Darnley could pull the rug quite effectively. Come on, now, just a drop more.'

He leaned forward with the bottle and replenished my tumbler.

'Darnley's too smitten with Kirsty to be taking any notice of Wimbish,' I said. 'They've left Wimbish to the mercy of this man Kirsty brought from Cambridge, Rice Robey who writes under the name of Albion Pugh. Now, the strange thing is, Sargie, this man used to know your brother Jimbo.'

'Plenty of people did.'

'I know, but he evidently knew Jimbo quite well. Jimbo was kind to him.'

'He *was* kind. One of the reasons I want you to write the book.'

'He thinks Hunter is a liar and worse than a liar.'

I was almost drunk enough to blurt out to Sargie the theory that his brother had been murdered; but I held back and spared him the shock. Sargie had no reason, as I had, to be interested in Rice Robey.

'Shall I say that you aren't up to supper? Someone could probably bring something up for you on a tray?'

'I say, Julie, this place is bloody uncomfortable. Let's do a flit, eh? Drive back to town. Only take us three hours at this time of night. You've got a car.'

Had I been my uncle Roy, I should probably have been immediately obedient to Sargie's whim, set off for London at once, and goodnaturedly turned the car round, somewhere near Fakenham, when he changed his mind, decided that Mallington was a 'dear old place' and that he could not face the solitude of his flat in Kensington.

'I'm leaving in the morning, Sargie, not now.'

'Please, Julian. I can't stand this place. I *know* Cecily is always coming here and it makes me sick. She tries to poison their minds against me. Pat doesn't need much persuading, you know.'

'I'm sure it's not true, Sargie.'

'Cecily still hates me, Julian, after all these years.'

Knowing nothing of the case, I could not comment. Sargie's wife had disappeared long before Uncle Roy, let alone I, had appeared on the scene, though she still kept in touch with the Lampitts, and Uncle Roy had, I know, met her on a number of occasions.

'Well, I must go now, Sargie.'

'Come back when you've had some grub, Julie, please. Don't leave me here all alone.'

The company downstairs was not the most alluring I had ever encountered.

'All right, Sargie.'

It was with a slight feeling of dread that I descended the stairs. I had not yielded completely to his caprice, but I had allowed him much more than I intended, to exercise his will over me, and I knew from experience how all-consuming and absolute that will was. I was wondering, by the time I joined the others, what I let myself in for. Going upstairs to tell Sargie that dinner was ready had seemed such a slight act when I had undertaken it. Already I started to sense that the conversation which had just taken place between me and the old man could change my life.

The others had finished their first course by the time I entered the dining room. Lady Augusta Wimbish alone was still eating what might have been her second, or even her third, helping. Mounds of piperade, sauté potatoes and green cabbage were rapidly diminishing beneath the jabbing assaults of her fork. I noticed that for the remainder of the meal, she made no efforts whatsoever to converse; her one, apparently desperate, concern was to fill her emaciated body with food. She ate as if she had been deprived of nourishment for weeks. While Kirsty – 'Poor you!' – lifted the lids of serving dishes in the hope of finding something for me to eat and Pat shouted about the possibility of running up an omelette, and I said I was perfectly happy to eat cheese and fruit, Lady Augusta shot me frightened, jealous glances, a starving squirrel anxiously guarding its pile of beechnuts against a predator.

The long oval dining table stood in the centre of a magnificent panelled room whose ceiling was encrusted with decaying rococo plasterwork. The centrepiece, from which depended a vast dusty chandelier, was carved with spears, drums and hunting horns, wreathed in foliage, grey with neglect. Most of the portraits on the walls, blackened with old varnish, were of Isleworths, but on either side of the chimneypiece hung pictures by an artist called, I think, Jackson, of Radical Jo Lampitt and his Quaker wife Naomi. How often Uncle Roy had spoken to me of these unremarkable productions, in terms which would not have been too effusive had he been describing the most sublime canvases of Titian or Tintoretto. For him, they were icons, these depictions of the ancestors of those generations of Lampitts whom he so dearly cherished, even down to

Kirsty and Jo, now placed on opposite sides of the table and beneath the gaze of their forebears.

Kirsty, still wearing her denims, was seated between Darnley and the place which had been set for me. Opposite her, Jo sat between Professor Wimbish and Sargie's empty chair. Jo stared impassively and glumly at her sister conversing with Darnley while Wimbish exclaimed about the magnificence of the library in which he had been working all day. Jo looked bored stiff by his praise of the copy of *Vetruvius Britannicus* to be found on the library shelves.

'Naughty me, you *see*! I should have been reading your grand-papa's political papers, but I just couldn't resist some of your folios, dear, and your positively delicious incunabula. But what a state they are in. . . .'

On her right, Jo had equally little luck with Rice Robey who was well into his stride doing what he had come to Mallington in order to do, buttonholing Vernon about this threatened henge. Vernon was nodding sagely and punctuating Rice Robey's impassionate talk with such phrases as 'We must see what we can do' and 'We're going ter stop all this wreckage of the countryside by the capitalists, you'll see.'

And Rice Robey was saying things like, 'But you don't under-stand! If you think it's just a question of keeping the countryside pretty and nice . . . it's not an aesthetic conundrum, it is one of the threatened sanctities, outraged divinities. No good will come of it if you disturb the ancient scenes of sacrifice.'

Arriving at the meal late and finding nothing much to eat when I got there, only increased my sense of alienation from the company.

'As soon as Augusta's finished we can. . . .' Pat was unashamedly impatient. Impervious to niceties, she piled plates (something which poor Uncle Roy had taught me never was done) of good Coalport much mended with rivets. She clattered them as if they were cheap crocks in the NAAFI. I sat awkwardly and nervously between Pat and Kirsty.

Some apples, oatcakes and an excellent cheddar were produced from a sideboard when Lady Augusta had wiped her plate clean with bread and made her only comment of the meal.

'Scrambled egg, isn't it?'

Pat offered me some rather sweet cider of which she, her daughters and Rice Robey appeared to be partaking in modest doses.

'Sargie's got drink up in his room, I suppose?' she fired at me.

'I've often seen him like this. A cloud suddenly descends. He can't face society.'

'Sitting on your own getting squiffy is no cure for the Blues.'

I thought that, with polishing, this could be the first line of a song, but there was no one round the table with whom I could share my thought.

'I'll take him some coffee later, if I may,' I said.

'Of course his mum spoilt him something rotten, that's the root of the trouble,' said Pat.

I had very often heard this explanation for the defects in Sargie's social behaviour, but I did not feel in a mood for a conversation about him. When Wimbish, who was an almost fanatical tee-totaller, caught wind of our talk, it was certainly time to change the subject.

'I can speak my mind freely to you, dear,' he said, touching Pat's wrist. 'Sargent is just a bloody fool, swigging all that al-co-hol. He was my tutor, you know, at Oxford. I'd seen enough of oafish, drunken behaviour before I ever came up. Men staggering out of pubs! A miner's son, an illiterate Welsh miner, swigging *his* stupid alcohol, you *see*! But even then, when I was eighteen years of age, I can remember Sargent Lampitt was a byword for *it*.'

Turning to Jo and prodding her with his finger, he smiled the smile of a pantomime dame momentarily employed as the madam in a brothel.

'You think I mean "it", you naughty girl, I don't think Sargent ever took much interest in "it", certainly not in me! But in stupid al-co-hol, yes. And I haven't touched a drop of it in my life. Do you see the very simple difference? I am the foremost historian of the Tudor Age, who has written over thirty-five books. What's *he* done, bloody fool, except write one book about the House of Lords, telling them to abolish themselves?'

As it happened, I felt a greater empathy with Sargie than with anyone else present; I regretted leaving him, and I wondered what I was doing there. The fact that, in its way, it was a convivial occasion, made me feel even more distant from it all. Darnley's various imitations – at that moment he was amusing the daughters of the house with a shameless parody of Vernon himself – had everyone at his end of the table in a roar.

Over coffee, when we had all arisen and wandered into the drawing room, Augusta Wimbish buttonholed me and said, 'I really prefer plain English food. There were things *in* that scrambled egg.'

'I think intentionally.'

'Gussy,' said Darnley, kissing her. 'Do you know Jason Grainger? From "The Mulberrys"?'

'What is "The Mulberrys"?'

We tried to explain.

'No, well, you see, I should love to have things like a wireless set, but Tommy simply *won't*.'

At this, she fell silent again, drew in her lips and looked furtively about the room, eyeing it possibly for some more food or perhaps just for other devices or diversions enjoyed by others but denied to her by the professor. I was surprised by Darnley kissing her, and turning out to be a relation.

Wimbish himself approached, with Vernon and Rice Robey.

'So!' he said to me. 'You are to be Mr Hunter's rival!'

I'd been that often enough; or, rather, Hunter had been mine. The observation made me start.

'So Sargie's spoken to yer,' said Vernon. 'Good, good. And yer like the idea? Excellent.'

I hummed and hawed. The idea that I should write a book about Jimbo, possibly a history of the Lampitt family, was evidently one which had been discussed before my arrival at Mallington, but it was still new to me, and I had not decided what I thought about it.

'It's quite an undertaking,' said Wimbish, 'but you must get me to help you. I had quite a lot to do with old Jimbo one way or another in the days when I was starting out in the literary world.'

'It's all very speculative, isn't it?' I said. 'Sargie has only just asked me. I'm not sure whether I even want. . . .'

'Splendid,' said Vernon, 'terrific.'

'I saw there was no point at all in my wasting all my talents on the academic fifth-raters,' said Wimbish. 'I shall read you the appropriate passages of my diaries. The struggle I had, you wouldn't believe it, coming from a filthy working-class home. Now, Jimbo saw my qualities at once. None of the academic fifth-rater about him. He was a very good *popular* historian, though it is a pity he wrote some of his books before I was born. Otherwise, I could have saved him from making some really silly howlers. That last book about him, though, rather missed the point, with all its *naughtiness*.'

He smiled archly and poked me with a long index finger. Kirsty came up breathlessly and said, 'There's going to be a full moon. We're going down to the beach. Come on, do.'

She tugged at my elbow excitedly.

'Oh come *on*.'

Darnley and she were so merry that I assumed that they were the only two going to the beach. I felt *de trop* and said that I had promised to look in again on Sargie.

'I'll say goodnight, then,' said Darnley. 'We might not meet before the morning.'

'OK.'

'I left that stuff in your room – the stuff I was telling you about in the car.'

'Which stuff?'

With comic movements of the head in the direction of Rice Robey, Darnley said no more. Rice Robey himself was excited by a not altogether affectionate rebuke from Pat.

'Here you, keep your hands to yourself and leave my daughter alone.'

He was stroking Jo's denim bottom as he waxed lyrical about the moon. He ignored Pat's suggestion that he was behaving improperly and she did not repeat herself.

'Come, Lady Lampitt, come with us to see the moon,' he said. 'The chaste huntress of the sky.'

I had not realised that there was to be a party accompanying Kirsty and Darnley to the beach but I was too proud to ask if I could after all join it. The elder Lampitts and the Wimbishes were (rather to my surprise) devotees of contract bridge. They were rejoicing, as such enthusiasts do, when a 'four' materialises. It was time for me to slink away.

I wanted to go straight back to Sargie and say that it was quite out of the question, my writing this Jimbo book. When I went to his room, however, I found him snoring sonorously on the bed, and any further discussion of the idea would have to wait. It was not long after 9 when I turned into my bedroom and found a brown paper envelope on my bedside table – the 'stuff', which I had supposedly discussed with Darnley in the car. I could not remember having discussed any stuff, and assumed that it was something to do with *The Spark*. I opened the envelope and found a bundle of extremely thin quarto pages closely typed on both sides. And I began to read.

•

Wild man, goat-man, scrawny fist uplifted,
Thin arm projecting from a shaggy sleeve.
He stood and ranted by the waterside.
'Be changed, O very surface of the earth!
Level each valley, low each hill and mount!
Before the great and terrible day shall come,
Before He comes, He mightier than I.'

He stood on level stones which jutted out
Into the Jordan water – desert man,
A coney among rocks and barren land.
His bearded face was gaunt and torn with grief,
Though scarcely thirty years, he was careworn.
Chronos had graven torture on his cheek,
All-Father, Zeus the Maker chose this out,
This locust-fed Joanes, desert man,
And scratched on him prefigurings of death,
A foredoomed martyr's death at Herod's hand.
Wild place for wild man, desert place apart.
Yet near the waterside the ground was green,
And here and there a tree put out its leaves.
And hither thronged the hearers to his rant –
Some merely curious about a spectacle,
Some openly derisive, others swayed
Desirous of a cleansing from their sin,
Healing in Jordan water at his hands.
'The leprous Syrian, Naaman, in his pride
Scorned to be washed and healed in Jordan's flood.
"Are not the Syrian waters, Abana,
And Pharpar greater than this trivial stream?
May not my rivers wash me, make me clean?"
So Naaman scorned Jordan – so scorn ye!
But not until his heart was humbled low,
And not until he washed in Jordan's stream
Could Naaman be rid of leper's sores!
And not until you all repent of sin,
Receiving metanoia's baptism,
Can you wash out the leprosy of soul!
Turn! Change yourselves! For one is coming soon –
Mightier, oh mightier than I! Turn! Turn!

And he will thresh his wheat and purge his floor
And gather good corn into garners – but
The chaff will burn in an unquenching fire!'

Swarming, hysterical crowd converge on bank,
To be baptised of Joanes in Jordan.

Aloof from mob, the learned stand apart,
The learned men of Zion watch with scorn.
One of them, Tentmaking Saulos, deeply read
In sacred Scripture and the Torah's Book,
Gazed with peculiar intentness now.

Seeing this group of scribes, the goat-man shrieked,
'Vipers! A brood of vipers! Who warned you,
To flee the certain wrath which is to come?'
'I have kept to the Torah since my youth,'
Saulos said quietly to a Pharisee.
'How dare he now instruct law-perfect me,
Me to repent and turn? I have rejoiced
In the way of Thy testimonies,
As in all manner of riches. . . .
So shall I keep thy testimonies, even for ever and ever.
Such as I need no repentance.'
Saulos' companion turned and quietly said,
'I fear this man, because he stirs the mob.'
'And yet,' said Saulos, 'should the words be true,
And should Messias step among us now,
Desire of all the nations, should he come,
And should the end of all days be at hand,
The day foretold in prophecies of old,
And should the number of the Lord's elect,
Be shortly now accomplished, should the Christ. . . .

'Come, Saulos, come!' smiled his urbane companion.
'Your head is turned by ranting such as this?
Look at the creatures splashing there below.
Dogs chasing birds have more solemnity.
Is this the following of holy law?
Is this religion – splashing in the sun?
They should not look to this unlettered loon.
We are the true interpreters of Law;

We studied Torah-books both day and night. . . .'
And still they watched the Baptist with disdain.
'What is he saying now?' Saulos enquired.
'The ranter is gone silent, muttering.'
'To such a one as he,' said Saulos' friend,
A haughty Pharisee in costly robe,
'See how he mutters to the ragamuffin,
Some fool who heeds his tricks of rhetoric.'

Saulos walked down towards the water's edge,
Leaving his wise companions in their place.
He wanted to be witness to this scene.
Thigh-deep in water the Baptiser stood;
His raucous voice was for the moment still;
No more cries of 'Repent!' and for the while,
No more immersions in the Jordan stream.
Joanes stood quite still. His hands, like claws,
Clutched at a neaniskos' collar-bone,
Angelic young one, angel in his flesh,
Fleshly in his concealed divinity.
The crowds encircled the mysterious pair,
Poised, as it seemed, for passionate embrace.
A love-moment in which two human souls
Are lifted from their self-containing lives
Into new unity at Love's decree,
Enveloped in the unselfing of the Divine Eros.
Saulos approached and felt this emanation,
This soul-entwining of Joanes and the Stranger,
Felt the rays emanate of the spiritual warmth and the love-god
    heaving his heart of love!
Was Saulos then in the spirit of evil, and was this Beelzebub?
Was there one here whom water could not wash?
Was there a sin here which could not be baptised?
'No!' said the Baptist to the Stranger's face.
He held his shoulders, and he shuddered, 'No!'
Saulos was close, could see the Baptist's eyes
Focused upon the naked stranger there.
Neaniskos in the water standing before the wild man,
Speaking in words too low to be audible.
Saulos could see the Stranger from behind.

99

He saw thick hair fall on to pale shoulder blades
He saw the line of the vertebrae come down the thin back
    towards white buttocks,
He saw the buttocks touching the water's surface.

Baptiser Goat-man made his stern reply
To the inaudible mutter of the Stranger.
'I must be washed by you, not you by me!
I must decrease, dear man, you must increase.'

But still the Stranger mumbled in reply,
And must at length have won the Baptist round.
Joanes threw his head back, rolled his eyes,
And passed into a frenzied state of trance.
He forced the Stranger's shoulders under water.
With violent pressing held the young man down,
As if to drown him, not baptise a penitent.
Beneath the bony hands the Stranger crumpled.
He seemed all weakness as he fainted down,
And those who watched let out a gentle moan,
As if indeed the young man had been drowned,
Or dragged beneath the waters by wild demons
Called up by shaggy Joanes in his frenzy
Of love-imprecation and harsh benediction.
Joanes opened wide his terrible eyes.
They rolled ecstatically, and from his mouth
There came loud shrieks of some unheard-of tongue.
He shook like an exorciser who wrestled with Power
As he held beneath the water the head of his catechumen.
Then he removed his hands, and up he sprang,
The Stranger leapt, not like a drowning man,
But like a giant spreading wide his arms,
Hands up, up, towards the sun in a mime of purest joy!
The immersion and its consequence became a dance
Communicating an erotic gladness which was bigger than Eros.
The naked man looked innocently at the sky,
And Saulos, rapt, stood by and looked at him.
Something about these happy outstretched arms,
The tautened thighs, the dancing of his legs,
Made Saulos see that all men, not just this,

All, had within them a divinity.
He felt he was not watching one young man,
Exuberant and dancing in the river;
Rather, it seemed as if the human race
Had made itself anew.
Out of the shallow waters, Adam leapt,
New Adam, newly dancing for a new dawn.
And as in Adam sinners all had died,
So in this dance should all be made anew,
And out of death would come a newer life.
He shuddered, Saulos, for what fiend of hell
Could have whispered such blasphemous nonsense in his ears?
And now with eyes aloft, the Baptist yelled,
'I see the Heavens opened and the Dove,
The Holy Wind of God descending here,
Proclaiming our Messias and our Prince!'
Saulos could see no dove and heard no wind.
He saw a young man, eternally youthful and eternally naked
Lifting strong arms towards the stronger sun.
The Stranger turned and waded to the bank.
He dried himself a little with his mantle,
Then slipped it simply over his wet hair.
Saulos watched the dressing of this mysterious being,
Who brought no scrip, no purse, no staff,
Simply a chasuble through which his head,
Fresh-washed with Jordan-baptism jutted with joy.
And Saulos watched the face as it emerged.
Long, bony, thin, akin to the Baptist's face,
It was quite different.
Saulos discovered himself applying to this face
A host of contradictory epithets.
Terrible, strong, but it was vulnerable,
And it was wise, yet simple as a child.
It stared as madmen stare, but it was sane.
It had no conventional beauty,
But its beauty haunted Saulos, it was an unforgettable beauty
And it had haunted him before, as the beauty of a woman
    haunts a man.
And as he watched the Stranger throw back his mane of hair,
His thick, lustrous black hair over the shoulders of his robe,

Saulos assured himself that he was not in love,
He fought back the presence of Eros, but shook to know
The presence of some other, greater God.
Joanes had returned to his task of baptising in Jordan-water,
And the air was loud with his voice, and the shrieks of his
    idiot-followers,
And the Stranger was silent, aloof from this religious scene.
And Saulos followed the Stranger with his eyes,
As he walked through the crowds, and turned from the
    Jerusalem road,
Taking his feet over stony ground and wilderness,
Towards the brow of the deserted hills.

Twenty years earlier, and in another world.
The scene: Albion, new-Roman-named Britannium!
'Tarry,' the man said, 'tarry with the ass,
While I go yonder with the weary lad.'
The bearers drew the ponies to a halt
At the base of the primrose-covered hill,
The round, green, buxom, undulating breast of a hill.
The ponies were squat and shaggy.
Like the ponies, the Celtic bearers too were dark and squat,
Speaking to these foreigners in a strange sing-song patois,
But speaking to themselves in a lilting native music,
Which sang with sea-echoes and danced like the movement of
    the sea in caves.
'Wait here we shall then,' said one of these men.
Another, who had led the boy on his pony,
Lifted the child down on to the brilliant green of the turf,
And as he did so spoke an endearment,
'Here, get down, my little Lamb.
There is a long journey home awaiting us,'
Said Yusif, the tall foreigner to the Little Lamb.
'Let us walk on this hill to refresh ourselves.'
Much-travelled Yusif, merchant in many lands,
Brought with him his cousin's lad, not long past his Bar-
    Mitzphah.
They had been many months among the heathen, buying and
    selling.
Bales of stuff, carpets and spices,

They had brought with them on the outward voyage
To western lands. And they had travelled far,
Far to the west, to Lyonesse itself,
And seen the tin-mines and the mines of Gold,
Where Celts had delved like dwarves Gehenna-bound
With picks and barrows, dug for yellow ore!
Half a century ago, Great Kaiser Julius,
Had brought to the unformed poem of Albion's sons and
    daughters
The order and magisterium of law,
And placed beside the tufty mound of intuition,
The rod of military strength.
And the corridors of Hades threw up their all-corrupting ore,
Which Imperial majesty and military avarice required.
'We give to Kaiser only what is Kaiser's,'
One of the toothless Celts of Lyonesse,
Had laughingly told Yusif and the lad.
And he had implied that there was some mystery which they
    retained,
Which Kaiser's legions could not buy or sell,
Something contained in songs they sang the Boy,
And tales they told of bird-gods, water-goddesses,
Of souls that slept in tombs a thousand years,
And then awoke to vitalise the world.
They sang, too, songs of sacrifice and death,
And told about the Coming of a King.
Returning from the west, and quite by chance,
Yusif and his companion had beheld,
Just such a heathen rite, horrid in blood.
As evening fell, they still were on the road,
And lighted on a certain place to sleep.
Waking before the dawn, they found themselves
Just on the edge of a great stone circle,
They heard within the enclosure of the high pillars,
Within the consecrated circle, petric and phallic,
The hierophantic wailing of the priests,
Hymning their Lord and Light before the Dawn.
And Yusif watched his boy-companion's face,
While these sounds, pregnant with the violence of mystery,
And the yearning of natural man for the religion of sacrifice,

103

And the hunger of the uninitiated soul for the satisfaction of a
  cult,
Broke the grey, misty silence of a British spring,
The darkness and dampness of the half-hour before dawn.
Yusif could see the boy's face taut with fear,
And staring too with fascinated awe.
They crawled with stealth up to the outer edge,
Where the turf sloped outside the inner circle of the henge.
From here, they could be unseen witnesses,
To what would happen when the sun was up.
They saw the figures standing in the henge.
A priest in long white robes, stood with an upraised knife.
Before him, was a naked boy-child, younger than Yusif's
  strange companion!
And the child was pinioned like a wild beast to a stake.
And other white-robed figures sung a dirge,
Until their Lord and Light the Sun came up.
And when the first rays of the rising Sun,
Caught on the shining blade, the knife came down.
He did not even scream, the little lad.
A whimper, a weak whimper, he gave out, before the blood
  flowed.
Far, far away at home, both Jews had seen,
The sacrifices in the Temple at Jerusalem,
Lambs, Kids and Doves, they took each year
To fall beneath the sacrificial knife.
But in this foreign morning, this cold dawn,
They saw a different blood-pouring,
The slaying of a different Lamb.
And the priestly murderers ran with their cups to catch the
  child's precious blood.

Yeshua, the lad, had turned away,
And retched and vomited on the grass.
Quick as they could, they'd woken up the guides,
And hastened on their pony-slow journey back, back to
  Londinium.

This brutally religious scene of blood,
Silenced the boy through all the journey back.
Each night, he anxiously implored Yusif,

That they should reach an inn and not sleep out.
Each night, he begged Yusif to sleep with him,
And through the hours of darkness the cousins clung.
Yeshua hardly spoke, but one black night,
Silently weeping, he said to his cousin,
'Yusif, that boy they killed could have been *me*!'
He said no more, but wept and wept and wept,
While his elder cousin held his quivering shoulders in his arms.

And then to Londinium they returned
And at their inn they met the tentmaker,
The first Jew they had met in Londinium,
A travelling merchant like themselves.
A tiny creature, not five feet in height,
Sure in his views and hasty in his speech.
Yeshua spoke to him, tried to make friends.
Saulos was young – perhaps five years older than Yeshua.
And he was a Turkish Jew, of Tarsus born,
But more a Pharisee than those at home.
And Yeshua spoke to him of heathen men, and heathen prayer.
There was a Temple not far from the inn –
The Temple of Mithras over the Hill of Lud.
There was the cup of sacrifice upraised,
The chalice of blood worshipped by the Roman soldiery.

NB. Some apostrophe cd be introduced here. The modern city. Lud's
Hill. The Temple of the tentmaker on Ludgate Hill?

Yusif heard with surprise that Yeshua
Had visited this Temple for himself.
So that was where he was in early hours,
When he had so mysteriously 'disappeared'.
Yeshua was 'famous' in the family for this,
Teased by his brothers and sisters for his disappearing tricks.
Miriam, their mother, Yusif's cousin,
Became wild with rage when Yeshua disappeared.
She was not consoled when one of the brothers said,
'Mother, don't fear, your boy will be returned,
He'll come back in three days, you mark my words.'
This was allusion to that passover,
When Yeshua had lost himself in the Jerusalem crowds,

Thousands of people, swarming on pilgrimage to the Temple,
And the little boy lost!
They found him after three days, sitting in the Temple.
Baiting the clergy by asking them difficult questions,
Interrogation was his only mode.
He showed no interest in answers, only in questions.
When the answers were given, the boy's face seemed
    abstracted,
Almost idiotic, as if the words of human discourse and the
    rationality of John Locke
Made no *impresa* on this, the first *tabula-rasa* mind since Adam.
Yusif thought of this incident now, far away in the inn in
    Londinium.
For Saulos the tentmaker was enraged, and Yeshua had on his
    face that idiot abstraction.
'You went to the Temple of Mithras!' thundered Saulos.
'Temple! No temple, that!
There only is one lawful sacrifice.
There only is one temple in the world.
Salvation cometh to the Jews alone.'
Yeshua sat and stared into his drink,
He held his goblet firmly in his palms,
And looked down into it, seeing his face reflected in the blood-
    red wine.
'The nostrils of the Almighty will not sniff
The meat that's roast for idols by these scum!'
Saulos explained the Torah to the child,
Reminded him of how *Leviticus*
Decrees that meats be cut and stewed and burnt
For the savouring nostrils of the all-devouring Jew-divinity,
Universal in power but worshipped alone through the formulas
    of his chosen priests and people.
And then the silence of Yeshua was broken.
He drained his cup and said, 'The time is coming,
No, the time is come, when neither in Mount Sion,
Nor in these temples of the Roman gods,
Will sacrifice be asked, nor blood outpoured.'
Saulos, astonished, asked the little boy,
'Do you deny the Covenant of God?'
'I do deny no covenants, but covenants

Are not fulfilled as partners would expect.
Our Father loves all men, He called the Temple
Built by King Solomon my ancestor,
A house of prayer for all men on this earth.'
'But only for the children of the promise.'
'And did your earthly father make such laws?
Did he distinguish one child from another?
If one child spoke to him and did not use
Precisely the same form of words as you,
Would then your father say he could not *hear*
The voice uplifted by his own dear child?
Surely Our Father hears the voice of prayer?
Whoever speaks, wherever it is raised?
For unto him shall *all* flesh rise and come:
Whether from the Mount Sion in Jerusalem,
Or from the Mount Lud in Londinium.
For if men lift up their voices to the throne of grace from
    Londinium,
Then is Britain Mount Sion and the Heavenly Jerusalem is
    found here!
Tentmaker's fury: 'This is blasphemous!'
Innkeeper comes to ask for no more noise.
''Ere, talking loud in all that foreign jabber!
Keep it quiet, will you, or I'll throw you out.'
And at a nearby table was a drunkard,
Who leaned towards them, and brought the flow of talk to an
    end.
Yeshua seemed to like this red-faced man.
He laughed at his jokes, and evidently enjoyed
His talk more than the earnest tentmaker's.
Saulos, indignant, rose and left the room.
They were not destined yet to meet until
Sixteen years later by the Jordan's bank,
When the eyes of Saulos the Pharisee met those of the anointed
    Messias.

Yusif disliked them both, the bigot Saulos,
And now this red-faced belcher with his jokes.
So, he proposed the ride, a few hours' air
Before the Tamesis tide allowed their ship

107

To sail for Gaul and turn their footsteps home.

From Hill of Lud, their guides led them north-west
Beyond the wattled walls and muddy streets
Outside the city wall, they rode through fields,
And from thick woods, finches and thrushes flew
Singing their bright songs in the grey cloudy air.
They passed through lush fields where the grass was thick,
Where green of bush and foliage was so bright
The colours shocked the eye. Much oak grew here.
May burst from bushes in abundant clouds.
Wild privet hedges burst with cow parsley.
High to the ponies' waists grew buttercups.
The boy's bare legs were brushed with wild barley-whiskers,
As they rode, rode, rode to the foot of a hill,
This round feminine hill, this breast on Londinium's edge,
Where they dismounted, and left their guides with the ponies,
And walking through the thicket, climbed the hill.
Beneath their feet the turf was soft and bright.
'This greenness soothes my heart,' said Yeshua,
'I still weep inwardly for that young boy,
Slain by the priests; now, I feel buffeted
By all the verbal onslaughts of that bore,
That bigot Saulos speaking of the Law.'
'There was no need,' said Yusif, 'for dispute.
Look at these flowers, this grass, these birds, this hill.
They do not argue, buffet, fight like men.'
Yeshua took in his hand the hand of Yusif of Arimathea,
And the two cousins who loved one another walked to the top
   of the hill.
The rain fell gently as they turned and looked,
Down on the city which they'd left behind.
The silver Tamesis wove like a snake
And slunk through fields and villas, camps and huts.
They saw the forts, the wooden palisades,
Built by the Romans at the water's edge.
They saw the temples, and the Roman walls.
Yeshua said, 'I love this little place!
It has no buildings worthy of the name,
No Temple like our own, Saulos is right!

The air's subdued, the light is dull and grey,
The population all seem mildly drunk.
But I don't want to leave . . . don't want to leave.'
Yusif replied in murmurs, 'Let my hand
Forget its cunning if I should forget
You, O Jerusalem, my mother, my city, my goal!'

The two stood silent on the fat green hill.
They watched a ray of sunlight penetrate
The lead-grey cloud and point into the Thames.
Over their heads from west to east there stretched
A rainbow, perfect arch formed in the sky.
Yusif felt bathed, suffused and washed
By this blest light and by these coloured rays.
He knew how heathen men could bow their knee
To worship the Magnificence of Light.
But as he stood in silence by the boy
He felt the light came not so much from the sky
As from this child himself. Yusif knew well
That he was standing on a little hill
On a grey day in a boring province of the Empire,
With a child born to his cousin Miriam,
Surrounded by bleating sheep and Lambs.
But his heart told him that he had come to the mountain of the
    Presence!
The light which he saw was no ordinary light, but the shining
    of the Unutterable!
And this was the *shekinah* of the all-mighty, the glory of the
    Lord,
And he felt that he was come unto Mount Sion, and unto the
    City of the Living God,
And to an innumerable company of angels.
And then a silence followed, unmeasured by time.
A silence of a most refreshing kind,
Leaving the person washed and the mind renewed.
They did not speak again, the man and boy,
Until they'd walked down the hill and stopped halfway,
Amid the shaggy ewes and bleating lambs.
Yeshua stopped and broke the silence then.
'Yusif,' he said, 'tell no one what you saw.'

Notes: All history is the reinterpretation of images. Memory the mother of the Muses. This supremely true in the true Mythos of the Anointed. Narrative to convey the actual numinous quality of Yeshua himself and the Mythos of Sacrifice and Atonement in the mind of Saulos. The Mythos takes over Yeshua, he is obliged to enact it, like a man upon whom a spell has been cast. This obligation comes from the human yearning for a religion, a cleansing, an atonement.

The Crucifixion itself a sadistic love-moment for Saulos. Its repetition at the stoning of the Protomartyr Stephanos enough to precipitate the crisis known to Christendom as the Conversion of St Paul.

The Mediterranean world adopted Paulism, the religion of the Atoning Death, the Resurgent Body from the Tomb. Yusif of Arimathea travels northwards to the grey half-lights of Ambiguous Albion. The thorn crown hidden in Glastonbury and blossoming.

The whole cycle to include all histories and mythologies. Odin on the Tree Yggdrasil offers himself to himself. Herne the Hunter hangs himself on a tree. Messias Yeshua's kinsmen, the Knights of the Round Table, Lancelot and Galahad, imprisoned in the eternal gulf dividing desire and achievement, moral aspiration and human appetite. The failure of the cousin of Christ by ninth degree, Lancelot, to see the Sangreal: indicative of an eternal conflict between flesh and spirit, love and betrayal. The Holy House of Nazareth built in the Vale of Stiffkey, Walsingham England's Nazareth. The religion of Paul brought to mammon-glutted industrial Albion by itinerant Wesley. Contrast the true Jesus of the Everlasting Gospel who found his resurrection in the prophecies and engravings of William Blake. Revolutions. The necessary overthrow of images. Voltaire himself an unheeding witness to the light.

Rector of Stiffkey and the harlots; his death in the lion's den. The Abdication of Edward VIII; the casting down of the magisterium of Caesar before the throne of the Divine Eros. Herne the Hunter is seen in the sky in Windsor Great Park.

'Was Jesus chaste?' (Blake)

The sex-impulse and the fire of divine love. The blessing of the harlot by Christ the beginning of a great process, unfinished when Lancelot lost his vision of the Sangreal, but achievable through the sublimation of Eros by the Embracing of the Divine correspondences. *She wiped his feet with her hair*. The eternal libido throbs through the heart of the creation, and is the creation. The Cross for Paul the contradiction of this principle, the demolition of the phallus; the Resurrection of Man in Eternal Day a liberation of all sexual impulse through the means of the new Agape. Paul fears his own nature; he projects it into the cosmos, peopled by demons, homoerotic orgies (see *Romans* i) a sinful race eternally punished by a vengeful All-Father who hates mankind. Jesus hates mankind. He loves the All-Father and melts the hard principle of *nomos* with the liberation of *agape. He is at the centre of the*

110

most highly charged scene in all literature, when the harlot wipes his feet with
her hair.

Our Father. God in creation is big with desire and makes love to our
mother the earth. Men and women are at one with this creative spirit
only when they have discarded the fear of Paul and Augustine and
moved with the Sun and other stars. It is sex which makes them anew
in God's image and likeness.

And from Galilee, riots, and tumults of the people, and mob-
    hysteria,
Such as possesses a tribe or *res publica* at certain seasons,
A huge uplifting of the collective soul, a great longing such as
    makes bloody revolutions, and brings down kings.

Marginal note: Lenin came to power when the Russian Church had
developed its holiest tradition of startsi, or enlightened ones. Cromwell
ushered in an era of the saints, ushered it in with blood.

And they, the Galileans, would make Yeshua their King!

Galilee not really converted to Judaism until two or three generations
before Christ. Galileans are not Jews, slaves of the law, but natural man
in his instinctive quest for the divinities.

He fed his folk with fish and bloated them with bread,
Five thousand at a sitting, as he preached to them the coming
    of the new Kingdom.

Saulos is far from the Kingdom, far in Jerusalem.
Punctilious civil servant in the palace of the High Priest,
Favourite protégé of the rabbis and the professors,
The rising promise of the Vatican secretariat.
What could they do, these men of greyness, these fillers of filing
    cabinets,
With the knowledge that a new King had come into their
    midst?
What if he seized, this Yeshua, his crown by force? for, he was
    of the blood royal and beloved of the people?
Saulos was in love with the face of Yeshua Bar Yusif whom
    they called Messias!
Yeshua's words and face made Saulos desperately afraid!
Ever since their first meeting, in Yeshua's boyhood,

111

Fatal encounter in the tavern in Londinium,
Saulos had been haunted by this elusive divinity,
And since the descent of the dove by Jordan water,
Shouted of by the shaman Baptiser, but unseen to Saulos,
He had followed the Son of Man, noted His preachings and felt
the power of his proclaimed freedoms!
Yeshua made crowds laugh with his satires against the
Pharisees.
He mocked the solemn faces of Saulos and his Sanhedrin
friends,
And imitated the way that they prayed at street corners,
And ridiculed their devotion to the Holy Torah of the
Almighty.
The sabbath was made for man, and not man for the sabbath,
Thus he overthrew the divinely given concept of Law, and
made men into gods!
For the Law was not made for men, to suit their pleasure,
Nor to provide them with some arbitrary sense of how to order
their lives.
The Law was the revelation of the mind of God; it was an
absolute and given thing,
Law symbolised and enshrined in *shabat*, in keeping of diet, in
recitation of set prayers.
The Jews were made and chosen by God to follow this Law.
Man was made for the *shabat*, not the *shabat* for man.
But Yeshua had set this at naught, and wanted to throw over
religion itself.
Saulos thrilled to contemplate the liberty of the sons of God,
But he hated this feeling of excitement, and fought against it.
It was so much easier, so much safer, to believe that man was
made for the *shabat*,
Than to think the *shabat* was made for man.
It was easier to believe that all our moral and spiritual
obligations
Can be fulfilled by following a religious set of rules,
Rather than leaping out to the great anarchic liberty which is
the birthright of the sons of God!

Today, Saulos had returned to the Jordan-bank, to the haunts
of the old Baptiser,
Joanes the ranter, whose head had been cut off by Herod,

112

To hear Yeshua preach to the crowds who came down from
    Jerusalem.
And with Saulos were some of his friends the Pharisees,
Hoping to heckle the heretic, and to catch him with subtle
    questions.
To none of his Pharisee friends had Saulos confided,
His strong feelings of attraction and revulsion,
And now they stood, Saulos and Shimon and Mordecai, and
    other scribes and Pharisees,
Listening once more to that maddening, beguiling voice,
With its succinct phrases, its humour, its innocence,
Speaking to the rabble, and making them laugh, with his
    absurd jokes and stories.
He told of a Jewish woman who had lost one small coin,
And searched her house through with serious diligence,
Turning over rugs and bedding, peering beneath cooking pots,
Until in her relentlessly serious quest, the coin was discovered,
On the muddy kitchen floor beside the sack of barley-meal,
And in the triumph of her finding, she summoned the
    neighbours,
To rejoice with her in triumph at this trivial finding!
Thus the Divine Love in pursuit of our little man-soul
Is reduced to a matter of laughter by profane analogy!
Shuddering at the blasphemy, Shimon by Saulos's side,
Catches the preacher off guard by changing his subject,
And calls out a question of Yeshua about marriage and divorce.
'Is it lawful for a man to divorce his wife? Tell us!'
And Yeshua turns the question back – 'My friend, you are
    young!
To ask such a question implies impatience! Live a while longer
    and she will get used to you!'
Shimon scowls with fury as the crowd yelp with laughter.
'Answer me the question,' he repeats hotly, 'is divorce lawful?'
'What? A Pharisee who does not remember the Torah? What
    did Moses command you?'
'Moses allowed that a man should put away his wife,' responded
    Shimon.
'Then for hardness of heart did Moses command you.
What God joins together can never be sundered.'
But this wasn't an answer, this was merely scoring a point!

113

For Moses merely decreed the Law of God, and did Yeshua set
   the Law at naught?
But in the heart of Saulos there stirred a deep yearning
For the law that was written in hearts and not graven in stone,
And he could not believe that Shimon had said anything
   serious,
Anything which described the human condition, or charted the
   mysterious prompting of God's voice in the heart of Man,
And when the meeting broke up, Saulos was still rapt in a
   daydream of thought,
And he allowed his friends to return to Jerusalem, leaving him
   standing,
Alone and aloof, watching the figure of Yeshua, who sat by the
   river.
Women approached him with children, and asked for his
   blessing.
And Yeshua picked up the infants and held them aloft,
And made each one laugh with a kiss or a grotesque grimace, or
   by tickling its ribs,
Each unwashed urchin-brat, he blessed them and held them.
And Saulos, who hated children, watched dismayed,
Jealous of the easiness with which Yeshua loved them,
And jealous of the children who received his love.
And then Yeshua arose, and set out with his followers,
Walking in a crowd down the dusty road to town.
Saulos was led by an impulse which he could not control
To run after the teacher, to run and to follow,
To push past the crowds until he was close to the Master,
And to throw himself, breathless, at Yeshua's feet.
'My good sir,' he uttered, 'my good. . . .' his voice faltered.
And 'Good?' answered Yeshua, 'why call me good? Only One is
   good, our Father in heaven.'
'Tell me,' said Saulos, 'what must I do to inherit
The eternal life of the Kingdom of which you speak in your
   teachings?'
'Why, follow the Torah,' said Yeshua, smiling. And Saulos felt
   mocked.
For dozens of times, he had made this reiteration.
And this seemed like a *shabat*-school answer in a synagogue.
Why did this smiling man treat him like a little child?

114

'Do not commit adultery, do not bear false witness,
Honour your father and mother – you must know the Law?'
'I do,' said Saulos, woundedly. He had hoped for an answer,
Glowing with subtlety, suffused with the love of God.
'I have kept all the law from my youth,' said the Pharisee
   Saulos.
Then Yeshua looked at him lovingly. Saulos felt then
All the love of the universe penetrate him through those dark,
   smiling eyes.
'You lack only one thing,' said Yeshua. 'Though you speak
With the tongues of men and of angels, you lack the divine
   love,
And you are imprisoned in possessions, and do not know the
   freedom of dispossession.
So, friend, go and sell your possessions and give to the poor,
And you will have treasure in heaven, and come – follow me!'
And Saulos looked down at his chest, and his clean, well-made
   tunic,
And thought of his house in the city, with its airy, spacious
   rooms,
And the money his father had made in the family tent-
   enterprise.
He knew that the words of the preacher were true, but they
   stung with their truth.
He had wanted to be confronted with a theological argument,
And he had been met instead by an all-embracing life-demand!
And he stood, and felt foolish to have come so close to Yeshua,
And foolish to have hoped that this man would take him
   seriously,
And homesick for his own kind, and his small collegium of
   confrères.
And he turned from the crowd and left Yeshua behind him,
   saying,
'You see how the rich cannot easily enter the Kingdom of God!
In this world, the bigwigs have lordship, but not in that
   kingdom,
And anyone wishing to enter the kingdom as a lord, must bow
   low as a servant,
The rich must be poor, and the great must be small, and the
   last must be first.'

These words Saulos heard as he hastened away, and his walk
   turned to running.
A mile down the road, he encountered a caravan of camel-
   drivers walking,
Who gave, for a fee, a rest to his limbs, and allowed him to ride
   to the city.
And as they ascended the hill to the city, he saw his young
   Pharisee friends,
And they too had camels, and rode them right up to the walls,
But had to dismount as they came to the foot-entrance,
Built in Jerusalem's wall, the small gate, and known as the Eye
   of the Needle.

Waking at 1 a.m., I found the leaves of Rice Robey's strange
effusion spread out confusedly across my chest, sheaves of almost
transparent paper, smudged with carbon. I put them into a pile on
the bedside table, lit a cigarette, switched off the lamp, and walked
to the window. My bedroom was in the eighteenth-century wing of
the house, overlooking the orangery.

A full moon lit the scene with eerie brightness. The branches of
the cedars cast long black shadows on the smooth silver lawn. There
were two figures discernible there, and in that strange light, they
were possessed of a non-human quality. It might have been almost
credible if they had turned out to be elves or fauns, or angels, they
seemed so colourless and silvery as they walked beneath the sky. It
was Kirsty and Rice Robey. He stood with both his arms above his
head, and I could hear that he was speaking, without being able to
make out what he said. He appeared to be looking up towards the
moon, and perhaps it was to the moon, rather than to Kirsty, that he
spoke. Then, in a moment of unforgettable intimacy, Kirsty, who
had been standing some yards apart from this hierophantic figure
with his outstretched arms, paced towards him, stroked his shoulder,
and buried her face in his collar. His arms came down and enfolded
her. I hastily withdrew from the window.

Earlier in the evening, Darnley and she appeared to be getting
along together so well. I felt sad on his behalf. Involuntarily, I
remembered the look of sadness on Darnley's face when I married

Anne for whom (I suspect, but will never know for certain) he had nursed a soft spot. His extreme emotional diffidence did not seem to grow less with the years. I hoped that Kirsty had not been cruel, on the beach, when, presumably, she had shaken loose of him in order to walk alone with Rice Roby.

Breakfast was a help-yourself affair in the kitchen. Jo was frying eggs and bacon when I came down at about half past 9. The older members of the party had all made a start on the day. Wimbish, who had no sabbatarian principles and to whom one day was exactly like another, was already at work on the Lampitt papers in the library. Lady Augusta had, I gathered, been to the early service in the parish church and returned, ravenous for the fry-up which she and Pat had consumed at about 9. Sargie had been taken a pot of coffee and some dry toast in bed. Kirsty and Rice Robey were not yet down. Only Jo and Darnley were in the kitchen when I entered it. Since I had not really eaten dinner, I ravenously accepted Jo's offer to cook me a plateful. I looked at Darnley pityingly. How bitter for him that, rather than sit with the clever, attractive sister, he should have been stuck there with Jo.

'I read that stuff,' I said to him.

'Great man, Pughie.'

I was not sure that this was true, still less sure that there was any evidence for such a belief in those crumpled quarto pages; but it wrung my heart to see that Darnley would be loyal to Rice Robey even though he had lost 'his' girl to him.

In the area of other people's emotional lives, one can leap to conclusions on no basis. Darnley had in fact given no indication that he was in love with Kirsty, or even that he found her sexually attractive. The fact that he had made her laugh at dinner did not mean anything. He was making Jo laugh now, and actually seemed in very good spirits, not in the least requiring my pity or sympathy.

Darnley was reading aloud from the Sunday newspapers in a different range of funny voices. It made Jo laugh so much that she broke my fried egg as she slithered it on to a slice of buttered toast. Absolutely anything Darnley said was capable of inducing in her new hysterics.

'Ah!' he said, in a simpering, Third Programme voice with a slight lisp on the 'r's. 'A new novel by Deborah Arnott . . . sensitive . . . the eternal triangle reworked in the setting of a Hampstead kitchen . . . a *tour de force*.'

Jo, who had almost certainly never heard of Deborah Arnott, found this so funny that she spewed out her coffee like a porpoise, a stream of brown liquid all over her jumper.

'Look . . .' she spluttered, 'I've spat all over my. . . .' She could hardly utter the word 'tits', so funny she found everything.

When two people are in the grip of truly uncontrollable laughter about matters not in themselves remotely funny, there is something embarrassing about it, you feel like an intruder.

'I thought I'd go about 11, if that suits you,' I said to Darnley. 'Give us time to reach Timplingham before lunch, and pick up Felicity as agreed.'

The arrangement had been perfectly clear, spoken about more than once on the previous day.

'You go,' said Darnley quietly and – for once – in his own voice. 'I'm going to stay on here for a bit.'

'But how will you get back to London?' I clumsily pursued.

'There are trains. I'll see, I'm staying a bit longer, that's all. You take the car – no difficulty about that.'

This was not meant as a joke, but it still made Jo guffaw.

When I had finished my breakfast, there seemed no point in hanging around. Vernon was having an interminable conversation with someone called Dick. I heard him saying, 'Yer should oppose it on the National Executive. . . . Granted, Dick, granted, but yer should oppose it now, or we'll have to carry it into the Election and it'll be a millstone round our necks. . . .' Pat had settled down in the morning room with Lady Augusta, who was reading a newspaper and silently munching her way through a plateful of custard creams, washed down by coffee. Kirsty had not yet come down; nor Rice Robey, nor Sargie. I was anxious to be on the road before Sargie surfaced, with more plots and schemes for a proposed biography of Jimbo.

'I think you should do it,' said Felicity, when we drove back to London together that afternoon. 'If Sargie helps out financially, that is. It might be absorbing and – perhaps it *ought* to be done. Perhaps you alone can set the record straight.'

'I hardly conceive it as a duty.'

'Telling the truth is always a duty. That sometimes takes the form of needing to contradict lies.'

Neither of us wished to discuss Raphael Hunter, so five or ten minutes of silence elapsed.

'Wasn't it a coincidence – Rice Robey turning up at Mallington?'

Had she known that Rice Robey was to be of the party, Felicity would no doubt have felt differently about coming along with Darnley and myself. I did not know how she would have responded to Rice Robey's evident *tendresse* for Kirsty Lampitt.

'He's so anxious to save Aldingbury Ring from this new road development. He's exploring absolutely every avenue – even Vernon! I don't know what influence Vernon has, or will have, when there's a new government.'

'That seemed to be the excuse for Mr Robey coming to Mallington.'

'Dear R.R.,' she said quietly. 'I do worry about him.'

'He seemed perfectly cheerful yesterday evening.'

'Well, you don't know him as well as I do.'

I freely admitted that this was so, omitting to mention that I was happy to leave it that way.

'I think Darnley may be a bit in love,' I said. 'I'm sure he's only staying on at Mallington because he's smitten with Kirsty.'

I don't know what, exactly speaking, 'happened' at Mallington that weekend. I do not know now whether Darnley ever felt remotely in love with Kirsty, or whether it was always Jo that he loved. Because I had it in my head that he loved Kirsty, I disregarded all the evidence, of Jo and Darnley laughing together and hitting it off so well.

'Are his feelings for Kirsty reciprocated?'

'Not exactly.'

Not wishing to hurt Felicity's feelings, I had given a heavily edited version of events, and made no mention of Kirsty's moonlit walk on the lawn with Rice Robey.

Felicity stared out of the car window with infinite sadness. Then she spoke with a false, brittle brightness.

'No doubt I shall hear Rice Robey's stories about the weekend when I get to the office tomorrow morning.'

THREE

Of my two small broadcasting jobs, I much preferred the work for the
World Service of the BBC. There was something different to do each
week for the literary programme on which I was engaged as a reader.
Sometimes I would be asked to read a poem, or an extract from a
recently published novel before the book in question was discussed
by a critic. Sometimes, Freddie Vance, who produced the programme, got me to read a passage from some well-established author,
or from a book which he considered ready for revival. One week I
might therefore be reading a few paragraphs from the latest Deborah
Arnott novel; the next, an ode by Keats or a passage from Sir
Thomas Browne. It was in the best sense of the word a bookish
programme, designed for those who enjoy reading, rather than for
those who merely wished to keep up with the latest publications.
Freddie was rather a charming man – a clergyman's son. He was
about ten years older than myself and his parsonage-upbringing was
more rarefied than my own, his father having become a Catholic.
We sometimes had a drink or a meal together after the recording.
We were not intimates, and we did not discuss our personal lives. I
think he was married to a schoolmistress in Amersham. I once knew,
but have now forgotten, whether or not he had himself once been a
teacher. If so, he would not have been a teacher like my own old
English master, Treadmill, with a gift for projecting his personality,
but instead, the quiet, colourless sort of schoolmaster of whom,
having left school, one retains no memory at all. He wore tweed
jackets, corduroy trousers and was half bald. His talk was punctuated
with archaic, sub-Wodehousian locutions. He tended to call me a
dear fellow. One could imagine him refereeing games of rugby
between teams made up of the less able players.

One day, when we were in the canteen of Bush House discussing the contents of future programmes, he put a couple of old green and white Penguins beside his plate of baked beans on toast and tapped them with stubby fingers.

'I'm wondering whether to do five minutes on this writer,' he said. 'There used to be a bit of a cult of his novels during the war – you're too young to remember that, my dear fellow. Oh, damn.'

A baked bean had fallen from his fork on to the back of *Memphian Mystery*. He retrieved the bean with his fingertips, ate it, and then, with a paper napkin, he rubbed at the small stain left by the tomato sauce just to the left of the photograph of the author on the back of the book.

'These are the author's own copies,' he said.

'Albion Pugh's?'

'Yes. I don't normally let my arm be twisted by authors – got to be tough with these blokes, my dear fellow, don't you know, but my missus has rather a thing about these particular books. Tickled pink when she heard I'd met Albion Pugh.'

'Where was this?'

'He didn't want to meet at our regular, and he wouldn't come and meet me here. Said it wasn't quite safe for him to be seen on Corporation premises. Said he needed to meet on neutral territory. All very hush hush. So we had gin at a strange old tavern behind Charing Cross station. Dripping old place, practically had stalactites coming down from the ceiling, or is it the stalagmites which come down?'

'Stalactites come down,' I said, remembering a useless piece of information which Lollipop Lew, a master at my prep school, had once taught us – 'Little mites grow upwards.'

'Eh? Oh, mites! Rather good. I'll remember that. Albion Pugh told me this bar where he took me had been there ever since the reign of Charles II. I think it was actually below the river. He said that the Popish Plot had been hatched there.'

'I thought the Popish Plot never happened – wasn't that the whole point of it – Titus Oates made it up?'

'Strange bird, Mr Pugh.'

'Really?'

'He was very keen that we should read his stuff on the programme; he brought along these two, and said I was to guard them with my life.'

121

'Oddly enough, I read *Memphian Mystery* for the first time not long ago. It's a favourite book of a cousin of mine.'

'What did you think of it?'

'A very gripping story, almost unbelievably badly written; so badly written, you could not imagine that it was not done deliberately, for some bizarre reason.'

'I told him my missus dotes on his books. He told me *his* missus loves "Bookrest". She particularly liked the one we did a few weeks ago about Pepys. By the way, Pepys used to go to this bar Mr Pugh took me on. I never knew he was a Rosicrucian, did you?'

'Albion Pugh or Samuel Pepys?'

'Pepys. Apparently, that cypher the diary is written in has all the hallmarks of a secret cabalistic cult or something. He had a whole theory about it.'

'Really?'

This was all too predictable. I was much more interested in the woman referred to by Freddie as Mr Pugh's 'missus', that is, 'the Great Attachment'.

'So he told you he was married?' The crude approach seemed easiest with Freddie.

'Had some name for her – what is it now? The Great something. Obviously very attached to her, as all right-thinking blokes are with their missuses.'

This was so much at variance from my own way of viewing human relations, this assumption that it was a matter of virtue, rather than of luck, whether one happened to enjoy the company of a domestic partner, that I said nothing.

'Full of weird talk, though.'

'About this woman?'

'Funnily enough' – Freddie's voice sank to a whisper – 'it was about the dear old Beeb. First there was some stuff about our esteemed D.G. Albion Pugh had some very wild things to say about him. You would think the D.G. was a communist agent to hear Mr Pugh talking. I shut him up pretty quickly, of course. We don't want that sort of talk. Oh, he's not really called Pugh, by the way.'

Freddie was one of those innocents who clearly did not enjoy, as, say, Darnley did, wild speculation about his fellow mortals, nor a suggestion that all is not as it seems in the various organisations and establishments (the Civil Service, the BBC) by which society is organised. I took it that there was some moral virtue in Freddie's distaste, without being able to see what it was. In spite of finding Rice Robey a strange bird, Freddie decided, in the event, to do a short feature on the Albion Pugh novels in a few weeks' time. There was to be a reading by myself and then a brief analysis of the books by a critic.

Much of the material for these programmes was recorded but Freddie liked, if possible, to assemble the separate items of his 'magazine' during the space of one afternoon; so, I quite often bumped into my fellow contributors. I was scheduled to read out the prepared passage – it was the moment in *Memphian Mystery* when the professor opens the mummy and finds the ark of bulrushes in which the infant Moses floated on the Nile – after the critic had recorded his say. I reached the studio and sat in the outer room with Freddie and the production team until it was my turn to sit in the sound-proofed glazed box with a microphone. The figure at present occupying this position, slouched at the round, baize-covered table and rustling his script nervously, was my old schoolmaster Treadmill, who quite frequently gave broadcast talks.

'If we can just have one more sentence for level, Val,' said Freddie.

Treadmill made the weary sound which one of my school contemporaries once described as an old sheep having an orgasm, a sort of 'yeair' sound, but muted, mumbled.

'I've already given you one sentence,' he said.

'Just a small technical difficulty. We weren't receiving you very clearly. Is that all right now, Jake?'

Whatever Jake, the sound recordist, had to say was drowned by a deafeningly piercing high-pitched squeak. There was then a silence. Through the glass which divided us from the studio I could see Treadmill talking but no sound communicated itself to the equipment on our side of the glass. Freddie good-humouredly made semaphore-like gestures with his script, and then spoke again.

'Bear with us, Val. Small technical fault.'

Treadmill was ageing. His moustaches were whiter, his skin sallower. His clothes, a capacious suit of stuff not unlike sacking, hung yet more loosely from his thin shoulders. He was by now glaring at Freddie. In a school setting, his cold rages, whether real or simulated, had a power to wither the most boisterous of childish high spirits. Nobody had ever been known to misbehave in Treadmill's classes. In this context, confronted by another grown-up supposedly in charge, Treadmill's display of wrath seemed merely petulant. When the sound mechanism was made to function properly, he read his well-turned four minutes of reflection upon the novels of Albion Pugh. The point he made about them was that they were a wartime phenomenon. At that date, the conflicts in which Europe was engulfed appeared to call for metaphysical answers. Fighting against Hitler, the Allies had felt themselves to be wrestling with principalities and powers of darkness. In such a world, a writer with a blatantly supernatural viewpoint made an immediate appeal. His stories all had the qualities of a good yarn, as if Rider Haggard or Conan Doyle had chosen to highlight the implicit moralism of their stories by the introduction of quasi-magical themes. He rounded off his four minutes with one of his favourite old chestnuts, Samuel Johnson's 'Nothing odd will do long – *Tristam Shandy* did not last.' Some oddities did, like Sterne's great novel, last, Treadmill stated, but it was too early to say whether the novels of Albion Pugh would sink without trace or be remembered, as he would think they deserved to be remembered, as one of the most distinctive contributions to English fiction during the Second World War.

It did not take long, when my turn came to sit in front of the microphone, to read the required passage. When recording 'The Mulberrys' in Birmingham, I never, strange to say, had much sense of the devoted audience who day by day lapped up the doings of the inhabitants of Barleybrook. With the broadcasts from Bush House, it was all different. There, the magic of radio often gripped me, the fact that sound waves could transcend time zones, land and sea and be picked up by transmitters all over the world. I sat in a studio in the Aldwych reading a book. Later that night, insomniacs like the Great Attachment could lie in bed at 2 a.m. and listen to my voice in Kentish Town or Cumberland. At the same time, with clocks set to different hours and with the sun in a different position in the sky, the voice would, or could, be heard in Malaya, Africa, the United States. Far-flung Lampitt cousins could hear it in Mombasa or Johannesburg. In the suburbs of Los Angeles it could be picked up in broad limousines gliding along the freeway. In some downtown bar in Rio de Janeiro the same voice, at the same moment, could be crackling out Albion Pugh's words, while simultaneously they could be heard in some mission hut in Borneo or a sheep station in New Zealand. It made me think of the evening hymn,

As o'er each continent and island
The dawn leads on another day,
The voice of prayer is never silent,
Nor dies the strain of praise away.

The voice of the BBC was similarly unstoppable, a disagreeable fact if considered in the wrong mood but by another token strangely consoling, bringing the sense that since the advent of this incomprehensible invention the inhabitants of our planet will never quite know solitude in the sense that their ancestors knew it. I did not delude myself into believing that everyone in the world tuned into 'Bookrest'. Of course, hardly anyone knew of its existence. It was not the numbers of those listening which moved me, it was the possibility of their doing so and their infinite distance from my own circumstances.

I handed back *Memphian Mystery* to Freddie who said, 'Now I've got to toil up to the blighter's house. He insisted on having the books delivered back to him by hand.'

'Where does he live?'

'Gospel Oak, roughly. Miles out of my way.'

'I could take them.'

'I say, my dear fellow, could you really?'

'If you could give me the address. It doesn't sound as if it is too far from where I live myself.'

A curiosity to see Rice Robey's ménage, more than any charitable impulse to spare Freddie trouble, explained my offer. It was soon arranged that I should deliver the books at 77 Twisden Road, NW5 on my way home.

'We had Albion Pugh down to speak to the Lampitt Club,' said Treadmill afterwards. We had woven a path through swing doors and subterraneous, ill-lit corridors to the canteen for a cup of tea.

'No one would say that his novels were – yeair – well *made*, but as Louis MacNeice, surprisingly an enthusiast, said in a pub not two miles from where we sit – as it happens, the Black Bottle which you know well; Joyce Cary was there, I remember, and Julian Maclaren Ross – "Pugh can hear the music of the spheres".'

'He can certainly hear something inaudible to the rest of us.'

'When I asked him to address the Lampitt, I had absolutely no idea – how could I? – that he had actually *known*. . . .'

'James Petworth Lampitt himself; he was something of a mentor.'

'Did he come to address the Lampitt, then, in your time in the school?'

'No. I happen to have met him since.'

Treadmill did not look particularly pleased by this claim.

'I wonder, though, if you were in the school when a very much *less* interesting writer, Raphael Hunter, came to give a talk on Lampitt himself?'

'That was when I first met Hunter.'

It was tactless to have intruded the word 'first' into that sentence.

Treadmill really preferred to be the one with literary acquaintances. For a second or two his face assumed the indignant expression it had worn if a boy had the temerity to be late handing in prep, or displayed some other failure to play life's game by Treadmill's rules.

'Don't overstretch yourself, Julian. I mean, *socially*. Was it Evelyn Waugh who said that only bores know everyone? The remark was not made to me by Waugh in person but quoted to me, when he came to address the Lampitt Club, by an old chum of mine and his, incidentally, called Henry Yorke.'

Treadmill seemed the natural person with whom to discuss my professional dilemma. As briefly as possible I explained that, a couple of months before, Sargie had asked me to write the 'official' life of his brother.

'I could give you a certain amount of help over Lampitt's schooldays,' said Treadmill. 'I investigated the matter in some detail. It's not all – yeair – as you would quite imagine. My only fear about a *book* on Lampitt is that he is not perhaps sufficiently a heavyweight. You perhaps remember the disobliging phrase used by D. H. Lawrence in one of his letters about J.P.L.'

'I don't remember, but I can guess the kind of thing.'

'I see the justice of the gadfly comparison, though the part of the sentence about excrement. . . .'

Treadmill laughed into his tea.

I continued to explain myself. It was not that I was burning with an immediate desire to write the life of Jimbo Lampitt. Sargie and Vernon between them, however, had made me a kind offer which was highly alluring. They would pay me a small retainer in exchange for being Sargie's assistant and secretary for two or three days each week. During those weeks when Sargie could find nothing for me to do, Vernon would enlist my help in making his own notes and papers into an orderly archive. In the meantime, they were scouting around the London publishers for someone who would take on, either a one volume life of Jimbo or – an idea which Vernon slightly preferred – a general history of the Lampitt family, from Radical Jo to the present day.

The objections to this scheme were obvious. I did not wish to be Sargie's creature and slave as, for years, my uncle Roy had been. Nor, if I wrote the book, did I want the Lampitts looking over my shoulder and determining what I said. If, upon investigation, it turned out that Hunter's 'hints' were accurate, for example, and if Jimbo had indeed led a very irregular sexual life, then I wanted to be at liberty to say so, regardless of the feelings of Pat, Sibs, Sargie, Vernon, Ursula and the rest of them.

On the other hand, if I wrote the book, it would provide me with the excuse to escape Jason Grainger. Treadmill was the man who had got me this role, being himself an occasional scriptwriter for 'The Mulberrys'. I knew that he would be able to offer sensible advice.

'"The Mulberrys" provide you with very regular work,' he said.

'But is it work I can continue for ever?'

'Your slightly bizarre friend Kempe has settled down very happily as Stan Mulberry, though in my consideration. . . .'

I always forgot how seriously Treadmill took this drama series. He brought as much critical weight to his analysis of Stan Mulberry's nature as to the many old essay themes, so endlessly rehearsed in his classroom, of character and motive in Shakespeare.

We wandered out together towards the Aldwych.

'And there's always the simple consideration, as Wystan, of all people, sensibly once said to me – *Never turn down easy money.*'

'I don't intend to.'

'Good. You never knew Aaron Samuelson at school, did you? He's a year or two older than you.'

'It's not a name that's familiar.'

'My God, what an able boy *he* was! Abler, if I may say so, than you were yourself. He was no mean poet as a boy, and then surprised us all by getting a job in the Bank.'

'Mr Eliot would have understood.'

'Indeed. Samuelson and his charming wife are – yeair – putting me up tonight. There'll be several old pupils coming to dinner. Do you remember Garforth-Thoms?'

'Yes. What's he up to?'

'A parliamentary career in prospect, though not, I regret to say, as a member of the party which I, and I suspect you, would support. Had I known I was going to bump into you, I should have suggested to Samuelson that you came along.'

'No, really.'

A reunion of old schoolfellows was not my idea of a congenial evening.

'I'm beginning to scent victory in the air. They'll have to have an election soon, and I think the Tories will lose. The tactlessness of appointing a fourteenth earl as our Prime Minister, the undemocratic way in which it was done, these things will have their just reward. . . .'

'I wish I found the Labour leadership more attractive.'

'One step forward, two steps back. I believe that was how Lenin defined socialism. I never knew Lenin, of course, but Beatrice Webb, who knew him well. . . .'

'This is my bus.'

It was rude of me to break him off in mid-sentence, but in those days Number 27s were a rarity. The appearance of one at the bus stop as we spoke was not an opportunity to be passed over lightly. I was particularly anxious to call on the Great Attachment.

I had not set eyes on Rice Robey in the months which had intervened since I stayed at Mallington. This by no means meant that he had been absent from my thoughts; in fact, he had been almost more vividly present to me through the conversations of other people than if I had been meeting him on a regular basis myself.

Human beings, particularly those of a vaguely mysterious character, exist for us less in their own impenetrable essence than in the mind of others. In the case of Rice Robey, my own inability to decide what he really like was increased by the extraordinary vividness with which others, notably Darnley and Felicity, had imagined him, so that in hearing their projections of his character, I was confronted by a far more assimilable figure than the man whom I had so fleetingly met. That is to say, they had a coherent picture of the man, whereas I, if I had to rely on my own impressions alone, could not put together the disparate signals which I felt myself to be receiving in his presence.

Jo Lampitt, who had thrown up her job in Ely and was now working in Darnley's office in some supposedly secretarial capacity, had a different vision again. When I met her and Darnley one evening in a pub, she spoke with a lack of subtlety which enabled me, at any rate, to adjust the figure of Rice Robey into some kind of focus.

'Kirsty's *really*, really' (she pronounced the word *rarely*) 'got the hots for him. You'd have thought he'd have done it with her by now, but poor little Kirsty! She thinks, now, he never will! He's the opposite of a cock tease.'

'You don't mean the opposite,' said Darnley, 'you mean the male equivalent.'

'Shut up, you.' She biffed him good-humouredly with an elbow.

'Cunt tease, I suppose it would be. I think Kirsty's nuts, but that's not surprising after the things they've been taking together.'

'What sort of things?'

'I wouldn't touch his concoctions, but Kirsty does, she's crazy! She offered him a joint, right, and he smoked it with her. But then he took her for this really, really creepy late night walk in Cambridge and they found these mushrooms he made her eat. They're really, really mind-blowing, apparently, and I think it's really, really frightening.'

It was a number of years before I heard of anyone else exploiting the hallucinogenic properties of mushrooms. Rice Robey did not regard it as a fad of the age. He thought it was a secret which had been transmitted, not through fashionable representatives of the 'drug culture' but through the same hidden oral traditions which handed down cures and spells, guarded the secret whereabouts of ley-lines and magic circles, or preserved the old tales of King Arthur, or of Herne the Hunter.

'They don't do anything, though!'

'Isn't this true of most people who make friends?'

'Of course it is,' said Darnley.

'Shut up, I tell you!' She was fiercer with Darnley now, and evidently felt that she should do all the talking. She certainly did not want to be contradicted. I do not know why it should have been so sinister that Rice Robey had not actually made love to Kirsty, but somehow this was what one did begin to sense, even before Jo's next revelation.

'You see, they have been to bed – he insisted. But nothing happened.'

'That was bad luck,' I said.

'It wasn't bad luck, dumbo!' I thought 'dumbo' was ripe, coming from her. At this point Darnley interrupted her narrative with a shorter version of his own.

'Rice Robey missed his train back to London from Cambridge and got Kirsty to put him up. It would seem that there was only one bed, which they shared, but with no intention on his side that they might have any leg-over.'

'Doesn't it give you the creeps, Mr Grainger?' Jo asked me, wide-eyed. 'Think of it, all night long, lying there. Kirsty really, really having the hots.'

'We've got the general idea,' said Darnley.

Jo put her tongue out at him and said, 'What's the matter, aren't I allowed to talk, or something?'

'I always knew that Pughie was a bit of a dirty old man,' said Darnley. 'But it's all slightly different with him.'

'You could say it was different! I wouldn't want to go to bed with a dirty old wanker if he didn't want to do it. Different! Kinky, more like.'

I saw what Darnley was trying to say, though I was not really convinced by his words. What was striking was that Jo so obviously missed the point. She genuinely supposed that 'different' was being used by Darnley to convey a bizarre erotic preference.

'Kirsty was practically starkers, and there he lay with his clothes on – that's different, if you like.'

I wondered how long I myself would survive with a girlfriend who did not quite understand anything which was said to her. Darnley appeared to be very happy. Her abrasiveness with him, and her willingness to speak so openly of matters which in grown-up life he had always seemed too embarrassed to discuss, seemed very congenial to him. He held her hand and smiled. I had never seen him hold anyone's hand before, or display any physical signs of affection for another human being.

'I've told Miles he shouldn't print this wanker Pugh's stories in *The Spark*,' said Jo. 'That one about the old poof being murdered – my cousin – there wasn't a shred of – Mama said he wasn't a poof anyway – always having it away with Sargie's wife.'

'I don't think that's quite true,' I said, with the condescending certainty of someone who regarded himself as an expert in the subject.

'We'll have to see about printing Pughie's stuff about Hunter,' said Darnley.

'Well, I say you're not to put it in.'

Three months earlier, if a typist in Darnley's office had offered her opinions on the verisimilitude of Rice Robey's stories, he would have laughed her aside. It was now obvious that he would take some notice of Jo's desires and opinions in the matter.

To Jo's disconcerting evidence about Rice Robey, I had to add the daily chronicles fed to me by Felicity. Jo Lampitt was too stupid to make things up. I was sure that there was something between Kirsty and Rice Robey. I was also prepared to believe that he was a person of intuitive power, an accomplished gossip and perhaps, in spite of Jo's malice about him, something of a sage. The fragmentary leaves of his religious epic, or however you chose to categorise it, were not in the least to my taste, but in their crude way they drew attention to a fundamental truth about the way we view the world, a truth which Rice Robey himself exemplified in his effects on those around him. That is, that it matters far more how a person is perceived than what they are actually like. However one viewed his theory that St Paul had a hand in the Crucifixion itself, it was incontestable that Christianity had begun, as far as the literary records shed light on the question, not with documentary or eyewitness memories of Christ, nor with any biographical details concerning his appearance, habits, marital status. Nor had this religion begun with Christ's reported sayings. As it first arrived in the Mediterranean ports of Asia Minor – Corinth, Ephesus, Thessaloniki – Christianity was something buzzing about in the mind of St Paul. It was Paul's perception of Jesus as a mythological being of cosmic importance which converted the members of the early church. They could not read the Gospels, which did not exist, and probably did not know stories of the goodness or wisdom of the actual historical personage who walked the roads of Galilee, teaching and healing. To the Thessalonians, Christ was a figure imminently expected to appear on the clouds to gather them up into the sky before they had known bodily death; to the Corinthians, he was the New Adam, the man who undid the death of the Old Adam by dying on a Forbidden Tree. It was Paul's capacity not merely to mythologise, but to communicate his vision, which transformed the world and brought Christendom to birth, with all its arcane theological preoccupations, its acrimonious councils about the exact nature of the person of Christ, its savagely cruel defences of intellectually untenable propositions, its persecution of heresies, its formulation of creeds, its wars of ideas, its sects, its factions. 'Albion Pugh', by contrast with the unbelieving bishops of the Anglican Church, could see that the craziness of St Paul did not, when recognised, diminish the Christian religion so much as place it within a comprehensible range of human experience. It was precisely because St Paul did not produce 'facts' which were capable of empirical discussion in the prosaic world of 'Either/ or' that he was able to revolutionise the world.

The journey to Rice Robey's house was rather more of a trek than I had foreseen. Between Tufnell Park and Gospel Oak, there is an infinite sea of dull Edwardian houses. Twisden Road was no nicer, if anything rather nastier, than the other streets in the vicinity; Number 77 (was the mystic number of importance to its occupants?) was much like all the other houses in the road. Darkness was closing in by the time I approached the front door, but by the garish street lamp, I could make out the diminutive front garden, the peeling paintwork on the front door (colour indiscernible in that light which made of everything a fluorescent orange) and window-boxes sprouting dried-out sprigs of plants which had long ago died of cold or thirst; the remains of Michaelmas daisies, swamped, like the good seed in the Bible, by weeds. Across the windows themselves were drawn greyish, yellowing Nottingham lace curtains, beyond which a chilly electric bulb was visible, shining unshaded.

My offer to return the two paperbacks to their author began to seem rash. Curiosity had prompted me to it, but now my intrusion on that scene filled me with foreboding. Rice Robey had never been quite a serious character to me. My failure to get him into any sort of focus, or to understand him, sprang largely from this fact; the knowledge that Darnley and Felicity took him on the whole completely seriously only increased my own inability to do so. Now, however, before his own front door, the joke wore thin, and evaporated altogether. Domestic unhappiness, the source of so many good jokes when viewed from the blessed distance where mothers-in-law, errant wives or husbands and sexual incompatibility are all matters for ribald laughter, cannot be enjoyed close up. Already, in

132

my various discussions about Rice Robey I had found myself censoring details and not passing on to one party what I had learnt from another; and this was because I could not mistake his power of making other people, especially Felicity, unhappy. I had told her nothing, for example, of Rice Robey's behaviour at Mallington except to report that he had badgered Vernon for promises that the Labour Government, when it came, would protect his beloved stone circle, and all other sacred and magical places of old Britain. Felicity therefore knew nothing of his midnight walk with Kirsty, of the girl pawing his arm and looking at him with such adoration, nor of his subsequent visits to Cambridge. My desire to protect Felicity had made me similarly diffident when talking to Darnley, the more so since Jo now seemed privy to all his thoughts, and I certainly did not want her crude misrepresentations of Felicity's devotion to Rice Robey to be circulated for the entertainment of Jo's friends. It was obvious that Felicity was suffering acutely. The office dramas which she recited to me nowadays had a much reduced cast-list. All the figures in it, from the Head of Department down to the office boys and, when she dared to mention them, the temporary typists were now brought in to her evening narratives not as characters in their own right but as extras in the grand Rice Robey play.

Darnley's hero-worship of 'Pughie' enabled him in effect to turn a blind eye to Rice Robey's foibles. Felicity's devotion to the man took the more dangerous form of believing that she saw his faults, but that she, and she alone, could cure them. His mischief-making in the office, his sense that the hierarchy of the Civil Service were out to 'get' him, his wandering hands whenever a pretty girl popped up from the typing pool, his stream of little letters, notes, quotations jotted on cards and memo-slips, to a wide variety of female acquaintance – were all signals to Felicity of his need to be loved. It was a need which she felt manifestly ready to supply. Abject love, when viewed from the outside, has something pitiable in it, even when it is reciprocated. It looks like a sort of lunacy. The cliché of popular phraseology seemed entirely apt to describe Felicity's position. She was 'mad about' Rice Robey, crazy on him. When I first became aware that her interest in him was out of control, I assumed that there was a level of artifice, even of playful deception, in her idea that Rice Robey and she positively *needed* to meet for snatched, semi-secret, sandwich lunches or drinks after work, in order to discuss office politics, or his famous 'ideas', or his state of mind. After a while, it seemed so obvious to me that they were just meeting for fun, because they found it emotionally compulsive and not because of the threatened henge nor because Rice Robey's battle with the Head of Department could conceivably have been advanced towards its conclusion by yet another three-quarters of an hour with Felicity.

'He *needs* to talk, he needs *me*,' she said.

I soon came to see that she believed this, and that she had come to see herself as his saviour, above all as his consolation for what Darnley called 'the wretched situation' at home.

'I think if we knew everything R. R. has to put up with from that woman, we should realise that he was a saint,' Felicity once remarked with quiet intensity.

Another time, she said, 'He stays with her out of pure goodness. Anyone else would have had her put away years ago. The strain of living with mental unbalance, paranoia on that scale, is bound to exact its toll. I'm just thankful that I've come into R.R.'s life at this juncture. I know it sounds conceited, but I honestly think he might have collapsed if it had not been for me.'

This sentence, not really characteristic of my cousin – one could not imagine her boasting about how good she was with her parents, for example – made me recognise how deep Felicity had plunged.

Now that I stood before the Great Attachment's front door, I felt every possible misgiving.

'She hated him to have friends,' Felicity had told me once of Mrs Paxton. 'If she hears he has been seeing a friend she really makes him suffer for it afterwards; even a male friend. Mentioning his friendship with me just wouldn't be *worth* all the tears, and shouting and explanations. That's why we meet in secret now.'

The bell which I tried at Number 77 did not appear to work, so I lifted the doorknocker, a cast-iron dolphin solid with paint, and gave three raps on the door.

A rasping voice, with the faintest tinge of the Edinburgh accent, said, 'I heard the bell. There was no need to knock as well.'

I looked about for the source of this apparently disembodied sound. It would have been fitting for Rice Robey to share his life with a spirit, a banshee, a poltergeist. An upstairs window was thrown open and the filthy lace curtain flapped in the damp evening wind. The voice came from behind this veil, and when I had taken a few steps backward and looked up, I could make out, behind the lace, the silhouette of a woman's head and shoulders.

'Is this where Mr Robey lives?'

'We don't belong to any Christmas Club. We don't fill in the football pools.'

'If this is the wrong address. . . .'

'You're not a Jehovah's Witness, are you?'

'No.'

'They *do* want shooting.'

Her tone implied that we had already been conversing for some time, that I had been consigning whole categories of comparatively innocent people to the firing squad, but that she had at last found some worthier candidates for this particular form of punishment.

'No, no. I've brought Mr Robey some books.'

'So you *are* a Jehovah's Witness. That was how you got in the last time.'

'His own books. This is Mr Robey's house? Mr Rice Robey? He lent them to the BBC. I've brought them back.'

'You see, this is such a very awkward time.'

'I'm sorry.'

'I don't know, really. You see. . . . Look, I'll come down.'

The window slammed. After two or three minutes, there was a sound from the other side of the door of bolts being drawn back, chains unhitched, the full paraphernalia of the suburban portcullis raised.

'Only,' she said as she opened the door, by way of explanation for the elaborate barricades, 'you get some funny people down this road.'

She herself was living proof of the statement.

Her shortish hair was iron-grey. A completely colourless face was brightened by a splash of scarlet applied to thin lips, lipstick which both in shade and texture might have been left over from the war. It was slightly smeared.

'Only,' she repeated (it seemed her sole conjunction), 'I have to listen in just now, if you will forgive me.'

It was years since I had heard anyone speak of 'listening in', the phrase my parents always used when preparing themselves for a session with the wireless.

Steel-rimmed spectacles gave her an intellectual appearance belied by her general manner and her talk. At first glance, she might have been some lesbian science professor, possibly German. She wore a severe navy blue suit on the breast of which had fallen a certain amount of cigarette ash. Ancient peep-toe shoes revealed the red-painted toe-nails, themselves ancient. I had not reckoned on her being so very old. We moved through the shadows of the hallway and into the back parlour at a tortuous pace, the Great Attachment with one mottled hand pressing the wainscotting for support as she went along; the other hand held the ignited cigarette.

'Silly, really,' she said, 'but I'm afraid I shall have to ask you to. . . .'

As we reached the back parlour she scanned the ludicrous Tudorbethan long-case clock of 1910 vintage and murmured, 'We're all right.'

She conveyed the sense that if we had not arrived in the room on time, it would have been a disaster.

'Could you? Thanks!'

The gnarled claws which clutched the cigarette gestured frantically towards a wooden wireless set which made my aunt Deirdre's obsolete Bakelite affair seem *à la mode*. The train of association was not inapposite; I realised a split second before turning on, and hearing the familiar Mulberry music, the reason for the Great Attachment's anxiety. Like Aunt Deirdre, and a million other people in the British Isles, she clearly found intolerable the possibility of an evening passing without tuning into the fictitious world of Barleybrook. She gestured me towards a chair, herself collapsing into a bulbous chintz armchair by the gas fire, stabbing her cigarette in the already brimming ashtray at her elbow and lighting another immediately as her face became abstracted, lost in Mulberrydom.

Jason Grainger was being a particular shit at that juncture of village history. I had been getting on badly with the ever-volatile producer, and it was touch and go whether, before I had decided myself to bow out of the series, Rodney would not have had one of his 'little words' with the scriptwriter, ensuring that Jason had an extended holiday or, if I was really out of favour, some nasty accident. The way Jason drove that E-type, it was always on the cards that he would crash it into the back of a horse-box or a tractor. It was one of the more curious features of the BBC stinginess that none of the actors on 'The Mulberrys' had any guarantee of tenure, nor even of regular work. This was as true of the national institutions, such as Stan Mulberry or Harold Grainger, as it was for the more peripheral characters in the drama such as Jason. If Rodney were feeling miffed, or if the scriptwriter just felt unable to write a particular character into the story-line for a few weeks, then the actor concerned went unpaid. The more colourless characters such as the vicar or the doctor sometimes had no work for months. I at least could not complain of Jason leading a dull life. Having tried to seduce Stan's daughter in a hayloft – she had run away screaming – Jason had consoled himself by smoking a cigarette and throwing the lighted butt into a bale. Thanks to the foresight of Stan's teenage boy Trevor, the extent of the fire damage was contained (what a crush Rodney had at that time on Johnny Bateman, who played Trevor), but there was talk of prosecuting Jason for arson; the further hint that Jason dealt in stolen property provided Rodney with another excuse, should he need one, to give me my marching orders.

That evening's episode found Miss Carpenter, the district nurse, local mercury and purveyor of gossip, with a gaggle of her fellow church-fowl cleaning the church in readiness for the Advent carols. A fairly boring antiquarian element had been introduced (the chief scriptwriter liked that sort of thing) but even this harmless tedium had been shaped, on Rodney's instructions, to point the accusing finger at Jason.

'They do say that old chalice the vicar discovered is medieval,' said Miss Carpenter. 'I say, Dol, you've left some polish on the eagle's beak.'

'Soon have that clean, Miss Carpenter.'

[Exaggerated huffs and puffs. The amount of energy the women were exerting in burnishing the brass eagle-lectern sounded as if it would have been sufficient to project the bird on to the church roof.]

'Much too valuable to be left lying for long in the vestry cupboard, the vicar says. That flimsy padlock on the cupboard door wouldn't deter a really hardened thief.'

'Oh, but Miss Carpenter. You don't get that nasty type of behaviour in Barleybrook.'

This was in general true. Barleybrook was an Elysian England almost untainted by the inheritance of original sin. True, the Swills ran a pretty filthy farm and had been known to water the milk. Reg, the landlord of the King's Head, drank too much and got on badly with his wife. The general impression conveyed by the programme, though, was of a bucolic paradise which would have been much to Shakespeare's taste when in Forest of Arden vein. There was no attempt to convey either the stultifying dullness of life in the real English countryside, nor the boot-faced oikishness of its actual inhabitants. Barleybrook had none of the smouldering feuds which I knew divided the farming people of Timplingham. No one in Barleybrook sodomised their sisters or their rams. Sheep could safely graze there. It is true that the villagers drove cars and tractors, and the women had perms, but nothing fundamental appeared to have changed in the rural paradise of old England since Justice Shallow sat in his orchard or Rosalind gambolled with Orlando in the woods. No one emphasised 'The Mulberrys'' place in the old pastoral traditions more exaggeratedly than the village blacksmith, Jason's Dad, Harold Grainger, whose memories of the place in the old days when swains sang folksongs and used hand ploughs owed more to the scriptwriter's weakness for minor Thomas Hardy novels than to any observed feature of behaviour among contemporary agricultural communities.

'Pointa scrumpy, ole dear,' Harold Grainger was saying to the barman at the King's Head, 'oh, 'ow oi loiks moy scrumpy.'

'There yar, then, 'Arold. 'Ear about this valuable goblet what the parson discovered?'

I mulled over this exchange as we sat, the Great Attachment and I, listening to her wireless, and I tried to imagine myself, during my own career as a barman saying it; tried to think of any bar in the kingdom where such a sentence could plausibly have been uttered.

'Oh, ar, the goblet. Moy Jason, 'eem a bin talking to paarson about it. Noice ter see the boy with a bit of an interest. Go all the way to Selchester 'e done to borra a book from the libree, primeval treasure or summat.'

'Medieval the vicar says it was.'

'Ar. Medi-um-eval, ole dear.'

We listened in reverent silence. Unlike Aunt Deirdre, the Great Attachment did not answer back to the Mulberry characters. No words escaped her lips. She sat rapt, until the last scene, which switched back to the church vestry where (a little predictably) Miss Carpenter found the padlock wrenched from the cupboard door, the ancient chalice stolen and a packet of flashy cigarettes of the brand smoked by Jason and no one else in Barleybrook, lying on the floor.

The Great Attachment sighed and smiled impishly.

'Hope he gets away with it – just between ourselves,' she said. 'It's only an old goblet, after all.'

'I'm sorry to have called at such an inconvenient moment.'

'I can't help having a very soft spot for Jason Grainger,' she said. 'Are you a regular listener?'

'Not really.'

138

'It was always the way when we ran our school that it was the naughty boys that you found yourself getting a soft spot for – the ones who really wanted putting across your knee and spanking.'

I found it difficult to reply to this.

'And I know someone else who'll get his botty spanked if he doesn't come home soon,' she added.

I assumed this was said in a spirit of pleasantry.

'So,' she continued, 'you've brought some books back for my boy.'

'For Mr Robey, yes.'

'And where are you from again?'

I gave a brief explanation of how I happened to have the books in my hand.

'Well, my boy's a dark horse! He never said anything about being on the wireless! And I like listening to the . . . you know . . . the one after the Home Service finishes.'

'The World Service.'

'Because it goes on during the night.'

'Yes.'

'Well, he *is* being a time. He works hard.' She smiled the same indulgent smile she had done for Jason Grainger. 'And then there are all the young ladies! They keep him busy.'

She seemed entirely untroubled by the idea. So much for Felicity's understanding that the Great Attachment was thrown into hysterical fits of grief by the mention of Rice Robey's female acquaintances. The Great Attachment was smiling at me innocently, or perhaps not so innocently. Darnley had been told by Rice Robey that his home life was 'wretched'. Felicity had been told that so much as to allude to his trysts with her 'would not be worth all the tears and shouting'. It was not for me to decide how unhappy Rice Robey might have been, but it became immediately obvious that he had, to put it mildly, adapted or edited the truth, and in a manner which was in its way more disturbingly disloyal to the Great Attachment than any physical betrayal.

'There are two main ones at the moment he likes to talk about,' she continued merrily. She lit another cigarette. 'But I must see to the toad-in-the-hole; he'll be home in a moment and wanting his tea. There's little Kirsty he likes to go to visit in Cambridge. She's rather posh. He's *shy* about her, bless him. I think he thinks I. . . .'

What Rice Robey thought Mrs Paxton thought was either

censored or forgotten, and she reverted to the urgent question of the evening meal.

'Only I've got to open a tin of peas. I don't suppose *you* are any good at tins?'

'Depends on the tin opener. I could try.'

'Could you? There's a step ladder in the cupboard under the stairs.'

'Will I need it?'

'Fetch it, will you.'

She spoke quite authoritatively and for some reason there seemed no option but to obey. Amid a clatter of buckets, mops, cardboard boxes containing pieces of wire and old tins, I found a very paint-stained old step ladder whose divided legs were held together by frayed pieces of rope.

'Only the light bulb's gone in the downstairs toilet, and it needs changing. If his nibs had been back, I'd have got him to do it.'

I changed the light bulb – it involved returning to the cupboard under the stairs to scrummage in one of the cardboard boxes for a 40-watt, and – 'while I was about it' – moved some surprisingly heavy flower pots from a high shelf in the lavatory wall. She wanted them for planting Christmas hyacinths. Then I came back to the kitchen to address myself to the tin opener. 'Only, he gives these talks, you know. Would it be ley-lines? And there are standing . . . They're very interesting, and he *so* often comes back from having given a talk and says he's met another little friend!'

'Lucky for him.'

She snorted with amusement.

The kitchen was steamy with the vapour of overboiled potatoes. With the cigarette between her lips, she drained off the potato-water into a pyrex jug with a Bisto paste lurking evilly at its bottom.

'That's the gravy made.'

This was very much Aunt Deirdre's approach to cooking.

'The tin opener's there. Thanks. You can't stop those men – unless they're like my husband used to be, they're romantic. You are, I shouldn't wonder. So at the moment, it's little Kirsty. Oh, dear, and next month it will be little someone else. And then there's this woman at the office.'

'Oh, yes?'

'Well, she's more of a friend. She sound a nice sort, and clever. Oh, *clever*! But a bit too intense, my boy says – wanting a bit too much, you know. I dare say she's been holding him up again tonight.

140

She makes little excuses to see him about things, says it's all frightfully important business, only she really just wants to be with him. Only, it's *understandable!*'

It was disloyal of me to allow her to tell me so much. I felt the sinking feeling of having been betrayed. It was also a feeling of embarrassment on Felicity's behalf. She had spoken so clearly to me about these trysts with Rice Robey. The version he gave to the Great Attachment was clearly very different. Where the truth lay, who could guess?

'But I'm thrilled,' said Mrs Paxton, 'about the wireless. He'll have been keeping that for me as a nice surprise. He used to be quite a well-known author – before the war, and a bit during. He was really ever so young when he first came to. . . .'

'To your school?'

'That's right. He came and helped my husband run the school; before it was all wound up.'

'Was it a Mr Lampitt who recommended him to you?'

'James Petworth Lampitt.' She said the words without looking at me, with one hand on her waist and the other taking the cigarette from her lips.

'Yes.'

'Now, he was an author, and he happened to know my husband. How odd that you should mention that.'

'I simply wondered if Mr Lampitt recommended Mr Robey for the job at your school.'

She either missed the point of this question or she did not think it was worth answering.

'He was always writing, you know. All those stories were written while he was working for us at the school. My husband ran this school.'

'Yes.'

'It was quite a *distinguished* school. Now, how are you getting on with that tin of peas? Don't cut your thumb.'

'Nearly there.'

'Oh, *good*. He still writes now, of course. Bits of poetry. And there's some great long thing he's planning. He won't tell me a *thing* about it. "Another mystery?" I'll ask him. "You could say so," he says. "Does it have a murder?" I'll ask, and he'll say, "You could say it has *the* Murder." Only, you see, the trouble is, he doesn't have the time for books now that he has all these other things. But it's nice to think – did you say, would it be, the producer, is that what you are?'

'No, I just help.'

'Oh, only I'd like him to make a name again for himself. And the money would be nice.'

The kitchen doorway was at that moment filled with Rice Robey. Presumably, he had come through the front door in the usual way, but I had not heard him do so and it seemed equally probable that he had simply materialised; or even that he had not materialised, that this was a spiritual emanation of his personality making its apparition while his body bilocated in another place.

'I'd nearly given you up,' said Mrs Paxton. 'Only it's Thursday.'

He bowed down to kiss her white cheek and I noticed how tenderly and lovingly he did so.

'Then it's toad-in-the-hole,' he said.

'This is Mr. . . . He's brought you your books. He says you are going to be on the wireless, boy, isn't that good?'

'Mr Grainger and I are acquainted,' he said.

'Grainger! I wonder if you're related to our friend Jason,' she said waggishly.

'I was going to tell you about the wireless programme, Audrey, only I didn't want to say anything until it was definite. You'd only have been disappointed. The Corporation of British Broadcasting can be very unreliable.'

'Perhaps your books will become real sellers! It would be nice to have the money. Have you ever read one, Mr Grainger?'

'I read *Memphian Mystery* not long ago. I was much impressed.'

This did not seem the moment to reveal that I had also read some fragments of his strange religious poem.

'Well,' said Rice Robey, 'it was very kind of you to bring the books, but we generally have our tea about now.'

Mrs Paxton moved over to him as he said these words, visibly delighted that he had shown the strength of character to bring my visit to an end. She stood very close to him. Her grey hair and ancient white cheeks reached his dandruffy shoulder. He spontaneously put an arm round her and squeezed her. It was not done for effect. The gesture could not have been made by a man who hated or feared his companion. I noticed too, that in her company, his voice was different. There was a cockney twang to it all the same, but it was not such a marked accent as it had been at Mallington Hall or the lunch in the Black Bottle. In the company of his admirers, I do not think he would have let fall a simple sentence about the hour when he preferred to eat. There would have been some Pugh-like phrase for it, and toad-in-the-hole itself would have become pregnant with mystic meaning. He appeared to be at ease with the Great Attachment in a way that I had never witnessed before during my other encounters with the man. It was also obvious that he could not wait for me to leave the house. My intrusion there had blown his cover, the secret of his domestic harmony, its ordinariness.

Since that moment of leaving Number 77 Twisden Road, and walking back through the dingy street, I have formed various theories to explain his shocking compulsion to tell other people that his home life was unhappy. One explanation was that they were fundamentally miserable together, that I simply happened to catch them on a good day when hostilities had momentarily ceased. Another possibility was that he chose to dramatise those periods of discontent which descend upon almost any pair of human beings living together; that, by making a story out of these bad patches, and depicting the Great Attachment as the cross he had to bear, he had mysteriously made life more bearable. The immediate explanation which came to me, however, as I made my tortuous way on foot and by bus to Camden Town, was that Rice Robey was simply a liar. He liked the company of young women; he was emotionally, if not physically, promiscuous, and he had discovered that the women themselves found it easier to square it with their consciences if he pretended that he needed their company since all was not well at home. Had they believed that he was perfectly happy with Mrs Paxton, then the more scrupulous of the adorers, Felicity above all, would surely have been inclined to keep their distance. I felt fury with him on this account. She would never have intruded upon him, and made herself so unhappy, had she known the truth. He seemed to be causing emotional havoc in Felicity's heart wholly arbitrarily. What was he gaining from their association if, as he told Mrs Paxton, it was not something he needed or wanted for himself? Was it simply the unclean pleasure to be derived by the exercise of power over another human being?

As a man who exercised a spell (perhaps in a literal sense) over a wide range of women, Rice Robey naturally invited comparison with Raphael Hunter. In both cases, I found it completely mysterious why otherwise intelligent women queued up to be treated so badly. The difference between the two men would seem to have lain in the area of emotional self-control. Hunter was a purely manipulative person. I do not believe that he was ever remotely in love with any of the women whose hearts he so easily broke. They happened, at whatever juncture they crossed his path, to serve some purpose. With Rice Robey, things were different, I am sure. He obviously had nothing to gain from displaying a passion for temporary typists. He must have been, for short spells at least, rapturously unable to stop himself doodling poetry on the blotter in his office and dreaming wild dreams about the latest girl.

At this period in my life I was in the strange position of having forgotten what love was like. I *had* been in love, or I supposed that I had been – with Miss Beach, with Barbara (a little), with Anne (besottedly). I did not wish to deny this, but I was unable to summon back any of the sensations which might have enabled me to empathise with the emotional predicaments of my friends. Why, for example, should a man with Darnley's intelligence, humour and melancholy good looks have 'chosen' a girl with Jo's apparent limitations? The question, which nagged me, was absurd. It implied that love was a matter of the will. The shock I so unreasonably felt was comparable to the first visit to the house or rooms of some new friend, whose good taste had somehow been taken for granted, and finding there shop furnishings and uncongenial pictures. Viewing the effects of love from the outside, it just seemed like a form of capricious silliness. Now, if Darnley had fallen in love with Kirsty. . . . Yes, of course. In the case of Felicity's attachment to Rice Robey, I felt not merely aesthetic disapproval, but also an appalled pity. I ached with pity, but at the same time I made the mistake (as with Darnley and Jo) of wondering why – why had she *chosen* Rice Robey? Why not choose some handsome, intelligent, presentable young man? Why fall in love with a scruffy, myopic man in his fifties who had an ugly voice, and a lot of bloody silly ideas?

Even to ask the question was a corrective to rationalism. *Incipit vita nuova* were words which Rice Robey had once written on a memo-slip and placed on the typewriter of a young stenographer to whom he owed a brief devotion. It had happened early enough in her acquaintanceship with the man to make Felicity laugh, and it was she who told me about it. Since the girl had been called Beattie, the highly charged Dantean reference had been apposite, though not one which the recipient of the note had understood. She had asked one person, and then another. Finally, she had asked Felicity, who

144

obliged her by translating the three words. As it happened, that morning, Beattie's boyfriend, a car salesman in Cricklewood, had been offered promotion by his firm on condition that he moved to St Albans. He had been sufficiently confident in his increased prosperity to be able to catch Beattie before she left for work and propose marriage, an offer which she had accepted. Her new life had indeed begun, and she had disappointed Rice Robey by the insensitive assumption that he knew all these things; she had taken the words to be an elaborate expression of pleasure at her good news. Rice Robey had felt crushed, so much so, that Felicity had bought him a drink at lunchtime by way of consolation. Perhaps her own New Life had begun on that day also, the establishment of herself as Rice Robey's confidante, and the incipient dawn of her own devotion to the man. In a way with which I had not yet come to terms, it was the beginning of a new life for me also. I found myself thinking about it all as I alighted from the bus in Kentish Town.

Drizzle fell through the darkness, lit up in mysterious shafts of sparkling light by the headlamps of cars. Light shone, too, from dusty shopfronts above which jutted the jerry-built houses of blackened brick. Here and there were signs of change. The first Chinese restaurant in that part of London, and a Laundromat. These were harbingers of some new creation, but already, after less than two years in the place, they wore the tired, dank aspect of the surrounding shops, the baker's, which still, after it had closed, left the less edible of its wares on display in the window, sticky buns erupting with currants which looked more like bread spattered with soot; or the barber's shop whose sun-faded Brylcreem advertisement grinned out to passers-by like a ghost, growing paler each hour it had been exposed to the light of day; or the pawnbroker's, stuffed with the merchandise whose value could not be redeemed in the betting shop next door. This was Kentish Town which William Blake (and perhaps Rice Robey) saw as a place where the pillars of an imaginative Jerusalem had been set up, ground trodden by the feet of the Lamb of God.

> Pancras and Kentish Town repose
> Among her golden pillars high
> Among her golden arches which
> Shine upon the starry sky.

145

Here, the imported labour force of the nineteenth century had crammed their sickly and ever-expanding families into mean terraced houses; here, ten-year-old factory hands had swarmed in tenement buildings. Sometimes, the sheer indignity of the life of the poor, even when viewed from a perspective in time or place where it might be imagined that life has improved, has a power to oppress and torture the soul. Lloyd George and Vernon's dad, and later Clem Attlee and Stafford Cripps and Vernon himself, had done their best to make existence more endurable for subsequent generations. That could not alter the fates of those who had lived and died like slaves in this place, their stomachs pinched with hunger, their lungs clogged with soot, their brains wandering through God knows what corridors of despair which only alcohol could numb.

Kentish Town deepened into brick-blackened Camden. On my left was the tube station, infested, as always, with human wreckage, blue-nosed contemplatives clutching ragged blankets to their shoulders and wodges of newspaper to their knees; shiny-faced inebriates, eyes swollen and cut, murmuring snatches of old songs; a woman who might once have been a flower-seller, a black straw hat rammed jauntily over scrubs of unwashed hair, sprawled in a pool of unidentifiable liquid, her neck and shoulders pressed against a newspaper-placard reading CLOSING PRICES, her bulbous legs spreadeagled on the chilling paving-stones and coming to a halt in a pair of dusty brown shoes from which the soles were yearning to part company. Could they, these people, remember who they were, or once had been? Was there any link between the bodies slumped there and the undeveloped limbs of their childhood, when their lives had been all in the future, rather than a fuddled nightmare past? I turned into Parkway, where more such figures lingered in doorways. The pavements were also full of sober men and women, all on the move. Thin-faced crones in headscarves, lighted cigarettes at ninety degrees to their sharp noses, paced homewards to evenings of solitude.

The comparative architectural elegance of Arlington Road, as I turned into it for the last few yards of my walk home, did little to console. Sadness in that sort of mood seems the only truth. To be conscious is to be sad, and anything else seems like an illusion. Approaching my own front door, I was visited by self-disgust. I had gone to Twisden Road as a voyeur, I had intended it as a guerrilla raid in some emotional war that I was fighting against Rice Robey inside my own head. Now, I felt merely that I had intruded on his privacy.

Having met Mrs Paxton, it was no longer quite possible to regard her as no more than a joke – 'the Great Attachment'; nor would I ever be able vicariously to enjoy accounts of her rages against Rice Robey, accounts which I would now believe to be lies.

Entering our common drawing room, I found Felicity sitting by the gas fire. A thick pile of foolscap typed pages was balanced on her knee.

'I'm just trying to work out next year's Budget Bids,' she said by way of greeting. She had not looked up from a page which had the word VIREMENT typed in capitals at the top of it. I resolved to say nothing to her about Rice Robey. Very likely, she would soon disappear into her own room or, as she quite often did, go out for the evening with a friend. If she *were* to discuss office politics, I hoped that it would be possible to vary our theme, and speak of other colleagues. I longed to hear more about Brenda and her friend Henri, and their dog-breeding life in Putney; or about Brenda's war with the surly Dr Jack, who countermanded her orders and proposals and made dark hints that paperwork had a way simply of disappearing when passed through her in-tray. Dr Jack was not saying in so many words that Brenda was throwing paper away, rather than filing it; this, after all, would have been in a civil servant the ultimate professional dereliction, the equivalent of a doctor disregarding the Hippocratic oath, or a Catholic priest celebrating a Black Mass.

These harmless matters were not, however, uppermost in Felicity's mind. She put down her work and sipped at a glass of pale sherry.

'I'm afraid that R.R. is in trouble up to his neck,' she said quietly. 'Our Head of Department . . . oh, Julian, it just makes me so *angry*. Rice Robey is worth ten of them. He is person of such talents.'

'Being the discreetly anonymous civil servant isn't one of those talents.'

'He isn't a civil servant. He is an inspector of Ancient Monuments with an unrivalled range of knowledge. He really does not *need* to waste his time in administration. It is all so footling. You know, quite apart from his work for the ministry, he is in constant demand as a lecturer; he gives guided tours, he. . . .'

'I heard of him going to Cambridge not long ago to give a talk: I think it was about ley-lines. Kirsty Lampitt was certainly much impressed.'

'He's respected. And yet these stupid people. . . . Since he isn't

147

a grey man in a grey suit, why should he behave as if he were one?'

'He is technically a civil servant.'

'True, he entered the Civil Service at the lowest level of the Executive Grade with no qualifications. It was towards the end of the war and they were glad of anyone they could get. But, he very quickly became involved in the practical supervision of these old sites. He never was a paper-pusher. He loves his work. And in this particular case, he is right to make a stink. The Ministry of Works holds these places in trust and what they are proposing is that Aldingbury Ring should simply be wiped off the face of the earth.'

'This is the cut-price Stonehenge which you have mentioned before?'

'He calls it his sacred grove,' she said lovingly. 'It's in Berkshire. R.R. thinks that it is an ancient sacrificial site. There is very little to *see*, it has never been dug. There is a strange slab of stone at one end of a grove of trees, and a little way away, there are the remains of a small stone circle. R.R. thinks that if it *were* dug, there is no knowing what might be found – swords, helmets, rings, human remains. . . .'

'If it has never been dug, how can he be so sure?'

'He works by instinct, but his instincts are often right.'

This was very like his approach to journalism, gossip, perhaps to religion. Like Darnley, Felicity seemed to place absolute trust in Rice Robey's hunches.

'Has he ever taken you to see it?' I asked.

She very slightly flinched. Doubtless she would have loved a day out with Rice Robey; in admitting that she had not so much as set eyes on the Sacred Grove, she was also having to admit that her association with Rice Robey was not as intimate as she would have liked. She did not answer my question. Rootling about in her capacious black bag she produced a cardboard folder, opened it, and took out a drawing of Aldingbury Ring.

'He gave me this,' she said.

Rice Robey was no draughtsman, but there was something un-deniably distinctive about the thick black pencil-work with which he depicted this strange place. The trees were after Palmer. In the sky above the grove, he had drawn an antlered figure hurtling across the clouds, accompanied by four-footed creatures, perhaps meant to be hounds but bearing more resemblance to goats.

'There's Herne,' I said, 'sometime a keeper here in Windsor Forest.'

'Aldingbury Ring is very near Windsor. That's the trouble. It's bang in the line of the new fast road they're planning to build between London and Bristol. That's the MOT's problem, though, not ours. It's the MOW's job to preserve ancient sites, not to allow them to be overrun by lorries and tarmac.'

'Can't the road be resited, so that it curves round the Sacred Grove?'

'It would wreck it if it did. R.R. takes it really seriously, Julian. He says that the Gods will exact their revenge.'

'That's certainly their usual way of behaving.'

'He thinks that the Head of our Department positively wants to destroy Aldingbury Ring, just out of spite against him. He has been out to get R.R. for years. Do you know, he had the cheek to ask R.R. to step into his office the other day and warn him that his Staff Report for the last six months was very unfavourable.' To speak the final two words of the sentence, Felicity adopted a mock-pompous tone reminiscent of her mother's 'joke' voice. 'The Head of Department is about ten years younger than R.R. I know that isn't the point; but it was a threat. They are afraid of him rocking the boat. They somehow know about his friendship with your Mr Darnley and they don't like it. Civil servants are terrified of journalists. They think R.R. will feed Mr Darnley with scurrilous gossip.'

'They would be right to think that.'

'It is almost a resigning matter. They want R.R.'s head on a charger; they won't be satisfied until they have destroyed him.'

We stared at the gas fire. It seemed so clear to me that, if I were in charge of a civil service department, I should find Rice Robey an uncongenial colleague; it was no surprise that they wanted to get rid of him, if indeed they did, and this was not merely a piece of persecution mania of Robey's own imagining. What was so eerie was to hear Felicity's account, and realise that she saw things so totally from Rice Robey's point of view. She was not even attempting to be rational or dispassionate.

'I believe civil servants are always made edgy by political change, and it does now look as if the Tories haven't got a hope of winning the next election.'

'I wouldn't be so sure. Think what snobs the English are. The clever journalists mock Douglas-Home, but I suspect he's really quite popular.'

'Rice Robey thinks Labour will win,' she said. She did not need to say that this was what she thought too.

She stretched and closed her eyes momentarily as she spoke. When she lifted her arms, the jacket of her navy blue costume fell open and I could make out the shape of her breasts beneath the sleeveless, schooly jumper which she had knitted for herself some months before.

I wanted to change the subject, but I also wanted to have the last word. I think that was why I made the next few tactless remarks.

'If they boot out Rice Robey, he'll get by perfectly well as a lecturer. You have said yourself that he is much in demand. Possibly, he'll do more writing. You shouldn't worry about him so much.'

Felicity had been looking at the floor. She lifted her oval, fleshy face towards mine and I could see that her eyes were full of distress.

'Get by? Get *by*?'

I saw that I had completely failed to come to grips with the reason for her sadness. The supposed persecution of Rice Robey was bad enough, but what truly distressed her was the prospect of losing him, the chance that he might no longer be a presence in the same corridor as her own, a head stuck round the door at periodic intervals during the day. It would spell the end of their secret little lunches and their drinks after work. Rice Robey would move on, and, of course, Felicity was realistic enough to realise that once she was removed from his immediate sphere of work, he would be unlikely to keep their friendship in good repair. He would find other women, other causes, other ruins and earthworks in which to be immersed, other audiences for his fantastical ideas; and she would be left alone. How bitterly this would pain her, was now written on her quivering strangely pale lips, on her harrowed brow, and in her tearful eyes.

'I've become very fond of him,' she said.

'Yes.'

'You probably can't see why. You probably think I'm just an hysterical middle-aged woman, past her best, fantasising about a much older man.'

'I don't think anything.'

'You suppose it's like women who fall in love with vicars. Do you remember Miss Dare?'

She sniffed, and we both laughed at this shared childhood

memory, a phase of two or three years when a spinster, living in a village quite some way away from Timplingham, formed an attachment to Uncle Roy. Miss Dare had come to Norfolk from London, where she had attended St Mary's Primrose Hill, and someone had recommended Timplingham church as an appropriate rural substitute. Here was the same loving reconstruction of an English ritual based on the Sarum Missal, with vestments modelled not on modern Roman Catholic rubbish but on illuminated Books of Hours from the fifteenth century. Miss Dare's addiction to apparelled albs, full, Gothic conical chasubles and the profound *inclinatio* (in preference to genuflection) had strayed into a devotion to the person of my uncle, who liked to talk of these rarefied ecclesiological matters in those very fleeting intervals of waking life when he was not talking about the Lampitts. Even here, Miss Dare had followed the form very closely and could claim to have taught in a school with a lady who had known Miss Bean, the very close friend of the unfortunate Angelica Lampitt.

'No, you're not like Miss Dare.'

'Oh, Julian.'

And she began to weep, copiously and silently, only occasionally letting out moans of grief. When she did so, I wanted to comfort her. She was sitting in the armchair where she had been working; it was not an object of furniture on which two people could sit and hold one another. Our embrace was clumsy. Perched sideways on the arm of her chair, I could neither kiss her, nor even quite fit my arm around her shoulder, nor could our faces meet without her jutting her chin almost vertically in the air. So we clutched one another awkwardly, lost for words as she moaned. I no longer thought especially of Rice Robey, still less held him responsible for the unhappiness of my cousin. Love had done this, not Rice Robey. Holding her as best I could, and putting my head on the top of her head, I realised that I was not doing this merely to comfort her. Something was awakening within me which had been dead for well over a year.

'Come on,' I said, 'I'll take you out for some dinner.'

'Couldn't. Couldn't face it.'

'It'll take us out of ourselves.'

'I don't want to be out of myself. I am more unhappy than I have ever been in my life, but I want to be hurting and bleeding with the pain of it. I don't want to be taken out of this state.'

I stroked her head. It was a signal for a change of posture. She stood to light up a cigarette from the matchbox on the mantelpiece and I remained sitting on the arm of the chair. For the first time in conscious memory, I found my cousin's calves in their thick tan stockings beneath the navy blue skirt hugely alluring.

'I've quite often been fond of men,' she said. 'You and I have never shared confidences, except once, when it was unavoidable' – she meant the affair with Hunter – 'but there have been others.'

'I guessed there might have been.'

One of my worst habits is stating, out of shyness, the precise opposite of what I think.

'But nothing like this,' she said.

'Is it worse because. . . . ' – I toyed with various delicate ways of asking her whether it was all made worse by the absence of sexual expression on both sides, the heightening of emotions which soared uncontrollably inside her head; or was it worse because he regarded her as no more than a friend, but had come to depend on her for friendship, so that she could not declare her love without destroying the friendship? Or was it something different, which made it worse?

'He set something free in my mind. When I gave up Oxford and went to the Ministry of Works I was determined to have a rest from thought. There seemed nowhere further to go, and yet my mind was still working away, hammering at a wall which contained no secret door, but which I had to get through. All the methods of penetrating this wall were either ineffectual or intellectually inadmissible. There was a very, very serious danger of my going mad, since the ratiocinative process continued in my head even when I was asleep. Nothing would stop it, not even work. It rampaged in my head like toothache. At first, I regarded Rice Robey as an entertainment, a sideshow to distract me from this fruitless intellectual churning. It was when I discovered that he was, in some sense, my saviour, that I knew I was lost. No, no. Don't worry. I'm not soft in the head. I mean, quite literally, that Rice Robey offered me salvation.'

'Would this have to do with his thinking Either/or the two falsest words in the English language?'

'Yes.'

She lit another cigarette from the glowing butt of the first. 'I thought – this has all been done before, it's back to Bergson, it is really a retreat from thought, the struggle between the idealists and

152

the realists was a true one and we must resolve it, either by an honest silence or an out-and-out empiricism; but the latter became as impossible as the former.'

'I don't really follow.'

'It doesn't matter. It does. It matters more than anything, actually, but it doesn't matter that you, individually, at this moment don't follow what I'm saying. I'm expressing myself badly. Rice Robey offered me a way of viewing things, of chucking ideas about at a simple level, which was liberating because it was totally unlike the way I'd been trained to think. I also began to see that in many, many areas he was right. So, all our early talk was about this philosophical stuff.'

'I see. Not office politics at all?'

'Well, yes, we talked about that; but the burning, essential thing we both needed to discuss each day was thought, ideas.'

Her hand was sweaty and she let me hold it in the way that people do hold hands, kiss, cuddle one another when sex is far from their mind.

'Then, quite simply, I became involved in his story.'

'There was a change,' I said. 'When you first met him, you found him tiresome.'

'I still do,' she said indulgently. 'It wasn't just pity for him. You know, he lives with this monster of a woman. He has not said so, but reading between the lines I can tell that she is actually mad. She would be locked up in a padded cell if Rice Robey weren't such a good Christian. She rails at him all the time. He has to do all the cooking – he has told me that much – but he never complains, not so much as a murmur. She has absolutely no interest in his work. There's no wonder he stopped publishing; she took no interest in his books, never read them.'

'You derive all this from reading between the lines?'

'He lets things fall sometimes.'

'I see.'

'You probably think that love has made me silly, but if you really knew Rice Robey, Julian, you would realise that he was practically a saint. Mrs Paxton is the cross he has to bear. She is the real torment of his life. The rest – the campaign against him at work, the destruction of Aldingbury Ring – that, I suspect causes less pain than the hell that woman has made for him.'

I urged her once more to come to the trattoria in Parkway and this time, somewhat surprisingly, she accepted the idea. (Felicity hated restaurants.)

As she was putting on her coat, she said, 'You must read something R.R. has written and tell me what you think of it.'

'Is it about Christ, because. . . .'

'I'll show it to you.'

The trattoria was five minutes' walk from the house, and we were soon established in the corner sipping a rather acidic Valpolicella and leaning backwards to allow a waiter to grind too much pepper into our minestrone from a huge phallic mill. We settled; we made no strenuous efforts to be cheerful; we reposed, conversationally, on the unplumbable store of Timplingham memories, which no one but ourselves could share. Neither of us could remember what happened to Miss Dare, but the mention of her name inevitably led us to talk of Felicity's parents, and to speculate how long Uncle Roy would stay in his parish before retiring.

'I don't think Ma's ever enjoyed being a vicar's wife; she's had enough of being a vicar's daughter.'

We left on one side the more general question of whether Aunt Deirdre had enjoyed any aspects of married life, or how far this was effected by her husband's choice of profession.

'She'd miss the garden if they retired,' I said.

'I say,' Felicity burst out impatiently, 'they're being noisy.'

A very pretty, animated woman, of about my age, was shrieking with laughter in the opposite corner of the restaurant. She was sitting facing us, and opposite a heavily built man with thick blond hair; she had heavily mascara'd eyes, and very full red lips, parted in her laughter to reveal magnificent even white teeth.

When her companion turned his head, I recognised him.

I said, 'That's Blowforth Bums, and he is meant to be having dinner with Treadmill.'

I explained that I had met Treadmill, and heard how much he was looking forward to a dinner with old pupils, Garforth-Thoms among them.

Like his friend, Garforth-Thoms was laughing fit to burst.

One felt excluded by the joke, whatever it was.

The waiters in the restaurant were being tolerant of their high spirits, but hovering, their smiles a little fixed, to make sure that things did not get out of hand.

Felicity said, 'I'm not up to joining them, Julian, I hope they don't notice you.'

'We can just wave at them as we leave. They won't want to join us.'

At that moment, a voice at our table said, 'Look at Hedda! My dear, I always told you my family were mad.'

William Bloom stood there.

I had never seen him on a regular basis since army days, when he had managed to make even the dreariest of occupations such as square-bashing, spud-bashing or cleaning equipment an occasion for high camp humour; very welcome it was, in those days. Inevitably, there had been some calming down since his return to civvie street and the passage of something like a decade. He had made such a success as the employee of a well-established London publisher that he had decided to set up on his own, in partnership with an Irishman called Byrne. 'Bloom and Byrne' had already made quite a solid reputation, and Bloom had been astute enough not to restrict himself to the 'literary' end of the market. It was said that they made most of their money from books about cooking and gardening.

'Hedda's meant to be giving a dinner party for her husband,' said William. 'I forget if you've ever met.'

'She's your sister?'

'She rang me at the office and asked me to buy her dinner. I said I couldn't – I've been entertaining an American author all afternoon – but she insisted. I see she's not been entirely without companionship in my absence. I wonder who that piece of beefcake is. Darling, where does she *find* them?'

'He's called Garforth-Thoms. He wants to stand for parliament.'

'You know everyone, darling, don't you?'

'I was at school with Patrick Garforth-Thoms.'

'Look at the way those lips of hers pout.'

I would have said that if this sentence had been spoken to Felicity in most circumstances, she would have frowned and been embarrassed. Two minutes earlier, she had been writhing with distaste at the behaviour of Bloom's sister, and preparing for a retreat from the restaurant had there been the slightest question of our joining the rowdies. Perhaps because she had so lately been weeping, and her emotions were wound up to an uncharacteristic pitch, she found Bloom's remark very funny.

'You haven't met my cousin Felicity?' I said.

'This is perfect. I've been *pining* for a philosopher all week.'

Bloom has a very good memory, which is one of the most necessary components of social charm. It is hard to warm to anyone, met three or four times, who has difficulty remembering the circumstances of one's life. By contrast, the man who after a couple of meetings, has an instant recall of where you went to school, the number and extent of your family, makes an instant appeal. Bloom had often talked to me about my family, and I must have mentioned Felicity to him dozens of times. On the other hand he had hundreds of acquaintances, and I thought it was impressive that he had retained so much information about her.

'There are plenty of philosophers about.'

'Listen, my dear, you can tell me, does anyone nowadays read G.E. Moore?'

'Fewer than read Agatha Christie or Deborah Arnott,' said Felicity.

'No, but be serious, my dear.' He explained that someone had asked him to publish a book about Moore and his Cambridge circle and he was uncertain until he had spoken about it to a professional philosopher. This was, as it happened, very much up Felicity's street – I rather think her PhD thesis had touched on Moore – and she spoke about the subject animatedly for about five minutes. Then Bloom asked her about various friends he knew in Oxford.

'How's Geoffrey Cormac?' he asked.

'Is he a rather cherubic-looking drunk in a leather jacket?' I asked. 'A strong Ulster accent?'

'He can be a bit tiresome,' said Felicity. 'He hasn't altogether mastered the difference between argument and fisticuffs.'

'Isn't he a great enemy of Professor Wimbish?'

'Tommy!' Bloom rolled his eyes. 'Isn't he divine! I want him to write a book for us when he's finished this boring history of the Labour Party. A nice sort of sex romp through the court of Henry VIII.'

'Hasn't he written quite a lot of those already?' asked Felicity.

Bloom bent double with a mirth at this question, shot out his tongue, rolled his eyes.

I was clumsy enough not to sense that there had been an immediate rapport between Bloom and Felicity, and I ploddingly continued to 'keep the conversation going' by spelling out the fact that I had met Professor Cormac and Professor Wimbish for the first time that year. I mentioned that Cormac had come my way at one of Darnley's lunches in the Black Bottle.

'Oh, that squalid little rag *The Spark*. I get more spark out of wanking. But I mean, darlings, it won't do will it – not quite?'

'I think it's pretty feeble,' said Felicity. 'Then you find, just occasionally, that there are some things in it which make you laugh.'

'Wish I'd found them. I suppose that pathetic "Diary" thing at the front is penned by our little friend Miss Malice herself?'

'Darnley?'

I could not help remembering the time when Bloom was so passionately in love with Darnley. 'The real thing,' he had said. 'Shakespeare's *Sonnets*, Tristan and Isolde, La Prisonnière, the whole horror story.' Now he spoke of Darnley as little more than an irritant, and I realised that in time Felicity herself would be delivered from the torments of loving Rice Robey, that this inexplicable pain which love brings does not last, any more than love itself lasts.

'Did you see their feeble thing last week about little Hedda?'

'About your sister?'

Bloom's sister had now spotted him and was waving, calling out, beckoning him to join them. Garforth-Thoms, at about the same moment, had noticed me and was looking, I thought, a bit sheepish.

'They made her out to be a sort of nymphomaniac. Her husband wanted to sue. Luckily, I managed to persuade him not to. As for Miss Malice.'

'Darnley?'

'You've heard the latest, I suppose?'

'What?'

'She's getting married. She may kid herself, but she doesn't kid Mother.'

'He's marrying the daughter of Vernon Lampitt.'

It took very little to persuade Felicity to cross the restaurant and continue our meal in the company of Bloom, his sister and Garforth-Thoms.

'Can you imagine anything more boring?' asked Bloom's sister. 'My husband Aaron had organised a dinner party consisting entirely of old school chums. No girls, just a lot of boring men.'

'Darling, I thought you were like me, I thought you never found men boring.'

'He didn't *want* me there,' said Hedda. 'It was perfectly obvious I was doing him a good turn, getting out of the house.'

'It was a dinner for Treadmill,' said Garforth-Thoms. 'You remember Treadmill?'

Having been accused of knowing everyone, I was almost non-committal in my reply, and certainly did not wish to advertise the fact that Treadmill had himself expressed the hope, that very afternoon, that he would be dining with Garforth-Thoms.

'He used to teach English in our school,' said Garforth-Thoms, ostensibly to Felicity, but partly, one felt, to me, in case I had forgotten. 'I should have gone to the dinner myself, but Hedda was bored and wanted. . . .'

It did not seem entirely polite to dwell on what Hedda, at any stage of the evening, had wanted.

'I think we'll find the pundits have got it all wrong,' he said confidently. 'Journalists get bored, they like a change, that's why they keep saying that Labour will win the election. If you look at the actual situation in the country, if you talk to people in the constituencies, as I have, you realise that there is a tremendous groundswell of support for the Conservative Party.'

'Yawn, yawn,' said Hedda, 'let's all go to a night club.'

This suggestion was repeated at various junctures until Felicity said she was tired and wanted to go home to bed. Hedda and Garforth-Thoms appeared quite happy to be left on their own. She was running through the possibilities, and had finally selected Ronnie Scott's as their next port of call. When we had parted from them, Bloom, Felicity and I walked slowly down the street together.

'I saw Sargie Lampitt last week,' Bloom said, 'so I'm glad I bumped into you. Isn't it a good idea, Felicity?'

'For Julian to write this book about Jimbo?'

'I want it to be a book about the whole tribe. It'll be *far* more interesting than Hunter's crap. The Lampitts are one of those great Victorian dynasties.'

'Radical Jo was dead fifty years before Queen Victoria,' I said.

'No, but by the time they were *established* – they'd married everyone, read everything. They're just a vanished phenomenon, families like that – the Bensons, the Sidgwicks, the Wedgwoods. They're not really aristocrats, they're the intellectual aristocracy of England. They're actually one of the best things this country has ever produced, those large educated, enlightened families, and I think you'd do it *frightfully* well.'

I had no such certainty, and it came as a surprise to realise that the idea for the book had advanced so rapidly in the minds of others. Bloom, who had shown no desire at all to publish my novel, would have been prepared, I felt, to sign me up on the street corner to write about the Lampitts. It did not occur to me to wonder whether money had passed hands during the conversations he had been having with Sargie.

'Sargie himself always meant to write the book,' said Felicity. 'It could be very good indeed.'

We lingered. The moment we parted from Bloom, both Felicity and I might return, not merely to our house, but to the painful preoccupation which had so wracked her with tears and grief before dinner. The meal had been an unreal respite, an interlude, the sort of holiday, which even in the most terrible emotional circumstances, the heart allows itself.

'I have to start early in the morning,' said Felicity, 'but I'm so glad we met.'

'Maybe,' said Bloom, 'you would let me buy you lunch, so that I can quiz you further about Moore?'

'That would be very nice,' she said.

When we had returned home, we made no more explicit allusion to Rice Robey; only, just before she went to bed, Felicity fished in her briefcase for a brown envelope and said, with a sad smile, 'You could read this if you liked.'

THE CONVERSION OF SAULOS

(Second draft)

On the beautifully unformed juvenility of the face of Stephanos could be read the terror of a cornered animal. His large dark eyes could not avoid glancing first this way, then that, as he looked at his tormentors, wondering who should cast the first stone. He had not been stripped quite naked. They had permitted him a loincloth before leading him down into the rocky hollow which dipped from the quarry on the edge of the Field of Blood.

The trial had been absolutely legal, inescapably conclusive. Stephanos was a blasphemer and the Law demanded the death, by this means, of those who took the Name of the Lord in vain. Stephanos, a young Hellenised Jew, was the most eloquent of the little gaggle of heretics who preached the error nicknamed the

Way. He had made fervent speeches, attracting considerable crowds, in which he argued with great erudition that Yeshua had been the fulfilment of all the ancient prophecies, the promised Messias of Israel, the dear Desire of all the Nations, Yeshua who had been crucified. Cursed is he who hangs upon a tree. No clearer manifestation could have been vouchsafed to Israel that Yeshua had been a pernicious corrupter of the Jewish faith than in the manner of his death. Would the Lord the Unutterable have allowed his anointed to perish on a tree? Why, even to admit the thought was to suggest that the Holy Torah could be disregarded; and this was to say the impossible, it would be to say that the Law of Moses was not the Law of God. Stephanos had maintained that the divinely ordered priestly hierarchy of Jerusalem had always persecuted the mouthpieces of the Most Holy, and that they had not heeded the prophets, and that it was no surprise that they had failed to recognise the divinely chosen Christ. He had even said that they had called down God's curse on their heads by murdering the Holy One of God. Such wild words called for blood-letting, not merely as a punishment to the blasphemer but as a Manifestation that the Holy Torah could not lightly be traduced. The trial, therefore, had been hastened to its conclusion and now the neaniskos, with wrists bound, was led outside the city as an example to the many. He had been pinioned to a stake on the edge of the hollow, and his accusers stood around him in a semicircle. Behind the judges and the guard, massed the crowds who saw here no more than a ghoulish spectacle such as might be provided by any criminal execution, for example the crucifixions which were carried out every week on the common criminals on Golgotha-hill by the imperial military.

Saulos had in his hand a rough boulder and for a moment the high solemnity of the occasion was lost for him by the self-regarding fear that he was going to miss his target and make himself look ridiculous. As a boy, with hoops and quoits, he had been clumsy and the other children had not wanted him as their companion. He had never been practised at such games as delighted the Hellenes. He had never in his life thrown a javelin or a discus. His delight, rather, had been in the Law of the Lord, which he had made his study both day and night. He could not waste time developing the muscles on his dwarf-like body, when he had more important things to think about, more demanding faculties to develop, such as his knowledge of the Torah, his capacity to understand its intricacies and to master the commentaries of the rabbis. Now, as he stood with a stone in his hand, he was conscious of the crowd at his back. They would jeer, as at the pagan games, if he threw and missed; thus the dignity of the Sanhedrin would be tarnished, and the high religious significance of the scene would be lost; for this was no secular punishment; it almost had the nature of a sacrifice, since this death, the atoning for a blasphemy, was an offering to the Unnameable and Holy One himself.

Then Stephanos ceased to glance this way and that, like a frightened animal. He looked up at the sky. Saulos saw the muscles of the youth's chin, throat and chest tauten as he stared upwards and intoned, 'I see the Heavens open and Yeshua at the right hand of God'.

With automatic horror, Saulos hurled his stone. It was as though he had been visited with strength not his own. The stone hurtled through the air and caught Stephanos on the temple, stunning him instantly. After this first stone had been projected, the others followed and before long, the animate beauty of the neaniskos had been reduced to a bloody heap of butcher's meat, a bruised bleeding *thing*, lying in its own blood like the carcases of the sacrificial lambs in the Temple.

Blasphemy called forth the necessity of blood-letting; it could only be appeased by the execution of the evil-speaker. Only the atonement of blood could pay for it. In all the weeks since the stoning of Stephanos, this thought had never left the fevered brain of Saulos. Inevitably, the young man's death recalled that other death, of Yeshua himself, some years previously, in which Saulos, still then a very junior member of Sanhedrin and secretary to the High Priest, had played a minor role. Yeshua had blasphemed. True, it had been necessary to bribe false witnesses to say so, but that was only because at the time of the trial, the Galilean had been so abominably silent. He who had disturbed the whole fabric of religion and society by his words during the previous three years would then say nothing to his accusers. The stream of jokes, stories and paradoxes with which his public speeches and his tavern-talk were larded had dried up. So, Annas had arranged for the usual false witnesses to come forward and claim that Yeshua had put himself on a level with the Almighty, or even claimed to

161

be the Almighty. Saulos could have saved Yeshua. He knew that this, most precisely, was what Yeshua had never claimed.

'Why call me good?' he had asked in that maddeningly quibbling, seemingly frivolous tone. 'No one is good but God.'

That made it quite clear that Yeshua did not think he was God; but when the false witnesses said otherwise, he would say nothing to contradict them; nothing to gainsay the preposterous claim that he had made himself the King of the Jews.

When they brought Yeshua back from the torturers, that was the last time that Saulos had seen the man at close quarters: the thorn crown rammed on to his bleeding brow, the robe of purple around his naked, bruised body. The rest – when they compelled Yeshua to drag his cross through the streets of Jerusalem out to the Place of the Skull – Saulos had been unable to watch. It was the just penalty of the law, of Roman *lex*, for by making himself a king, Yeshua had defied the authority of Imperial Kaiser. From a window in the High Priest's house, Saulos could look out of the city towards the hillside where the crucifixions took place. There were always crosses erected there, holding up their victims like bloody scarecrows until sundown. He had not needed to watch. He knew that somewhere among the forest of crosses, the divine Jester of Nazareth was receiving his reward. It had been the ending, as Saulos believed, the purging of a lifelong obsession. Until Yeshua was dead, the faith of Saulos would never be safe. It had become as bald a choice as that. The love-hate which he felt for Yeshua would not rest. The humour of the Carpenter was one of the things which most disturbed Saulos. Someone would ask Yeshua to explain the love of God. Yeshua would describe his mother fussing because she had lost a coin she put down on the kitchen table for the shopping, and how no one in the household was allowed to rest until she had found it. And then when she found it all her agitation turned to joy and the neighbours would be asked to celebrate as though the discovery of one lost coin were worth a festival of rejoicing. And Saulos could see that the story, as told, was funny; not because he himself laughed, not because he had himself ever found anything funny in his entire life, but because it made the crowds laugh. And their laughter, and his inability to laugh, made Saulos pine to be a part of the accepting and good-humoured moral world which Yeshua inhabited, even though with another part of himself it made Saulos shudder, to

162

hear Yeshua speak so familiarly of God. The Galilean had taught illiterates, buffoons who could not possibly understand all the implications of the Torah, to believe that they could approach the unapproachable majesty of the Almighty Mystery, and call It, 'Our Dad'.

Saulos had wanted Yeshua dead, and when there seemed a danger that Yeshua's followers would revive his heresies and group themselves together in a new movement called the Way, he had been uncontrollably anxious that they should be eliminated. Gamaliel, his old teacher from university days, had been puzzled by his fury. Was it not better, and kinder, to let the Way die its own death, in the manner of all previous such enthusiasms? There had been so many other prophets, particularly from Galilee, troubling the tranquil surface of life for a while, attracting followers by their supposed miracles, and then passing into the obscurity of the grave. Their credulous disciples claimed for them miraculous powers, the capacity to heal lepers, or to give sight to the blind. Who could know the truth of such things? The air was full of demons, spirits and powers, which could be harnessed for the good or evil of mankind, and wizards and shamans had always been able to harness them, just as in times past, the Witch of Endor had brought back King Saul from the dead. Safe, cynical, religious old Gamaliel had been in favour of allowing the Way to go its way. To persecute would merely make its adherents into martyrs.

Gamaliel had put his scrawny old arm round the small simian shoulders of Saulos.

'Let it be, let it go,' he had counselled. 'You have this man of Galilee in your mind, and he is swelling out of all proportion. Perhaps, my dear, you feel guilty about your part in his trial. It was a shabby business, if the truth is told.'

Saulos had stiffened.

'There was nothing shabby about it and I feel no guilt. The Torah had to be defended against blasphemy.'

What business of Gamaliel's was it, how Saulos *felt*? Part of Saulos had wanted to disclose his heart to his wise old tutor. In his awkwardness and uncontrollable anger, he envied the old man's urbanity.

'Yeshua was a very good man,' said Gamaliel. These words were a bitter gall to the young fanatic who wanted to block his ears as the old man continued. 'I am thankful that in the end it was the Romans who executed him and that he was not given the Jewish condemnation of stoning. We should all have known that that was wrong. Even Caiaphas was saying to me the other day that the thing should never have come to trial. Maybe it never would have done so, my dear, if you had not made friends with Judas Iscariot, and started that rumour that Yeshua was in league with the zealots and planning an uprising against the Romans. It was that which tipped the balance against Yeshua in the mind of Pontius Pilate. I am sure of that. You, though, became too involved emotionally.'

'It was simply a matter of law, of principle,' said Saulos stiffly. Gamaliel smiled at him kindly.

'You know, Saulos, I think you envied Yeshua.'

'Why do you say that?'

'Because Yeshua was one of that rare class of being, a man who was at one with himself and at one with God. He had somehow learnt the secret of how to live, how to be simple. That was what made him invulnerable, even when he had been beaten by the soldiers and dragged out to die on Skull Hill he was still in his own mysterious fashion strong, because he had never been, as most men are, at war with himself. He had always been the same person. I've known the family for years. He is a cousin of Yusif of Arimathea, you know, that charming man in the treasury who arranged his funeral.'

'I know.'

'Oh, I can remember Yeshua coming to argue with us when he was just a little lad, preparing for his Bar-Mitzphah. He *was* a clever little thing. He knew the Scriptures as well as the wisest doctors of the Law, and yet he had an almost idiot simplicity. Miriam, his poor distracted mother – you know it is always said she has blue blood in her veins – a direct descendant of King David.'

'I've heard that.'

'I remember her, anyway, saying to me, Yeshua says that we should live like the birds. "What, I say to him, do we do for money, answer me that?" "God feeds and clothes the birds," said Yeshua, "why should he not feed you, Mother?" Yes, Yeshua was at one with himself and at one with God. Most of us are at war with ourselves. We want to be chaste, but we find it hard; we want to live simply, but we crave riches. When we meet a figure like Yeshua in whom these conflicts do not seem to exist, we find it disturbing. That happened to you, didn't it, my dear? And so you wanted to kill him; you wanted to kill his freedom, his ability to live without conventions, his natural goodness. If all men were like Yeshua, there would be no need for laws, or the Law.'

'He mixed with harlots,' said Saulos, 'drunkards, quisling collaborators with the Roman authorities, as well as with the zealots whom you mentioned, hothead terrorists who are willing to put innocent civilian lives at risk for the sake of their political ideas. Yeshua had no morality at all.'

'No,' agreed Gamaliel. 'None at all. That is what I have been saying. Morality is only for sinners. Do you remember how he broke up the rabble when they were going to stone that adulteress?'

'Typical interference in the due processes of the law.'

'And he said, "Let the man who has no sin cast the first stone".'

'The casuistry is typical of the man,' said Saulos. 'That is the sort of thing he was always saying. But it is all perfectly clear. The Law prescribes, in cases of flagrant adultery. . . .'

'Yes, yes, the Law prescribes. But I wonder if you would have thrown a stone at that woman after Yeshua had said those words.'

'Certainly I should.'

'Saulos – my dear – what is the Torah?'

'That is a schoolroom question. The Torah is the mind and will of the Almighty, graven on Sinai stone by His own right hand, the gift of the all-Holy to his chosen people, written in our hearts and inscribed in the holy scrolls of our scriptures. He has spoken to our race, alone and select throughout the entire world. While the rest of humankind sank into moral chaos and depravity, the Jews have kept alight the sacred knowledge of how mankind should live.'

'True, the Jews are the conscience of the human race. But even the sacred Torah itself is no more than a shadow, an echo of God's mind in man's mind. It was drawn up because men and women are sinful. But if there were another way, if there came among us a man who was so in tune with the mind of God and so at one with God, that he felt no instinct to murder, to steal, to commit adultery, what then? Would he not be entitled to show no interest in what you and I call morality?'

'There is no such man and never was,' said Saulos, but the words scalded him as he spoke them.

'I think we might have wanted to kill such a man if he had been born of our race,' said Gamaliel. 'That is why I ask you, "What is the Torah?" There are the laws of the schoolmasters and the armies and the judiciaries. Those who break them are punished and in time, those who exercise authority come to believe in law for its own sake. They fall in love with punishment itself, they enjoy condemnation, they forget that Our Father in Heaven is a loving God who forgives our sins and cleanses us from all unrighteousness. There are other sorts of law, however, and those are what we call the laws of nature. Fire burns, so it is not wise to put your hands in the flame. Weights fall to the ground, so it is not safe to step off a cliff top. What if the laws of morality were really laws of this order, part of His loving care, mere warnings to us that we shall suffer in our inward selves if we seek only to live for ourselves, if we nurse anger or pursue greed and lust? Then, could we not feel that these laws, implanted in the hearts of all, and not just in the hearts of Jews, were not the end of life, but merely the beginning of wisdom, and that those who transgressed these laws were not to be punished but to be pitied, as we might pity the folly and carelessness of a child who had thrust his hand into the fire? You remember what they reported Yeshua as saying when he was lifted up on to the cross?'

'Yes.'

'They are not easy words to forget, are they, my son?'

'No.'

'Father, forgive them – they know not what they do.'

Gamaliel was right. The words could not be forgotten. They were intolerable. Saulos did not want such forgiveness. He did not want the liberty of living as Yeshua had taught us to live. If there was need for forgiveness then this was only another way of saying that there was a cause for condemnation. If those who condemned Yeshua to die on the cross needed to be forgiven, then they were guilty of a terrible crime, at best the killing of an innocent man, at worst, something much graver and more mysterious. Stephanos in his homiletic martyrion had declared the crucifying of Yeshua to be the killing of the Holy One of God, the slaying of the Christ. Among those who followed the Way there was even talk of Yeshua himself being the promised Messias. The wilder among them even claimed that they had been granted visions of Yeshua after he had died, but since a large proportion of these were women there was no need to take them particularly seriously.

So, Saulos had led the persecution of Stephanos and yes, yes! Saulos had cast the first stone. Saulos had torn with a boulder at that smooth skin and cracked the beautiful temple of the young man. And he would go on killing followers of the Way until he had stamped them out and rid the world of their immoral poison.

'Father forgive them for they know not what they do.'

Yeshua had been speaking, presumably, only of his persecutors as they nailed him to the Cross at Passover time. Saulos had subsequently come to believe that the utterance was of a far broader consequentiality. If the race of mankind knew not what it did, if they were in fact a race of moral idiots, ethical imbeciles, then forgiveness or contempt were the only possible reactions they deserved. But, if that were the case, what was the position of the Jews, who were very far from being moral idiots? For they *did* know what they were doing – they had the Torah! Was their self-discipline, honesty, sobriety to count for nothing in the eyes of the Almighty? And if virtue counted for nothing, what *could* win God's favour and love? Yeshua, in his stories and apothegms spoke as if we could not, did not need to, bargain with God. His love was poured out for us without our asking for it, like the love of that father in the story of the prodigal son. The boy did not have to earn his father's favour when, having wasted all his substance, he turned for home. The father was awaiting for him at the gate, ready to kill the fatted calf and put the best robe on his lost child, now found again. Saulos had so easily identified with the elder brother in that story who sulked and refused to come to share in the festivities of the fatted calf. The father seemed to want to place the two brothers on the same moral level. The love of the father was not won or earned by all the loyalty and hard work of the good elder brother. Did this mean that the sin of mankind was not going to be *paid for*? Surely, Saulos believed, there must be punishment for wrongdoing? The patterns of natural justice demanded it. And if the words of Yeshua had been true it was hard to see how moral imperatives had any seriousness, how, indeed, they remained imperatives at all. If the reward is fatted calf, whether you work hard or waste your substance, what is the point of working hard?

Such questions throbbed through the mind of Saulos in subsequent weeks, as he continued to persecute the followers of the Way. He found it extremely easy work to persuade most of the fools, when they were arrested, to recant the error of their ways. He began to notice within himself the capacity to persuade people. The more simple-minded ones, in particular, were putty in his fingers. It interested him, moreover, that none of these enthusiastic followers of Yeshua and his Way even began to see his religious significance or importance. Of course, this was chiefly because they were too stupid, but even the intelligent ones like Yeshua's cousin Yusif of Arimathea seemed woefully unable to concentrate on the central, pivotal thing. Yusif believed that Yeshua offered a new Way of living, but this was little more than an extension of the baptism of Joanes the Baptiser. Turn again! Change! Find newness of life in the knowledge that God is Abba, Father.

Did they not see the paradox in Yeshua's vision of the universe and of the human race, that such a turning was impossible? Oh, men could turn, but they could not change what they were inside. Saulos remembered the scorching love in Yeshua's eyes when he said, 'You lack one thing – go and sell all and give to the poor.' Always, in Yeshua's vision of mankind, it would lack one thing.

Chastity, as defined by any sane or legal definition must mean an abstention from lustful behaviour. 'But I say to you,' Yeshua had proclaimed, 'that anyone who looks at another to lust after her, has already committed adultery in his hearts.' It was not enough to abstain from violence. Yeshua searched out even the involuntary anger of the human heart. 'Be ye therefore perfect, even as your Father in Heaven is perfect. . . .' 'Why call me good? No one is good, only God. . . .'

Precisely by his goodness, and by his searching reappraisal of the very nature of ethics, Yeshua had revealed the great ache in the universe, the gulf between our good desires and the divine perfection. He had placed the virtuous Pharisee and the sinful publican on the same level before God, because both fall short of the divine perfection. His shortlived popularity with the mob could partly be explained by his humorousness, his attractiveness, his apparent easiness. 'Learn from me – my yoke is easy and my burden light.' And they had been drawn to that, the fools, and not realised that this was itself a condemnation of the human race, a nullifying of all the ethical codes and moral systems which good men had been painstakingly devising since the dawn of consciousness.

Yeshua's religion derived from the Psalter and explored with relentless and unsparing extremism the implications of those haunting songs. The relationship between God and the Psalmist was that of a tempestuous love affair, a catalogue of reconciliations, estrangements, battles, tenderness, desolation. Yeshua's last words on the Cross were reported to have been a quotation from the Psalms – 'My God, my God, why hast thou forsaken me?' In those words, Saulos now began to see, Yeshua had spoken not only for himself in his loneliness, he had spoken for the entire human race. Why were the race of men God-forsaken? Had the Psalmist not also written that God was a loving father who forgave men their sins? As far as the east is from the west, so far hath he set our sins from us? But how, how, was this forgiveness to be achieved? 'Thou desirest not sacrifice, else had I given it thee. . . . The sacrifice of God is a troubled spirit, a broken and contrite heart, O God, thou wilt not despise. . . .' Yet the voice of the Almighty in the face of sin must always be the same: 'Forty years long was I grieved with this generation and said: it is a people who have erred in their hearts and who have not known my ways, unto whom I swear in my wrath, that they should not enter into my rest.'

This was the rub. Even God could not undo sin. Merely to say that God *forgave* would be to destroy all moral imperatives in the world, for if God merely forgave and overlooked all wrongdoing, why should we esteem virtue more than vice? Why not steal?

'Why call me good? Only God is good!'

'Thou desirest not sacrifice, else. . . .'

God did desire sacrifice. Of this, Saulos became increasingly convinced. He felt that he, and he alone, could see clearly what Yeshua had been saying, and more than saying, what Yeshua had been doing. During those final ignominious days of Yeshua's life, Saulos and the others had collected the witnesses against him, had him arrested, beaten, tortured, killed. . . . Ever since, Saulos had lived with the guilty knowledge that he had condemned an innocent man. But there was something further, a feeling of disjointedness about the whole experience, and he now began to ask himself whether Yeshua had not in some mysterious fashion been in control, whether he had not wanted this death, whether this death of a pure, innocent victim, this offering of a perfected humanity, was not the arcane healing for which the universe yearned and travailed. No one is good but God. We can only call God Abba if we are reconciled to him through the death of Yeshua. . . .

Saulos felt the attractiveness of these new and wholly strange ideas as others might be drawn to the sensualities of Eros or to the lure of narcotics. He knew them to be a terribly, explosively dangerous set of assumptions. He felt that he himself, and all his religion, and the very Temple itself at Jerusalem with all its hierarchies, laws, rubrics and formularies, its priests and levites, its screaming goats and birds spattering their blood in the area of sacrifice, its money-changers and treasurers, would be overthrown if Yeshua had been right. By Yeshua, Saulos meant his vision of Yeshua. This was what made it so imperative to destroy the religion of Yeshua, the followers of the Way. Yeshua was not merely an itinerant exorcist, who told people funny stories in order to inspire them to become better Jews. If Saulos was right . . . . If Saulos was right, Yeshua was not merely claiming to be the Anointed Messias of God, but in his deliberate act of self-sacrifice on the Cross. . . . Such thoughts stopped being thoughts and became wild visions in which Yeshua had a superhuman status, in which his death had undone the profound ache in nature's heart and reconciled the erring hearts of men to the fountain of goodness. And this was to make him into a being of divine power. Saulos thought of that long, strange face which he had first seen as a little child in Britain so many years since, and then of Yeshua the man, the disturbing combination of absolute love and absolute knowingness in those dark, humorous eyes. Even to have the thoughts which were now possessing Saulos was an act of blasphemy. The thoughts held out to him the supreme temptation. His guilty part in the Crucifixion would become, not the worst thing he had ever done in his life, but the best. The murder of the innocent of Golgotha became a triumph of God's purposes. He could positively glory in the Cross!

No, no, no! He must suppress these thoughts, and he must suppress the followers of the Way before they realised its significance. The heart of the Way for these simpletons consisted in brotherly love, holding things in common, being diligent in their Temple-observance, and generous in alms. They still spoke of the death of Yeshua as a disgrace to those Jewish authorities who had not recognised him for the great prophet he was. These fools thought that Yeshua had been teaching them a simple ethical system, and they were trying to put it into practice. They did not see. . . . Pray God, they would never see. . . . It was Saulos's own secret, the knowledge of what Yeshua had been doing, alone in the darkling desolation of Golgotha. It was the ultimate witchcraft, the deepest magic, the strangest and most terrible, and most wonderful idea, one which would transform the world even as it was trying to transform Saulos. But he would not let it, he would not.

The Way was even attracting adherents in the Diaspora. Saulos heard a rumour that it was infecting the synagogue at Damascus. Gamaliel and the older members of the Sanhedrin had laughed when Saulos had announced this. So, a few Jews in Syria were being kind to the poor, and living in a commune where they shared all their few possessions! Was that a reason for becoming so angry? What authority did the High Priest in Jerusalem have over Damascus? Saulos spoke as if it was the end of the world. Yes, he had retorted, furiously, to Gamaliel. 'It *is* the end of the world!'

'Oh, let him go,' said Gamaliel. 'There is a good Jew there called Ananias. He'll explain what they are doing.'

Saulos had insisted on getting letters from the High Priest to the leaders of the synagogue in Damascus, telling any followers of 'the Way' that they must return at once to Jerusalem and justify themselves in Sanhedrin.

It was an excessively hot day, one in which the sun dazzled, the dust choked and merely to be out of doors was a species of torture. Saulos felt heady in such weather, though frightened that he would be revisited by the mild epileptic convulsions with which demons had tormented him since childhood. If it had been possible to stop thinking, if only it had been possible to stop thinking for five minutes about Yeshua, and the Way, and the Cross. . . . What peace would follow. But his brain raced and churned with it. Sometimes, within the space of a minute, Saulos had experienced violently contradictory emotions: sentimental piety for kind, humorous Yeshua being killed on a cross; gnawing guilt for his own part in that death; certainty that it was all for the good, the more so if it were a death of necromantic power in which Yeshua was himself summoning up great strengths and powers by his sacrifice. And all the time, throbbing through his whole being, Saulos had the appalled and grief-stricken knowledge that he loved Yeshua, he loved that man as he had never loved anyone before and now he was separated from the possibility of that love for ever. . . . Jangling of bridles, flash of sunlight on the horse-furniture of the servants who accompanied Saulos on his journey, high sun and further along the road, a figure. . . . A beggar – the roads were dotted with them, always. A leper? Saulos blinked and the man was no longer there. He blinked again and his eyes were dazzled by the sun. There *was* a figure, standing now directly in his horse's track. The beast reared. Saulos gazed towards the sun and saw the face of Yeshua Messias.

'Saulos, Saulos, why are you persecuting me?'

'You? Who are you?'

'Yeshua Bar-Yusif, whom you are still persecuting. But it is hard for you to go on fighting. . . .'

Saulos had fallen from his horse. He lay on the road with his eyes closed, but he could still see that beautiful face and it no longer caused him any torment. It was looking at him with absolute love.

FOUR

A year passed, possibly a little longer. I had not got very far with my book on the Lampitt family, but I now made a weekly visit to Sargie – notionally to 'help with his letters'. His correspondence was in fact negligible, and on most weeks, my secretarial duties did not extend beyond a walk to the local off-licence where I was expected to procure half a dozen bottles of 'what killed Auntie'. Of course, no reference was implied, by Sargie's rather hackneyed kenning, to either of his actual aunts, Gloria Boyd-Fleet, his mother's sister, nor to old Michael Lampitt's sister Lavinia. [I remember her architectural water-colours hanging on the rectory walls. 'Well in the Shotter Boys league' was Uncle Roy's verdict on these accomplishments. Critical rigour was never brought into play when surveying the achievements of Sargie's family. Uncle Roy, for example, was the only person whom I ever heard to praise the Symphonic Poems of Campbell Dilkes, Lavinia's husband, a minor musician, a friend of Elgar's, and a collector, with Vaughan Williams and Cecil Sharp, of English folksongs. (Strangely enough, Campbell Dilkes achieved immortality through one air, though few who listen to it know the name of the composer: the melody from his 'Surrey Rhapsody' is used as the theme tune for the Mulberrys.)]

After a session with Sargie the essential difficulty of the man would sometimes overwhelm me. His whims and violent mood-swings would have repelled any but one like myself who had known him a long time and fallen into the habit of making repeated allowances. On that particular afternoon, when my narrative resumes, Sargie had been shedding gin tears on my arrival (supposed fear that I had forgotten the appointment, certainty that no one really liked him, fury with Vernon for having Cecily to stay at Mallington the previous week) to a quite different mood. Within half an hour of the deep, self-pitying melancholy which greeted my arrival, he had been cackling with ruthless glee at the latest edition of *The Spark*. He flung it across the room for me to read.

'Second para, my dear, on the gossip page, the "Diary" thing. What's Lover Boy going to make of that, do you suppose?'

The paragraph read as follows:

To the House of Lords to lunch with my old friend Lord ('Ernie') Lampitt to commiserate with him for not being chosen as a member of the new government. Harold, it would seem, had more or less promised him a Cabinet post, but a certain lady who has the Prime Minister's ear was said to be opposed to the appointment.

Ernie can perhaps turn his attention to family matters. Jason Grainger of 'The Mulberrys' (otherwise known as Julian Ramsay) is to undertake the history of the Lampitts, and looks likely to drag many skeletons out of the family cupboards.

We have not been able to gauge the reaction to Mr Grainger's work by that other Lampitt biographer – televisionary and man-about-literary-London Raphael Hunter. No doubt Mr Grainger will be able to shed light on the mysterious death, seventeen years ago, of James Petworth Lampitt, the bachelor man of letters, who fell to his death from a fire escape into the area beneath his flat in Manchester Square. Did Lampitt fall, or was he pushed? Since only his biographer, Mr Hunter, was present on this occasion, he is perhaps in a position to supply this vital information. We wonder how many cases there are in which a biographer has been the agent of his subject's demise?

I was astonished that Darnley had chosen to print all this stuff. My first reaction was one of selfish annoyance that he had somehow involved *me* in the story. I was in no better position than anyone else to know how Jimbo died, and by suggesting that I would tell the story, *The Spark* managed to implicate me in their scarcely covert assertion that Hunter had murdered the old man. Since it was over a year since Robey had begun to voice this thought, it seemed extraordinary that Darnley should have chosen now, of all times, to print the story.

When I had absorbed the surprisingness of the story being printed, I was able to feel further surprise at Sargie's reaction. Probably there is no appropriate reaction to the discovery, or suggestion, long after a brother's death, that he had in fact met a violent end. I was shocked, none the less, by the absence of sadness in Sargie as he crowed over the story. He appeared to view the whole matter as a weapon against Hunter, detestation of whom grew with the passage of time.

'So – Lover Boy's got his come-uppance at last!'

'I don't quite see that, Sargie.'

'He's only been exposed as a murderer!'

'Accused, not exposed. He's bound to sue the paper for libel, and I should think he'll make a lot of money out of it.'

'Wouldn't dare, my dear. Your friend Darnley's got him on toast. If he comes to court, Darnley will produce evidence. Vebba clebba febba, Darnley. I'm only sorry they've abolished the rope. Perhaps Harold will bring it back; he seems so bloody keen on giving the IP what they want, and apart from an indoor topos, it's the one thing most English people most ardently desire, the restoration of the gallows.'

'Darnley hasn't enough evidence to hang his hat on, let alone hang Hunter.'

'You'll see, my dear. Lover Boy won't sue, too much of a coward, and that'll be an admission of guilt. You'll see – he's guilty as hell.'

There were the words which were still repeating themselves inside my head as, one evening, I stewed in the Miller Street baths. For some time, I had been a devotee of Turkish baths. To be lightly poached in the steam rooms, to be so intensely hot and moist that all physical strains and all thoughts were purged by the mere concentration of breathing in that atmosphere, produced sensations of well-being which were incomparable. I would always emerge from the baths with my worries in better perspective and the general melancholy of life momentarily assuaged. I had tried several Turkish baths, but the Miller Street ones were my favourite, not least because they were only a very short walk from my home. That proud old Victorian building off Camden High Street was pulled down long ago. It constituted a weird place of architectural eclecticism. Outside, its plain brick façade and pillared portico suggested the Queen Anne revival of the 1890s. Inside, you passed through a sitting-out room lined with cubicles and divans whose décor blended music-hall and pub in its riot of Edwardian baroque, its gilded electroliers and lamp brackets, its green flock fleur-de-lis wallpaper. Changed, wrapped round with towels, one descended the gradual stairs to an area of cold

175

pools, a poor man's version of the Arab hall at Leighton House, where a fountain splashed against sub-de Morgan turquoise tiles. Beyond the cold baths, the showers, and beyond them, the steam rooms, Vales of Lethe where libel, *The Spark*, the emotional lives of friends, the problems of what to do with one's life, all slowly sweated themselves into nothingness and evaporated in the steam. The atmosphere was as thick as one of the old pea-soup fogs evoked in the Sherlock Holmes stories, or as the profoundest sea-mist in a late canvas by Turner. One was aware that there were electric lights shining somewhere, giving a yet more ethereal quality to the thick vapours, now purest white, now evanescent silver, through which the eye was aware of other human figures, but so dimly aware that it would not be quite true to say that one *saw* them. Only thick smudges of grey appeared to the sight, sometimes assuming form, sometimes fading to whiteness again, as, in the first shock of extreme heat, I breathed through my mouth and peered about to find my way to the edge of the room and the benches which lined the wall.

The room, for all I knew, could have contained two or twenty people. It was impossible to gauge. Only when my nose was almost touching the wall tiles could I discern a patch of empty bench and deposit myself upon it, waiting for the next faint evaporation of the steam to see whether I could stretch myself out without kicking another man in the face.

One's eyes accustom themselves gradually to such an atmosphere. It grew more possible to sense, at least, if not to see the presence of others. Then the steam lessened for a while to the point where the grey smudges took human shape and colour and one saw here a scarlet pot-belly, there a hairy shoulder blade. There is a passage in the Bible which Uncle Roy enjoyed declaiming where the prophet Isaiah had a vision in the Temple: the Holy of Holies is filled with smoke, and through the fumes and the rays of light he makes out the presence of six-winged angels. Miller Street baths conjured up visual experiences comparably remote from everyday. I knew that there was a figure quite near me, and when the mist cleared and I could make out its shape, younger than the last pot-bellies glimpsed but not unflabby in its soft sloping shoulders and rather full breasts, making me have a moment of wondering whether I had accidentally strayed into the baths during a women's session, and whether the hirsute limbs half glimpsed earlier had been figures of my imagination. The figure who had arrested my attention was, I decided, just too close to me on the bench for it to be easy to stretch out my legs, so I swivelled myself once more into a sitting posture and buried my face in a towel for a further five or ten minutes of pure thoughtless sensation. (Keats, in the mood which made him exclaim, 'O for a life of sensations, rather than of thoughts!' would have been happy in the Miller Street baths.)

When I removed the towel from my face, it seemed as if the soft, womanish body on my left had edged nearer. Certainly now, there would have been no question of stretching out horizontally on the bench, as I had originally considered. He was so close that he was visible all the time, even at the thickest swirling of the steam, close enough for me to be able to see him, and to be aware, though I could not make out his face, that he was peering intently in my direction. Moreover, his hands clutched the edge of the bench, and one of them, his right hand, was now within inches of my thigh.

I was not so naïf as to suppose that everyone attended Turkish baths purely for the enjoyment of steam and heat. The proximity of scantily clad sweating male bodies never happened to be a temptation to myself, but – *chacun à son goût*. I had never seen any man at the Miller Street baths behaving in a remotely suggestive manner, but for some reason on this occasion, the hand of my near neighbour, even though it was not yet touching me, made me think that I was unquestionably in the presence of a man on the prowl for a sexual partner. It seemed the moment to cross one's legs and fold one's arms. The only irritation it caused me was that it forced me to think, or to have semi-coherent thoughts, until the remedy occurred. I could stand up and find a space on the bench on the other side of the room. I did so, wandering somewhat more cautiously now through the Dantean fogs and half-embodied shapes on the mosaic floor. It was only when I crossed the room and found a completely empty bench, where I could stretch out with ease, that I realised that I had been followed. The womanish form was there at my side. In quite insistent, nasal tones, it spoke.

'Shall we sit down together?'

'I don't think so,' I said.

As I replied, the steam cleared momentarily to reveal our faces to one another and I found myself looking into the eyes of Raphael Hunter.

The embarrassment of the situation was potentially enormous, not least because I had an irrational fear that he might think I had been pursuing *him*. As a young man, I worried very much about how other people would assess my own sexual proclivities; it is one of the blessings of age that one ceases to mind about these things.

My ex-mother-in-law, Sibs Starling, used to assert that 'there was a pansy on the top of every omnibus', an article of faith not often substantiated, I should guess, from a personal experience. She considered herself rather an expert at nosing 'them' out, and often hinted that she thought Hunter was 'one of them'. When her daughter Anne formed her disastrous infatuation for Hunter, about a year after I married her, I had given little credence to Sibs's suggestion that Hunter was ambivalent in preference. Bloom had once told me that Hunter was homosexual, but Bloom believed that this was true of most men, even though some, for their own baffling reasons, chose to conceal this taste by the casting up of contrary smokescreens. The fact that a man like Hunter had a string of female conquests behind him (I myself knew, from first-hand observation, of Miss Beach, Vanessa Faraday, Felicity, Isabella Marno the actress, and my wife Anne) was all the more reason, in Bloom's eyes, for guessing that Hunter's interests really lay elsewhere.

'It stands out a mile, darling.'

'What does?'

This, on my part, entirely unintentional *double entendre* provoked one of Bloom's explosions of abandoned mirth, tongue out, eyes rolling, a laugh which seemed to bear relation to narcotic or religious ecstasy.

'Well, perhaps not a mile. Not on that young lady. O, darling, you'll kill Mother if you make too many cock jokes.' He dabbed the corner of tearful eyes with a red and white spotted handkerchief. 'But those women in Miss Hunter's life – little lesbian affairs for her – they don't fool Mother. They never last, you see. A whole string of women, all for show like a little string of pearls on her little twinset. It's the way queens behave. We can never be happy with a good thing when we see it. Straight men give up the chase eventually.'

'Not always. What about Casanova?'

Another pause for manic eldritch laughter.

'By this view, any deviation from pure, heterosexual, lifelong monogamy would really be a sign of. . . .'

'Don't be shy, darling, you can tell Mother.'

Bloom patted my hand.

'Mind you,' he added, 'I think that's true. Faggots flit from flower to flower, busy little bees that they are, cruising down the river, popping in and out of the cottages.' His eyes rolled at this strange pair of expressions, more redolent of *Wind in the Willows* than the actual range of activities denoted. 'You know, I think the straightest guy I've ever known is you, Rikko.'

He stroked the shoulder of Rikko Kempe's windjammer. Everyone else with us at the pub that evening had laughed. Rikko patted a violently blonded perm with his carefully manicured hand, pursed glossed lips and fluttered mascara'd eyes crossly.

'This is a very boring subject,' he said in his gravelliest, most manly, Stan Mulberryish tones.

Fenella, his wife, never quick on the uptake even when sober, had stirred herself on her bar stool and grinned winsomely at Bloom as if imploring him to hold the lid on this Pandora's box and keep his reflections to himself. She began an anecdote about Lord Kitchener.

'Shut up, Fenella, you did not know him,' said Rikko petulantly.

'My father and he were best friends. They knew everything about one another.'

'Lord Kitchener liked buggering women, we know,' said Bloom. 'That's not what we're talking about.'

'Oh,' said Fenella.

She grinned yet more fixedly, hoping that no one would ask her at that vodka-soaked stage of evening, to make any comment to demonstrate that she had been following the previous line of argument.

That conversation with Bloom, and the judgements of Sybil, probably came to mind after my Miller Street encounter with Hunter, but the essence of their theme, and the whole question of the ambiguity of human emotions, and the fallibility of judgements based on appearances, did sweep into my mind there and then.

Hunter, however, was nothing if not brazen in his approach to social difficulties. How else could he have smiled in the faces of so many men whom he had cuckolded, or heartbreakingly contrived to offer friendship, the very last thing they at that stage wanted, to women whom he had discarded as sexual partners? So now, semi-naked in the steam, and very nearly unmasked as the sort of faintly pathetic individual who might risk arrest and imprisonment for making a nuisance of himself in a public place, Hunter stepped back from the moment and resumed control. It had, after all, only been a split second during which his guard had dropped and, if his next sentence were true, then his first – 'Shall we sit down together?' – was stripped of any suggestive purport.

'I was fairly sure it was you, Julian. Well met.'

This was a matter of opinion. I considered walking away from him into the steam. Certainly an encounter with Hunter was calculated within seconds to undo the therapeutic effect of the steam room and to bring to mind not merely the women he had made unhappy, but also, all those Hunterish questions about life itself, the extent to which one was a success or a failure, the degree to which one had got on.

'We could go and sit in the hot rooms where there is no steam.'

He spoke quietly. We could, I thought, do as he suggested. Alternatively, he could stick his head in the toilet and pull the chain on it.

Strangely enough, though, it was impossible, in Hunter's presence, to allow the slightest unpleasantness to show through. His own smiling gentleness of manner neutered all situations, making them pappy as his prose, pasty as his skin. I found myself obediently following him into the hot rooms.

He held the door open for me as he said, 'You will have guessed that there are a couple of things I wanted to talk about.'

His words and manner put the embarrassing moment of a few seconds earlier firmly out of mind, implying almost that I had come to Miller Street baths specifically for the purpose of talking literary 'shop' with Hunter, even, perhaps, that this was something we did together quite regularly.

'First let me say, I'm thrilled, truly, about the idea of your Lampitts book,' he said.

'Who told you I was writing it?' I asked, hoping very much that he had not read about it in *The Spark*.

'Madge' (his publisher) 'keeps her ear to the ground. Now, some people have already spoken as if you been setting yourself up as my rival. They'll say anything to create mischief. I've already made it clear that I regard you as a friend and the book you are writing will complement my more *literary* biography of Petworth.'

To whom had these assurances been made? For a few more sentences, he prosed on about his own difficulties in getting started with Volume Two, his readiness to help me in any way he could, for example with introductions to Virgil D. Everett, the American collector in whose archive the papers and literary remains of Jimbo were, thanks largely to Hunter's machinations, deposited.

'The Everett Foundation have already said that I can see the Lampitt Papers,' I said. 'Sargie has squared it with them.'

'Oh, he *has*?' That weasely look came into Hunter's face. 'Good, good. I'm not saying this *will* happen, but just in case Sargent has unintentionally queered your pitch. . . .'

'How could he have done that?'

'He may think he has arranged everything with the Everett Foundation, but in fact, by the terms of the purchase, I have the ultimate say-so about who is permitted to consult the Lampitt Archive.' He paused for a while so that I could gasp at the production of this trump card. 'No one can lay a finger on the Lampitt Papers without consulting me, and in this case' – Hunter's voice always became more nasal when emphasising a point – 'no one has in fact consulted me.'

'I thought Virgil D. Everett might have some say in the matter,' I said shortly. 'After all, he owns the Lampitt Papers.'

'I'm sure there'll be no difficulty,' said Hunter. 'It's just a good example, that's all, of how one's got to be – shall we say' – he smiled that indulgent, amused smile of his, creasing and half closing his eyes with mock, or perhaps actual, affection – 'a *little* cautious with some of Sargent's wilder utterances.'

It was hardly a wild utterance of Sargie to say that he had written to the American who had bought his brother's literary remains. I had typed the letter myself and we had received a reply, which I now only understood for the first time, stating that Sargie's request (permission for me to visit New York and read through the manuscripts in the Everett Collection) would almost certainly cause 'no problems' and that the letter had been passed on to the Custodian of the Lampitt Papers to whom all future correspondence should be addressed. Until this encounter in the Miller Street baths, I had forgotten that the Custodian of the Papers was Hunter himself. It was, on the face of it, unlikely that anyone had ever asked before to consult the Lampitt Papers. This was another thing which only began to occur to me then. I had breezily assumed that people were coming into American libraries all the time, leafing through documents for their own obscure purposes, perhaps for no purpose at all other than to pass the time. I had therefore assumed that 'the Custodian' was a busy person, dealing with such requests as my own

181

on a regular basis. But who, now one came to think of it, would wish to consult the Lampitt Papers? The Everett Foundation was in any case a private collection, not a public library or an academic institution. Virgil Everett bought literary manuscripts in the way that other men bought blue chips, as an investment. Hunter had persuaded Everett to make him the 'Custodian' of this particular archive solely to safeguard his own position as Jimbo's biographer. Since my own enterprise could be regarded in some sense as a threat to Hunter, I was not optimistic about my chances of his allowing me to see the papers. I had that feeling which had visited me before in his presence, if not quite of being in his power, at least in a position where he could make a fool of me.

'I've been absurdly busy as usual,' he said, appearing to answer the question I had not asked; more, seeming to indulge me with tit-bits of information for which I was open-mouthed, ravenous. 'The London Library Committee takes up a lot of time, and I've been co-opted on to the Leverhulme thing, and I'm judging no less than six prizes this winter. Then the Government – this is rather between ourselves – wants to set up a committee to advise the new Arts Minister.'

'I think poor Vernon Lampitt was rather hoping for that appointment,' I said.

'Is this another of Sargent's ideas?' He smiled good-humouredly, making me feel that I had made a rather feeble joke which he was trying to find amusing, for politeness's sake. 'Thank goodness, anyway, that we have an Arts Minister at last. 'I've been pressing to have one for years. Jennie is somewhat at sea, which is why I – she – think that such a committee would be no bad idea. I've talked to Charles Snow a certain amount about it, and we've been throwing some very interesting ideas about.'

He shrugged and smiled. Where there were twenty blotters around a table, with Minutes and Apologies for Absence and Any Other Business, there would be Hunter in the midst.

'It leaves little time for writing,' he added. For a moment, as if consulting an order paper he looked down at his navel. 'The other thing which I wanted to pick your brains about is rather more delicate.'

For a moment, I expected an embarrassing confession, a description of the compulsion which led him to follow naked men about steam rooms.

'I know that you are a friend of Miles Darnley,' he said. 'The last time I was in Malvern, Robbie Larmer told me that you and Miles were at Seaforth Grange together.'

Hunter was at least ten years my senior, so we had not overlapped as pupils at Seaforth Grange. He had evidently been one of the headmaster's favourites. In common with most people who attended this hellish establishment, I regarded Mr Larmer as an almost criminal monster, and I could not imagine wishing to remain on terms with him in grown-up life.

'Margot's very much crippled with arthritis.' He sighed to contemplate the sorrows of the headmaster's wife, a figure if anything more insufferably cruel than the Binker himself.

'They are thinking of moving into a bungalow down on Barnard's Green. Robbie's as alert as ever, still manages the *Telegraph* crossword each morning.'

'Surely not a very difficult accomplishment?' This observation of mine sounded harsh, ill-mannered.

'Naturally,' Hunter said, 'I talked over with Robbie what to do about Miles.'

Hunter was leaning forward now, pressing his palms together.

'I've nothing against Miles personally. Nothing. Robbie's view is that I must sue, however, in order to establish the truth. It's a very serious charge, Julian.'

The idea that libel trials clear the air, or establish the truth, is not one borne out by a study of legal history. I did not then know enough to be able to say so to Hunter. I was chiefly arrested by the thought that he still regarded the Binker as a friend and confidant. The Binker had made life insufferable for generations of boys at Seaforth Grange. He was a pervert and a sadist, a criminal whose activities should by rights have been brought to the attention of the police, not a wise old Nestor to whom one would naturally turn in grown-up life for advice about how to conduct one's affairs.

'I suppose Miles wrote the piece himself,' said Hunter. No aggression was visible in his features. He wore the same impassive smile, and spoke in the same toneless voice which would have been adopted had he been presenting the cheque at a poetry prize-giving or making a speech at the AGM of the Royal Society of Literature or the PEN Club. 'I simply have no idea how he could have got hold of such a story: that I, who did so much for Petworth, and so much for his reputation after he had died, that I could have. . . .' Words failed him. 'We've got nearly all his stuff into paperback now, many of them with introductions by myself.'

His tone implied that not marble nor the gilded monuments of princes could be a more enviable memorial for a deceased writer.

'I think they felt. . . .'

'They?'

I was completely convinced, by the testimony of all the Lampitts who had spoken to me about it, that Hunter's claims to have been very close to Jimbo were fraudulent. This was not to say that he was a murderer. I did not know what to think about it all.

Years had passed since I had trusted Hunter, or taken him at his word, but it was perhaps not until this meeting in the Miller Street baths, talking of James Petworth Lampitt, that I reached the view that Hunter was through and through a creature of artifice, a person whose true identity, if it existed at all, had never been displayed and whose projected self, offered to the world as a substitute for actual encounter with a real man, had as little substance as vapour. So forcibly did this image present itself to me that I would hardly have been surprised, now that we were in the dry room where the air was clear and the outlines of benches, chairs, lockers and other bathers were sharp, had Hunter's form evaporated from my sight as it had done in the Stygian fogs of the steam room. The absolute non-existence of the self he had been presenting through the years, and the capacity for inflicting suffering which his fraudulence had explored, had a curiously weakening effect on me. For years, I had supposed that I hated Raphael Hunter, because women I had loved had loved him so distractedly, because his presence in my life had created so much suffering; but I did not really hate him. I realised that for all those years I had been peering into an abyss, confronting an emptiness. My 'jealousy' of Hunter, for example, my obsessive certainty that he had had an affair with my wife, had been hatred of a phantom. I felt, sitting with him, tricked and puzzled. I also felt the extraordinary contrast between Hunter and Rice Robey, the new bane of my life. Both men, certainly, were capable of an impressive series of emotional conquests, but Hunter's success in this area was explained (I now felt) by what he wasn't, not by what he was.

Some great paintings convey their effect by leaving everything out; much oriental art depends on such a principle. This was Hunter. Rice Robey, by contrast, was like some full-square grotesque primitive painting, perhaps one of those curious Ethiopian renderings of

Coptic saints or biblical characters, strong in outline and colour. There was nothing subtle about Rice Robey. Perhaps the confrontation between the two men was an archetypical clash of opposites, just such a conjunction of thesis and antithesis as Rice Robey liked to describe and expound. Undoubtedly – as I will now admit to myself, though I would not admit it at the time – I wanted a confrontation. I had come quite bitterly to resent Rice Robey's power over Felicity. I was jealous of it, though this was something which I did not fully appreciate. Instead, I told myself that I found it *boring* that she spoke of him all the time, tedious that she was deeper in with him as month succeeded month, and that he was not worthy of her, not quite clever enough, not quite something. In fact, I was simply jealous of his hold over her, and over Darnley. It was only during that conversation with Hunter in the Turkish baths that I realised that my feelings about Rice Robey were not in control. I was ready, if necessary, to destroy him. Hunter was fishing for information about the authorship of the libel in *The Spark*. My motives from now onwards became base; I cannot defend myself, but any reader may be puzzled by my behaviour unless recognising that I did not understand the law of libel. I thought – it was probably a measure of my obsession with Rice Robey – that in a case such as this, the litigant would select the author of the offending sentences. It did not quite occur to me that several parties might be sued for the same offence – that Darnley could be sued for publishing the article, the printers for printing it, the newsagents for distributing and selling it. I thought that if responsibility and blame could be shifted to one man – the actual author of the story – Darnley and *The Spark* would escape Hunter's lawyer.

'When you knew Lampitt,' I began. I was never able to indulge in the absurdity of referring to Jimbo as 'Petworth'.

'Yes,' came Hunter's suspicious, nasal reply.

'How much part did a novelist called Albion Pugh play in his life?'

Hunter's smile momentarily vanished; then he laughed nervously.

'Oh, dear,' he said. 'I might have known that *he* was behind all this. You think it is likely he wrote the piece?'

'Certain.'

An expression passed over Hunter's face which made it clear that he had received the information he wanted. It was not an expression of triumph, so much as of finality. The chairman, having seen that there was no more to be discussed under the heading AOB was about to bring the meeting to a conclusion. We parted very shortly afterwards, I to the showers, he for another session in the steam.

I spent that evening dining at a cheap Greek restaurant with a girl. Our affair was not going well, and would soon come to an end. Since my moment of awakening with Felicity – when I held her and tried to comfort her some twelve months earlier, and she admitted to being in love with Rice Robey – girls had come back into my life. There was nothing worth writing down here. It is simply worth noting that life was once again punctuated by affairs. Evenings now were likely to include the cheapest restaurant supper I could find, or a visit to the cinema. I was back into the routine of looking for the perfect mate, an everlasting quest. In my case, ordinary standards disappear when I am engaged in the pursuit: that is, in seeking or finding friends, I have been guided by fondness, liking or shared interest. Many of the girls I saw during that year were, by contrast, not necessarily people I would otherwise have liked. I do not think any of them fell in love with me; they certainly failed to engage my imagination.

Falling in love is the greatest imaginative experience of which most human beings are capable. What happened between myself and my Greek restaurant companion possessed as much imaginative significance as an encounter between two cats on a dustbin lid, possibly less. It was not to be compared with the Wagnerian opera which must have played inside Felicity's head whenever she thought of Rice Robey, a figure with whom she had indulged in no physical intimacy.

I envied Rice Robey's capacity to mythologise existence, to draw out of it shapes, stories, significance. I envied him his charm and his whatever it was he had instead of genius. I was also, as I have indicated, simply jealous of the devotion he excited in Felicity. Since the conversation in which she wept and we had hugged one another, everything had changed between Felicity and me. I saw no signs that she was aware of this. She still came and went. We still ate an evening meal together if no alternative materialised, but continued to have an independent social life. She had quite a number of friends, and I am sure that I was not the only ear into which she eagerly poured her stories of office gossip and the latest utterances or adventures of her sage. But life in Arlington Road was utterly different for me. What had been a companionable, cosily domestic arrangement, had turned into a torment. Visits to the bathroom, for example, were now charged with potential shocks. The size of her large wet footprints on the bath mat caused me paroxysms of frustration, and I more than once caught myself out in strange fetishistic and secret gestures, such as removing my own shoes and socks so as to place my own bare feet in her damp footprints, or taking one of her stockings from the towel rail where it hung to dry and pressing it to my lips.

Felicity, since confiding in me the state of her heart, had settled down. I was her Dutch uncle, and she still spoke obsessively about Rice Robey, but I think she had begun to be able to accept that their relationship would never go further than it had done already. What I had not fully absorbed, since I am not a philosopher, was Rice Robey's importance to her as a man of ideas. He had, though, effected in her an intellectual transition which was as extreme as could have been. My puzzlement, my inability to take in what was happening, could not be blamed on any reluctance of Felicity's to talk about it. Some days, she talked about it for hours at a time. Put simply (which she always refused to do) Rice Robey had converted her to a belief in God. As far as I am aware, this is a belief which has never left her and since religious conversions, in my circle of acquaintance, are rare, I wish I could provide a more coherent account of it.

The subject is one which interests me extremely, not least because I fail to understand it. I suppose that Felicity must be one of the most intelligent people I ever knew, perhaps the most intelligent. It is a pity she was so unwilling to put her ideas in a form which would have been intelligible to the layman. To my untrained eye, it seemed as though what happened was like this. When she withdrew from her job at Rawlinson and entered the Civil Service, she seemed to have reached the limits of her own rigidly empirical view of the universe. Rice Robey's idiosyncratic world-view had an effect on her which I felt to be highly comparable with the effect which reading William Blake had had on me several years before. Felicity denied the points of comparison, insisted that I did not begin to understand the religious viewpoint and further insisted, truthfully and not meaning to be unkind, that my use of language was too imprecise for it to be worth discussing the matter. Blake had changed and enriched my way of viewing life. I supposed that his conflict with eighteenth-century rationalism was comparable with the movements of Felicity's mind as she thrashed around the problems of logical positivism. Blake's importance for me was to make me see that the world of

187

phenomena and of other people is not a fixed set of *things*, to be described or investigated in only one particular manner, but rather, a story which we tell to ourselves, a set of impressions capable of an infinitude of explanations or non-explanations, but which can only be intelligently perceived through the exercise of the imagination. Thus, for each of Sir Isaac Newton's scientific explanations of how the world appears to us, Blake provides an irrational but imaginatively satisfying alternative.

> The atoms of Democritus
> And Newton's particles of light
> Are sands upon the Red Sea Shore
> Where Israel's tents do shine so bright.

I took it that Rice Robey's unfinished scraps of verse and prose about St Paul were exploring similar territory. The significance of St Paul was not that he knew more about Christ than Caiaphas or Pontius Pilate had done. His importance, rather, was imaginative. Questions of theology were not empirical ones. I thought I now saw the point of Rice Robey's distrust of those two words Either/or. *Was Christ Divine?* was a question which deceived us because it appeared to be grammatically comparable to sentences such as *Was Napoleon a Corsican?*, an enquiry which could be settled one way or another by empirical analysis. Had the question of Christ's divinity been like this, his advent into the world could not conceivably have haunted the imagination of mankind for 2,000 years. I could not admire the style of Rice Robey's new book, but I was excited by what seemed to be the central idea, an idea which had application far beyond St Paul: *Each of us comes to fullness of life only when we have learnt how to mythologise it.* My own experience had been shaped by the intricately extensive Lampitt drama being played out inside Uncle Roy's head, a vision wholly at variance with Hunter's plodding account of the same events and people. The Lampitts themselves hated Hunter's book because of its inaccuracies, or what they would see as downright lies. This was certainly one way of viewing Hunter's claim to have been Jimbo's secretary and years-long companion.

I believed Rice Robey's doctrine that we need stories by which to live. Each life needs, and probably creates, a mythology. For me, this makes sufficient sense of the religious question to enable me to leave it alone. For years, I was puzzled by the fact that religious opinions for which there was no shred of evidence or justification were those to which people clung most tenaciously, being prepared to die, or kill, for them. How could this be? In a suffering universe, why had religious people chosen to add to the suffering by resorting to physical violence, torture, wars and murders over such questions as whether the Holy Ghost proceeded from the Father alone or from the Father and the Son; or whether certain legends about the prophet Mahomet were true; or whether men and women were predestined or elected to divine grace. These were things in which it was not, strictly speaking, possible to believe; not in the sure and certain way we can believe in observable phenomena. Then I read in a book that 'religion is what we do with our madness', and I began to understand. The activities of the uncontrolled and unexplored self create religious belief, and it is in this unexplored area that we are most vulnerable. We protect the cloud-capp'd towers and gorgeous palaces of that insubstantial pageant more fervently than we would protect the quantum theory or Newton's Law of Thermodynamics because that is where we have learnt to come to terms with life's pain and muddle, if we have come to terms, which perhaps we never shall and perhaps we should not hope to do. That was what I had come to feel, anyhow, reading Blake, and recognising within myself all kinds of religious impulses which I knew could never honestly be translated into belief.

But Felicity had been rather quiet when I tried to put this point of view to her. This was partly a polite quietness since she evidently did not want to show up the inadequacy of my language, my looseness of expression; but there was more to it than this, for after a while she had quietly said that we evidently had rather different views of the religious question.

It was on some other occasion that she told me why. Apparently 'my' idea that the world is really something which we make up inside our own heads had been in circulation for centuries, certainly since Samuel Johnson refuted the ideas of Bishop Berkeley by kicking a stone. *I refute him thus*. The point, Felicity laboured it, was that there really was a stone, it really existed. I have never said that the stone did not exist, of course, but Felicity said that the logical corollary of my position was that truth did not matter, that we could, if we chose, decide that the stone kicked by Dr Johnson was a phantom, or a spoonful of mashed potato, and once you had gone down that path, Fliss said, of truth not mattering, there was no point in having any discussions or views about anything. And then we had a brief moment of agreeing that probably 'views' weren't very interesting, certainly less interesting than gossip; and we talked of the novels we liked reading, and remarked on the fact that in English, 'gossip' or interest in human character had called forth all the best writing; that even writers who could easily have devoted their writing lives to the cerebral exploration of ideas, like George Eliot, were at their most riveting when discussing and describing human character, and though 'ideas' might come into their books, they would not spoil the narrative flow by long disquisitions on metaphysical subjects. And at the mention of metaphysics, Fliss returned to the fray and said that I entirely misunderstood Rice Robey, probably misunderstood William Blake too, and that I had certainly misunderstood the nature of the things I was discussing. The fact that these things were so intensely difficult to grasp with imperfect linguistic tools did not diminish the supreme importance of trying to do so, which was what philosophers ever since Pythagoras and Plato had been trying to do. And this was one of the reasons that philosophy was so supremely important. The mystery was, that we do not, in fact, make up the world out of our heads. We receive it. We find ourselves in a universe where stones are not mashed potatoes, and there is an all-but-universal consensus of agreement about which is which. Much more intensely important and mysterious, we find ourselves in a universe where there is a similar consensus about the difference between good and bad. We cannot claim that this is just something happening inside our own heads. From the beginning of time, no one has been able to invert moral value. Different societies and religions might differ over inessentials such as the legality of eating pork or sleeping with a sibling, but the universality of moral values was far more striking than the minor points of difference. Here was something which was outside ourselves. It required our patient homage and intelligent attention. Perhaps too it required our silence, and our contemplation. And another thing, she had then surprisingly interjected, I had been quite wrong to think that Rice Robey suggested, in his writings, that Christianity was no more than some crazed fantasy buzzing about in the mind of St Paul, utterly wrong. The reverse was the case. All that Rice Robey was exploring in his book was the manner in which the imagination of St Paul worked on certain facts, certain given and authentic data. (I did not agree with her then, and I don't agree with her now about this matter, but this was how she argued.) She said that when Paul spoke of Christ as the Eikon of the Living God, he was presenting the authentic and revealed doctrine of the Incarnation – what Rice Robey called the God-enfleshment. You could not escape this, any more than you could escape the challenge to the imagination which it presented. Rice Robey believed, Felicity said, with Coleridge, that the primary imagination was the repetition in the finite mind of the eternal act of creation in the infinite I AM. I take it, this really means that the pictures drawn in our minds, the stories we tell ourselves, are not, as I would contend, internalisations; they are actual invasions of the consciousness from outside. If I say that St Paul *imagined* his theology, I mean that he created myths about Christ which were a response to his own profoundest psychological needs (Rice Robey's speculation that it began with a guilt complex about the Crucifixion would make some kind of sense to me) and to which, for various reasons, many, many human beings have responded at the same deep level ever since. The myth that Jesus would come on the clouds to take the living and the dead to live with him in the sky was the first central story of Paul's message to the world and it set the tone for all the rest. Biggest and strangest myth was the idea that the Cross of Jesus itself had been able to remove the sin and guilt of the human race, or the guilt of those people who turned towards the Cross in faith. For me, the meaning of this idea will always be elusive, but I see that it can only be explored on an imaginative level. Clearly, when I thought of all the millions of human beings for whom the Cross has been the symbol and focus of salvation, I did not dismiss lightly what St Paul had set in hand. I did not think, and never have thought (since the coming to an end of my early adolescent quarrels with Uncle Roy about religion) that Christianity was a mere sham, or lie. I considered it a profoundly important thing, but something which existed on the level of the inner being, so that its truth could not be regarded as universal, it was not a commanding, undeniable truth before which everyone must bow, like the truth of mathematics. If an imaginative life has been focused on the Cross, then to kiss a crucifix or to sing 'When I Survey' might touch the deepest part of a person's soul, and be the most important thing in their lives. But for someone whose imagination had been shaped in a different way there was no obligation to believe in the Cross, or, indeed, in any of St Paul's other myths. It was not a truth which compelled.

This was not, however, how Felicity viewed the matter. She said that there were not various sorts of truth; it made no sense to talk of imaginative truth, or of things being true for one person, but not for another. In the case of Christianity, it ultimately came down to something unknowable, that is, whether God himself had actually been enfleshed, and entered history, and been born of Mary. This could never be investigated as an historical phenomenon, but in Felicity's mind it related to her increasing sense that truth is not something inside ourselves which we are fashioning out of our own psychological experiences as much as something utterly external to ourselves and which, in the case of great truth, religious truth, for example, or ethical or aesthetic truth, can only be perceived by the exercise of virtues, such as patience and humility. So, slowly and inexorably, she moved towards the acceptance of Belief – though it was some years before she joined the Society of Friends. I remained, and remain, on the borders, revering Felicity's mind as much as I revere her heart, but wondering, always, how truly intelligent and grown-up people could believe in stories of Jesus ascending into the clouds, or walking about in water, or rising from the dead – and if they did not believe these things, why did they call themselves Christians? It is rather an Anglican question, and no one quite seems able to give the answer, since Christ and Christianity continue to exercise such a benevolent and powerful hold on the human heart that some men and women will never leave go of Jesus even if they did cease to believe in miracles, or angels or perhaps even in God.

I do not mean to disparage Felicity's religious journey when I say that it had largely to do with Rice Robey. Her obsession with the man made it quite natural that she should follow his intellectual interests; to some degree it was inevitable that she should have come to think his thoughts, just as it sometimes happens when a person falls in love that, all unconsciously, they come to imitate the mannerisms, locutions, even on occasion, the handwriting of the adored one.

From Jo Lampitt, either direct, when I met her in pubs with Darnley, or through the indirect intermediary of Darnley himself, I gathered that Rice Robey's association with Kirsty had fizzled out. The last time he had tried to visit her in Cambridge she had pleaded a prior engagement, or pressure of work.

'She should have told him to piss off,' Jo opined, 'from the very beginning.'

'But presumably she found him charming.'

'He's a prize wanker.'

There seemed no point in rehearsing with Jo, whose approach to human psychology Darnley at least found reassuringly unsubtle, the possibility that charmless behaviour had never yet been an obstacle to strong attraction growing up between the sexes. I wondered slightly about Jo's reliability as a witness. She varied her accounts of what Rice Robey did or did not do with Kirsty. It may be said at this distance of time that it did not really matter, but I am one of those who is never reluctant to know these details about my fellow mortals, provided the information is authentic.

Felicity had for some time known of Rice Robey's visits to Cambridge, and she had duly absolved him. He had expounded to her the view which is mentioned in more than one of the Albion Pugh novels, of Sexless Eros, a doctrine which I think he invented, but which he claimed to derive in slightly wobbly descent from the writings of Plato, St Paul and Dante. According to this view, when two people fall in love, or grow fond of one another, they immediately involve themselves in the chemistry of mutual attraction which was called in Pugh-language 'the Mutualities of Unselfing'. Part of the boy flies off to join the soul of the girl and vice versa in a process he called 'the Coition of the Psyches'. So lofty a view did he take of these fleeting moments – indeed, for him, they held the seeds of the secret of the universe – that he enunciated the view that all those who had been involved in such feelings were held together in a perpetual spiritual link, of sexless Eros.

Why sexless? He pointed out that Plato's *Symposium* recommends passing on from adoration of a boy's beauty to the contemplation of spiritual love. 'At no point,' Rice Robey would insist with eyes ablaze behind his thick lenses, 'does Plato recommend a free-for-all of the homosexuals.' St Paul urged virginity on his followers. Dante had not bestowed so much as a kiss on the face of his beloved Beatrice. Of course, Rice Robey had not invented the idea of chastity as an important adjunct to spiritual advancement but he added refinements of his own to the traditional notions. Sexual energy in his view was a divine fire which could be harboured. As the professor states in *Memphian Mystery*, 'Man and woman, when seized by the divine fire of mutually experienced carnal attraction may choose to dissipate and waste it by unchastity, but if they choose to cherish the fire in the crucible of chastity they will become as gods, empowered to see mysteries, to exercise psychic control, to call down angelicals to the terrestrial plane and to raise up their confused consciousness to high knowledge.'

Poetry, the intellectual achievements of philosophers and scientists, the insights of mystics, all sprang from the human ability to link up with the Divine Energy, and this ability was intensified, he believed, by the Mutualities of Unselfing. Assuming that he practised what he preached, it did not suggest that Felicity, the Great Attachment, or any of his other female admirers could look forward to a very vigorous sex life. Perhaps this was part of his charm.

For Felicity, a large part of the attraction appeared to be the belief that she was rescuing a fallen archangel, so that the most glaring contradictions in his character, and the most off-putting faults positively increased his attractiveness to her. She even seemed to relish the fact that he was, by any ordinary criteria, a quite stunningly bad writer, and to blame this fact on Mrs Paxton.

'The early books are half formed; they are brilliant but they do not add up. He should still be capable of writing a book which brings together his great spiritual and intellectual powers, his imaginative powers. That woman just fails to stimulate or expand his imagination. Do you know what he had to do all last week?'

'I can guess from your tone that it was something tedious.'

'Go round the shops and buy her a washboard.'

Felicity's laugh at this point was both girlish and conspiratorial: it could have been a confidence shared after lights out in the dorm or the girl guides' camp. 'Of course he could not find one, they went out with the Ark. People have washing machines now.'

'We don't.'

'We don't have a washboard either. He had to go to umpteen hardware shops in Kentish Town and Holloway.'

'Skiffle groups had them. They must still be around somewhere.'

'Julian, that isn't the point. What is a man of R.R.'s distinction *doing* in a hardware shop searching for washboards?'

'Presumably, Mrs Paxton felt that she needed one.'

I had not met the Great Attachment since my visit to Twisden Road of a year before. I wondered if Rice Robey had ever mentioned to Felicity my visit to his house. I had said nothing about it, and continued to allow her to repeat her stories of 'R.R.''s domestic hardships without overtly suggesting that the man told lies about

194

them. Felicity herself found all domestic chores tedious. I had once suggested to her that many people positively enjoy shopping, cooking and indulging in humdrum household chores. I enjoy it myself, and thought it possible that Robey did too.

'He's trying to read his way through the *Enneads* of Plotinus but he can't concentrate because she insists on having the wireless on all the time, and she makes him sit and listen to it with her. If his attention wanders for an instant, she flies into a rage. If he goes out for half an hour to take a turn in the open air, she suspects him of having an affair with another woman. No wonder there's so much unresolved anger in R.R. I told him the other day that he should pipe down about Jimbo Lampitt, and all that business.'

I somehow guessed that Rice Robey knew nothing of Felicity's former attachment to Raphael Hunter and that she did not intend to confess it to him. There was no reason why she should have done, but it is always a little surprising to think, when two people develop deep emotional bonds, how little each knows of the other, compared with old friends and family. That Hunter had 'jilted' Felicity was one of the great unmentionables in our family. It lay behind all our thoughts about James Petworth Lampitt. Since it was in the past, and since it was unmentionable, Rice Robey knew nothing of it. He had his own personal memories of Jimbo and it made sense to suppose that he disliked Hunter for reasons of his own which had nothing to do with Felicity.

I made some remarks to the priggish effect that, if Rice Robey was so anxious to pursue his study of Plotinus, he should have not wasted so much time on gossip. And I developed the theme by suggesting that two aspects of his nature sat oddly beside one another: his mystical and religious interests in private and the unbridled malice of his journalistic pen.

'R.R. is never malicious,' she said. 'I never knew a less malicious man; but he is angry, which is different, and sometimes the anger is misdirected. If he expressed to that woman Mrs Paxton the anger which he actually felt – why, he'd kill her!'

'So, he libels Hunter because he doesn't want a row with Mrs Paxton?'

'He has rows with Mrs Paxton whether he wants them or not, poor lamb.' She did not develop or take up my question. She had once told me that she hated Hunter, and at the time of the abortion this was probably true. The quality of hatred which we nurse for those

195

who have caused us pain in love is unlike any other form of hostility: it is in fact just a continuation of love itself, nothing less, and I wondered whether some of the old flame for Hunter did not continue to burn in Felicity's heart and make sad clashes with her new fondness for R.R.

'I wish he hadn't written that thing about Raphael,' she said quietly.

'Do you think it's untrue?'

'No *good* will come of writing like that.'

That was as much as we said about the matter before Darnley's wedding party, a function to which both Felicity and I were invited. The union which (to my mind, so unaccountably) he had finally decided to make official, between himself and Jo Lampitt, had been solemnised at a register office earlier in the day, and friends and relations were bidden to celebrate the occasion at a party in the Savile Club, beginning at, roughly speaking, the cocktail hour, and continuing through dinner. Darnley was my oldest friend, and I wished him well; there would have been no question of my staying away from such a gathering, even though I knew in advance that it would be one of those parties where as much energy would be devoted to the avoidance of those whom one did not want to see as to devising themes of conversation with those whom one liked. Such forebodings were well judged. Within seconds of stepping into the room I found myself standing next to my ex-wife.

After we ceased to 'get on', Anne had more capacity for communicating anger than any other human being I have ever known. Encountering her, I at once felt waves of it, and remembered the disastrous evening, the beginning of the end really, when we had gone backstage after a particularly good production of *Uncle Vanya* and discovered Raphael Hunter in the arms of the actress Isabella Marno, a conjunction which had plunged Anne into a moody rage from which she could not escape. There was no guessing what had set her off this time. Perhaps she by now made a habit of fuming disgruntlement. The most obvious explanation, namely that my own appearance on the scene embarrassed and irritated her, or at the least awoke painful memories, oddly enough did not occur to me.

'I can't think why Vernon and Pat have asked all these people,' she said by way of greeting.

'To swell the throng? Because Jo and Miles wanted them?'

Anne's taste for the company of the human race, never marked, was fast evaporating into non-existence. The thought that people might choose, actually choose, to see one another in great numbers, was puzzling to her. She knew about families: *they* saw one another, naturally, and one saw a very few old friends, in her case, her poisonous friend Lesley, a fellow student at the Courtauld, or the slightly less poisonous Elizabeth, with whom Anne had been at school, and who was Darnley's sister. She was worlds away, Anne, from my feeling that the circle of acquaintanceship was infinitely extensible, that it was always interesting to meet new people and that, as far as something like the present party was concerned, the more the merrier. She stared bleakly at the people who milled about on the upper floor of the club. It was a place where I had more than once seen Sargie become drunk. It was in fact, though I did not witness this, the place where Sargie and Uncle Roy ate lunch on the day of Jimbo's funeral.

'It's an entirely unsuitable place for a party,' said Anne.

There was space, elegance, beauty. Waiters were moving gracefully among the guests distributing glasses of wine or fruit juice. A female trio, bespectacled, crop-haired, all girls with pale, intensely serious faces (they looked like girls who might have got on well with Simone Weil) played a jaunty selection of tunes, ranging from nearcontemporaneous favourites like 'Fings Ain't What They Used to Be' to revivals such as 'Pasadena'.

One of the girls, fascinatingly plain and serious-looking, occasionally abandoned her mouth-organ or clarinet (she played both) so as to croon into the microphone in an icily academic, tuneless whisper.

I was unable to see what made this an unsuitable place for a party.

'How are you, Anne, anyway?'

Her silent shrug told me that the banality of the question did not even compel good manners on her behalf, still less a reply. She walked away from me without a word. I wondered, since she seemed so determined not to enjoy herself, why she had troubled to attend the party. Possibly Sibs, her mother, had put out what she would have termed a three-line whip and insisted that all her family should be there, lest Darnley's friends and relations be seen to swamp the Lampitt contingent.

When I approached Darnley himself he was standing with Jo and a soignée blonde whom I took to be aged about forty.

'Mr Grainger!' he said. 'Excellent! Mummy, you remember Julian Ramsay.'

'It is funny that we have never met before,' said Darnley's mother, whose name at that point was, I think, Mrs Fitzgerald.

'We saw you!' Jo interrupted.

'When?'

'Just now, trying to chat up that dark-haired piece.'

Darnley's grin became a little fixed and he shook his head to indicate that she was being tactless and should shut up. Either she did not read these signals, or she chose not to do so.

'You didn't have much luck, did you, Mr Grainger?'

'I'm sorry?'

'Chatting up that bird. Nice tits, boring dress, though, you're better off without her. . . .'

I could avoid the embarrassment of telling Jo her mistake since she continued to prattle without a pause.

'. . . Frances has asked me to call her Frances, haven't you Frances – Miles already calls Dad Ernie, some call him Ernie, some call him Vernon. Bit of a pose, calling himself. . . . But what do you think of Frances, Mr Grainger, eh? Nice mother-in-law for me? Do you think?'

The directness of the interrogation made any response impossible, anyway in Mrs Fitzgerald's hearing. There could be no doubt that Darnley's mother was beautiful. Whether she would be a 'nice' mother-in-law, not the easiest of roles in which to exercise pleasantness, remained to be seen.

'I think we met a number of times actually, when I was at Seaforth Grange. You kindly bought me lunch at the Foley Arms.'

She seemed ageless. Her cool smile implied that if the rest of the human race knew her secret formula (frequent divorce? vitamin pills?) they too could defy the ravages of time. When she had entertained me as a schoolboy twenty years earlier, her head had appeared to be encased in a helmet of mouse-coloured perm. Now her hair was drawn gently back from her forehead in loose swathes of platinum blonde. The suggestion that she had once bought me lunch did not disconcert her. Certainly she saw no need for the elaborate apologies which most English peopole, quite insincerely, would have introduced into conversation at this point.

'Miles said you were married to a Lampitt once.'

'To Anne Starling, standing over there.'

'Would you recommend it?'

'Say you do, Mr Grainger,' said Jo eagerly. For the first time in my life I felt tenderly towards her. Mrs Fitzgerald had turned the tables on Jo's tactless prattle (whether she herself would make a nice mother-in-law) and was showing her mettle in retaliation, by holding up for assessment the Lampitts and all their tribe. Were the Lampitts marriageable? Perhaps this was an example of the empiricist fallacy and the falsehood of the words Either/or.

'They vary,' I said.

'You can give it a go, darling, anyway,' said Mrs Fitzgerald, stroking Darnley's cheek.

'Oh, do shut up, Mummy.'

'Come on, Julian,' said Mrs Fitzgerald, lightly taking my arm. 'You'll know far more people here than I do. Show me round.'

There was no evidence in her gait or speech to make me suspect inebriation; in fact, I am sure she was not drunk, but she seemed, in her poised, quiet way, to be in an anarchic frame of mind which most of us are only able to achieve with alcohol. The suggestion that I would know more people than she did was a ludicrous one, and her request for me to show her round had the sort of condescension which one would display to a child. Perhaps she really did remember our lunches together on exeat from Seaforth Grange and still, subconsciously thought of me as a little boy. I record these feelings as I believe I had them at the time. It was years before I heard the strange stories about her very distinctive predilections, and the impressively varied catalogue of men who had submitted themselves to her charm.

'He can be so prickly, can't he, Miles?' she said as we left her son alone with his bride. 'You've known him for ever, I know. Do you think he's doing the right thing?'

'He and Jo seem very fond of one another.'

This was no answer, but she must have been pleased that I did not reply in the negative. As it happened, I thought that anyone who wanted to marry Jo Lampitt was raving mad, but one could hardly say this on their wedding day to the bridegroom's mother.

'You see,' she said, 'you *do* know everybody.'

As we walked through the room, I had nodded here and there to the arbitrary miscellany of people there assembled. Presumably, Mrs Fitzgerald herself had been consulted about the guest list, or perhaps Vernon had approached Darnley himself. One saw some strange conjunctions. Peter Cornforth, his existence only semi-imaginable outside the Black Bottle, was resting his full weight on his metal foot and holding an ignited Park Drive rather threateningly close to the nose of Dame Ursula Lampitt, who giggled appreciatively at what he had to say. They both waved to us as we glided past. The best parties provide the chance for such surprising confluences. Was Pete treating Ursula to one of his usual foul-mouthed diatribes against her sex – is that why she was laughing? Or was she telling him about the latest fruits of her research into Anglo-Norman literature? Or were they both revelling in the chance to talk to someone of a kind they would never normally meet, and had they found some common ground which the rest of us could not guess at? We did not stay to discover.

After the celibate years, in which sexual feeling had been all but quiescent, I was easily over-excited by discovering that I was attracted to someone else. It tended to make me behave in a way that Aunt Deirdre, perhaps others, would have categorised as 'silly'. Mrs Fitzgerald certainly made me want to be very silly indeed. The last girlfriend whom I had entertained at cinemas and Greek restaurants had lasted about a fortnight. I was feeling, on that evening, game for anything. Between Mrs Fitzgerald and myself, there was, undoubtedly, what Sibs would have called (and oh, dear, there *was* Sibs at the top of the stairs talking to the Home Secretary) chemistry. Mrs Fitzgerald's light touch on my arm seemed charged with significance and when I reached up to strengthen my hold on her elbow and lightly to squeeze her fingers, she made no resistance.

'That's Lady Augusta Wimbish,' I explained. 'She is married to an historian.'

'She's my aunt,' said Mrs Fitzgerald. 'It would be a cruelty to disturb her while she's at the trough.'

Not much in the way of a buffet had been provided, since there was a dinner afterwards for twenty or thirty of the guests. Lady Augusta had none the less managed to arm herself with a side-plate and heap it with some salted nuts, about eight olives and some sausage rolls. She was the only person in the room who was eating. Perhaps she had brought the sausage rolls with her in her pretty silver-mail reticule which was suspended from one tiny, bony wrist. Upon the comestibles assembled on her plate her entire attention was fixed. Thin, tall and pale, she stood firmly in the middle of the floor eating with nervous speed and occasional glances to left and right. It would certainly have been an unkindness to approach lest she mistook a harmless social advance as a covert attempt on her salted peanuts. Her husband, the professor, was not far away, and I saw that he was accompanied by William Bloom.

'Are these two men screwing?' she asked me quietly, as they approached.

'I've no reason to suppose they have even met before this evening.'

'That's not a reason for not doing it.' Her fingers squeezed mine in return.

'George is just making a fool of himself,' said Wimbish, loudly. The only reason that he addressed us was that we happened to be there. The remark would have been made had Wimbish been standing on his own. He made no distinction between conversation and monologue, dialogue and soliloquy.

'Just look at the bloody fool! Thank goodness our party for once in its life saw some sense and voted Harold into the leadership. Can you imagine if that buffoon over there were now our Prime Minister.' He pursed his lips in mock-dowager distaste. 'Very Prime Ministerly behaviour, that!'

It was a surprising sight, certainly to me, but then, in spite of the impression I hoped I was making on Mrs Fitzgerald, I was unused to the ways of the world. George Brown, the Deputy Prime Minister, and at that stage in charge of the newly formed Ministry for Economic Affairs, was attempting a dance. He was generously undiscriminating about his choice of partner. When a waiter had shaken free of him he had seized a potted bay tree near the piano, and after a few steps he had swayed into the arms of my old landlady, Fenella Kempe. Rikko, standing by, was pinching his forehead. I don't suppose that he minded anyone being drunk. He was doubtless dreading the incident being exaggerated in the telling by Fenella when she described it to their friends and lodgers.

'It's a bit early in the evening for all that,' I said.

'I wonder,' said Mrs Fitzgerald, 'where Vernon and Pat found that extraordinary band. I know quite a lot of good musicians. They should have asked me.'

Wimbish's smile was unamiable, even threatening. It suggested that, just this once, he would brook interruption, but in future would we jolly well shut up and listen to him.

'I believe they're friends of Kirsty's,' said Bloom. It was clear that he knew Mrs Fitzgerald quite well. Did she know that, in army days, Bloom had been so much in love with Darnley?

'I love the fact that they don't smile,' he said.

The palest and most humourless of the girls, the one who sometimes played the mouth-organ, was whispering,

> My love for you
> Makes everything hazy
> Clouding the skies
> From view--oo-hoo.

'And Hugh, you see, bloody fool, was the same, always swigging from the bloody bottle.' Wimbish was allowing himself to become quite worked up. 'Thank goodness we've got Harold, who in my view is one of the most distinguished leaders this country has ever had since the Tudor Age. I don't know if it has ever occurred to you, but Harold Wilson is just a *tiny* little like Henry VIII. . . .'

'My dear!' said Bloom, 'does this mean that poor Mary is going to have her head chopped off on Tower Green?'

He made some other remarks which made it clear that Mrs Wilson was something of a friend of his.

'Who writes that thing in *Private Eye*?' asked Mrs Fitzgerald. 'It's meant to be Mary Wilson's diary. It's screamingly funny.'

'. . . a man, you see, of brilliant intellectual accomplishments. He knew French, Latin, Italian. He could compose music and songs. . . .'

'It's funnier than Miles's paper really, *Private Eye*, wouldn't you say?'

'And yet with this vein of tremendous ruthlessness. Really, Machiavelli might have been thinking of him when he wrote. . . .'

'They're called the Newnham Norns,' said Bloom. 'Aren't they heaven? I must apologise, my dear, for the other evening.'

'What on earth for?'

'Now, you see, no one would have been able to predict that he would dissolve the monasteries. What? Catholic Henry? Author of a book on the Seven Sacraments . . . ?

'My sister and I spoiled an evening for Julian and Felicity some months ago,' Bloom explained.

'Who's Felicity?' and 'You did not spoil it at all,' said Mrs Fitzgerald and I in unison.

'She's married to the most extraordinarily boring man called Aaron Samuelson,' said Bloom. 'At the moment she seems to have lost her head to an old schoolfriend of Julian's called Patrick Garforth-Thoms.'

The evening in the restaurant, which I had already begun to forget, had ossified in Bloom's mind into an anecdote. He changed a lot of details, but his description of Garforth-Thoms's raucous behaviour was quite funny. Aeons later, someone told me that Mrs Fitzgerald herself nursed a *tendresse* for Garforth-Thoms, even that he had at one stage been one of 'her boys'. This discovery made sense, as nothing did at the time, of the momentary spasm of distaste which disturbed the haughty passivity of her face. At the time, I barely noticed it and certainly failed to interpret her reaction, a good example of the fact that we frequently fail to catch the meaning of events until years after they have happened, and also of the fact that our interpretation of the past depends on more than mere powers of recall.

'Come on,' said Mrs Fitzgerald. 'Let's go and talk to Mia Eggscliffe.'

She began to walk away before Bloom had finished speaking, which provoked him to an exaggerated shrug, hunched shoulders, pouting lower lip, palms upturned, for five seconds the parody of a stage Frenchman.

'Funnily enough,' I said to Mrs Fitzgerald, 'Miles and I were at school with Garforth-Thoms.'

'Mia!' exclaimed Mrs Fitzgerald, 'how wonderful to see a sympathetic face amid all these *strangers*.'

As we drew level to the celebrated Mrs Eggscliffe (as Bloom used to say, 'one of the last great hostesses, present company excepted,' a phrase he managed to make even cheaper than it looks by emphasising the second syllable of the word *hostess*) a cruel alchemy took place in my perception of Mrs Fitzgerald. In the twinkling of an eye, I realised that these two women were roughly of the same generation, if not an age. Mrs Eggscliffe's bouffed-out dyed black hair encased a thin face fast turning to scrawn, though gallantly disguised by well-applied make-up. Already, however, she seemed poised to enter that penultimate phase of human decrepitude when a face has become prune-like, a phase which in women can last as long as twenty years. As soon as Mrs Fitzgerald approached Mrs Eggscliffe, her own face appeared to age, like the countenance of 'She' in Rider Haggard's story when the spell of her agelessness is broken. The platinum streaks in Mrs Fitzgerald's blonde hair now seemed like wisps of grey and the blue-grey eyes were visibly edged with crows' feet which I had not noticed before. With the complete heartlessness of youth, I released the pressure of her fingers in mine. The strange ten minutes or so in which I had found Darnley's mother the most beguiling being in the universe had passed.

If I knew how you did it to me

sang the Newnham Norn,

I would do it to you.

'I've asked a waiter to take George in hand,' said Mrs Eggscliffe, speaking of the Minister for Economic Affairs whose light fantastic with the bay tree had been resumed. 'It was Vernon's responsibility, I suppose, but I took it upon myself.'

She was manifestly incapable of behaving in any social setting other than as a hostess, giving orders to waiters and gazing about the room to make sure that the 'right' people were talking to one another. Seeing a roomful of people, instinct made her speak as if we had all been summoned at her command. This fact was emphasised by the roll-call which was now fired at myself and Mrs Fitzgerald. Since I never moved in the world, I had no idea who the people were that she was talking about. It was a rapid rehearsal of names, not unlike the roll-call at school with which each day began and ended, almost like the low-toned announcement of the dentist to his assistant as he makes a rapid survey of one's mouth and declares, for the record, which teeth are missing, or which require attention since the patient's last session in the chair. In this litany Mrs Fitzgerald was cast in the role of acolyte or assistant, giving me no more than a minimum response before the rapid interrogation continued.

'Is Frank here?'

'Over there.'

'He's so dotty. With Elizabeth?'

'In every sense.'

'Where's Isaiah?'

'Couldn't get.'

'Naughty. Now, Dick I've seen, but. . . . '

'Oh, he's somewhere.'

'I suppose the PM. . . .'

She smiled with triumphant malice.

'My dear.'

Mrs Fitzgerald whispered something to Mrs Eggscliffe, who responded by talking down the back of her hand, which she held up to her lips. This gesture evidently announced that her words were supposed to be 'classified information'. They weren't exactly whispered, but they looked as if they were being spoken from behind an arras in some Renaissance tragedy.

The two women were discussing Vernon's political disappointment. Since his failure to be chosen as a member of the Cabinet, there was bad blood between the Prime Minister and the Lampitts; Harold Wilson's failure to choose the second Baron Lampitt as a minister, however lowly, was now being reinterpreted as a danger signal to the left. Not to have chosen Ernie, the people's man, marked down the Prime Minister as at best a fair-weather socialist.

I was naive enough, since they were discussing the matter, to suppose that this was of interest to Mrs Eggscliffe and Mrs Fitzgerald. I assumed, since Mrs Eggscliffe was evidently on such easy terms with so many senior members of the new government, that she was herself a committed Labour supporter. I did not realise that she had just as many friends, probably more, in the Conservative Party, and that her *salons* (it almost seems appropriate to use such an obsolete term), though frequently places where politics were discussed, were far from being easy to classify in political terms. She chiefly loved the pursuit of success, the worship of chic and the exercise of power. Hence her preparedness to be married to rich men who bored her (two of them had been newspaper proprietors) but who provided her with the means to exercise her curious range of influence.

It was something of a concession that Mrs Eggscliffe had accepted the invitation to these nuptials. Several years afterwards, Darnley used, laughingly, to relate that she had 'had her eye on him for one of the Rothschild girls'; since the surname was pronounced in this phrase in the continental manner, he assumed that the girl in question belonged to a French branch of that illustrious dynasty. Mrs Eggscliffe was related by blood neither to the Darnleys nor to the Rothschilds. This did not prevent her from believing that the marriages of members of these families somehow fell under her responsibility. The Rothschilds and the Darnleys both belonged to the elect, as far as Mrs Eggscliffe was concerned, a category which it would be difficult enough to define. Being rich, or famous, or aristocratic, or all three, were by no means qualities which Mrs Eggscliffe undervalued, but you might possess all three and still be regarded by her as 'a bore'. Others, such as the columnist Godfrey Tucker, hardly conspicuous for any obvious style or breeding, was one of the men on whom Mrs Eggscliffe most doted, insisting, in those phases of life when she was married to Fleet Street magnates, that Tucker's columns of opinionated reflections be given pride of place in whatever newspaper the husband of the day happened to own.

The Elect were present at the wedding party but by Mrs Eggscliffe's mysterious but also, one suspected, rather rigid standards, their number had been almost irredeemably diluted or coarsened by the admission into the assembly of riff-raff such as myself. I slightly hated Mrs Fitzgerald for introducing me as 'a madly famous radio actor' before mentioning my name. Mrs Eggscliffe's 'Oh?' made it excruciatingly clear that my name meant nothing to her, a fact which is hardly surprising when it is remembered that 'The Mulberrys' so invariably clashes with the cocktail hour.

'Sargie here?' she continued.

'No,' said Mrs Fitzgerald, 'but one would not expect him to turn out.'

'He comes to my parties,' said Mrs Eggscliffe. No one had in fact tried to excuse Sargie's absence, for example by the suggestion that he feared crowds or was of a generally unsociable disposition, but she spoke as if wholly inadequate excuses had been offered to her. 'I got him round the night we really badgered Harold to give Dora a peerage. My dear, is that Violet Bonham-Carter?'

'Talking to the clergyman?'

'Canon Collins – he's an ass, but a bit of a charmer. I wonder who that handsome man is with them, the one with the sort of metal frame on his foot; looks frightfully uncomfortable. I wonder who chose this *ghastly* music! No, you're right, my dear, Sargie would never come to a clan gathering like this. Too many skeletons rattling in cupboards.'

'Sargie said to me this morning that he never attends weddings,' I volunteered. 'He finds them too depressing, can always see what is going to go wrong for the bridal pair. . . .'

Mrs Eggscliffe stared at me as if she wished that I would simply go away, possibly as if my claim to know Sargie was spurious.

'I haven't seen Cecily for ages,' said Mrs Fitzgerald. She had lit a cigarette, and her words seemed to be borne on the two perfectly straight diagonals of nicotine smoke which issued from her nostrils.

'I met *the* most extraordinary man just now,' said Mrs Eggscliffe, 'but he was really very charming. I asked him to one of my parties at once, he's coming next Tuesday. He was dressed in a sort of demob suit, my dear, you never saw anything like it, and he was telling one of the Know-Dutton twins, Jilly, the pretty one, the one I call Tinkerbell, how they practised human sacrifice in the ancient pyramids of Mexico.'

'Poor Jilly.'

'Lapping it up.' Mrs Eggscliffe let out a short barking laugh, a strangely countrified noise, the sort of sound you might have expected from a distinguished MFH if you had told him that you had moral objections to field sports. Young girls, her tone suggested, jolly well should learn about human sacrifice, if necessary, perhaps, even offer themselves up as candidates if the occasion, or Mrs Eggscliffe's social arrangements, demanded such a thing.

'What was so interesting about this scruffy man, my dear, was that he knew all about. . . .'

Once more, Mrs Eggscliffe lifted the back of her hand to her mouth and spoke down her flattened knuckles like Midas whispering secrets to the earth. Whatever it was that Rice Robey had said, it made Mrs Fitzgerald roll her eyes and gasp with astonishment.

'No!' she said.

I now felt like an eavesdropper.

'He's great friends with Miles,' said Mrs Fitzgerald.

'And he's a poet isn't he?' said Mrs Eggscliffe. 'I must get hold of some of his stuff before Tuesday. I'll ring up Heywood Hill in the morning, and they can send the books round.'

'He writes under the name of Albion Pugh,' I said. 'Even though his name is Rice Robey.'

Grateful for this information, Mrs Eggscliffe said, 'I must remember that. Albion Pugh. I think people talked about his novels during the war.'

'That's what everyone seems to say.' Her facial expression made it possible for me to imagine that I had said something to offend Mrs Eggscliffe. First I had claimed acquaintance with Sargie, she seemed to think, and now I knew about Albion Pugh. Enough was enough. I did not particularly wish to attend one of her famous parties, but I could not help wondering what it was about Rice Robey which had made her so instantly desirous of his company. I had been standing beside her for ten minutes, and I knew that she was never going to suggest that I dropped in to see her.

'I wonder how he could have *known*,' said Mrs Fitzgerald.

'You won't say anything?' said Mrs Eggscliffe.

'Of course not.'

Darnley had been afraid, and said so several times before his wedding, that Pat and his mother between them would manage to fill the party with 'awful people', by which, roughly, he meant relations, and those individuals whom Mrs Eggscliffe would have regarded as most acceptable. It was to offer some kind of antidote to 'awfulness', thus defined, that he had scoured the hedgerows and ditches for such a wide variety of unfashionable characters, many of whom could have been no more than casual acquaintances of his or Jo's: hacks, barflies and oddballs. Fenella Kempe was there, for example. I saw her shouting something in the ear of Godfrey Tucker and went over to join them; as I did so, I heard Mrs Fitzgerald repeating to Mrs Eggscliffe that I was a schoolfriend of Miles.

Fenella was boasting about Rikko's national fame as the son and heir to Dick Mulberry.

'It's absolute rubbish,' said Godfrey Tucker in his voice which recalled sacksful of gravel being emptied into trucks. 'It's completely beyond my comprehension why anyone should be fascinated by such a concentration of pure gibberish.'

After five years of acting in 'The Mulberrys', this had become more or less my own view of the series, so I waved aside the heavy-handed apology with which he concluded his diatribe when Fenella reminded him that I was the man who played Jason Grainger.

'I'd better watch what I say,' he reflected.

'So you'd better,' said Rikko hotly. He had come up to join us and looked extremely displeased by Tucker's opinions.

'Who are you?' asked Tucker incredulously. For the previous sentence or two, Rikko had been standing by Fenella's side, one hand on a hip and the other holding a wineglass at shoulder level. He resembled some slightly overweight Renaissance sculpture of Bacchus. When Fenella explained that Rikko was her husband, Godfrey Tucker spluttered with astonishment.

'Then what did you let me go on for, you stupid woman?' he grumbled. Probably, like most successfully opinionated journalists, Godfrey Tucker did not entertain any sincerely held views at all. The regular production of strongly worded observations on the world was his means of livelihood and had become habitual to him. He could not help doing it. If the views expressed provoked a response, he had done his job, whether the response was one of outrage or of rapturous agreement. He deftly demonstrated this facility by sketching out aloud an absolutely opposite viewpoint from his earlier assessment of the series.

'If it gives a lot of people completely harmless pleasure,' he began.

'Which it does,' said Rikko.

'You could almost say that it was the closest thing we have in our culture to the Pastoral. *Some Versions of the Pastoral*, now who wrote that?'

This question, being put to Fenella, produced in her a frightful fit of coughing until the moment passed in which she might be expected to answer it.

'Within a certain conventional framework, it works extremely well,' said Tucker. 'And don't let's forget, the real tests of a thing like that are, Has it lasted? Do people still want to go on listening? To which we must answer a triumphant Yes!'

Though pretty bored with my role as Jason Grainger, I was at that stage in a state of suspense, not having been 'used' for some weeks. Rodney, our producer, had no qualms about leaving a story-line in the air. This had happened the previous year with the Mystery of the Stolen Chalice. It looked as though Jason had been responsible, but no one pinned it on him. The latest thrilling possibility was that he might become a reformed character and attend a horticultural college with a view to becoming a landscape gardener. Listeners agog to discover whether he would pursue this harmless avocation were now to be left uninformed for some weeks, perhaps for ever. Interest had switched to an outbreak of fowl-pest at Daisy Farm, the chance that little Ginger – Reg's daughter – would be bought a pony for her tenth birthday, and a bumper dairy yield at the Swills' farm, leading to a repetition of the perennial suspicion that they watered the milk.

'I was talking quite seriously to Rodney the other day,' said Rikko. 'He really shouldn't do this to well-established members of the cast.'

'Kind of you,' I said. 'As a matter of fact, I don't really know how much longer I shall be going on with it all anyway.'

The time would have been, in his early days as Stan Mulberry, when Rikko would have seen some of the absurdities of the series, though he was always impressed by its power to attract a large and faithful audience. His touches of merry cynicism had, however, vanished with the years, together with any discernible ambition to pursue a career as a serious actor.

'What on earth do you mean?' he asked. 'You are surely not contemplating leaving "The Mulberrys"?'

I mumbled something about the Lampitt book taking up a lot of time, and how my conscience was pricked by my failure so far to settle down to any research into the matter. Meanwhile, Sargie expected me to call once a week, and I was still doing my book programme for the World Service.

'But none of these compare with being . . . a national institution,' he said earnestly.

Rikko was no less effeminate in manner than when I had first known him, but over the years there had been a perceptible transformation. He no longer said 'your'. There was a touch, in the way he pronounced the word, of Vernon's mock-earthy 'yer'.

'It would be madness to give up yer part in the series now.'

Stan Mulberry was quietly taking him over. Perhaps in some moods, he thought he was Stan Mulberry. Fenella and he even spoke of giving up the house in South Kensington where I had lived as a lodger and taking a cottage in Worcestershire, to be within easy distance of Birmingham and the recording studios. Stan Mulberry was not simply a voice speaking into a microphone. He had begun to do such things as open village fêtes, and to reply to fan-mail in his own name.

'I'm not sure that I want to be in "The Mulberrys" for ever,' I said.

Rikko believed himself to have been instrumental in having secured me the role of Jason Grainger in the first place. I now felt him bridling, and I had not quite realised how he had come to take his own part in 'The Mulberrys' with complete seriousness. It was like the moment, after an uncongenial year working at Tempest and Holmes, the shirt factory, when I had tactlessly told Mr Pilbright that I wanted something more interesting out of life. Pilbright had worked for the firm for the greater part of forty years. To admit that I did not take 'The Mulberrys' seriously was to suggest that I did not take Rikko seriously. It was understandable that he pursed his lips. I could tell that he was on the point of saying, in one of his habitual phrases, that some people did not know what was good for them. By rational standards, the various other activities in my life were not so serious or exalted as to justify the sense of superiority to Rikko which had so embarrassingly been allowed to show.

'What an unusual band,' I said.

'She can't sing,' said Rikko peevishly. 'I can't think why they've hired her.'

'Isn't the point that she's not even trying to sing?'

The vocalist now looked really cross, far crosser than Rikko. Barely bothering to project her voice into the microphone, which she was almost kissing, she whispered,

> I don't stay out late,
> Nowhere to go,
> I'm home about eight,
> Just me and my radio.

She injected into these words a desolated sense of the tedious manner of life which they depicted.

'Good heavens,' I said, 'I've just seen my uncle Roy.'

'Then you'd better go and talk to him,' snapped Rikko, and he turned aside to tell Fenella that if they did not go soon, the Afghans would have shat all over their drawing-room carpet. I heard him saying, 'I sometimes think you simply don't care about my Persian rugs.'

Since schooldays, when Uncle Roy sometimes helped me to change trains from Liverpool Street to Paddington or, later, Euston, I had hardly ever seen him in London. I thought of him primarily as the *genius loci* of Timplingham and his appearance at a gathering such as this was almost like an apparition of the dead.

He looked, however, far from moribund. His cheeks were as pink and his smile as fixed as I had ever known them. He was almost the only person present, apart from the waiters, and the Secretary of State for Defence (just leaving) who wore evening dress, so that he cut a conspicuous figure in the throng as he leaned slightly forward, cocking an alert ear to the neat little woman with whom he was conversing. She had a short bob of white hair, rather mischievous eyes and a sharply intelligent face which could have been peering at you out of a burrow or a sandy hole. To say that she was rodent-like would mislead if it suggested anything unpleasing in her appearance.

It was simply that she seemed like one of the smaller mammals, though not necessarily one which you would want to keep as a pet. Her clothes, her neat paisley blouse and her rather long black skirt had a faintly incongruous air, somehow recalling the world of Beatrix Potter, where hedgehogs, rabbits, rats and mice disport themselves in human garb.

'I don't *think*,' said Uncle Roy laboriously, 'that you've met. . . .' He looked at me and paused. I wondered if, in the excitement of being surrounded by so many Lampitts, he had in fact forgotten my name. 'Er, my nephew, er Julian.'

'No, but you're the one who's going to write the book,' she said with almost exaggerated directness. 'Is it the family as a whole or is it mainly about Jimbo?'

I half guessed at once who she was, but no explanation or introduction were offered. I suppose that Uncle Roy thought that all members of the Lampitt family were as instantly recognisable as film stars or royalty and did not need the superfluity of an introduction.

'It's really. . . .'

I hesitated. She was not asking out of politeness – there was far too much eagerness in her tone for that – and I did not want to commit myself too far before knowing why she was so interested.

'I so hope, that's all, that you won't be too much in Sargie's pocket,' she said. 'It was entirely because of him that we had that *frightful* book about Jimbo, *wicked* book, scandalous book.'

She spoke very emphatically, gabbling the words which were not important, but stabbing the air with a finger when she wanted to underline part of a sentence which demanded close attention. Her vowels were strangely coy. For all its vehemence it was a cooing voice; the sort of voice some people might have thought appropriate for reading aloud to children.

'Dear Sargie!' said Uncle Roy, who had now been excluded from Sargent Lampitt's company for years. 'He *can* be maddening!' I could see that he would be unable to resist telling the very old chestnut about his drive to Cromer, and Sargie's belief that the tyres of the car were first too hard, then too soft, all the way to the coast.

Our companion's method of listening to Uncle Roy's anecdote differed from, say, Aunt Deirdre's, who was anxious to cut these stories as short as possible, or from those others who listened, either in amusement or lost in their own thoughts, until the narrative was done. This lady had no sense of anecdote, no idea that this particularly deadly conversational mode requires nothing except an audience on the part of the speaker. She would not play the game. She punctuated Uncle Roy's story with repeated interruptions. For example, when our heroes had reached the garage in Fakenham, and Sargie had leaned over my uncle to sound the horn in the middle of the steering wheel – thus throwing the garage-man into a fury – she did not laugh. Instead, she said, 'That's one of the things I find so *hard* to *understand* about Sargie, that he has always been so rude. Do *you* understand it?'

Uncle Roy, I could see, found these interruptions trying. By the time he had reached his punchline, the discomfort of Sargie's bedroom and his insistence that Roy change places with him, the lady had made so many interjections that her identity was plain to me. She was Cecily, Sargie's long-estranged wife.

'Typical! It was the Hotel de *Paris*, I expect, overlooking the pier.' (She pronounced the word pee-er.)

'I think it was. Yes.'

Since no one else laughed, Uncle Roy did so. This particular narrative was one of his favourites. During my childhood, I heard it on average every ten days.

'He liked going to Cromer with *me*,' said Cecily. 'Once upon a time. You see, the *trouble* with Sargie, and Jimbo used to be driven *mad* with *rage* about this, was that he was always spoilt. That was why I couldn't live with him. No one *could*.'

She glowed at this confession.

'Extraordinarily difficult,' Uncle Roy agreed, only he said it as though being difficult was the most charming quality in the world, the one thing we should all look for in a friend or life's companion.

'You should have been *firmer*,' she said. 'Firmer with Sargie. I should have done. We *all* should. And now, you too, Julian. You must be firm with Sargie. Oh, Julian,' she suddenly changed gear, 'I've just had the most *extraordinary* thought. Over there with Vernon. The man with the crumpled dark blue suit. . . .'

'His name is Rice Robey,' I said.

The effect on Cecily was electrifying. She brought a mottled hand to her quavery lips and her dark eyes shone.

'Oh, but he is so *old*,' she moaned. 'It couldn't be *our* Rice Robey, could it? Mine and Jimbo's? Our little urchin boy?'

I remember now Sargie's repeated assertion that Cecily and Jimbo had been thick as thieves, and his paranoid claim that they plotted against him. My uncle had barely known Jimbo, nor Cecily, and so it was hardly surprising that he had never come across Rice Robey in his juvenile incarnation; but when I explained that he wrote under the name of Albion Pugh, my uncle's interest quickened.

'The very best is about Herne the Hunter,' said Uncle Roy. 'It is a most remarkable book. That opening chapter of a gamekeeper thinking he has surprised some poachers in the wood at night, the sudden rustling of branches above his head and then his sighting of this terrifying antlered creature, silhouetted in the sky against the pale moon. . . .'

'I've not read that one.'

'We've got them at home. We all read them during the war, though,' he smiled, 'they weren't really your aunt's cup.'

'I would imagine not.'

Cecily was almost dancing with excitement to have discovered that Rice Robey was at the party.

'We must go and look for him, Roy, we *must*, oh this is *too* extraordinary, it's years, *years* . . . Jimbo was heartbroken. . . . We just felt, you know, that we had lost him. We found him this little job at a prep school, oh, out in the sticks.'

'Was it in Chorleywood?'

'It might have been. It seemed perfect, for him. He wrote his books, which of course Jimbo got published for him. Oh, I remember the Egyptian one, and his coming to us for the books, you know, that he had to read and saying, "Oh, Mr Lampitt, my hieroglyphs are rusty, they need burnishing!" Wasn't it wonderful? And then he just got swallowed up, he just vanished from our lives. There was no explanation, but this *ghastly* woman took him over *completely*. He came to Jimbo's funeral, of course, but I was too distressed to talk to anyone that day. . . . Oh, where *is* he?'

In the minute or two that it took Cecily to utter these words, I realised how very little I knew about Jimbo Lampitt. I had read all his published works, and some of his books, such as the biography of Prince Albert, I had known so well that I knew paragraphs of it by heart. Of his life, I knew little. Hunter's published account of Jimbo's early years, discounted by the family as inaccurate, largely failed to bring him to life, since, in spite of the reputation which it created for Hunter – a fearless exposé, etc., etc. – it is in point of fact a very wooden, inanimate sort of book. For the rest, I knew only a few snatches of information about Jimbo. I knew that he spoke with a high squeaky voice, that he had an old-womanish manner (about which Harold Nicolson made that famously barbed comment) and I knew that he had a fondness for Italy. The personality who survived in his books was powerful enough, but it was chiefly a style, a voice, a way of describing the world and people which had bowled me over when I first read Jimbo's books. Yet, I had no sense of what it would have been like actually to spend a week in Jimbo's company. I realised for the first time, what must always have been known in the family but never openly discussed, that Cecily must have been very close to Jimbo, perhaps in love with him. The idea that any woman (apart from the 'extraordinarily nice' old Mrs Lampitt of Timplingham – 'what a woman') had ever been involved with this famous bachelor man of letters had never once crossed my mind. All the testimonies I had heard had suggested to me an emotional history in which women played no conspicuous part; and this was true even before Hunter's book came out, with its hints at emotional conquests, on Jimbo's part, as varied and surprising as Cardinal Manning, Lloyd George and Lawrence of Arabia. It now occurred to me that the Lampitts had always cast a certain veil over the story of Jimbo's life, which was not really to be explained by the rumours of his homosexuality. Now I came to consider the matter, it struck me as odd that they were so united in the certainty that Hunter's allegations were untrue. It was not as if they regarded homosexuality as an entirely unmentionable subject in the family. One thought of Angelica and Miss Bean; or Frankie, the one who was so keen on the Boys' Brigade, and had to leave the country for a while before settling in, I think, Eastbourne. Would they have all been so sure about Jimbo, if they had not possessed evidence that Jimbo's emotions were in fact engaged in some other area? That evidence, I now realised, stood before me. Cecily's association with Jimbo was no secret, but, as so often in families, its nature was unexplored. Some time later, the whole story was told me, partly by Cecily, and partly by Pat Lampitt, of Cecily falling in love with Jimbo not long after she married Sargie, of Sargie's desolation, and the beginning of this worst period of depression and alcoholism, of Jimbo's devoted attachment to Cecily which did not, in either of their minds, rule out the possibility of emotional attachments being formed for members of his own sex (though they seem always to have been emotional rather than physical attachments) and of the curious ménage which they retained, never quite living together, never quite apart, for at least a quarter of a century.

Before we found Rice Robey at the party, Cecily let fall another piece of information which strengthened my strange feeling of life possessing a shape which I had only begun to understand or interpret.

'You must remember, Roy,' she said, 'when you were looking about for a school for this one.'

She tapped my arm.

It was the first I heard that the Lampitts had played a part in the choice of my prep school, though I knew that my public school had been chosen because of its Lampitt associations.

'What did Albion Pugh have to do with it?' Uncle Roy asked. 'I rather forget now how Seaforth Grange was chosen. . . .'

Uncle Roy was unable to refer directly to his dead brother, my father.

'Your brother wanted advice about a school for Julian,' said Cecily, 'and you asked Sargie and Sargie asked Jimbo, and Jimbo suggested sending the little boy – that's you, Julian – to this place in North London where Rice Robey was teaching.'

It was a strange thought that, had this plan been put into operation, I might have been taught by Rice Robey, and that those hierophantic cocknified utterances might have become part of the inner world of childhood memory and imagination, never lost in after years, like the sayings and mannerisms of Treadmill. What Cecily continued to say, however, was even stranger.

'Your wife – where is she, by the way?'

'Deirdre?'

'That is your wife's name?'

'Oh, she's not one for parties.'

I wondered whether Aunt Deirdre had excluded herself from the evening or whether Uncle Roy had simply chosen to come on his own. It is perfectly true that my aunt would have hated it all.

'*Deirdre* said you *couldn't* send the boy to school in London, with the *Blitz* going on, and most of the boys were being *evacuated* anyway, or transferred to that woman's brother's school. It was in the West Country, wasn't it?'

'Malvern,' I said. 'Seaforth Grange.' A name of dread to me still. I shudder slightly even to write the words on the page. 'But are you saying that Mrs Paxton's brother. . . .'

'Mrs Paxton, that was her name – she took Rice Robey over *completely*.'

'She was my old headmaster's sister?'

'I think that was right.'

There was no time to develop this now, nor to make sure whether it was true, which it was. It merely accentuated my sense of destiny having fewer cards in the pack than I had supposed, and of life having a shape which is hidden from us except in strange moments of illumination such as this, which we label coincidence.

'There's Rice Robey – there!' I said.

He was standing in a group which contained Vernon, Darnley, Jo and Felicity, who kissed her father and introduced him to her beloved.

Rice Robey looked hard at Uncle Roy.

'Felicity's sire!'

He was rather red in the face as he said this, and sweat had formed globules on his Shakespearian brow which were running down his temples.

'You can always tell, with a woman,' he added, 'when the blood of the sacerdos runs in her veins.'

This was mere Robey talk for saying that Fliss was a vicar's daughter. I did not know whether my uncle was more disconcerted by the words themselves or by the accent in which they were delivered, having striven so successfully to banish from his diction all trace of the London vowels which still lingered in the voice of his mother, and which my father had had.

'Good ter see you, Roy, good ter see yer,' said Vernon, pumping my uncle's hand. 'Fliss said yer were here.'

My uncle fell at once to Lampitt talk with Vernon, leaving me to take Cecily by the elbow – she seemed in that moment very small – and introduce her to Rice Robey. When he recognised her, he folded her in his arms and clutched her for a full minute of silence.

'It's an *age*,' she said.

'I wanted to write to you, Mrs Lampitt.'

'Lost your pen?' she asked sharply.

'I mean, lately,' he said.

'I suppose you mean, about *The Spark*.' She turned to Darnley, whom she evidently knew a little, and said, 'Did you write it?'

Darnley smiled in a non-committal way. So much had passed through my mind since meeting Cecily that I had not yet allowed myself to speculate about her likely reactions to the allegations in *The Spark*. The idea that someone we love has been murdered, could not, one supposed, have failed to be upsetting. Sargie, however, had been so oddly elated by the suggestion that his brother had been pushed off the fire escape that I no longer knew how anyone would react to the story of Jimbo's death.

'No one could have written that paragraph unless they *knew* something, you see. Oh, it's so *long* ago, so *long*, but darling Jimbo. . . . I could say so much about it all, if I wanted. I wouldn't *speak* to that man who wrote the book, I wouldn't *see* him. He's insufferable, with all his claims to have known Jimbo so well. I saw Jimbo every day of his life, every single day in those last years, and I should think he met Mr Hunter at most six times. He was an. . . .' She dithered for a sufficiently devastating word, 'an upstart! I know it sounds awful to say that, but that's what he *is*. But the idea that he had *killed* Jimbo. . . . And in cold print. . . . Rice Robey, it wasn't you wrote the article, was it? Or who told Mr Darnley the story?'

'I'm sure it's true,' said Darnley before Rice Robey had the chance to reply. 'It has the ring of truth about it.'

'After all these *years*, to have it raked up again. I'd always supposed that it was the most terrible *accident*. *No one* knew Jimbo better than I did, and I'm quite sure he would never have. . . .' The word suicide would not quite come. 'He just wasn't the type. He loved life! But, oh! If the dead could only rest in peace!'

The air of theatricality in Cecily – Sargie had sometimes made disobliging comments about it – was never more marked than when replaying her memories of Jimbo. Conversation in the little group had rather stopped. We all looked and listened, except for Vernon, who was talking to Felicity about the virtues of a planned economy.

As Cecily was speaking, a young man came to join our group, evidently unknown to the company, a pale young man with a lot of spots on his forehead and a strangely elderly manner of dress – a dark suit and a watch chain. He moved awkwardly from one foot to the other. Sometimes a smile played across his weasely face and sometimes he held his mouth open as if, should anyone care to listen, he was about to speak.

'Oh but I miss him, I miss him,' Cecily was saying.

And Vernon was rubbing pipe dottle on his fingertips and saying,

'Ur aim shud be to take all manufacturing industry into public ownership within the first three years. There's no good in beatin' about the bush.'

'I think this young man. . . .' said Felicity.

She did not develop what she thought about the stranger.

Vernon slapped the youth on the shoulder.

'Good ter see yer, good ter see yer. Friend of Miles? Where's yer drink? There's lemonade if, like me, yer a teetotaller.'

'I haven't come for a drink,' said the young man, now gulping with embarrassment.

'And look, um forgottin' me manners. Um Ernie Lampitt.– Roy Ramsay, Julian Ramsay. . . .' He began a round of tedious introductions. 'Miles Darnley, yer know.'

'My name is Tongue,' said the young man, blushing at the admission. 'I represent the firm of Widdell and Blair.'

Jo Lampitt, silenced for the previous few minutes by her inability to say anything sufficiently fatuous about either the planned economy or her great-uncle's demise, squealed with merriment at the mention of the word Widdell.

'I see in you,' said Rice Robey to Mr Tongue, 'the neaniskos of Gethsemane, the unknown young man who appeared at the arrest of Christ and who fled naked when the guards seized his outer clothes.'

Mr Tongue blinked like a cornered rabbit at this assertion which might well, in the circumstances, have been the prelude to debagging him and sending him out naked into the night with no clothes.

'Mr Rice Robey?' he tentatively enquired.

'Yes.'

Without another word, Mr Tongue reached into his pocket for a folded paper and placed it into Rice Robey's hand.

'Mr Miles Darnley?' enquired Mr Tongue again.

'This is like Christmas,' said Jo. 'Little cards and prezzies for everyone.'

'Who are you?' asked Felicity fiercely. 'Are you from a lawyer?'

Mr Tongue placed into Darnley's hand a document identical to the one which he had given to Rice Robey. Darnley smiled, but I felt it was a stung sort of smile, and I remembered Rice Robey's very odd assertion, made to me long before, that Darnley had in him something of John the Baptist, a prophet doomed to martyrdom. By the time we had all absorbed the fact that these pieces of folded cream paper, sealed with scarlet wax, were writs for libel, Mr Tongue (in

219

this respect, at least, like the biblical young man who so interested Rice Robey, though fully clothed) had vanished through the throng.

Because of the creakingly slow processes of the law, it was at least eight months before Rice Robey's case came to court. At Darnley's wedding I had assumed, knowing nothing of such matters, that the police might arrive at any moment and prevent the newly-weds from departing for their honeymoon. In fact, for a long time nothing much seemed to happen. I was not, of course, privy to the long exchange of solicitors' letters between the various parties concerned. I felt intensely embarrassed by my own part in the affair, and, in the way that the marriage of one's friends can make them into strangers, Darnley did not bother to keep in touch with me. My life was taken up with other things – with 'The Mulberrys', with Sargie, with unattainable girls.

The first I knew of what had happened in the case was on a blustery evening the following April. I had returned from Birmingham (a recording session of 'The Mulberrys' during which Jason had started an improbable flirtation with the Barleybrook village schoolmistress) and found Rice Robey sitting with Felicity in the downstairs sitting room of the house in Arlington Road. When I entered the room, they were sitting next to one another on the sofa, and she sprang up with such nervousness that I wondered if I had surprised them in an embrace.

'Julian! I wasn't expecting you so soon.'

'The intrusion is my own,' said Rice Robey.

'Sit down, R.R.,' said Felicity sharply.

'If you'd rather I went out again,' I said, awkwardly, not knowing how I should finish the sentence. I saw no reason why I should be driven from my own home by Rice Robey and Felicity having yet another of their little trysts.

'We'd better tell him,' said Felicity.

For a second of horror, I guessed that she was going to announce her intention of marrying Rice Robey.

'Mr Darnley has settled,' he said, instantaneously putting my mind at rest.

'Settled the case with Hunter? Oh, but that's marvellous news.'

'How can you say that?' asked Felicity reproachfully. 'You see where that places R.R.?'

'I don't see anything.'

As far as the intricacies of law were concerned, I was an innocent. They patiently explained to me that Hunter had issued three writs. He intended to sue Darnley and Rice Robey as individuals, and also the small limited company that owned *The Spark*, which consisted of Darnley and a couple of 'backers'. Darnley's family lawyer had eventually put pressure on him to settle the case with Hunter out of court. It was not, apparently, something to which Darnley agreed very readily, but when he had realised the extent of the likely damages and legal costs, there was really no alternative. His mother and the family lawyer did not wish Darnley's assets (which I was somehow not surprised to learn were considerable) to be poured into Hunter's bank account in a limitless flow. They had agreed to pay Hunter £10,000 and to close down the paper – which could not by any standards hope to sustain a loss of this magnitude. (At that date £10,000 could buy you a substantial house in the middle of London.)

These were big stakes. As I heard the story, I felt crushed by self-hatred; by the knowledge that my indiscreet words to Hunter in the Turkish baths had helped to bring about the downfall of my friend and the closure of *The Spark*.

Since the whole painful business began, Rice Robey had refused to employ his own legal adviser. Any letters which had been written to him by Hunter's solicitor had been answered by himself – no doubt in his own distinctive manner. When, however, Darnley's solicitor reached a settlement with Hunter, they approached Rice Robey and asked him to come in on the deal. Darnley had generously offered to pay all Rice Robey's costs; and I have no doubt that he would also have paid any out-of-court settlement in lieu of damages on Robey's behalf out of his own pocket however much this was frowned upon by the guardians of the Darnley family money.

This development was not to be. Robey had spent about three hours with Darnley's solicitor. It had been pointed out to him that he had only two alternatives. He could issue a full retraction of the libel, and come in under the umbrella of their collective settlement with Hunter, or he could be left on his own. Since his legal liability was inextricably linked with that of Darnley and *The Spark*, Darnley's lawyers were skilfully anxious to distance themselves from the risk which Rice Robey now constituted. In spite of Darnley's protests, they warned Rice Robey that if he did not accept the settlement, he would be on his own. The prosecution could sub-poena Darnley as a witness *against* Rice Robey, by making it clear that he had published the accusation in good faith, and that the libel, the suggestion that Hunter was a murderer, was a lie originating solely with Rice Robey. Hunter was evidently in no mood for clemency. He would sue Rice Robey for all he was worth, perhaps more. Robey and the Great Attachment faced total financial ruin, and Robey could very well face a prison sentence.

This was the sobering news which Rice Robey had come to my house to relate to Felicity.

Now that Darnley was out of the running, it was more than ever clear to me that I was directly responsible for the case having been brought. If it had not been for the fact that, in his guileless letters to Hunter's solicitors, Robey had already admitted to the authorship of the articles, I might have myself been summoned as a prosecution witness.

'So, what are you going to do?' I asked.

'*Magna est veritas*', Robey intoned, '*et praevalebit.*' The shock of the whole experience had made him momentarily forget his own language, and it seemed that he was only capable of speaking in Latin – pronounced, as always, in his highly idiosyncratic tone. When I asked – 'Apart from anything else, how will you pay for your trial?', he merely smiled and said: '*Deus providebit. . . .*' Even I knew how that quotation ended – God would provide a victim for the slaughter – whatever deities of wrath had been unleashed by the libel, they would exact their revenge.

The trial, when it happened, was conducted in a small room in the Courts of Justice in the Strand. Cinema-going had led me to believe that trials – however few the participants – happened in vast theatrical settings – a crowded public gallery, rows of bewigged clerks and counsel, a judge on his bench set apart like Zeus in a Greek drama. In reality, the whole place had an almost embarrassingly intimate air. There was very little space for spectators, and these benches were filled to capacity, partly by journalists, partly by myself, Darnley, Cecily – who put in faithful and regular appearances on each of the three days of the trial – and Felicity. The jury were squashed into benches on the other side of the court.

The judge was a man called Mr Justice Howell, a small-lipped, scarlet-cheeked Welshman whose face suggested that he might at any moment become uncontrollably angry. His appearance on the Bench, for which we all respectfully stood to attention, did not bode well for Rice Robey's chances. Hunter sat behind his own counsel, a clever barrister called Oliver Leslie. He did not, as Rice Robey did, look around the courtroom or attempt to catch anyone's eye. He sat pale, and impassive, as the proceedings got under way.

There was a great deal of palaver before the trial proper began. The judge greeted the prosecution counsel with effusive good manners which were immediately switched off when he came to address the defendant.

'I employ no counsel, my lord,' Rice Robey said. 'Partly because it is beyond my means to do so, partly because the Truth needs no. . . .'

'Please do not try to explain yourself to me, Mr Robey,' said the judge.

'I thought that this was the function of the present assembly, my lord – that I should explain myself to you.'

This sally of Robey's made the judge's already scarlet face deepen to the colour of purplish bricks.

'Since you clearly have no idea of what constitutes the law, Mr Robey, I should leave it to me to decide what the function of this assembly might be,' he snapped.

'As your lordship pleases. Except to say this.'

'What is it now, Mr Robey?'

'We were not forbidden to judge one another because it is improper – merely because it is impossible.'

'Forbidden? Forbidden? What on earth are you trying to say, man? Who has forbidden me to judge you?'

'Another judge, my lord,' said Robey with his mysterious, and on this occasion infuriating smile. 'Another Judge.'

'I should be interested to know his name,' snapped Howell. 'Whoever he is, he has no function in this court. I am trying this case. I apologise to you, Mr Leslie' – once again, he switched on an ingratiating smile – 'for the amount of your valuable time which we are wasting.'

'I'm sure it is valuable time, my lord, for which my client will not be paying,' said Oliver Leslie smoothly.

'I'm sure,' added the judge, thus making it abundantly clear, before a single word of the trial had begun, how he intended that it should be concluded. Since Rice Robey was no lawyer, he did not pick the judge up on this, and so the farce began without further interruption.

Oliver Leslie QC arose, and began to explain to the jury the nature of the libel. He told them that Raphael Hunter was well known to them, a proposition with which I am not sure that they agreed. He told them that they had all seen Raphael Hunter on television, and admired his 'many contributions to the arts'. (It made it sound as though he was recommending Hunter for a knighthood in the New Year's Honours rather than defending his good name in court.) Some of them would read Hunter's column in a Sunday newspaper. Others would have read his biography of James Petworth Lampitt.

'It could be said,' pontificated Oliver Leslie, 'that Lampitt was a distinctly minor writer, who owes his survival very largely to my client. When he died, I should say that very few people read the works of James Petworth Lampitt. Very few indeed. His was a vanished reputation, if, indeed, ladies and gentlemen of the jury, it was a reputation at all. He was, I gather, a lonely man. He was what you could call the literary world's equivalent of a has-been – if I may use so vulgar a phrase. And this was the man, ladies and gentlemen, whom my client, out of the goodness of his heart, befriended, the man whose loneliness he. . . .' Olive Leslie paused. It was by no means clear what Hunter had done to the supposed loneliness and neglect of Jimbo.

'After he died,' continued the QC, leaving the loneliness and neglect somewhat in the air, 'Mr Hunter, my client, worked tirelessly for the restitution of his work. It is entirely thanks to him that some of that work is now available in paperback. It is thanks to him that the name James Petworth Lampitt is known. And it is known, very largely, I should submit, because of Mr Hunter's magisterial biography of the man – a man whom he knew, and whom he respected, and to whose friendship and conversation, he owed much.

'Ladies and gentlemen, this is a libel trial, and not a murder trial. There is absolutely no question that James Petworth Lampitt died an accidental death, on that April day in 1947. You will hear from my client, when he takes the stand, how that death occurred. A coroner returned a verdict of accidental death on the man, and accidental death it unquestionably was. If – and of course, the very possibility is unthinkable – if anyone has suspected otherwise, there would have been every possible opportunity for them to state their suspicions to the police at the proper time, and in the proper manner. Of course, no such suspicions existed. It was only after sixteen years had passed – sixteen years, ladies and gentlemen of the jury – that the defendant chose to perpetrate this foul and damaging libel on my client, the very direct suggestion that he had been responsible for the death of the man whom he so much revered and to whom, as I have already stated, he owed so much.'

Mr Oliver Leslie QC proceeded to acquaint the jury with *The Spark* – which he described as 'a vulgar news-sheet of which they had probably not heard'. He told them that it was now defunct but that it developed a reputation for printing scurrilous verbal attacks, often upon persons unable or unwilling to defend themselves. He described the magazine as 'malicious with the malice of the school playground – and we all know how cruel that can be'.

It was, he stated, an open secret that Rice Robey was the author of many of these items which appeared in the anonymous 'Diary' item at the front of the magazine, and that he had enjoyed extraordinary good luck in not being prosecuted for some of the libellous things he had printed about other well-loved and much-respected figures in the public eye.

Rice Robey smiled through all this. He did not rise to his feet, or object that he was being tried for a libel upon Raphael Hunter, rather than upon these putative and unnamed public figures. He did not even protest as Oliver Leslie began his description of himself.

'Mr Robey, it would be true to say, ladies and gentlemen of the jury, is a bitter man. He is a failure. You will learn how he wished to pursue a career of learning and literature, but that poverty and various character defects made this impossible. He was in early days a protégé of the late Mr Lampitt's and he would dearly have loved to enjoy the same position in Mr Lampitt's affections that was occupied by Mr Hunter. He was, in short, envious of Mr Hunter, eaten up by envy and malice for sixteen years, and probably for longer. He had known when he published his libel in *The Spark* that it was the most dastardly libel, and he had still persuaded the editor, much against his better judgement, to print it. He had done so for reasons of envy and pique and malice, knowing them to be foul lies. There is no worse libel than to accuse another man of having killed one of his best friends. This is a very simple case, ladies and gentlemen; an

225

extremely simple case. I have absolutely no doubt how it will be concluded.'

I gather that it was not Oliver Leslie at his best, but the judge seemed to like it. He beamed solicitously at the barrister as he sat down, and then said, with ill-concealed distaste, 'Mr Robey, you may make some statement for the defence if you wish before the case proceeds.'

Oliver Leslie had been a little verbose, but his manner had been reasonable, his tones quiet. His eyes had moved from his papers to the jury, and back; he spoke as a reasonable man speaking to other reasonable beings. It was obvious from the moment that Rice Robey rose to his feet that this was not to be his technique.

Thrusting his head right back so that he looked at the ceiling, and raising both arms in the air, he called out, 'What is truth!'

Such a long silence ensued, that one wondered if this was to be his defence. Then he turned, not to the judge or jury, but to Hunter himself, who refused to meet his gaze, but sheepishly examined his finger-nails as the Robey harangue unrolled.

'It is a good question at a trial, and you will recall at which trial the question was first posited, by the representative of the *saeculum*, by the *magisterium* of Empire, what is truth? And he managed – I speak of Pilate – to find no answer in his process, and so through the hand-washing ritual he demonstrates the impotence of the empirical lie, and the illegality of the Roman *lex*, and the worse emptiness of the Torah, written in scrolls and not on hearts. . . .'

'Mr Robey,' said the judge, 'this is nothing to do with the case.'

'Ah! We shall remember that, your honour, and so will the jury when they come to their verdict: that the question *What is truth?* has nothing to do with the case.'

'Mr Robey, you are here to defend yourself against a very specific and I might add a very serious charge. I really must insist that you restrict your remarks to what is relevant to the charge against you, and not treat us to this – *generalised* tirade.'

'My lord Caiaphas, my lord Pilate, I stand rebuked,' said Rice Robey.

'I am sure that the jury agree with me that it is extremely improper, not to say blasphemous, to introduce all these other considerations into the case,' said the judge testily.

'*I'm sure this Jesus will not do – Either for Englishman or Jew*,' agreed

226

Rice Robey. 'Very well, I shall present my defence in terms which even a judge might find comprehensible. I feel no malice towards friend Hunter – merely a confidence that he shed innocent blood. I knew Mr Lampitt – Mr James Petworth Lampitt – for many years. Witnesses will be called who knew him for much longer.'

There was a rumble of excitement in the courtroom at this news. We had all assumed that there would be some witnesses for the prosecution, but (in so far as Felicity would let me be privy to details of Rice Robey's plans for his own defence) I had not heard that there would be any defence witnesses.

'James Petworth was no self-slayer. He was possessed with no suicidal *daimon*. He was not – though you could consider this, O Pilate, to be an irrelevant detail – he was not the watery figure whom we meet in the pages of Mr Hunter's compilation, published some winters since. He was, for one thing, not homoerotic.'

'Mr Robey, I have warned you,' said the judge.

'But have you warned *him*, O Pilate?' and Robey pointed a long and hieratic finger at Hunter. 'Have you warned him of the consequences of shedding innocent blood? No! For the judgement is not yours or mine to give. All we are here to do is to arrive at the truth; and we shall! We shall!'

The sing-song manner of Robey's delivery – and the volume (he spoke, for that little room, far too loud) did not seem to have made a very favourable impression on the jury. They looked distinctly as if they were in the presence of someone embarrassing and distasteful, and there was laughter among them – the embarrassed laughter of relief when the comparatively 'normal' judge spoke and the trial went on.

It was during that first day that Hunter took the witness box. Whereas Robey was wild and mad-seeming, Hunter, particularly when cross-examined by his own counsel, was quiet, and his smile suggested that he was being extraordinarily good-humoured about a matter in which other men, less reasonable or kind, would have been violently aggrieved.

Mr Oliver Leslie QC did not have many questions to ask of Hunter. He took him through the article in *The Spark*.

'Mr Hunter, it will distress you if I repeat that sentence once more, that foul libel, but I feel that I must do so. Here it is: "We wonder how many cases there are in which a biographer has been the agent of his subject's demise." Those are the words. Do you believe that these words can be interpreted in any way other than to make it seem that you murdered James Petworth Lampitt?'

'No, sir,' said Hunter. 'I do not.'

'And, in order to save Mr Robey the trouble of asking you the question, let me, Mr Hunter, ask you the question myself: did you, sir, murder James Petworth Lampitt?'

'No, sir, I did not.'

Quiet, hushed, reasonable. It was an odd occasion for one of Hunter's smiles, but he did smile at the jury, with an almost flirtatiously nervous curl of the lips.

'No, sir,' Rice Robey repeated, as he rose to cross-examine Hunter, 'you did not. And that is your reply.'

'Mr Hunter's reply was perfectly audible, Mr Robey,' interrupted the judge, 'without your repeating it. I must also remind you that you must address the bench with an appropriate deference or I shall punish you for contempt of court.'

'A not inapposite description of my feelings, m'lord,' said Robey, which caused laughter in the public benches.

'Now, Mr Hunter, may I ask you some questions?'

'Mr Robey,' said the judge, 'we know that you have stood up to ask Mr Hunter some questions. That is all we wish you to do. Kindly hurry up about it.'

'Do you believe in God?'

'Mr Robey, really!' exclaimed the judge.

'I think I am entitled to the question, my lord.'

'I consider it improper,' said the judge.

'Perhaps I may ask some other questions of you, Mr Hunter,' continued Rice Robey, who was fishing in his pocket and produced from the inside of a dirty cheque-book some yellow newspaper cuttings. 'Did you, in a review in the *Sunday Times* last summer, review a book about the modernist movement in poetry?'

'Yes,' said Hunter. 'I did.'

'Did you write these words: "I" – referring to yourself, Mr Hunter, "must be one of the many who found 'The Four Quartets' an inspirational work while being unable to share T.S. Eliot's religious beliefs"?'

'Yes,' said Hunter. 'I wrote those words.'

'Did you, in a review in the same newspaper of a biography of D. H. Lawrence dated some months earlier, state that "few intelligent people nowadays accept the old religious orthodoxies"?'

'Yes,' said Hunter, 'I wrote that.'

'And would you consider that you are among the few or among the many?'

'Mr Robey,' said the judge hotly, 'I must warn you that I see no relevance in this line of questioning.'

'My lord, Mr Hunter has made it very clear in his journalism that he is not a religious believer. He makes it clear, I should say, by every uninspirational sentence that he pens. . . .'

'I should remind you, Mr Robey, that this is not a symposium on the merits of Mr Hunter's prose style.'

No one except the judge laughed at this pleasantry.

'Mr Hunter began his evidence, my lord, with an oath. He swore by Almighty God that the evidence he would give would be the truth, the whole truth. . . .'

'We all heard Mr Hunter take the oath, Mr Robey.'

'I think, my lord, that the ladies and gentlemen of the jury might be illuminated to discover that the man who swore by Almighty God does not believe that Almighty God exists.'

The judge turned to the jury.

'You may disregard all those questions,' he said hotly. 'Now, Mr Robey, will you kindly get to the point?'

'I cannot get to the point, my lord, if you and I do not agree as to what the point is,' said Robey. 'I began by asking – What is truth? I was told that it was of no interest in an English court of law, and that will be an interesting lesson to have learnt, if nothing else is to emerge from these proceedings. I then began by asking if Mr Hunter's oath was to be understood to have the slightest meaning. You directed the jury to disregard my question. Now we know where we are. We are in a room where it is not considered important whether there is such a thing as truth, or whether we live in a godless universe. And in this place, this infernal place I should say, we are required – by what means I do not know – to establish truth by some means which will be beyond me.'

'If it is beyond you to establish the truth, Mr Robey, you had better shut up and sit down,' said the judge.

'Not yet, my lord. I have some more questions for Mr Hunter.'

Hunter smiled patiently. I noticed, as on the first occasion that I met him, and he was describing the death of James Petworth Lampitt to a small literary society at my boarding school, that he pressed his hands very firmly down on the surface in front of him, in this case, the wooden railing at the front of the witness box.

'Once again, I ask you – were you alone with Mr Lampitt when he died?'

'I was not with him. I was in the sitting room of his flat. He had gone into the kitchen. He liked to stand on the fire escape just outside his kitchen and look at the sky. I heard a crash – a cry – and I ran out to the kitchen to see what had happened. He was not there. I looked over the balustrade at the top of the fire escape and saw that he had fallen into the area below.'

'And nobody else was there?'

'No.'

'How high is the railing outside his kitchen?'

'My lord, this incident happened seventeen years ago,' said Hunter. 'I seem to remember that it was about waist-high, but I could not be certain.'

'How tall are you, Mr Hunter?'

'Five foot ten inches.'

'And how tall was James Petworth Lampitt?'

'I do not know.'

'You wrote a very long book about him, but you do not know his height. You knew him well, but you do not know his height. You were, according to a recent paperback of his life of the Prince Consort, his close friend and private secretary, but you did not know his height.'

'I meant that I do not remember his exact height.'

'Quite so, Mr Hunter,' said the judge sympathetically. 'There is really no need to submit to this hectoring from the defendant.'

'He was five foot five inches in height,' said Rice Robey. 'Would you agree that he could not have fallen over the railing. He could have climbed it – a very unlikely eventuality – or he could have been helped over it. Would you agree?'

'There is no need to answer that question,' said the judge. 'It was an impertinence even to have suggested it.'

'Thank you, my lord,' said Rice Robey. 'And it is an impertinence to suggest that a man fell over a railing which he would in point of fact have had the greatest difficulty in climbing. I have no further questions of this witness.'

*

It was on the following day of the trial that Robey made his most dramatic coup.

'My lord, I call Mrs Sargent Lampitt.'

In the witness box, Cecily looked smaller than she was. More than on previous occasions when I had looked at her, I was put in mind of the dressed animals in Beatrix Potter's illustrations. Her pretty rodent-like eyes darted sharply about the court, and then fixed themselves accusingly on Raphael Hunter.

Cecily did not take the oath. She made a declaration that she would tell the truth, but that she would not invoke the deity in whom she did not believe.

'Your name is Cecily Horatia Lampitt.'

'It is.'

'And you are married to the brother of the late James Petworth Lampitt.'

'I was. I am.'

The judge leaned forward and peered at Cecily contemptuously.

'Well, are you or aren't you married to him?' he asked.

'In law, I am still married to Sargent Lampitt.'

'Speak up!' snapped the judge.

'I said in law, my lord, I am still married to Mr Lampitt. We have not lived together for many years.'

'Why waste words?' asked the judge. 'How else can you be married to someone except in law?'

This rebuke excited Cecily's indignation. Her lips pursed, and then she said vehemently, 'There is no need to be so *rude*! Just because you are a judge. . . .'

'I must remind you, madam, that if you do not restrict yourself to answering the questions, you could be in very serious trouble.'

Rice Robey smiled and stared at the ceiling as he said, 'Mrs Lampitt, you knew your brother-in-law very well, and for a long time.'

'Yes,' said Cecily.

'When were you married?'

'1917.'

'And James Petworth died in 1947.'

'Yes.'

'So you knew one another for at least thirty years.'

'Most of us can count,' said the judge.

'Did you read the biography of James Petworth Lampitt by the plaintiff Mr Hunter?'

'I did.'

'Did you consider that it provided an accurate account of the man?'

'No, I did not. I considered it a mean book, a cruel book, a foolish book. It was not the man I knew so well. It wasn't him at all. It was full of innuendo. No one in the family liked it. None of us recognised James Petworth Lampitt in Mr Hunter's book. No, we did not.'

'In particular, you were displeased that Mr Hunter made James Petworth Lampitt out to be of homoerotic proclivities; is that not the case.'

'I have said, there are many innuendoes in the book which I disliked.'

'And that was one of them.'

'Yes.'

'And you considered that this was unture – that James Petworth did not indulge in the vices of Alcibiades and Alexander the Great?'

'If you mean did he make love to boys, then I would say very decidedly not.'

'And you knew him very well – you knew him well enough to feel confident about this?'

'I do feel confident. Mr Hunter told lies. He pretends that he knew James Petworth Lampitt really well and this wasn't true, it wasn't *true*. I used to visit Mr Lampitt many times, oh, often each week. And yes, in the last few months of his life, I heard him mention Mr Hunter. I forget where they had met: at some literary party, I believe. They certainly did not know each other well. Mr Hunter used to come to tea with Mr Lampitt sometimes, that was all. He came to tea on the day that Mr Lampitt died.'

'And you were due to call on Mr Lampitt later that afternoon, were you not?'

'Yes, yes I was.'

'Can you tell us what happened that afternoon?'

'I arrived at Jimbo's flat – at Mr Lampitt's flat, as I often did, and let myself in, I had my own key, and I was astonished.'

'By what?'

'I was astonished to find that Mr Hunter was sitting in the flat on his own. He had been going through Jimbo's desk.'

'How do you know?'

232

'Jimbo was a very neat man. He never left papers or notebooks lying about, he never left drawers open. But when I came into the room, his bureau was open, and there were papers spread out all over the desk. Mr Hunter had obviously been going through his things – going through Jimbo's things, Mr Hunter. He was, he was.'

'What did you say or do?'

'I challenged him. I said – "Where is Mr Lampitt? You aren't supposed to be here on your own"' (hee-er). 'He said that Jimbo was dead, that he had fallen from the balcony at the back of the flat, and that he was very glad that I had come. He said he had wanted to tell me in person.'

'Did you believe him?'

'No, I did not. Why should he wish to tell me anything? He was surprised by my coming into the room, startled – he looked fishy, guilty, up to no good. He was not shocked by Jimbo's death, not at all. But he was shocked by my appearing. He was trying to rifle through Jimbo's desk, and he was trying to cover his own tracks.'

'Can you guess what he was searching for in James Petworth Lampitt's bureau?'

'No.' She paused. 'I have often wondered.'

For me, who had so often thought about the day on which James Petworth Lampitt died, all this had an extraordinary interest. Since Cecily was not really on terms with Sargie, it was not surprising that her presence in the flat, so soon after Jimbo's death, had never been mentioned by Uncle Roy.

As Mr Oliver Leslie QC was soon to demonstrate, Cecily had not provided any new evidence of a kind that would, as the phrase goes, 'stand up in a court of law'. She had not proved that Hunter had murdered Jimbo. But in an imaginative sense, as far as I was concerned, she had changed the whole of that day for me. I now saw it, and all the actors involved, and to some extent everything which had happened thereafter, in a different light. It was the little details which changed things – the fact that she had her own key, for example; and her vivid word-picture of Hunter, startled like a guilty thing surprised as he sat at Jimbo's bureau. And it was all so long ago, and yet it all had such power, still, to change us.

Mr Oliver Leslie QC was not kind in his cross-examination of Cecily. I do not know whether the judge knew what was coming, but he leaned forward as soon as the prosecuting counsel was on his feet, and a malign smile lit up Howell's mean little features.

233

'Mrs Lampitt, your brother-in-law was a bachelor, was he not?'

'Yes.'

'He had many friends in the literary world, I believe.'

'Yes, he did.'

'Stretching back over a number of years?'

'Well, yes.'

Mr Oliver Leslie QC picked up a fat paperback edition of Raphael Hunter's biography.

'For instance, I believe he knew slightly Henry James.'

'Yes, he did.'

'And Hugh Walpole?'

'Yes, Jimbo knew Hugh Walpole.'

'Is it true that he also knew Baron Corvo?'

'I can't remember. I did not know all of Jimbo's friends.'

'Ah. That is very interesting. You were close to Mr Lampitt, but you did not – er, know *all* his friends.'

'I don't see what's wrong with that!' Again, Cecily was losing her temper, and she turned to the jury for support. By now, it was clear in what direction Mr Oliver Leslie QC was leading his inquiry, and Cecily was presumably angry that she had allowed herself to be led into a trap so easily.

'We are told in Mr Hunter's book that, as a young man, James Petworth Lampitt even went to Paris in order to meet Oscar Wilde. That was an event which took place, would you not say?'

'Yes. He described it to me.'

'Mr Lampitt told you he had met Oscar Wilde.'

'Oh, really, what's all this got to do with it?'

'I'd like to ask you a few more questions, Mrs Lampitt. Do you remember that James Petworth Lampitt wrote a short introduction to the sonnets of Michelangelo?'

'Yes, I do. It's a very fine piece of work.'

'And do you remember that in that introduction he described the love of Michelangelo for his own sex as "an ennobling thing, this love which Shakespeare celebrated in his Sonnets, and Plato in his Symposium, a love, perchance, which can never be found between a man and a woman". Do you remember that sentence, Mrs Lampitt?'

'The substance of it, yes.'

'And do you remember the sentence which appears in a later paragraph – "It is not merely in the pages of the sacred texts that we find love 'passing the love of women'". A reference of course to the love in the Bible between David and Jonathan.'

'I am perfectly well aware of the Bible story,' snapped Cecily.

'Do those sentences please you, Mrs Lampitt?'

'I think they are very interesting,' she said.

'And you think they are true?'

'I beg your pardon?'

'Do you think it is true that for certain men, there is a love which is "passing the love of women"?'

'You have just told us that there is. In the Bible.' She smirked, as if she had scored a point, and not realising that he was about to pounce on his prey.

'Were you in love with your brother-in-law, Mrs Lampitt?'

A pained silence fell on the courtroom. Rice Robey jumped to his feet.

'My lord! This is not relevant to the case. My witness is being subjected. . . .'

'It is of great relevance to the case, Mr Robey, to know in what direction witnesses are biased,' said the judge with a satanic gleam in his face. 'Please answer the question, Mrs Lampitt. We are all agog for the answer.'

'Why should I answer such a question, in such a place?' Cecily asked furiously.

'Because I have said that you must,' said the judge sharply. 'Were you in love with James Petworth Lampitt or weren't you?'

Another aching silence. Then, Cecily's voice, very quiet, and serious and low.

'Yes. Yes, Jimbo and I loved one another.'

'That is not what I asked you, Mrs Lampitt,' said Oliver Leslie. 'I put it to you that you were in love with James Petworth Lampitt, but that your affections were not returned.'

'That's not true!'

'I put it to you that you knew James Petworth Lampitt was homosexual by inclination, and that you had a jealous hatred for the young men to whom he formed attachments. I put it to you that you suspected him of loving my client Mr Hunter, albeit in a platonic sense. I put it to you that you were jealous of Mr Hunter and that you are still jealous of him, and that in all your remarks about him you are motivated by sexual jealousy. I put it to you that you are a bitter woman whose judgement is clouded by years of nursing a foolish and

235

hopeless passion for a man who had no interest in you whatsoever.'

'No, no, no. . . .'

But Oliver Leslie had sat down. He had no further questions.

The summing-up occurred on the following day. As Oliver Leslie had said in his opening speech, it was a very simple case. Rice Robey had accused Hunter of murder. The coroner's verdict on James Petworth Lampitt's death had been produced, and they had even managed to find the doctor who had performed the autopsy in 1947. No evidence had been produced that Jimbo's death had been other than accidental. Therefore, Rice Robey was guilty of libel. In his own summing-up, he was crushed. He still looked aloft, and he still waved his hands in hieratic gestures, but he knew that he had no case.

'Ladies and gentlemen of the jury, I began by asking you Pilate's question – "What is truth?" And like jesting Pilate, our learned judge would not stay for an answer. You have heard the testimony of Mrs Lampitt which Mr Leslie has attempted to twist and distort. She knew James Petworth Lampitt; and I knew him too. We knew he was not a suicide. We knew that he had not died by natural means. There was only one who could have hastened his end, and that one is Mr Oliver Leslie's client, the plaintiff in the case today.'

The jury were out for about twenty minutes. They found him guilty, and Rice Robey was ordered to pay £1,000 damages, and almost as much again in costs.

It was from Felicity, in the subsequent days, that I heard the last details of these costs. I had gone away again to Birmingham, and did not follow the final stages of the drama. Darnley's offer to pay Rice Robey's costs had been refused. Nobly, but surely foolishly, Rice Robey had said that he had got himself, and Darnley, into the case and he would pay his own way out of it.

'Julian – it was so wicked: when one thinks of that rich judge, and that rich barrister, being prepared to reduce R.R. to ruin. He would barely have got £2,000 for that house in Twisden Road.'

'So, what happened?'

'I went through a terrible twenty-four hours of believing that R.R. wanted to go to prison, wanted to become a martyr for the cause of truth. Oh, Julian, he is a noble man.'

'What saved him? – or should I say – who saved him? Felicity – you didn't. . . .'

'I offered, of course. I haven't quite got that money, but I have about £1,000. Of course I've made it available to R.R. from the beginning of all this.'

I did not know this fact and it made me furious; but I kept my counsel.

'So, who bailed him out?'

'Guess.'

'I can't.'

'The Great Attachment.'

'I thought that she was as poor as he was.'

'They are both desperately poor – particularly now that he has lost his job.'

'It's not certain that he's lost his job, is it?'

'They'll get him out,' she said with great sadness. 'He was so unpopular with those *fools* in the Ministry that they can easily get rid of him now. It is really because he was going to stop them building a road through Aldingbury Ring. But now that this case has come to light they can dress it up as a disciplinary offence. They can say that he was leaking secret, civil service information and writing in *The Spark* about things he could only have known from classified documents.'

'True?'

'It's so unfair.'

'But, how did the Great Attachment come to have two thousand quid?'

'Julian, it is such a strange story. They had a couple of really hideous paintings by this man that you used to work with in the shirt factory.'

'Not Mr Pilbright?'

'Yes. The one who's just been "discovered" after a lifetime of obscurity. One of them in particular – R.R. calls it the Woolworth Magdalene – is said to be a really "important" Pilbright. Mrs Paxton sold it a couple of months ago. Apparently it will pay for the damages and the costs and leave a little over for' – she smiled wanly – 'a washing machine.'

FIVE

William Bloom's large flat overlooks the Westminster School playing fields in Vincent Square. In idle moments, of which, for both of us, there are nowadays so many, he can gaze down on the boys at play, occasionally even lifting field glasses from his desk to survey, in summer, some particularly decorative figure in white flannels at silly mid off, or, in winter, the more tempestuous beauties of a Rugby scrum.

Quarter of a century had passed since Rice Robey's trial for libel. I was lunching with Bloom that day I saw the 'Mr Pilbright at Home' exhibition at the Tate, and we fell to talking, inevitably, about our lives, the forty or so years we had known one another, the singular threads of cognition and coincidence which had run through experience like Blake's Golden String.

'Extraordinary to think of all those years that Mr Pilbright worked at the shirt factory,' I said, 'and the total obscurity of his life when Daddy worked with him, then me. . . .'

'You'd still be working in a shirt factory today, my dear, if I hadn't talked you into lodging with Rikko and Fenella, and set you on the move, so to say.'

This was true. As we spoke, sipping coffee (how abstemious we have both become – no smoking, and barely any desire for alcohol) I thought of all the parallels between Mr Pilbright and Rice Robey. Not only were they both men with an idiosyncratic religious vision, translated without apparent awkwardness into their chosen medium; they also both achieved their effects of imaginative projection entirely uncowed by the way in which 'the world' expected them to earn a living. Rice Robey's career in the Ministry of Works is now remembered as little as Pilbright's forty years in Accounts at Tempest and Holmes. What remained was their imaginative achievement, Pilbright's hundreds of canvases, Robey's Albion Pugh novels, which still have their admirers, not to mention the charismatic effect which Rice Robey was to make as a minor cult figure in the late 1960s – something which lies outside the scope of the present volume.

Speaking of Robey, Bloom said, 'All that mingling of sex and religion – my God, he had it *made*!'

He threw back his snowy head and his wrinkled old face (the same age as mine – it is incredible!) creased into its familiar manic laughter.

'The chicks couldn't have enough of it!' he guffawed. 'His great secret was never for one instant doubting his own fantasy life. A very rare quality, that. Most of us lack faith in ourselves and call that process of disillusionment growing up. Not Robey-baby. Nor old Pill-prick. I haven't seen this latest exhibition, but I remember the important one at the Hayward Gallery which they put on after Raphael Hunter did that big interview with Pilbright on telly.'

While Bloom talked, I looked about his flat and tried to fashion into words what it was about these figures which had become significant for me with the passage of the years. My eyes fell on the comfort of Bloom's huge room, its wall lined with books, and the impressive Matthew Smith nudes, the gleaming, slightly too new leather sofas and armchairs, the huge round table where we sat alone, the two of us, looking out over the treetops and the boys in the distance playing hockey. The point at which I identified with Pilbright and Rice Robey was precisely in this area of the disparity between their imaginative and their workaday lives. Bloom was probably right to say that they had never grown up, never doubted their fantasies, always lived, as William Blake had done, within the self-confidently discovered borders of their own imagination, and refused to accept any second-hand vision of the world doled out to them by others.

My imaginative history lacked such cohesion. Mine had been a story of many visions and revisions, a chronicle of doubting everything, especially myself. Yet, when it occurred to me that my life was defined in anyone's eyes by the way in which I earned a living, I experienced the same sense of shock which could have been felt if Pilbright's life-story were told with no reference to the paintings, only to Tempest and Holmes, or if someone were to write the story of Rice Robey, schoolmaster and civil servant, without ever mentioning the Albion Pugh novels, the cult following, the pursuits in mind and on foot of legendary Britain.

Bloom had asked me to write a short book about my thirty-five year career as Jason Grainger. 'The Mulberrys' are as popular as ever, and Jason, as I need hardly remind regular listeners to the programme, is barely the same man as his youthful self. Successive scriptwriters have been sentimentalising his role to the point where all that remains from the bad old days is the occasional expression of verbal cynicism, which does not really conceal a heart as nauseatingly warm and loving as that of his sainted father, old Harold. Since the Mulberrys are so popular, and Jason Grainger is one of the longest-surviving members of the cast, it was not surprising that some publisher should see a saleable book in the subject.

William Bloom's idea was that I should actually write the book in the persona of Jason, describing his early adolescent quarrels with dear old Harold Grainger, his sorties into criminality, the unscrupulous affair with the lady of the manor turning into a love match, his mysterious absence from the village (during that period when I really believed that I had shaken free of him and might pursue my own career – he was meant to have gone to Canada, but Bloom wondered whether he might not have had a spell in prison for the sort of sexual aberration which is now regarded so much more sympathetically than then) right down to the present when, after Lady Tredegar's demise, Jason found himself the heir to Barleybrook Manor which he promptly converted into a 'country-house hotel' with himself as the increasingly oleaginous proprietor.

Bloom's money tempted me, but I could not write the book. After several false starts, I realised why. I wanted, before I died, to explore another story. It was not an urge to pure autobiography.

> I will give you the end of a golden string,
> Only wind it into a ball:
> It will lead you in at heaven's gate
> Built in Jerusalem's wall.

All lives are intertwinings of such golden strings. Mine, thanks to Uncle Roy and the way I was brought up, had been peculiarly connected with a family which was not my own – the Lampitts – and in particular to Sargie's brother Jimbo. James Petworth Lampitt had been the first writer to fill me with the desire to be a writer myself.

Reading his work had produced in me an epiphany to which I had never lived up, a vocation to which I had been unfaithful. I had allowed life to float by, never disciplining myself, as Professor Wimbish was said to do, to 3,000 words a day, rain or shine. Had I pursued a 'literary' career, I suppose I should have been able to improve on my first disastrous autobiographical novel and to produce books which might have been in the same fashionable league as, say, Deborah Arnott's books, reasonably well-turned stories of domestic life in contemporary Britain. Looking back, I realise that it was not what I wanted to do, and that James Petworth Lampitt had haunted me all my life, not simply because of his writings, but because of the Pandora's box opened up by contemplating his death. I find myself increasingly interested in the past, in the way that the past, just as much as the evanescent present, is always on the move, always changing, only perceptible by imaginative means. Blake distrusted representational art. 'I question not my corporal or vegetative eye any more than I would question a window concerning a sight. I look thro' it and not with it.' This vital perception illuminates everything for me, though it illuminates in the manner of a child's kaleidoscope, shaking all the constituent ingredients into shapes which will never stand still. The Petworth Lampitt created by Hunter in his fat tome was said by one reviewer to have 'a full square reality', comparable with the subjects of other great biographies, Froude's *Carlyle* or Sartre's *Flaubert*. This illusion of reality, just like the realism of Sir Joshua Reynolds so much abhorred by Blake, was achieved by Hunter's invariable ability to look with a window, not thro' it. In this connection, it makes almost no odds that most of the 'facts' in his biography are untrue, any more than it would matter to subsequent generations who had not known the original sitters, whether the canvases of Reynolds were true likenesses. Jimbo Lampitt, then, began to acquire a significance for me which Rice Robey, using the term in his own distinctive way, would have described as mythological. Jimbo's reality was beyond question. I knew two of his siblings well, and I came to know Cecily, who had loved him for more than a quarter of a century. In time, I would visit the United States and open those notorious boxes, labelled THE LAMPITT PAPERS and discover what they revealed. The whole experience of reflecting upon Jimbo, and by extension upon my own experience of the Lampitt family, not to say upon my own life, has caused me to make endless readjustments of vision, with which I can

241

only come to terms by writing them down. This act is itself an act of 'mythology', a fixing of things which are fluid, a series of still photographs of moving objects. Felicity, when I have discussed it with her, reverts to her merciless belief that there is no point in writing about such subjects unless one can, in her terms, *think*. My own ratiocinative defects, and my consciousness of them, have deterred me again and again from the task. In other moods, however, I have believed that it was precisely because I can not approach the matter as a philosopher that qualifies me for the task. Very few human beings can think, and perhaps those rare ones who can, like Felicity, necessary as they are as puncturers of nonsense, will never be able to understand, as intuitive artists can do, the way that reality presents itself to the human imagination. What nagged me about Jimbo, and the Lampitts, and my own past, turned out, the more I considered them, to be perennial questions with which Rice Robey, and other Christians before him, had been wrestling for 2,000 years. We inhabit a world of facts, a world where things either are, or are not, the case, where events did or did not happen; but facts and events actually possess no significance until they have been lit up by imagination. Truth-telling is impossible unless we see thro' and not with the eye. And yet I could not entirely sympathise with Rice Robey's dismissal of 'the empirical fallacy'. There are facts. There is Either/or.

Death, my own approaching and certain death, sharpens all this. My days are empty enough now, but I am haunted and terrified by the greater emptiness which stretches ahead, when my sentient being has ceased to exist and there is nothing. Memory floods back. I am one of those who 'lives in the past', and whole phases of existence come alive while I go about humdrum domestic chores or lie awake at night, phases which I had imagined were lost and forgotten. My early childhood in London, life in the rectory at Timplingham, the awakening of love, the dawning of my obsession with the story of Jimbo Lampitt, all these swirl into the brain, sometimes welcome visitants, as often not. Each time they do so now, I am stung by the knowledge that all these experiences are lost and irrevocably past. I know that the return of these memories does not mean that they can truly, still less permanently, be recalled. They are not for me intimations of immortality; nor are they hints that, after my bodily death, all such consciousness, refined and purified, will remain with me for eternity. (This, presumably, or something like it, is what religious people believe when they speak of the survival of consciousness or of the soul.) I feel reasonably certain that there is nothing to look forward to but total blank. At the end of the day, before the mind drifts off into the oblivion of dreamless sleep, half-dreams come, and the preoccupations of the previous twelve hours flit in and out of the mind, sometimes assuming playful shapes and muddling themselves into fantasies. The mind thus automatically stretches its limbs before the dark unconscious. In the same way, before the endless sleep of death, whole tracts of experience resolve themselves into stories in the mind. The cards are being reshuffled before they are put back in the box. I cling to them. I do not want them to go.

During childhood, I would become hysterical at the prospect of returning to boarding school. My grief was not wholly rational. 'You'll be all right once you are back at the school,' my exasperated aunt would say briskly to me as I sobbed and moaned and struggled. This had a broad truth. I did not cry because Seaforth Grange was horrible, though it was. (In many respects, the company of Darnley and my other friends there was more congenial than that of my uncle, aunt and cousin at the rectory.) It was the separation itself which terrified me. Awaiting death is much worse than the 'back to school' feeling. What is there to dread if there is no future consciousness? Such common sense should console more deeply than the belief, at an earlier stage, that I should be all right when I got back to school. But I am not ruled by common sense; and it is precisely the nothingness, the non-being, the absence of thought, memory or desire, which fills me with terror. In this state of mind, it no longer matters whether I have had a happy life or whether there is not much of it which I should prefer to forget. In such a mood I cling to memory as to the only thing, in my remaining years, which can ward off the emptiness of eternal death, and I cling to it with a horrified desperation, unable to tolerate the knowledge that it will go. In reality, the years have passed, the time is gone, and writing about it all will not bring experience back.

The last time I saw Mummy was on the railway platform at Paddington station before I went back to school. She thought it would upset me less if she left me there before the train pulled out, but I implored her to stay, which she did – quarter of an hour's anticlimax in which we had nothing to say to one another, nothing to do but cry, until the carriage juddered into motion and I pulled away, separated from her for ever. My present existence, the writing of these pages, has something of the same pointlessness, I know. Soon the guard will wave his flag and the train will pull out, and what will have been the use of clinging to these memories until the last moment? No use, but compulsion, a necessity like love. So long as I write, my aloneness, and my sense of the future abandonment of consciousness itself, are held in check; but, together with the self-indulgence of the exercise, I feel a duty to tell it all as honestly and truly as I can. These compulsions inspired my first volume of childhood reminiscence which Bloom had just read and which we had met that day to discuss.

Throughout our meal, we had tiptoed around the subject, swapping memories and gossip as we ate an excellent goulash and looked out at the bleak magnificence of the wet afternoon sky.

'Well, my dear, it's not what we had in mind,' he was eventually brave enough to say. 'I'd thought you were writing a book about "The Mulberrys".'

I think the phrase 'Christmas market' came into the next part of the sentence, reinforced by the earnest hope that I wasn't planning, in my old age, to turn into 'Miss Proust'. This transposition of the sexes, which used to be a regular feature of Bloom's conversational style, had now largely been abandoned, and 'Miss Proust' was a deliberate allusion to the old days, a plea based on old friendship that I was not going to land him in grave financial difficulties.

'I mean,' he said, 'it's just going to be this one volume?'

He eyed me suspiciously.

'I thought, as many volumes as it would take.'

Bloom sipped his coffee and stared out of the window.

'You'll get piles if you lie in bed all day long – scribble, scribble, scribble!'

Bloom's wife (a perhaps surprising addition to his ménage, but they seemed very happy together in a slightly quarrelsome way) entered the room to help herself to coffee and to join in the laughter.

'I read your book,' she said shyly. 'Hope you don't mind. I've told William he ought to be bold and publish it – even if,' she added with dispiriting realism, 'not all that many people will want to buy it. Who wants to hear about the fucking Mulberrys?'

She squeezed her husband's ear before going back to her desktop printer in another part of the flat.

One of the reasons they got on well together was that Alice seemed totally unabashed by the flare-ups of anger which so often occur when two strong characters are sharing one another's lives.

'Only about two million people, who listen to the fucking programme every fucking day!' Bloom yelled at the door which Alice had just shut.

She opened it again. She is about thirty years younger than Bloom, tall, pretty, fine-boned.

'Why publish crap?' she asked hotly. 'Isn't there enough crap in the world?'

Her high-pitched New York voice rose to a squeal at the end of the question.

When she had slammed the door again, and begun to tap and whirr with her computer in a distant room, Bloom grinned. In that over-emphatic way he has of speaking, he slapped the forefingers of one hand into the palm of another in time to his words, as he enunciated, 'Because crap, as she calls it, is what people want to read. Look, Julian. Here you are. My dear, a national institution.'

'Hardly.'

'You'd make so much more money if you'd do a nice little Jason Grainger book.'

The glacial silence after this felt like eternity.

'Are you saying that you don't want to. . . . ' I could not quite bring myself to suggest that he did not want to publish my book, lest this make it easier for him to slither off the hook.

'The *fleuve* novels have to be *bloody* lucky to make publishing sense.' He prodded his hand once again. It was a gesture more suitable for soap-box oratory than for private discussion. 'You pick up Volume Five or Volume Seven and ask yourself, "Who the fucking hell *are* all these people?" It's like arriving at a dinner party a couple of hours late and not being introduced to the other guests and spending the whole evening picking up the fag-end of their conversations.'

'I first got addicted to Proust by dipping into the middle. It didn't matter that I had not been introduced to Mlle de Vinteuil or Saint-Loup. . . . One picked it up after a page or two.'

'Authors expect readers to make such *efforts* these days.'

'You mean, actually *read* their books?'

'It's years since William read a book,' said Alice, re-entering in search of cigarettes.

'Oh, rubbish, Alice, you know that's rubbish,' he added crossly,

245

'Over *there*! They're on the arm of that chair. And stop interrupting us. This is important. Julian is on the verge of conning me into losing money so that he can lie in bed scribbling about the old days.'

'Thanks.' She retrieved her Marlboro Lights. 'I read aloud to William in bed. Beatrix Potter. I'm quite sure, they're the only books he reads now.'

'They're *heaven*,' he purred. The eyelashes of his old face were still abundant and boyish. Unlike the rest of his features, they had not altered, and they provided one of those little shocks which I frequently have when looking in a glass, bafflement that one should have come to inhabit this prune-faced old carcase while still remaining in many observable areas the same person who once had smooth cheeks, some white teeth, ungnarled knuckles, cornless toes and the same vulnerable emotions.

I probably have Alice Bloom to thank for the fact that her husband accepted my book. As I had already written the second novel in the sequence, it would have been disconcerting if he had turned down Volume One. From this point of view, the problem was how to make each separate division of the *fleuve* into a plausible unit which could be sold on its own.

'Each book must be able to be read in its own *right*,' he has kept saying defensively, since he started to publish the story.

For me, the problems have been more technical; wondering how much to leave out, which scenes to place in which order, how much to reveal without burdening the reader.

There could have been much to say to Bloom that afternoon about the architectonics of the projected work, had I thought that he would be remotely interested. I might have wanted to explain that he was wrong to think of 'Miss Proust' as the only possible structural model. His own preferred Beatrix Potter could be another, a writer who, like Balzac, wrote a series of separate chronicles in which we might meet as major protagonists figures who in previous volumes of *La Comédie* had only walk-on parts. Within the over-all structure of my Lampitt obsession and my desire to snatch some parts of my own experience back from the consuming entrails of oblivion, I intended, should fancy take me, to turn aside and to relate stories which were extraneous to what might be regarded as the main story. A church-crawling analogy occurred. The visitor to a large church which had been a long time a-building, might never take in the whole edifice at once, but on one visit might find a single place in which to beguile half an hour, now the Lady Chapel, now the choir. On one visit, he will want to sit at the back and gaze at the light pouring from the east window and take in the edifice as a whole. On another visit, it will be the detail for which he searches; turning up a misericord in order to concentrate on one carved scene from medieval life, a housewife at her distaff, a monkey-faced demon tormenting a lecherous friar, a drunkard downing his knobbly, black carved pot. Then, looking up from these tiny intricacies, the eye might take in the structure, and in some transept arch see how each piece of carved stone or wood formed part of the whole. In any human life viewed from a long perspective there may be found these linking points, analogous to roof-bosses or the meeting points of the arches, where different parts of the building are held together, and where, in medieval times, the craftsman might have chosen to place some grinning face or winged angel.

A case in point would be the Great Attachment. I have not written much about her in the previous pages, and indeed I hardly knew her, but in some ways she is as interesting to me as Rice Robey himself. As first depicted to me, in Felicity's accounts and Darnley's, Audrey Paxton had been no more than a grotesque gargoyle in the edifice, a monster of domestic horror who kept Rice Robey in her trivial thrall, forcing him to perform menial tasks when his mind might have been given to supposedly more important concerns. I had accepted that Rice Robey was completely miserable with her, and that this in some way excused or explained his wide circle of female acquaintanceship beyond the confines of Twisden Road. When I actually visited their house, and saw them together, and discovered that other women were not unmentionable in her presence, I had felt a considerable shock. It made me believe that Rice Robey was purely a bogus figure, stringing all the other women along. Then I came to realise that human relationships are never simple and that his projected descriptions of Mrs Paxton as a tyrant whom he hated probably would not have been necessary to invent unless they corresponded at least some of the time to a felt reality. Probably, he did hate her, as well as love her. With part of himself, he must have resented the limitations on his freedom which followed their elopement from the school. Cecily's vision of things, that Mrs Paxton had wilfully cut off Rice Robey from his friends, broken his association with Jimbo, deprived him of all imaginative and intellectual stimulus, and prevented him from developing as a writer might have been true, but whether he considered this a price worth paying for the emotional fulfilment which she, and perhaps no other woman, provided, we shall never know.

Cecily had astonished me, at Darnley's wedding party, by revealing that Mrs Paxton was the sister of the Binker, my old headmaster at Seaforth Grange. In itself, there should have been nothing so surprising about this. What more probable than that her husband and her brother should both have pursued the same unpleasant Dotheboys line of business? When Cecily told me this, however, it was one of those moments when the eye strayed from mere detail, the grotesque gargoyle or carved misericord, and took in the structure of the whole edifice. My vicarious interest in Rice Robey's ménage had already changed by the time that I realised that Felicity was in love with the man. It was a shock to discover that this bogus gargoyle, who had so beguiled my friend Darnley and my cousin, who had appeared arbitrarily and suddenly on the scene like a comet flying across the night sky, was not, in fact, a man who had arrived in the drama from nowhere. He had been part of that interconnected pattern of personal destinies which were one of the given truths of his own metaphysic.

'Branches and shoots of the *arbor cognitionis!*' he had intoned one night in the Spread Eagle, when Felicity had persuaded me to meet him there for a pint. 'Each of us has a tree of cognition, which we could sketch and trace; no uninteresting exercise for a winter night – how meeting X led us to know Y and love Z and change our views about ABC. In most lives, the relation of the branches to the parent stem is uncomplex. Your life, I suspect, Mr Ramsay, has a number of interstices which are somewhat further from the central trunk.'

'I'm always amazed,' said Felicity, 'by Julian's capacity to remember trivia about the people he meets.'

Rice Robey had launched into a far from trivial disquisition on the transmigration of souls.

The fact that Rice Robey was a branch of the tree who connected my Lampitt life with Seaforth Grange was odd enough in itself, but I had been even more surprised to discover that Mrs Paxton was the owner of two or three important Pilbrights.

I have already said enough about Pilbright to convey how astonishing it was when he burst upon the world as a stupendously successful painter. I had known him, as my father had done before me, as an infinitely tedious office companion, to whom I would have

248

attributed no powers of imagination, let alone artistry. For forty years or more his painting life and his copious work were unknown to the world. The secret was contained in his dingy house in Balham, where he worked during the evenings and at weekends. Then, just as he was retiring from Tempest and Holmes, he was 'discovered'. Raphael Hunter made him the subject of one of his 'Perspectives' programmes on television, and there followed that huge exhibition at the newly opened Hayward Galleries.

That day I lunched with Bloom and discussed my literary future, the day I had just been to see 'Mr Pilbright at Home' in the Tate, it was inevitable that I should recall this earlier and showier affair.

Merely to get there, to reach the newly built gallery itself, was an experience which jolted eye, mind, heart, into a recognition that a great change had occurred in England, and perhaps in oneself. Vernon was not in the Cabinet, and the Socialist Government had disappointed those of us who voted for it by being scarcely distinguishable, in most of its attitudes and policies, from the previous administration. This did not matter. The changes which were coming upon us all did not need to be authorised by government. The excitement of walking to the South Bank to see that exhibition was intense. The boldness and apparent anarchy of the vast expanses of concrete offer numberless visual delights, an effect partly achieved by the varieties of level on which the even grey lines of rough-hewn planes are arranged. The particular walkway which I crossed was from Waterloo station. Behind me, was an old railway bridge, where commuter trains still rattled in and out of the terminus. The blackened London brick of the railway bridge, the train, even the faces of the travellers, seemed, in scale, to be like a child's toy. Old London, old England, old Life were swept behind us; we were all soaring to something newer, freer and infinitely more exciting. Gulls circled above my head, letting out their poignant seaside sounds, and the sun shone brightly. Now and then, the clean sweep of concrete, which from some aspects appeared to stretch for numberless yards, gave place to a little gap through which was momentarily visible a Canaletto scene – the Thames as blue and clear as in some idealised canvas, and, beyond, the dome of St Paul's. To one's left, there was a different vista, of buses and cars passing at eye level, and for this reason seeming, as the trains did, like toys. The world itself seemed like a plaything.

> Then felt I like some watcher of the skies
> When a new planet swims into his ken:

but the new planet was earth, and life was now possessed with a thousand exciting possibilities, not so much of action as of sensibility.

That the new gallery should, within months of its opening, be housing a large exhibition of P. J. Pilbright, was symptomatic of this change which had come upon myself as well as upon the world. Hitherto in my mind, Pilbright had been the embodiment of everything that was inimical to imaginative release. He was a man who stood for plodding work, slavery to routine, unbounded domestic dullness. Of no one I had ever met did I feel more confident that he was a slave to dullness, a man without a soul. The fact that he had pursued a secret artistic life for the previous forty years, covering canvas after canvas with his strangely self-assertive projections, was cause for reassessment not merely of Pilbright, but of the world itself. At first seeing, probably because I was simply jealous of the talents displayed on wall after bare concrete wall of the new gallery, I could not throw off my dislike of Pilbright the man. I did not like the pictures, even though I could see that such huge set-pieces as *Matthew Forsakes the Inland Revenue to Follow Christ* had an undeniable originality. In the many interviews which he gave about his work, Pilbright fought shy of defining his own religious position, and I suppose that it is possible that he did not really have one, the paintings being their own statement, and not requiring a theological justification. Seeing them at that particular juncture of life was to be reminded of the powerful hold which the Christian story exercised on my friends, notably on Felicity. Pilbright did not paint exclusively religious scenes but when he did so, it was to represent Christ as a contemporary figure, the events in the New Testament occurring in the setting of London and its suburbs. (Critics at the time of the exhibition at the Hayward Gallery made much of *The Marriage Feast of Canonbury* in which the Virgin Mother, far from demurely wishing that the other guests be given more wine, is herself a chaotic, plump cockney girl, not unbrassy, with one hand reproachfully holding out an empty glass towards her son, and with the other clutching a cigarette. The empty glass might once have contained white wine or champagne, but from her general appearance – there were affinities with the fat women in Donald McGill cartoons and postcards – I would guess that hers was a port and lemon.)

Not all Pilbright's representations of the human form were so earth-bound. I was haunted at once by the so-called Woolworth Magdalene whom he painted more often than any other female form. It is hardly original of me to say so. She became the favourite of everyone who saw the exhibition. Sometimes the pictures have no obvious biblical link and appear to be simple portraits of the girl, sitting on a chintz sofa with her scarlet-varnished toes tucked under her buttocks, or standing beside some municipal flowerbed admiring the zinnias. She is also to be seen as the girl in a hat in that picture so strangely full of movement, about which the critics differed. Some wanted to call it merely *Girl Running for a Bus*. Others accepted the judgement by the author of the exhibition catalogue that the bundle under her arms was not laundry but a baby, and that this was the picture referred to by Mr Pilbright in a notebook as *The Flight into Egham*.

Her most celebrated appearance at a bus stop, of course, is as *The Angel of the Resurrection Informing the Balham Bus Queue, 'He is not Here, He is Risen!'* Her short dark hair and gamin features might almost make the spectator believe that the angel was an androgynous creation of Mr Pilbright's fantasy, or perhaps, even, a boy. Turning to the justly famous Woolworth Magdalene, however, you see this figure (same face, larger breasts) as unmistakably feminine. In her role as the penitent, she is kneeling on a pub floor at an angle of three-quarters to Christ. Her eyelids are beguilingly cast down in an expression of self-reproach. Are the eyes shut, or does she gaze, as we do, on that half-buttoned blouse, and the perfect moulding of her young breasts? Everyone when looking at the picture (now part of the permanent collection at the Tate) always notices the torn big toe of the fishnet stocking, the scarlet toe-nails jutting through, the peep-toe stiletto cast aside as she bathes with tears the socks and sandals of her Redeemer who looks as though he might have been a schoolmaster, possibly with a fondness for the Aldermaston March where Vernon made so many friends, demonstrating against the existence of nuclear weapons.

Since first seeing the picture, I have often wondered about its significance and formed my own ideas about the biographical sources for its inspiration. As with so many other depictions in art of Mary Magdalene, one wonders quite how penitent she feels, and whether, in the light of the liberal absolution she receives from her Master, it would in any case be appropriate to feel abject misery. My own feeling is that the title of the picture is only half serious. (That's another matter which divides the Pilbright critics, the extent to which he expects us to take the religious content of the work seriously or whether, as some believe, the pictures do not betray a perkily irreverent not to say blasphemous point of view.) She is sorry, the Woolworth Magdalene, but she is also resolute, sad more than penitent and more than a little angry. Are we quite sure that the young man in the picture is in fact meant to be Christ? Might she not be more of a Guinevere than a Magdalene or (the reader will have guessed my reason for asking the question) a wife or a mistress, sorry that she now has some other attachment, but taking leave of the figure at the pub table? Take a closer look, if you will, at that pub table. Critics have neglected it. Only one figure is sitting there – the bearded man. The other characters in the bar are all holding their drinks. In front of him on the table, however, we see a barely sipped half and several glasses which have obviously contained 'shorts', probably whisky.

['Medieval man,' said Abbot Denys to the ex-garage mechanic, *castrato* novice in *Glastonbury Tor* by Albion Pugh, 'made the drunkenness of Noah a type of Christ's Passion and since then, we have been blind to the complementary verity, that Christ's drunkenness is a redeeming answer to the lonely passion of Noah. The Celestial All-Father poured out his promise of benediction in the bow of rain and the rainbow of his wrath. But the Divine Humanity came to birth in a tavern and he was condemned in life as a wine bibber and a drunkard since the innocence of the inebriate abandonment releases the glad heart of redeemed humanity and numbs the mind which poses those questions which would rend in twain the Temple veil. For only one could challenge the All-Father for the broken promise of the rainbow, the promise to withhold pain from the sons of men on earth. Only one could turn water to wine, and wine to his own blood, a chalice which he wished could pass from him, but which he raised in the noonday on a lonely hill as a salutation to suffering mortality and a reproach to the indifference of the Father who forsook him at the last. The sun of nature turned the grape to wine, and the indifference of Zeus turned the wine to vinegar on the lips of the Crucified' etc., etc.]

Supposing, in other words, that the Woolworth Magdalene is in the presence not of Christ, but of the very man she has wronged? Or, by total contrast, could she be kneeling at the feet of a serious young man whom she is about to seduce?

The reader will have seen the way in which my mind is moving; though, when I say 'mind' I mean that curious and intuitive part of consciousness which prepares the ratiocinative faculty for the absorption and comprehension of surprising pieces of information. Before reason could possibly deduce the facts from a given set of information, instinct has helped us to knowledge. On a trivial level, it is manifested in the phenomenon of discovering the answer to crosswords momentarily before understanding the clue. In this case, the clue was, I suppose, the scarlet nails poking through the Woolworth Magdalene's torn fishnet stockings. I did not 'place' the scarlet nails, nor realise that I had seen them in the gnarled and ancient flesh some twelve months before.

'Hallo. It's Mr Grainger, isn't it?'

I swung round on hearing this voice, deeper and throatier than when heard in the domestic context, because for an instant, I believed it to be that of the Binker, my old headmaster at Seaforth Grange. It was a misapprehension which called up a succession of painful reactions; for a split second, I was at school once again, locked in the never-forgotten fear of the Great Dictator, before I recognised his sister, the Great Attachment. And then I looked at the feet, which were enclosed in soft suede bootees trimmed with lambskin at the ankle. When I had last seen those feet, the scarlet toe-nails had been visible.

'Mrs Paxton.'

She smiled conspiratorially.

'You're too modest. That day you came round. You should have said. You know, when you came round with his book.'

'I felt a bit shy.'

'And to think we sat and listened to "The Mulberrys" together. I was so *cross* with him when he told me – not for weeks afterwards, mind. I said to him, "Why didn't you *tell* me that was Jason Grainger. You know I've got a soft spot for Jason."'

Rice Robey had already left the Civil Service. Felicity and he now saw one another less often, but, in view of my obvious feelings about the man, she did not always tell me when they had their little trysts and lunches. I half wanted to know very much, and half did not want to know at all. He had managed to get a number of engagements as a

lecturer and guide to the sites of legendary Britain. There was some
travel agent who employed him, I believe, to inform or entertain
American visitors, and I was told that he was not above placing
advertisements in the newspapers, proposing walks, for interested
clients, around Blake's London. I had not been on one of these walks
myself. Apparently, he had been known to attract as many as a dozen
followers. The advertisement requested that any interested party
should convene at the West Door of Westminster Abbey at 11
o'clock on Saturday mornings. There, apparently, he would show
them the Gothic tombs of the old church where the young Blake had
studied when an engraver's apprentice. A bus ride would take them
to Soho and if there were few enough, they would repair to the Black
Bottle in Poland Street. Darnley had come across him one morning,
annoying Cyril's regulars by declaiming the Songs of Innocence to a
bemused gaggle of Blake enthusiasts. Then, if time and weather
allowed, he would take his followers north of Regent's Park to stand
on Primrose Hill and look down on London.

> The fields from Islington to Marybone
> To Primrose Hill and Saint John's Wood
> Were builded over with pillars of gold
> And there Jerusalem's pillars stood. . . .

One of these days, I half intended to join this walk of Rice Robey's
myself. Thinking about it at the Pilbright retrospective, I could see
the many points of comparison between the painter's view of
London and Rice Robey's own. Mrs Paxton, however, was obviously
under the impression that I shared her purely commercial view of
Pilbright's pictures.

'Wasn't it a stroke of luck! To think of those pictures hanging in
my bedroom since – oh! before the war. The funny thing is, I never
particularly liked it. Nineteen thirty-four. No, three.'

Her little shoulders hunched. Her teeth were very brown when
she grinned.

'It was Mr Pilbright himself who approached us,' she said. 'He
thinks it is his best painting. Well, you know the rest.'

In my foolish way, I grinned, shy to admit that I knew nothing at
all.

'It was the Tate Gallery who wanted to buy it,' she said.

For a few moments of silence we stared at the canvas together. I

254

was still slow to realise that she was the Magdalene in the foreground. Grey, and small, and wizened, she no longer bore any resemblance to this sulkily voluptuous woman, kneeling on the pub floor. Even if she had been instantly recognisable, it was not possible to deduce how she and Pilbright had met. It was later that I heard about it all from Rice Robey himself. She and Pilbright had not met very often; most of Pilbright's pictures of her, and there were dozens, had been done from memory, becoming increasingly stylised over the years, icons more than portraits.

'It was my husband, you know, who *knew* Mr Pilbright – not. . . .'

'I thought perhaps that Mr Robey and Mr Pilbright. . . .'

What did I think?

'His nibs? Oh, no. Only, my husband was always very particular about his shirts. He always bought them at a particular shop, usually patronised by the legal profession, in High Holborn. He liked black and white striped shirts, and a clean collar every day. Now, one day' – her voice, like that of her brother, entirely lacked euphony, and I could imagine the shirt anecdote lasting for ever. She did spin it out much longer than necessary – her husband's penchant for a particular type of stiff round collar which had become obsolete before 1939, the retailer's inability to procure the desired item, Mr Paxton's decision to write to the factory – Tempest and Holmes. She did not explain, and I now kick myself for not asking, how Mr Paxton and Mr Pilbright became friends, or what it was about Paxton which enabled Pilbright to reveal his secret: that he was not simply the man in the Accounts department at Tempest and Holmes, but also a painter. As she told the story, I was distracted by the curious thought that all this was going on when my father was still alive and working with Mr Pilbright. Perhaps it was Daddy himself who opened Mr Paxton's first letter about the collar, and took it over to Mr Pilbright's high clerk's desk. The upshot of Mrs Paxton's tale was that Pilbright was able to get hold of some of the preferred collars out of 'stock'.

'There were dozens of them, dozens. Only, my husband had a bit of a thing about shirts, you know. I took some for his nibs to wear after we, you know. . . . Well, he's still *wearing* some of them. And that's what? Thirty years?'

I would give anything now to have the much more interesting part of the story filled in: that is, how Pilbright met Mrs Paxton, and persuaded her to sit for him. I do not think she was being secretive.

She probably assumed that I knew it already. Rice Robey said that he thought the Paxtons had occasionally asked Mr Pilbright to Sunday lunch in Northwood during the school holidays. Presumably, while Mr Paxton quietly drank himself under the table, Mr Pilbright produced a sketchbook and began to immortalise the female form who plays so important and repetitive a role in his work.

When I told Bloom that I wanted to bring some mention of Mrs Paxton into the present story, he said, 'There must have been *something* about this woman, and you haven't said what it is! She inspired these two crazy geniuses, Pilbright and Pugh. . . .'

'Half geniuses.'

'She inspired them. Pilbright made her the Angel of the Resurrection – what *was* it about her?'

I agreed that there must have been 'something' about Mrs Paxton, and I freely admitted that Bloom was right. I had not captured the 'something' because I had insufficient faith, or vision, to see what it was. Presumably, sex played some part in her power over Pilbright's imagination, but having said that, one has not said much. Pilbright must have seen hundreds of young women in the course of his life, on his bus journeys between Balham and the works. Many of the girls at Tempest and Holmes were probably prettier and cleverer than Mrs Paxton; none of them had been transformed into the Woolworth Magdalene.

The modernist outlines of the Hayward Gallery provided an incongruous enough setting for Pilbright's pictures. Mrs Paxton seemed even more out of place there than her images on canvas. I found, having fallen in with her, that I was stuck with her; and perhaps in an infinitesimal degree I recognised how she had managed to keep Rice Robey in thrall for thirty years. After five or ten more minutes looking at the pictures, she was announcing that she was ready to go, and making it clear that I was responsible for seeing her safely on her way.

'You don't have to see me all the way back to Twisden Road,' she said, with the air of someone who was offering a tremendous concession. Since I had met her in the gallery purely by chance, it had not crossed my mind that I had any responsibility to convey her several miles across London. I had, after all, only met her once before. As soon as that sentence had been uttered, however, I felt mildly guilty and bowed to her superior willpower. It felt as if the very least I could do was to walk her to the train.

'I had a job finding this place,' she said. 'Only, it's a long walk for someone my age.'

By now we were hobbling along the concrete walkway in the direction of Waterloo. I was carrying her bag, which she had chosen to weigh down with some potatoes and a change of shoes, and a large frayed umbrella.

'I tried to put it up, there was a nasty shower earlier, only the wind nearly blew me away.'

I wanted to ask her why it had been necessary to bring a bag of potatoes to the picture gallery, but instead, I tottered obediently at two miles per hour and allowed her to hold my arm.

'You must remind me to get toilet paper,' she said, 'only we're running out.'

Why was this obligation thrust upon me? In a cowardly way, I murmured an assurance that I would, at some later stage, remind her of the necessity.

'Only, I really wanted to take our electric kettle to be looked at on the way home, only I couldn't carry that *and* the potatoes. I suppose you wouldn't come back and fetch it?'

'The thing is, I've promised to be somewhere else.' The lie flew out desperately, and I felt an absolute brute for suggesting unwillingness to become her slave.

'Some of the girls gave it to, you know, his nibs when he. . . .'

'Left?'

'No, no. It's up there, Waterloo. To the right.'

We veered slowly over a footbridge.

'I mean, when he left the Civil Service?'

'I said it wouldn't work.' She did that laugh which I remembered from my first meeting; perhaps it was what she did when Rice Robey's female acquaintances were under discussion: a sucking-in of spit and air through brown teeth. Her lips curled into an impish grin.

'I'm much happier using, you know, our big old. . . .'

'Your old kettle is working, then?'

Having established this fact, there seemed no urgency about the electric kettle which she had already admitted to not liking.

'Only, we'll have to get it mended. No use having it if it doesn't . . . . And in the early morning, it saves a thermos. Bother!'

'Are you all right, Mrs Paxton?'

She had stood quite still and her face had become concentrated with anxiety.

'Knew there was something else. Hot water-bottles! You see, it's just as well I bumped into you!'

The previous night, Rice Robey had screwed the top too tightly on to her hot water-bottle. He was not expected back until late that evening, and it was essential that she had a fresh hot water-bottle for her afternoon rest. It was an inevitability that I offered to traipse all the way back to Twisden Road.

'Only, now he's a free . . . free agent, you might say, he is busier than ever. He's taken the bus to Glastonbury today to show. . . . And they were anxious, you know, to see. . . .'

I have no idea what he was up to in Glastonbury, nor who 'they' were. Evidently, being sued by Raphael Hunter and being made to give up his job had not after all done much damage to Rice Robey's career.

Ever since I had heard that Mrs Paxton had sold a Pilbright to the Tate, I had ceased to regard her, or Rice Robey, as figures of pathos. And anyway, had she known it, financial considerations were not to bother her much longer. That journey to see the portraits of herself in the Hayward Gallery must have been one of her last major expeditions.

It was not simply infirmity, however, or old age, which allowed Mrs Paxton to dominate the rest of my day. She was a time-waster of a stupendous calibre. Effortless expertise is always recognisable: the difference between a good average cook, who has plodded along with the help of cookery books, and the magician like Thérèse before whom soufflés obediently rose, fowls grew golden and pastry delicate, soft. Compare the heavy thump of a child practising its scales and the rippling diapason as another set of fingers runs over the same ivories five minutes later. All of us have made bids for sympathy or have wanted at some stage to enlist another person to help us mend a fuse, wash up our dirty dishes, take a cat to be wormed or injected, or to unscrew a too tightly done-up hot water-bottle. Few of us have had the cheek to ask even our nearest and dearest to perform such menial tasks on our behalf. With the abolition of the servant class, everyone does these things for themselves. Not so, Mrs Paxton, the *maestra* in this department of life, who effortlessly established a situation in which I should have felt churlish to refuse any of these chores. By the time I had taken the kettle to the electrician (an awkward journey by bus and not made easier by the presence of Mrs Paxton's cat Smudge, mewing at the prospect of the vet) most of the day had gone by. Her secret, I suppose, was that it never crossed her mind that I should refuse. When it was allied to sexual attractiveness, as in earlier years with Rice Robey, it must have been a powerful combination. Ever since Darnley had begun to speak to me of 'Pughie' and Felicity's Rice Robey obsession began, I had been told that his domestic life was hell; and yet this had not been the impression I received when I saw them together. The mystery had remained in my mind, why had he *chosen* to be her domestic slave? A few hours with Mrs Paxton made me see that choice did not really come into the matter.

When I returned to Twisden Road with Smudge, Mrs Paxton insisted in reimbursing me for my troubles and a tediously exact calculation was made – nine and six for the veterinary fee, eightpence bus fare each way, one and three for a magazine called *Woman's World*, which she had requested me to purchase at a newsagent en route. Needless to say, she did not have the exact money in her purse and she would not hear of merely giving me a pound note and owing me the rest. I was sent out on another expedition to the newsagent for change, and while I was there, I was commissioned to buy some sweets. Having destroyed the better part of my day, Mrs Paxton glowed with satisfaction, smiled with the look of an artist who had achieved particularly satisfying results. While I ran my errands, she had been recumbent with a hot water-bottle. On my return from the newsagent with the Chewies and the change, she was in the process of making tea, and we were soon settled in the back parlour with cups, milk, cigarettes and some rather stale buns.

'Kind of you to make the tea, only my wrist. . . . That big steam kettle is so heavy. That's why I wanted the electric. . . .'

'The man said it would be ready in ten days.'

She grinned at me through fumes of Fragrant Cloud. She smoked desperately, hurriedly. There was so much that I should have liked to discuss with her: her importance in the life of Mr Pilbright, her life with Rice Robey. . . . And there was her brother to talk about, too, the criminally sadistic headmaster of my old school, Seaforth Grange.

'You know the man who sued Mr Robey,' I said.

'Would he have been a Mr Herne?'

'Mr Hunter.'

'His nibs has just a slight bee in his bonnet.'

259

'About Raphael Hunter? He wouldn't be the first.'

'Well, as you know, he came to us on the recommendation of Mr Lampitt, you know, when we ran. . . .'

'You mean Rice Robey came to you: when you ran your school.'

'Graham knew Mr Lampitt, of course, that was how it happened.'

'Graham was your husband?'

'Mr Paxton to you,' she said sharply. 'I don't like this Christian names thing, do you?'

I was not suggesting for an instant that, had Mr Paxton been alive, I should have aspired to be on Christian name terms with the man. I had merely been establishing his identity. An awkward little silence followed. She had lost the thread of whatever it was she had been about to say.

'His nibs has had . . . since our little bit of money with the, you know, with the. . . .'

'With the money from Mr Pilbright's pictures?'

'He didn't want a whole book, but he's had a poem published. I shouldn't think he'd mind if you took one. There they are on the table.'

A pile of about fifty pamphlets stood on the table, bound in stout purplish card. I accepted Mrs Paxton's gift as a reward for my day's labours. I was not to receive any more confidences. Seeing me to the front door, she said, 'Only Graham always thought that Mr Lampitt was just a bit *too* fond of his nibs. . . .'

They were the last words which I heard her utter.

On the bus which took me southwards to Camden Town, I opened the purple pamphlet, which had been rather handsomely printed and which was entitled *A Return to Glastonbury*.

Yusif began to hear the silence now,
The silence of Yeshua, the silence Yeshua enjoined.
'Tell no man.' 'Say nothing.' How often had such words
Parted from Yeshua's lips after moments of strangeness,
When the corner of the created curtain had been lifted up,
And the brightness beyond had been revealed!
In the days of his flesh, the friends of Yeshua,
Yusif among them, had tried to explain the silences.
'He is modest,' Yusif had said, 'it is part of his modesty.'
But since the dark day of Golgotha and the in-tomb-laying,

Yusif had pondered the nature of Yeshua,
The boy he had loved since childhood, the man whom he
    buried in tomb;
And 'modesty' was not a quality Yeshua had, nor diffidence
    either.
He had loved verbal quips, and the engagement of debate.
He was not short of words when the Pharisees were present.
Only in moments of secret glory with those whom he loved
Did he say, 'Silence! Tell no man. Say nothing.'
For some new believers who never knew Yeshua, silence meant
    'mystery'.
They believed that Yeshua Chrestos had made a cabal.
'Tell no one' meant 'Keep the cabalistic lore
From those outside our secret confraternity.'
Just such cabals had now been started up
By little Saulos whom the church named Paul.
Yusif had journeyed round the Great Sea's coast,
Before in Spain he reached his greater ship
And sailed back to Britannium in rain.
He had seen Mediterranean synagogues,
And heard in gentile towns the word as preached
By Paulos of the mysteries of Christ.
In some such towns, new 'synagogues' arose,
And followers of Yeshua's simple way
Were dubbed the Men of Chrestos, 'Christians'.
Corinth had been the very worst of all.
The drunken love feast there had taken place
In some rich merchant's house. He'd never heard
Of Yeshua's injunction to sell all, and give to the poor.
The 'gathering together' in this house
Disgusted Yusif with its vinous din.
The merchant lolled in the triclinium,
Surrounded by inebriated friends.
And there a Greek – Apollos was his name –
Held up a cup of wine, and said it was
The Fruit of Gnosis – 'Who would drink thereof
Would know the secret given to the world
By Yeshua the secret-bearing, messenger of God.'
Part mystic orgy, part erotic feast, the dining room.
Outside, the fountains gurgled in the Atrium.

261

Throats gurgled too, when incomprehensible slaves
Shouted out incomprehensible sounds, gibbered with tongues.
Another slave vomited on to the mosaic floor.
A wild-eyed youth explained it to Yusif.
'He drink the blood of Yeshua, but he no good.
He drink unworthy like Lord Paulos say.
He cursed. He have bad spirits, so he spew.'
Another figure (female) stood and wailed.
A mirthless glossolalia made her laugh.
Yusif had left the merchant's house displeased.
How well he saw why some of his fellow-Jews
Wanted to silence Paulos and his mysteries, Paulos and the
    Secret Chalice.
At Thessalonika, he landed next.
Much smaller there, the little Paulist band.
Fifteen or twenty followers of 'the Way'.
They welcomed Yusif to an evening meeting.
He did not tell them he had known 'the Lord',
Known him in his enfleshment, shared indeed
Kinship with Miriam the Mother of the Christ!
The Thessalonians had made of Yeshua
A demi-god who rode upon the clouds.
Soon, soon, he would come, on his chariot in the sky!
Soon, he would come and gather them up to meet him!
And then, beloved Yeshua would call
The dead in Christ to meet him in the clouds,
And then the end would come – destruction fierce
Of world, and all the race of human kind.
No need to ask who first had brought this word
To Thessalonika – 'Lord Paulos said.'
Paulos had told them all they had to know.
They knew no saying of Lord Yeshua's lips,
None of his parables or witty tales,
None of his moral paradoxes, none of his high comic jokes,
Only the manner of his dying they knew,
And the fact that he would return on the clouds,
And save their souls from certain death and hell, so Paulos
    said.
Paulos had not been there for several years.
He was, men said, en route to mighty Rome,

262

Led as a prisoner for his lord the Christ.
In Sicily, when Yusif landed there,
He met some women who had heard the word,
Imbibed from Paulos the great Mythos which would transform
    Europe
More than the journey of Aeneas to the Latium shore.
The universe was doomed, the women said.
The God who made it cursed it in his wrath!
Only the blood of Yeshua could avail
To quench the anger of Jehovah's heart.
Their certainty wrung anger from Yusif.
He spoke! 'Yeshua was my friend –
He loved the Psalms of praise, the songs of love,
God was a father, loving to us all!
Forgiveness was the message that he preached!
He has not dealt with us after our sins!'
There was a story Yeshua had told,
Yusif repeated it in Sicily.
A father waiting by a garden gate,
Yearning with love for his rebellious child,
Kissing the boy on his crestfallen return,
Kissing his neck, killing the fatted calf.
There was no need for sacrifice for sin.
'Thou desirest not sacrifice, else had I given it thee.'
The women of Sicily heard the tale impassively.
Paulos had said, Paulos had said. . . .
Their God and His was not a loving Father,
But a monster of Cosmic wrath and malice,
Placing the universe under his inescapable curse!
The blood atoned, the mystic blood of Christ –
Else were the universe consigned to hell.
So Paulos said, and Paulos they believed.
Yusif had said no more. 'Say nothing to any man.'
'Tell no one.' 'Hearing they do not hear.
And seeing with eyes, they do not understand.'
He thought of Yeshua the little child,
Disputing with the doctors of the Law,
Wrangling with the hard men, the men who lived by rule,
He remembered the raised voices in the Nazareth home,
He remembered the overturning of the money-changer's tables.

These outbursts of noise and rage had all occurred
When Yeshua spoke to the hard men of malice who worshipped
   the Cosmic Sadist.
And by contrast, Yusif remembered Galilee.
Those hours of silence in the flower-strewn hills,
The silence of the blue sky, and the lake.
And nothing had been gained by the words, for men and
   women would not hear them,
And everything had been contained in the silence,
And the 'Consider the lilies of the field'.
There was no need to fashion into words
What need not be said and what could not be articulated.
Miriam the Harlot had run from the garden terrified.
The tomb in which Yusif laid the body of his friend
Was empty on the first day of the week.
Its emptiness was what was frightening.
Before long, the stories had begun,
For it was easier to fashion into stories
Something which could never be understood.
Yusif had heard the tales of resurrection.
The followers of the Way had pitied him
Because he had not seen the risen Lord.
Yusif preferred the silence of unknowing, and the mystery of
   emptiness
And the non-knowing to the knowing, and the not-seeing to
   the seeing.
And now, in Mediterranean ports and small towns of Italy or
   Asia Minor,
Those who had never known Yeshua heard the words of Paulos
   and Apollos,
And sang to a mystic Christ, a demi-god.
Yusif did not suppose that it would last,
This cult of Paulos. Even now, the dwarf
Buzzing with tales of a redeeming god,
Who sacrificed himself on Calvary's hill
And poured his blood out for the sins of men,
Would be confined in Rome, out of harm's way.
Mercantile interest gave the first excuse
For Yusif to return to British soil.
But memory took him, too. He would go back

To those grey, misty, ambiguous lands where he had travelled
With Yeshua the boy,
Back to the land before it all began,
Where he had made his promise not to tell
The unutterable mystery which shone forth
From the height of Jerusalem's mount on Primrose Hill.
Back to the Western Lands he'd travel too,
Die there, perhaps, and bury with himself,
The object which he carried in his bag.
For twenty years, he'd kept it,
He could not throw away something so hauntingly sad,
A symbol of all that was most pointlessly cruel,
Of all that was base in human nature, he could not destroy it.
For Yeshua had worn it at the last,
Worn it as if it was a triumphal crown.
Yusif could not forget the darkest hour.
He lived with it for every day he breathed.
Nothing could be more abject, pitiful
Than that pale body, bloody, thin and bruised,
Which Yusif and the women had wrapped round
With winding sheets and laid within the tomb.
This was the reward given by men to one
Who saw what could not be uttered and refused at the last to
    utter it,
Who preached only by riddle and story the divinity of man,
Who saw the human face divine in children and lepers,
Who loved the drunkards and harlots because they did not
    believe that goodness consisted in the following of ethical
    codes,
Who challenged the malice of the All-Father with a grand
    gesture of impenitent defeat!
And from the body, from the battered head,
Yusif had taken it, the cruel thing,
And now would bury it in Glastonbury.
Blackened and dry it was, the crown of thorn
Which thugs long dead had forced with brutal hands
On to the temples of the Son of Man.

*

I did not read more that day. I put the poem in my mackintosh pocket when I got off the bus, and did not discover it again for several weeks.

Not long afterwards, Mrs Paxton died of some pulmonary conditions. They took her to the Royal Free Hospital in the end, the place where my old friend Day Muckley had died. Rice Robey was in the north of England at the time, conducting a coach party of Americans to the Roman wall, and probably giving them an oration laced with his thoughts about the Celtic divinities, about Mithras God of the Morning, and about the arrival of Cuthbert and the other Christian missionaries in Northumberland. No doubt, in some sense, his audience would get their money's worth. I forget if it was this particular American party, or another, who had been spotted by Darnley in Trafalgar Square during the London leg of their tour. One of the party, a septuagenarian curly-haired woman clad in tennis skirt and shoes, was attempting to record the Speaker's reflections in note form, perhaps for personal perusal during the winter months in Ohio, perhaps for regurgitation to some group of interested coevals on her return home. She was looking up at Nelson's Column.

'So, let me get this right. It's a phallic symbol, it's a ship's mast with an eyeless boy at the top of it? Eyeless? Have I got this right? And. . . .'

'In the death of the great, there is a perfect marriage between the heroism of sacrifice and the sacrifice of the hero,' Rice Robey had replied. 'I mean sacrifice in its pure, ritual and arcane. . . .'

'*Ark*-ine. What's ark-ine?' another member of the party had enquired.

The old lady in tennis shoes had relentlessly returned to her spiral-bound pad. 'And a totem-pole? Right? It's a totem-pole?'

This was one of the many snapshots which Darnley preserved of 'old Pughie' and which he would produce for the entertainment of anyone who was interested in the pub. I imagine that Rice Robey was almost perpetually engaged in such conversations, baffling most of those whom he met but exciting a gratifyingly intense appreciation from the Faithful Few.

Felicity certainly belonged to this latter category however fiercely she would defend her own independence.

'Rice Robey has brilliance, but he has not actually got this matter right,' she had said to me about some esoteric metaphysical concern. What was memorable about her saying it was the brave expression on her face. She obviously thought that it was daring, almost out-rageous of her, to disagree with the Master. There can have been few *cleverer* Robey-maidens – 'daughters of Albion' as Darnley had dubbed them – than Felicity, and the book on which she now laboured was perhaps the highest compliment that anyone ever paid him.

Felicity was to rewrite the book many times, and I found the work, when it was eventually published under some academic imprint, totally impenetrable. It had chapters about Frege, Heidegger and Wittgenstein. The second half of the book was devoted to Felicity's own thoughts or notions about the Metaphysical Question. It was couched in terms which the ordinary intelligent layman could not possibly have understood. In some circles, however, it was regarded as a philosophical breakthrough, rescuing the subject from the arid borderlines in which, in England, it sometimes too readily rejoiced. Evidently, to judge from things people in the academic world have occasionally said to me over the years, the book was 'difficult' even for professional philosophers to grasp. I believe that there is even some dispute about whether the book was the ultimate refutation of Theism or an extremely subtle justification for it. I assume, the latter – but perhaps there is more mystery than my mind can grasp in the hours of silence which Felicity, nun-like, has spent in her attendance at meetings of the Society of Friends.

The book's dedication–'To R.R.'–also tells its own tale. Until she had met the 'really rather awful man' on her corridor at the ministry, Felicity had been interested in very different philosophical con-cerns. I do not know whether he took this fact as a compliment or whether he was so consumed with egotism that he assumed that any woman would wish to conform her way of thinking to his own.

Jo, who improved on closer acquaintance and whose marriage to Darnley seemed very happy at that date, used to complain that a faraway look still came into Kirsty's eyes whenever she received one of Rice Robey's strange postcards or letters, even though a consider-able time had elapsed since their brief period of intimacy. I began to think that Kirsty was entirely typical of the 'daughters of Albion', and that there might well be dozens of such women, dotted about the country though mainly in London, whom he had loved intensely for about a fortnight, and who still gazed dewy-eyed at the coconut matting if the postman delivered on to it one of Robey's communications in his large babyish handwriting.

In the bosoms of all these Daughters of Albion, there must have been a certain relief, if not actual hope, when the demise of Mrs Paxton became known. It had not been my intention to attend the obsequies of the Woolworth Magdalene. I had only met her twice in my life, and it seemed intrusive to go to her funeral. During the singing of the hymn, I asked myself why I was there. Was it really, as Felicity had said, that we owed Rice Robey our support and comradeship at this time of trial? Or was it somehow the egoism of the Great Attachment herself which drew me there? I am sure that she would have been delighted to know how extremely inconvenient it had been to rearrange life in order to be present at her funeral. It meant cancelling a visit to Sargie – with all the emotional upheaval which that provoked – and missing a rehearsal in Birmingham for 'The Mulberrys'. (Tight lips from Rodney.)

Felicity had wanted to be at the crematorium, however, and I had accompanied her, not sure whether I did so to lend her support or to keep a jealous eye on her. We had been lovers ever since the night of Darnley's wedding, and the affair had now entered the phase of wondering whether it was what either of us actually wanted, or whether we had been duped by physical attraction into a state of things unconducive to personal happiness.

One of the least pleasing aspects of this, on the whole, rather happy period, had been her continued obsession with Rice Robey. It baffled me completely. Felicity and I did not pretend that we were, exactly speaking, in love with one another. But it had been a surprise to find, after we had been lovers for a few weeks, that her pillow-talk consisted almost entirely of the saying and doings of 'R.R.'. Because of his famous devotion to the Sexless Eros, I was apparently supposed to find acceptable her continued devotion to him. The fact that she had no chance of going to bed with him made it wholly acceptable for her to continue regular trysts with the man when he was available for them, to exchange long letters with him when he was not, and to discuss his genius and character with me for hours, when I should rather have whispered sweet nothings or read a book.

I had assumed, and certainly hoped, that when they ceased to be colleagues, Felicity and Rice Robey would see less of one another. I thought the preoccupation would somehow simmer down to more manageable, less boring proportions. At the time of Mrs Paxton's funeral, there was no sign of this happening. During the hymn – 'Lord Dismiss Us' – my lips were sealed. I thought of the conversation which Felicity and I had had the previous evening.

'This of course has solved nothing.'

Felicity's words had implied that we had a shared problem to which all manner of solutions had been sought, the present activity, that second over, being one of them. I had not been aware that we were seeking to solve anything, but her stiff shoulders and her serious eyes looking up at the ceiling told me that all was not well.

'Not that it isn't very nice,' she had said.

'Good.'

'I could make us both a pot of tea.'

'That would be nice too.'

She had turned once more to hold me in her arms. When I kissed her naked shoulder, she murmured, 'Earl Grey, or Indian?' And when she had returned with a tray, and a pot of Indian, she had said, 'If he wants to be alone with me after the funeral tomorrow, you won't mind, will you?'

'He?'

She ignored my absurd implication that she might be discussing anyone other than her hero.

'He might prefer to be alone with me, that's all,' she had said.

'You do what you like.'

Beside me in the chapel of the crematorium, I could hear Felicity's tuneless voice singing

> Pardon all, their faults confessing
> Time that's lost may all retrieve . . .

a school hymn perhaps appropriate in Mrs Paxton's case. We had sung it at Seaforth Grange on that speech day when Darnley used my five pounds – a present from Sargie – to order a ton of manure to be delivered outside the marquee during the Binker's sermon.

Felicity was not the only Daughter of Albion to imagine that Rice Robey would want a shoulder to cry on after the service. Considering the fact that Mrs Paxton was a virtual recluse, seldom leaving 77, Twisden Road in latter years except to remonstrate with the newsagent for failing to deliver the *Daily Mail*, I could not believe that many of those present at her funeral had been closely attached to her. The chapel, though, was quite full. We had arrived late and found places at the back. We watched the proceedings over twenty or thirty heads, most of them female. Beyond the hats and scarves and perms, I could make out the back of Rice Robey's Blakean crown. He stood entirely alone in the front pew on the right. On the other side of the chapel, another group of mourners were huddled, but I could not see them very clearly from where I stood.

The parson who conducted the service was a fat, bespectacled figure with a red face and sleeked, possibly brilliantined, hair framing a podgy brow. The lubricious self-importance of his tone was not unfamiliar, but I could not place him until the end of the service when he began to read some prayers.

The congregation was kneeling. At that stage of my life, I had not abandoned the adolescent feeling that unbelievers such as myself should not compromise, when attending church services, by bowing head or knee. I was prepared to take my shoes off in a mosque, but I would not kneel in church. Sitting upright, I was therefore able to get a better view of the assembly.

'Shall we pray for Audrey's family . . . and in particular, at this time, our thoughts go out to Robbie . . . ', there was a significant pause, ' . . . and Margot.'

Not being a praying man, I have never seen the point of these meaningful pauses during extempore prayers. They somehow imply that the Godhead is rather slow on the uptake, and needs a moment – as I did not – to recall who Robbie and Margot were. There they were, in the front row, the Binker and his horrible wife. The parson, I instantaneously realised, had been the head boy of Seaforth Grange in my time, a bloke called Timpson.

Someone (Bloom?) once told me that clergymen who find employment in crematoria have usually been withdrawn from regular parochial life to avoid scandal. During the unctuous prayer for my old headmaster, I allowed myself to speculate about the nature of Timpson's indiscretions. To have landed up, at a comparatively early age, as a functionary in this dismal suburban furnace, the offence must have been glaring. If Darnley had been there, perhaps one would have found this thought funny; as it was, the picture of Timpson indulging in any erotic activity was unpleasing. Public lavatories? Choirboys?

In fact, of course, Timpson did not work at the crematorium. He had come along at the Binker's request to take the funeral. When he had finished begging the Almighty to soothe the supposedly grieving hearts of the Binker and Mrs Binker, Timpson pressed a button, and we waited for the coffin to disappear through the hole in the wall which, now I come to think of it, resembled the food hatch in the dining room at Seaforth Grange. I remembered reaching through that hatch for a dish of vegetables (we all took turns to wait at the table), and Mrs Binker, who happened to be standing there with a ladle, arbitrarily rapping my knuckles and drawing blood.

The button which Timpson had pressed produced a recorded rendering of 'Sheep May Safely Graze', but the coffin refused to budge. I was delighted to see Timpson's face become cross and flustered in a manner which recalled his losing his temper with Darnley and myself aged twelve.

'There appears to be some fault,' he said. One of the undertaker's men came forward to the little desk where Timpson stood and indicated the button to push.

'I've already done that,' said Timpson hotly. 'It simply makes the music play.'

'It looks as though. . . . ' said the undertaker's man awkwardly.

He retreated to the back of the chapel while we waited for something to happen. Then he came back up the aisle with a workman in overalls, who disappeared into the pale oak pulpit or lectern where Timpson waited.

Timpson, I thought rather foolishly, had opened his floppily bound leather Bible, and was reading a passage at random from one of St Paul's epistles. It was an apostolic utterance which I thought showed particular confusion of mind, but it was hard to concentrate on it very carefully, since everyone was by now desperate to see whether the coffin would finally shift, or whether Mrs Paxton's mortal remains would be stuck in the chapel for ever.

While Timpson read aloud, one couldn't help hearing the man in overalls, who had been tinkering with a screwdriver, observe, 'It looks to me like a faulty connection.'

Probably only a few minutes passed in which Timpson continued, with smarmy false emphasis, to harangue us with suggestions about how to behave at a dinner table in the event of being offered meat which had previously been sacrificed to idols.

Then, in his front pew, the Binker stood up.

'There appears to have been,' he said, and then he cleared his throat. 'If Timpson would kindly turn down the music – thank you, Timpson. There appears to have been a mechanical difficulty. I think it might be a more fitting conclusion to the ceremony if we were simply to leave our places now and. . . .'

And, what? We all wanted to know what was going to happen to the coffin.

The Binker did not look in the least grief-stricken; he looked pleased, if anything, to be given the chance to address us. It was school all over again. One half expected him to tell us to leave the chapel in twos, and that anyone seen talking would have to come to his study afterwards for a thrashing.

It was presumably because Mrs Paxton had not been married to Rice Robey that her family had taken charge of the funeral arrangements, a fact which would have accounted for their extreme dreariness. We shuffled out with a sense of profound anti-climax. Even as we did so, two more workmen in overalls and the undertaker's men were advancing on the coffin. It seemed appropriate that Mrs Paxton was causing maximum trouble to the last.

Outside, in the arcade, the congregation stood about in awkward little groups. Some members of the party leaned over the pathetically few wreaths and bunches of flowers which had been sent to attend Mrs Paxton's last journey to the flames. Natural curiosity made me lean forward to read the labels attached to these tributes, and my eye fell on words and handwriting which were immediately familiar.

With deepest sympathy and all good wishes from P. J. Pilbright

These words were identical to those with which Pilbright had concluded his letter of condolence to Granny when my parents had been killed during the war. Similar formulas adorned the Christmas cards which he still regularly sent to her. One might have supposed that something more heartfelt would have been appropriate for a painter's leavetaking from one of his greatest sources of inspiration, but it would not have been in Pilbright's nature to stray outside the borders of convention.

'Oh good,' he said, 'mine arrived! You never know with florists.'

And there he was, looking as he had always looked when we worked together in Accounts at Tempest and Holmes: white hair *en brosse*, steel-rimmed spectacles, a very good colour in his unlined faced. Retirement and fame were evidently congenial.

'I saw Mrs Paxton not long ago,' I said to him, 'at your exhibition.'

'Oh, yes?'

He looked a little quizzical, but from an emotional point of view quite unmoved. There was nothing in his face to suggest that I was talking of a huge exhibition which had whisked him from total obscurity to prodigious celebrity, nor that I was discussing a person who had been of immense importance in his imaginative life.

'She was always a very good friend, Mrs Paxton was to me,' he said. 'And, of course, Mr Paxton. Mr Paxton was also very kind.'

Once this fact had been established, there seemed no more to say. This was certainly not the moment to talk about the Woolworth Magdalene. I was not even completely sure that Mr Pilbright knew who I was. I asked him if he knew Kirsty Lampitt, who was also leaning over to look at the floral tributes.

'No,' he said crossly, 'no, I can't say I do.'

'Hallo, Julian.'

'Hallo.'

'I thought I'd come,' she said quietly. She looked as if she might have been crying. The resemblance between her and Jo was certainly very striking. I had now spent a lot of time in Jo's company, and almost none in Kirsty's, so it was hard to remind myself that they were in fact different people.

'That was P. J. Pilbright,' I said, adding slowly, as if to a dim-wit, 'he is a painter.'

'Wasn't the exhibition extraordinary,' said Kirsty. 'Did you read the catalogue? He'd been working in total obscurity for years, until he was discovered by Raphael Hunter. The man Mama and Papa blow so hot and cold about.'

'I know.'

'Good news about Jo-Jo, isn't it?'

'What news is that?'

'Hadn't you heard – she's having a baby.'

'That's marvellous.'

Kirsty did not want to be wasting time talking to me. Her eyes were darting around nervously in search of Rice Robey. The Binker and Mrs Binker were now emerging from the chapel, treading short, slow steps and looking about them timorously. Raphael Hunter held the Binker's arm. To Kirsty, and to anyone else who did not know them, they probably looked like a couple of harmless old people being helped along by a middle-aged man. For me, there was something about the defiant way in which the Binker looked about him which recalled the behaviour of impenitent war-criminals seen on those newsreels of the Nuremberg trials.

'I think I can say, a very beautiful ceremony,' said the Binker.

'It was lovely,' said Hunter. 'Just as Audrey would have wished.'

'A pity about the mechanical failure,' said the Binker, sounding more than usually Scotch.

'Can't stand gloomy funerals,' barked Margot Larmer with some savagery.

'Just mind that step, Margot, dear,' said Hunter, carefully guiding Mrs Binker every inch of the way.

The Binker turned aside to thank Timpson for the manner in which he had conducted the service.

'I can always rely on my boys,' he said.

'Very good to see you,' said Timpson to me, pumping my hand and staring into my face without a glimmer of recognition.

I could not tell whether the Binker recognised me. I thought on balance that it was unlikely. Hunter, who clutched his elbow, certainly did know who I was; since, until a few moments before, I had been accompanied by Felicity, it was not surprising that he decided to cut me. Soon, he, the Binker, Mrs Binker and Timpson were piling into the back of a hired limousine. The funeral party was beginning to disperse.

'Phew,' I heard one of the undertaker's men say to another as they re-emerged from the chapel. 'Never had to do that before – shove 'em through *by hand*.'

Kirsty and Felicity had both made a bee-line for Rice Robey, who was bending over to kiss a woman in a headscarf. As I approached, he was saying to her, '. . . just such an immortality as Plato evisaged, a striving for the union of the Psyche with the eternal Agathon, the melting away of *sarx* to be reborn in *gnosis*.'

Not being a Greek scholar, and never being quite used to Rice Robey's strange vowels, I thought he was telling this lady that divine wisdom came after the dissolution of *socks*.

'Remember, dear man,' she said, 'any time! You have my number.'

They were all queuing up to say the same – Kirsty aged twenty-two, Felicity at forty-odd, this older woman, who was perhaps sixty.

'Mr Grainger – Felicity – it was kind of you to come.'

'I couldn't have stayed away,' said Felicity.

Even as she said this, and Kirsty made some almost identical remark, I was saying to Rice Robey that I had seen Mrs Paxton at the Pilbright exhibition. I was going to remark on Pilbright's presence at the funeral. (Where was he? Presumably, he had walked briskly to the nearest bus stop or to Golders Green station.)

We had seldom slept together, Felicity and I. After an hour or two in bed, I would get up and return to my own room. Sometimes, in the mornings, we would greet one another as lovers, and hold one another tightly in our pyjamas and dressing gowns. Sometimes, more often, we would be overcome by shyness, by wondering, quite, whether the previous evening had actually happened.

I felt paralysed, humiliated, by her continuing need to be a Daughter of Albion. She had no treachery in her nature; and we were both perfectly well disposed towards one another; but I knew, as she stood there beside Rice Robey, that our lovemaking of seven hours before meant absolutely nothing to her.

She did not need to say anything. Without speech, she could convey to me an overpowering desire that I should be gone. She wanted to be alone with Rice Robey. In spite of the others who hovered with similar attentions, I could see that Felicity rated her own chances high, of being able to take him home in a taxi, and spend an evening cooking for him and listening to his talk.

I began to wish that I had teamed up with Mr Pilbright and gone home with him on the bus. It would have been interesting to renew our old acquaintanceship.

'You'll be wanting to take a taxi,' I said to Felicity. 'I'll go. Kirsty, if you're not. . . .'

'I'm fine,' said Kirsty, who also waited by Rice Robey's side with a hopeful expression on her face.

I half thought of walking home across the Heath.

Rice Robey was seriously discomposed. He looked more than usually peculiar, since the blue pin-stripe had been discarded for a suit of deepest black fustian, the property, I suspect, of the late Mr Paxton, to judge from how very short the trousers seemed on Rice Robey's legs and how bulkily the coat sat upon his shoulders. His cheeks were wet with tears, and he was shaking.

'You look tired, R.R.,' said Felicity. There was something bossy and school-matronly in her tone, something falsely no-nonsense, a manner which she was adopting, partly to put him at ease, but chiefly, I felt, to differentiate herself from the more gushing or quasi-mystical of the Daughters. Some of these looked like very strange creatures indeed. I thought that the one with a woolly hat and spectacles wore such an idiot smile that she could only have been released for the afternoon from some institution. Another figure, with iron-grey shoulder-length hair, had, one assumed, arrived at the funeral by broomstick. Neighbours in Twisden Road? Members of his lecture audiences?

It was humiliating enough to know that Felicity yearned for Rice Robey's company rather than my own; but I also felt humiliated on her behalf, to see her competing with this gaggle of slightly strange individuals: secretaries from the Ministry of Works? Deaconesses? What about the heavily moustached young woman with red hair and a shopping bag from Harrods? And what did *that* contain? Rat's bane? A pot of basil? Or some sacred relics?

'I think I should perhaps be going,' I said. 'Mr Robey, I'm. . . .'

The conventional words of condolence seemed more than usually pointless on this occasion.

'We shall meet again,' said Robey. 'You were very kind to Audrey.' It looked as if he might be going to weep again. Perhaps to guard against such an eventuality, he changed the subject, and his face assumed some of that malicious glee which Darnley always found so infectious.

'You saw our friend – with Audrey's brother? Mr Hunter! Sometime a keeper here in Windsor Forest!'

'Hunter was at Mr Larmer's school,' I said. 'I was there myself, though at a later date than him.'

'Those people did nothing for Audrey.' He fumbled in his pocket as he spoke and produced a packet of cigarettes. When he had got one alight, he spoke with it still between his lips. 'Through all her years of unhappiness with her husband, through all her years of poverty, they did nothing.'

'Come on, Rice, you need a drink.'

This sentence was uttered by the young woman who now came to join us, and who was waving her car keys temptingly in the air. I had not seen her at the funeral, but she had presumably been there. Her dark hair was shorter than when last seen, as the lead vocalist singing at Darnley's wedding. She wore jeans and a black T-shirt.

'R.R., you're very welcome to come back to my house,' said Felicity, shameless now, flushed with disappointment. 'We could share a taxi, or we. . . .'

'Miss Nolan has a conveyance,' he said quietly. He had perhaps hoped to shake off the Daughters of Albion and leave as a mystery his manner of getting away.

Miss Nolan obviously did not wish to waste any further time on conversation. She looked as pale and plain and cross and mysterious as she had done that evening when she had sung. Her spoken tones were no less educated, but, without a microphone, almost inaudible. In fact, as a passing aeroplane flew overhead, it was impossible to hear what she said, though her lips were visibly moving.

Rice Robey could hear her and was apparently turning down, on our behalf, an invitation from Miss Nolan to drive us back to Camden.

'It's hardly out of our way,' whispered the Newnham Norn.

'Felicity and Mr Grainger will have their own arrangements,' said Rice Robey firmly. 'And, anyway, we shall meet again soon.'

'Oh, R.R.!' With a sudden gush of affection, Felicity placed her hands on Robey's shirtfront and buried a kiss on his neck. Miss Nolan watched with the impassive distance of a dog-owner waiting for its charge to empty its bowels before resuming a walk.

'Ready?' she said to Rice Robey when Felicity had blushingly stood back from the kiss.

'I'm ready,' said Rice Robey.

We stood, Felicity and I, both for differing reasons vaguely shocked, and watched him climb into the front seat of a van adorned with the legend PSYCHEDELIC LIGHTS. It was a primrose yellow van, and the letters, of varying shapes, colours and scripts, danced unevenly over its side. Rice Robey did not acknowledge us as he sped past, in the passenger seat, though Miss Nolan gave a little wave, not entirely unable to banish a smile of triumph, as she turned her van left, out of the crematorium gates, and into the afternoon traffic of Golders Green.

No logic could explain this, but as I watched Rice Robey and the Newnham Norn lurch away in the van, I knew that Felicity and I had ceased to be lovers. From the beginning, it had been a somewhat questionable development. We still loved one another, and would always continue to do so, but this particular period of life, during which – not all that often – we had wandered into one another's bedrooms, had now come to a close, like a phase of childhood. We never discussed the matter, never alluded to it in any way, but the night before Mrs Paxton's funeral was the last which we spent in the same bed.

Watching the Newnham Norn's departure, I felt a great surge of jealousy, and once again asked myself, as I had often done in the preceding weeks, whether I had gone to bed with Felicity simply in order to compete, emotionally, with Rice Robey. Certainly, there was satisfaction to be gained from the knowledge that whatever power he exerted over Felicity, here was one Daughter of Albion who had come, albeit physically, albeit for a brief half hour or so, beneath my imaginative thrall; yet, even here I could not be consoled, for who could guess what had passed through Felicity's mind as we made love?

'What a rude girl,' she said.

'A woman of few words, certainly.'

'I *hate* unnecessary rudeness.'

'I vary. Most unfairly, I know, I rather like rudeness in girls; some latent masochism, I suppose.'

'She's just a *silly* pesron,' said Felicity vehemently. 'All the same, it is a pity to see. . . .'

She did not finish the sentence. Was it a pity to see Rice Robey, as usual, making a bit of a fool of himself over a girl? Me, slightly, ditto? (Already, in my fantasy life, I was concocting plans to pursue the Newnham Norn.) Pity that Mrs Paxton was dead, and that we never appreciated in her what it was that had inspired Pilbright's artistic vision? Pity that Felicity was in love with Rice Robey, and was doomed to be one of the Daughters of Albion for the rest of her life, her heart – however much she told herself that she had 'got over' the experience of Robey – always missing a beat when she heard his name or saw one of his books? Pity to see that people age, but they do not grow up? Or that England ages, and is being, has been, destroyed? Pity to see the world, turning on its sad old axis, learning no lessons, solving no problems, and increasing, with each of its revolutions, the sum of human misery? I do not know how Felicity's sentence would have ended. Some time, not long after that, she returned to Oxford: not on a permanent basis, but for a space of several weeks, in order to get started on her great philosophical treatise.

I missed her. Before her arrival in Arlington Road, I had luxuriated in my solitude. Now it hung upon me like a burden. I wandered the streets in the evenings, rather than to endure the oppressions of my own society in my own room. I became, then, one of the night people, the men and women who for some reason or another are out when the rest of the world is indoors. Some of them are insomniacs searching for late-night cigarette vendors. Some are dog-owners with an obvious need to pause at lamp posts and street corners. Some, however vaguely, are searching out some sexual encounter, and some are strayed revellers, too drunk to know where they are or why they are there. I felt a kinship with all the night wanderers whom I passed, even those whom I suspected of being violent psychopaths, prowling in search of victims to cosh or knife. Sometimes, sexual feeling would be so heightened by the night, and the gloom, and the fear, that one could imagine oneself inside the skin of a rapist, whose needs were momentarily so intense that the humanity and fear of their prey become entirely forgotten in the overwhelming need to assuage lust. Sometimes, these lusts could, on my night prowls, be satisfied, usually for an exchange of cash, and I would return home, hoping that sleep would bury the experience, blot it out, make it as if it had never been. Then dawn would come, and remind me. During my nocturnal walks, my mind would normally become so confused that its movement could not be dignified with the name of thought. Impressions, sometimes of the day just past, sometimes of my life would jumble together, and mingle with the immediate sensations of the night. On other such walks, however, particularly if I had reached just the wrong stage of drunkenness and begun to sober up, I would be confronted by a vision of life's emptiness, of the terrible pointlessness of my own way of life. This made returning home even harder, and when the cruelty of the perception was sufficiently strong, I would pace and pace until dawn, sometimes finding that I had walked for miles, across the entire expanse of London. On one night, having set out from Camden Town, I found myself breakfasting at a workmen's café in Wimbledon.

Self-estimation, my good humour in general, were low at this point, so low that I did not voluntarily seek out those friends and haunts which would restore to me my sense of common belonging to a world of good humour and sense, a world of day, not night. A telephone call out of the blue from Darnley restored these things instantaneously.

He said, 'I've tried you several times. You always seem to be out.'

'I've been busy.'

'You wouldn't like a drive in the country tomorrow, would you?'

'Love one. Where to?'

'Jo and I think we've found a house.'

'That's good news.'

'We thought we'd drive out and have a final look round before making up our minds. Before that, I thought of having a squint at Aldingbury Ring.'

'The threatened henge?'

I heard Darnley laughing down the line.

'A friend of mine went there the other day. . . .' He paused for more laughter. 'They found this party of Americans gazing up into the trees. Pughie said there'd been a sighting of Herne the Hunter there during the previous week. They were all looking to see if they could see him. . . .' Darnley switched to his 'Pughie voice', which had become eerily accurate. 'The Hunter appears in the skies at times of spiritual undoing and rebirth. . . .' Darnley added in his own voice, 'He also appears when you've had one too many drinks on a Friday night.'

The next morning, early, Darnley and Jo appeared at my front door. Jo, heavily pregnant, seemed to fill the Morris, and it was with some difficulty that I clambered on to the back seat. As we drove out of London westwards, she prattled excitedly about the new house.

'There are two spare bedrooms, Mr Grainger – aren't there, darling –'

Darnley assented with a nod of his head.

'One for junior' – she touched her belly – 'but one for our friends, so you must come and see us often if we buy it. And there's a garden – huge garden – and it's near Henley – and you see, there's an old garage which I think we can convert and make into a sort of study, lair thing, for Miles. It'll be perfect.'

'We shall see,' said Darnley.

He was glowing with happiness, and for a period, as the car bowled along, and they talked intimately among themselves in the way that married couples do, I felt wholly excluded by it, more of a pariah than I did on my night prowls. I knew that they were doing what the human race naturally wants to do – settling down, buying a house, starting a family, declaring their belief in the future. Something within me held back from wishing to join in, and I felt it to be my loss not theirs.

'Darling, you put the rubbish out before we left?'

'Yes, yes.'

'And you moved those chops from the meat safe to the fridge?'

'Yes, yes.'

'Thank you, darling.' She leaned over and kissed his cheek.

'We'll drive through Windsor,' said Darnley, 'and then out by the road which is going to go smack through Aldingbury Ring – if they get away with it. Pughie was organising some sort of protest. He was telling me about it last time we met. Real Gandhi stuff – lying down in front of the bulldozers if necessary.'

'He would enjoy that.'

'Darling,' said Jo, 'tell Mr Grainger what Pughie said that time we bought him lunch in the Café Royal.' And she burst out laughing.

'Julian knows that story,' said Darnley.

'Darling – what was the word he said – the word Pughie used for rent-boys?'

'It wasn't quite rent-boys. It's any young man, really – *neaniskos* – it's a Greek word. It's even used for angels in the Gospels.'

'Anyway, Mr Grainger. . . .'

Jo relentlessly pursued this little piece of narrative – it was not strictly speaking a story – about Rice Robey's behaviour at the lunch table in the Café Royal, and his speculation that Oscar Wilde might have sat just at such a table with a neaniskos. He himself had been an angel there in younger days, dining and lunching with Jimbo, who went on patronising the Café Royal long after it had ceased to be fashionable among literary or theatrical celebrities.

'Oi think the roast fowl with bread sauce,' she spluttered, in a very inaccurate imitation of Rice Robey ordering from the menu. Darnley was visibly delighted by her chatter, certainly did not manifest any of the irritation or embarrassment which would have come over me if I had elected to share my life with Jo.

'I think if we drive up this little road here, we come to Aldingbury Ring from behind,' said Darnley.

There was no sign of the earthworks until we were nearly upon it. Darnley parked the car in a lay-by of a narrow road, and it was only when we had climbed a stile into a field, that we could see, on the brow of the gentle hill, surrounded by trees, a row of mounds.

'The Ministry of Transport say that they aren't burial mounds.'

Darnley sniffed hard and long. 'Old Pughie says that if they dig 'em up, they'll find a dragon's hoard or something!'

'Just before he was sacked – I remember Felicity telling me – he went to his Head of Department and asked him if he had ever read *Beowulf*. The Head of Department asked him if he had read such and such draft memo or report which referred the whole matter to such and such committee.'

Darnley laughed.

'Typical Pughie, that. Still' – sniff – 'I shouldn't be in the least surprised if that hill was not stuffed with Iron Age treasure.'

'Anyway,' said Jo reasonably, 'it's a shame to build a road there.'

None of us at the time could have guessed how prescient Rice Robey had been about this ring. The Ministry of Works and the Department of Transport had both insisted that it was not an 'important' site, and that the extension of a motorway to ease London's traffic problems was of far greater importance than some low-lying grassy mounds which might simply, in their view, be the remains of a badly ploughed field.

'No good can come from raping the earth,' said Darnley in his Pughie voice, 'From disembowelling the earth, and disturbing the dragon's gold. They should read *Beowulf* (pronounced *By-a-wolf*).

Now, as we know, there is a whole room in the British Museum containing artifacts bulldozed up at the time of the destruction of Aldingbury Ring: well over thirty complete swords and daggers, and the fragments of dozens more; an eighth-century BC bronze helmet – the oldest military headgear to be found in Britain; bracelets, pins, brooches, rings, harness fittings, were, if we had only known it, but a few inches beneath our feet as Darnley, Jo and I paced the turfy slopes. Archaeologists seemed, after twenty or more years of research, to accept Rice Robey's hunch that Aldingbury Ring was a sacrificial site. Perhaps the most haunting, and painful 'exhibit' in the Aldingbury Room in the British Museum is the tiny skeleton, thought to be that of a child, with a fractured skull, preserved by chance in what had been a peat bog, long since hardened.

I can certainly testify that Aldingbury Ring possessed an 'atmosphere'. As we climbed the gentle slope towards the copse, Darnley, Jo and I became silent. It was a palpable silence, as if some unseen presences commanded it: the sort of silence which comes upon all but the most insensitive visitors to a great cathedral. Behind us, fields stretched through Windsor Forest towards Eton, and in the mist we could make out the outlines of the College chapel, and on the further hill, the turrets of the Castle. Nearer, there was a nondescript row of houses; a gas works, where large iron frames encased the huge grey cylinders and stood out against the pale misty sky like the buttresses of a gothic church. On our other side, there was an illusion of open country, and a bluish smudge of forest, whence, presumably, the antlered figure of Herne could be seen flapping his bat-like wings by night and driving his hounds of destruction across the sky. Hedges gave way to open land. The Thames snaked into invisibility, streaked with silver from the sun which now began in arbitrary shafts to penetrate the clouds. The sun was invisible, but the sky was filling with light. We had reached the first of the stone circles. By the standards of Stonehenge or Avebury, it was small. Some of the stones were little more than boulders. Others, vaguely phallic in shape, poked up from the tufts of grass some four feet in height. One of them, from an angle at which I first glimpsed it, suggested a gaunt face with high cheekbones.

'They can't be going to destroy *this*!' I exclaimed.

'Shh.'

It was Darnley who hushed me. I thought at first that he was objecting to my speaking because it was no place for idle chat. Certainly, the atmosphere was potent, the ancient presences induced a gooseflesh. But Darnley wanted us to be quiet so that we could catch the mysterious noise which came to us on the cold air.

'Listen!'

A thin, high-pitched voice, euphonious but not especially tuneful could be heard. It would have been credible at that point if one had been told that it was the song of the elves, disembodied or invisible to mortal sight.

When we left the small henge behind us, and tramped through the copse at the brow of the little hill, the song grew more audible, and one saw that, just beyond the trees, the ground sloped with some abruptness towards the west. Just out of sight, but somewhere down that slope, someone was singing.

Following a small mud track through the bracken, we came upon the source of the song. It was a mysterious incantation, and I guessed that the words might have been Welsh.

Two figures were sitting on the grass at the mouth of a miniscule tent. One of them, the one who sang, wore a tweed cloth cap, a blue jersey and trousers, and seemed to be a young boy. The other was much older – a balding mage-like man who sat hunched in meditation against the boy's knees. The pair were immediately suggestive of figures from old stories: Merlin and the boy Arthur, or the prophet Samuel with David the young shepherd-king. The misapprehension was dispelled in an instant when I recognised Rice Robey and Miss Nolan.

When he stood up, Rice Robey showed absolutely no surprise at our presence. Indeed, his opening sentence implied that Aldingbury Ring was his own personal domain, to which he was welcoming guests.

'I knew that I could rely upon you to appear,' he said. 'It is at such time that the loyal *animae* conjoin. We came last night.'

Miss Nolan scowled silently. She looked thoroughly displeased to have been interrupted.

'It is any day now,' said Rice Robey. 'They think to take us by surprise, which is why Persephone and I have encamped. Lord Lampitt has said that he will join us, and Kirsty is hoping to come; I had not thought it right to enlist her sister in view of her condition.'

'Enlist them for what, Pughie, old boy?'

I was glad that Darnley asked this blunt question, since I was beginning to wonder myself why Rice Robey should be so pleased and unsurprised to see us.

'The engines of destruction and rape are poised – just down the road. You probably passed them as you came.'

'No,' said Darnley, 'we drove by the back way.'

'Darling, we can't stay here all day and wait for the bulldozers,' said Jo. 'We promised Mr Fanshawe – he's the house agent – that we'd get to the house by half past ten.'

'But Mr Grainger will stay and support us?' asked Robey.

It soon became clear that Rice Robey had organised a 'demonstration' against the proposed road development, and was planning to camp in the line of the road until the Ministry of Transport changed their plans or until the police came to carry him away. I cannot now remember exactly how it came about, but within minutes – as it now seems to my memory – Darnley and Jo had driven off to keep their appointment with the house agent, and I was left sitting on the hillside with Rice Robey and the Newnham Norn. This seemed to please her even less than if we had made up a party of five. She said nothing at all, even when Robey praised her singing, and explained to me that it was an old Irish song, something to do with the Daughters of Cohoolin. Miss Nolan did, however, consent to boil up some cocoa for me on their spirit-stove. When she handed me my mug of steaming chocolate, our knuckles touched. She wore black woollen mittens and the fingers which obtruded from them were small and cold and white. Her round petulant face must have been as cold; her little snub nose was quite pink. She refused to meet my gaze during this transaction, and this somehow heightened for me her attractiveness.

In the course of the morning, a group of about thirty people assembled there on the hillside. Some of them seemed like professional vagabonds, weighed down by haversacks, pots, pans, tents. Others, like Vernon Lampitt, obviously had no intention of sleeping there and had come dressed as for a vigorous hike. The dignity of Vernon's appearance was somewhat diminished by his wearing a bright red woollen hat, not unlike a tea-cosy, with a pom-pom on top. He did not remove it as he explained to a group of the protesters why he was there.

'I'm not against progress, I'm not against roads, but I am against *people* not being consulted. I'm against the present government. I'm ashamed of it, ter tell yer the truth. Like a lotta me comrades, I'd thought it'd be a socialist government. . . .'

'. . . a place of sacrifice,' Robey was saying to another gaggle of young people. It occurred to me that these older men, who believed themselves to be engaged in discourse, were in truth little more than sideshows, engaged in entertaining the demonstrators until the more exciting action began. That such action was about to start could not be doubted. In the course of the morning, we heard that the bulldozers, only a few hundred yards away from us, had begun to gouge out the earth, and at about midday, a police van appeared containing ten or fifteen uniformed officers.

'It is my intimation – something stronger than what the world would call a hunch – that here was a place of sacrifice. Indeed, I have even written about it as a place where Yeshua Himself witnessed the slaying of a child in a sacrifice of the old dispensation.'

'It's an interestin' theory,' said Vernon, 'but yuv got ter admit that the issue which confronts us ter-day is one of accountability. Government accountability.'

One of the policemen was advancing towards the huddle of protesters, of whom I now realised myself to be one.

'Now, we're not tryin' ter stop yer doin' yer duty,' said Vernon to the policeman.

I wonder what it was about Rice Robey. Although Vernon was trying to make it clear by this intervention that he regarded himself as the senior person present, the officer took no notice of him at all. Uncle Roy would no doubt have considered this extremely surprising. The policeman spoke to Rice Robey.

'Are you the leader of this lot?'

'Not the leader, though it is my idea that we should convene here.'

'Now we don't want any fuss,' said the policeman, 'but in half an hour, the bulldozers are coming through this site and they are going to continue with building this motorway. As I say, we don't want any fuss. You are obstructing, and if you don't move quietly, we'll have you for obstruction.'

'I'm pleased to be obstructing,' said Rice Robey, 'because I can tell you what it is that I, and my friends here are obstructing. We are obstructing the obliteration of the sacred past.'

'That may be your opinion, sir. In our book, you are obstructing what might turn into a public highway.'

'Every valley shall be exalted,' said Rice Robey, 'in this Satanic New Jerusalem, which you are allowing to be built. But no new Jerusalem can be built without stretching forth with faltering hand to touch the old Jerusalem.'

'I must warn you, sir, just as politely as I can, that if you aren't out of here in half an hour we'll put you under arrest.'

Vernon began talking about Magna Carta and the rights of an Englishman, but Rice Robey was still intoning, 'The past is what helps us to define ourselves, to define the present, which is why it has to be continually rewritten, revisioned, retold. For you, my friend, this is just a piece of rough ground, with a few stones and a few trees, and doubtless, when its rough places have been made smooth, a few old swords and shards and helmets. I do not doubt that it is a place of what some might denominate a site of archaeological interest. But that is not why we are here. We are here because it enshrines our true past – the past which your empiricist academicians would define as fantasy, but which we know to be. . . .'

His voice was drowned by the noise of the vans and lorries and bulldozers which relentlessly, though slowly, were churning and trundling in our direction.

We had been given our instructions by Robey, and some instinct in all of us recognised him as a figure of authority. We closed ranks and sat down: a crowd of about forty by then. The bulldozers came closer and closer, but still we sat down. Then two large white police vans, with sirens screeching, came bumping over the field, and at that point, in a vigorous, rollicking loud voice, Robey began to sing. Like Uncle Roy on the Day that God Pulled the Plug Out, he had found that William Blake's words matched the hour. The first few lines he sang as a solo –

> And was the Holy Lamb of God
> On England's pleasant pastures seen?. . . .

but by the time he had reached the end of the first verse, we had all joined in, and our voices made the sort of raucous but moving noise that I associate with chapel at school, when as boys we roared out hymns during the morning service. A disproportionate number of policemen had been assigned to the task of bundling us into the vans. One officer took my feet, and the other was holding me under the armpits as I continued to sing

> I will not cease from mental fight. . . .

Vernon was being carried into another van, and he too sang –

> Nor shall my sword sleep in my hand. . . .

Inside the van, as it rolled away, we were squashed quite tightly together. Most of them were a hippyish rent-a-crowd whom I don't believe I have ever met since: but good fortune had allowed me to be dumped by the policeman next to Miss Nolan. Her thighs and legs squashed beguilingly against my own. In the van, we sang 'Jerusalem' again. This time, because her delicately formed, boy-like lips were so close to my ear, I could hear her tuneless, breathy voice chant –

> Bring me my arrows of desire. . . .

I knew in that way one sometimes does that we were destined for further intimacies.

READ MORE IN PENGUIN

In every corner of the world, on every subject under the sun, Penguin represents quality and variety – the very best in publishing today.

For complete information about books available from Penguin – including Puffins, Penguin Classics and Arkana – and how to order them, write to us at the appropriate address below. Please note that for copyright reasons the selection of books varies from country to country.

In the United Kingdom: Please write to *Dept. JC, Penguin Books Ltd, FREEPOST, West Drayton, Middlesex UB7 0BR*

If you have any difficulty in obtaining a title, please send your order with the correct money, plus ten per cent for postage and packaging, to *PO Box No. 11, West Drayton, Middlesex UB7 0BR*

In the United States: Please write to *Penguin USA Inc., 375 Hudson Street, New York, NY 10014*

In Canada: Please write to *Penguin Books Canada Ltd, 10 Alcorn Avenue, Suite 300, Toronto, Ontario M4V 3B2*

In Australia: Please write to *Penguin Books Australia Ltd, 487 Maroondah Highway, Ringwood, Victoria 3134*

In New Zealand: Please write to *Penguin Books (NZ) Ltd,182–190 Wairau Road, Private Bag, Takapuna, Auckland 9*

In India: Please write to *Penguin Books India Pvt Ltd, 706 Eros Apartments, 56 Nehru Place, New Delhi 110 019*

In the Netherlands: Please write to *Penguin Books Netherlands B.V., Keizersgracht 231 NL–1016 DV Amsterdam*

In Germany: Please write to *Penguin Books Deutschland GmbH, Friedrichstrasse 10–12, W–6000 Frankfurt/Main 1*

In Spain: Please write to *Penguin Books S. A., C. San Bernardo 117–6°E–28015 Madrid*

In Italy: Please write to *Penguin Italia s.r.l., Via Felice Casati 20, I–20124 Milano*

In France: Please write to *Penguin France S. A., 17 rue Lejeune, F–31000 Toulouse*

In Japan: Please write to *Penguin Books Japan, Ishikiribashi Building, 2–5–4, Suido, Tokyo 112*

In Greece: Please write to *Penguin Hellas Ltd, Dimocritou 3, GR–106 71 Athens*

In South Africa: Please write to *Longman Penguin Southern Africa (Pty) Ltd, Private Bag X08, Bertsham 2013*

BY THE SAME AUTHOR

The Lampitt Papers sequence

Incline Our Hearts

'An account of an eccentric childhood so moving, so private and personal, and so intensely funny that it bears inescapable comparison with the greatest of childhood novels, *David Copperfield*' – Selina Hastings in the *Daily Telegraph*

Bottle in the Smoke

Julian Ramsay pursues love, art and fame in smoke-wreathed Soho in the Fifties. 'Stunningly funny . . . Wilson's knowing mockery of the viler aspects of the London literary world and the "insane vanity" of authors is spot-on . . . But there is a redeeming idea behind it all, about the fantasies people live by' – Victoria Glendinning in *The Times*

Gentlemen in England

Gentlemen in England is both an accomplished and wonderfully satisfying novel of a family in turmoil and a stunning exposé of Victorian manners and mores. 'A delicious confection . . . some wildly funny moments' – Jane Ellison in the *Evening Standard*

also published:

The Healing Art
Love Unknown
Penfriends from Porlock
Scandal
The Sweets of Pimlico
Tolstoy
Wise Virgin
Who Was Oswald Fish?